"I've been thi

Oh, he'd been think

would have done if ~~in the dark.~~

Garrett looked at her and knew instantly thinking about it had been a mistake. Desire glittered in her eyes. He recognized it, because the same thing was happening to him. He couldn't seem to fight it. More, he didn't want to.

He hadn't asked for this. Didn't need it. But the truth was, he wanted Alexis.

The worst part? He couldn't have her.

He was working for her father. She was a princess. He was responsible for her safety. In the real world, a holiday romance was right up his alley. No strings. No complications. But *this* woman was nothing *but* complications.

Good reasons for avoiding this situation, he told himself. For keeping an eye on her from a distance.

And not one of those reasons meant a damn thing in the face of the need clawing his insides.

Dear Reader,

I *love* old movies. From romantic comedies to thrillers to ghost stories. The old movies—and I'm talking really old movies from the forties and fifties—all had a kind of magic you don't see very often today.

And one of my absolute favorites has always been *Roman Holiday,* the story of a princess who runs away from her royal duties for a day of freedom.

In *To Kiss a King,* I was able to change that idea up a little and give it the romantic happily ever after it deserved. My royal princess, Alexis, escapes palace life to experience real life. And she starts out with her dream trip to Disneyland. Which, of course, since it's my book, is where she meets Garrett King.

Garrett's a security expert, and when he discovers that Alex is a runaway princess, he's torn between protecting her and seducing her.

And that, I think, makes for a whirlwind romance filled with secrets, lies, seduction and—I sincerely hope—a wonderful love story.

I hope you enjoy *To Kiss a King* and I'd love to hear from you! Find me on Facebook or Twitter and e-mail me at maureenchildbooks@gmail.com.

Happy reading!

Maureen

TO KISS A KING

BY
MAUREEN CHILD

Published in Great Britain 2012
by Mills & Boon, an imprint of Harlequin (UK) Limited,
Eton House, 18-24 Paradise Road, Richmond, Surrey TW9 1SR

© Maureen Child 2012

ISBN: 978 0 263 89343 4
ebook ISBN: 978 1 408 97206 9

51-1112

Harlequin (UK) policy is to use papers that are natural, renewable and recyclable products and made from wood grown in sustainable forests. The logging and manufacturing processes conform to the legal environmental regulations of the country of origin.

Printed and bound in Spain
by Blackprint CPI, Barcelona

Maureen Child is a California native who loves to travel. Every chance they get, she and her husband are taking off on another research trip. The author of more than sixty books, Maureen loves a happy ending and still swears that she has the best job in the world. She lives in Southern California with her husband, two children and a golden retriever with delusions of grandeur. Visit Maureen's website, www.maureenchild.com.

To Susan Mallery, a great writer and an even better friend. For all of the shared dreams, all of the good laughs and all those yet to come.
Thanks, Susan.

One

Garrett King was in Hell.

Dozens of screaming, laughing children raced past him and he winced as their voices hit decibels only dogs should have been able to hear. Happiest Place on Earth? He didn't think so.

How he had let himself be talked into this, he had no idea.

"Getting soft," he muttered darkly and leaned one hand on the hot metal balustrade in front of him only to wrench his hand back instantly. He glanced at his palm, sighed and reached for a napkin out of his cousin's bag to wipe the sticky cotton candy off his skin.

"You could be at the office," he told himself sternly, wadding up the napkin and tossing it into a trash can. "You could be checking invoices, keeping tabs on the new client. But no, you had to say yes to your cousin instead."

Jackson King had pulled out all the stops getting Garrett to go along with this little family adventure. Jackson's wife, Casey, was apparently "worried" because Garrett was alone too much. Nice woman Casey, he told himself. But did no one ever consider that maybe a man was alone because he *wanted* to be?

But he still could have begged off if it had been just Casey and Jackson doing the asking. But Garrett's cousin had cheated.

He had had his daughters ask "Uncle" Garrett to go with them and frankly, when faced with three of the cutest kids in the world, it would have been impossible to say no. And Jackson knew it, the clever bastard.

"Hey, cuz!" Jackson's shout sounded out and Garrett turned to give him a hard look.

Jackson only laughed. "Casey, honey," he said, turning to his stunning wife, "did you see that? I don't think Garrett's having any fun."

"About that," Garrett cut in, lifting his voice to be heard over the raucous noise rising from the crowd, "I was thinking I'd just head out now. Leave you guys to some family fun."

"You *are* family, Garrett," Casey pointed out.

Before he could speak, Garrett felt a tug at his pants leg. He looked down into Mia's upturned face. "Uncle Garrett, we're going on the fast mountain ride. You wanna come?"

At five, Mia King was already a heartbreaker. From her King blue eyes to the missing front tooth to the dimple in her cheek, she was absolutely adorable. And not being a dummy, she knew how to work it already, too.

"Uh…" Garrett glanced behind Mia to her younger sisters Molly and Mara. Molly was three and Mara was just beginning to toddle. The three of them were unstoppable, Garrett told himself wryly.

There was just no way he was getting out of this day

early. One girl pouting was hard to resist. Three were too much for any man to stand against.

"How about I stand here and watch your stuff while you guys go on the ride?"

Jackson snorted a laugh that Garrett ignored. For God's sake, he owned the most respected security company in the country and here he was haggling with a five-year-old.

Garrett and Jackson had been good friends for years. Most of the King cousins were close, but he and Jackson had worked closely together over the years. Garrett's security company and Jackson's company, King Jets, fed off each other. With Garrett's high-priced clients renting Jackson's luxury jets, both companies were thriving for the loosely defined partnership.

Jackson's wife, Casey, on the other hand, was one of those happily married women who saw every determined bachelor as a personal challenge.

"You going on the Matterhorn with us?" Jackson asked, plucking Mara from his wife's arms. The chubby toddler slapped at his cheeks gleefully and Garrett watched with some amusement as Jackson practically melted. The man was a sap when it came to his family. Funny, because in business, Jackson King was a cutthroat kind of guy that nobody wanted to cross.

"Nope," Garrett told him and lifted the baby out of his cousin's arms. With the crazed population explosion in the King family, Garrett was getting used to dealing with kids. Comfortably settling the tiny girl on his hip, he said, "I'll wait here with Mara and the rest of your—" he paused to glance down at the stroller and the bags already piled high on it "—stuff."

"You could ride with me," Mia insisted, turning those big blue eyes on him.

"Oh, she's good," Jackson whispered on a laugh.

Garrett went down on one knee and looked her in the eye. "How about I stay here with your sister and you tell me all about the ride when you get off?"

She scowled a little, clearly unused to losing, then grinned. "Okay."

Casey took both of the girls' hands, smiled at Garrett and headed for the line.

"I didn't ask you to come along so you could just stand around, you know," Jackson said.

"Yeah. Why did you ask me along? Better yet, why'd I say yes?"

Jackson laughed, looked over his shoulder at his wife and then said, "One word. Casey. She thinks you're lonely. And if you think I'm going to listen to her worry about you all by myself, you're nuts."

Mara slapped Garrett's face. He swiveled his head to smile at the baby. "Your daddy's scared of your mommy."

"Damn straight," Jackson admitted with a laugh. He headed off after the rest of his family and called back, "If she gets cranky, there's a bottle in the diaper bag."

"I think I can handle a baby," he shouted back, but Jackson was already swallowed by the crowd.

"It's just you and me, kid," Garrett told the girl who laughed delightedly and squirmed as if she wanted to be turned loose to run. "Oh, no, you don't. I put you down, you disappear and your mommy kills me."

"Down." Mara looked mutinous.

"No."

She scowled again then tried a coy smile.

"Man," Garrett said with a smile. "Are women *born* knowing how to do that?"

Bright, cheerful calliope music erupted from somewhere nearby and the smell of popcorn floated on the breeze. A dog wearing a top hat was waltzing with Cinder-

ella to the cheers of the crowd. And Garrett was holding a
baby and feeling as out of place as—hell, he couldn't even
think of anything as out of place as he felt at the moment.

This was not his world, he thought, jiggling Mara when
she started fussing. Give Garrett King a dangerous situation, a shooter going after a high-profile target, a kidnapping, even a jewelry heist, and he was in his element.

This happy, shiny stuff? Not so much.

Owning and operating the biggest, most successful security company in the country was bound to color your
outlook on the world. Their clients ranged from royalty
to wealthy industrialists, computer billionaires and poli-
ticians. Because of their own immense wealth, the King
brothers knew how to blend in when arranging security.
Because of their expertise, their reputation kept growing.
Their firm was the most sought-after of its kind on the
planet. The King twins flew all over the world to meet
the demands of their clients. And he and his twin, Griffin, were good with that. Not everyone could be relaxed
and optimistic. There had to be people like he and Griff
around to take care of the dirty jobs.

That was his comfort zone, he told himself as he
watched Jackson and his family near the front of the line.
Casey was holding Molly and Jackson had Mia up on his
shoulders. They looked…perfect. And Garrett was glad
for his cousin, really. In fact, he was happy for all of the
Kings who had recently jumped off a cliff into the un-
charted waters of marriage and family. But he wouldn't
be joining them.

Guys like him didn't do happy endings.

"That's okay, though," he whispered, planting a kiss on
Mara's forehead. "I'll settle for spending time with you
guys. How's that?"

She burbled something he took as agreement then fixed her gaze on a bright pink balloon. "Boon!"

Garrett was just going to buy it for her when he noticed the woman.

Alexis Morgan Wells was having a *wonderful* day. Disneyland was everything she had hoped it would be. She loved everything about it. The music, the laughter. The cartoon characters wandering around interacting with the crowd. She loved the gardens, the topiary statues; she even loved the smell of the place. It was like childhood and dreams and magic all at once.

The music from the last ride she'd been on was still dancing through her mind—she had a feeling it would be for hours—when she noticed the man coming up to her. Her good mood quickly drained away as the same man who had followed her on to It's a Small World hurried to catch up. He'd had the seat behind her in the boat and had come close to ruining the whole experience for her as he insisted on trying to talk to her.

Just as he was now.

"Come on, babe. I'm not a crazy person or anything. I just want to buy you lunch. Is that so bad?"

She half turned and gave him a patient, if tight, smile. "I've already told you I'm not interested, so please go away."

Instead of being rebuffed, his eyes lit up. "You're British, aren't you? The accent's cool."

"Oh, for heaven's sake."

She was really going to have to work on that, she told herself sternly. If she wasn't paying close attention, her clipped accent immediately branded her as "different." Though it would take a much better ear than that of the man currently bothering her, to recognize that her accent wasn't British, but Cadrian.

But if she worked at it, she could manage an American accent—since her mother had been born in California. Thinking about her mom brought a quick zip of guilt shooting through her, but Alex tamped it down. She'd deal with it later. She was absolutely sure her mother would understand why Alex had had to leave—she was just in no hurry to hear how much worry she'd caused by taking off.

After all, Alex was a bright, capable adult and if she wanted a vacation, why should she have to jump through hoops to take one? There, she was feeling better already. Until she picked up on the fact that her would-be admirer was still talking. Honestly, she was trying to stay under the radar and this man was drawing way too much attention to her.

Trying to ignore him, Alex quickened her steps, moving in and out of the ever-shifting crowd with the grace earned from years of dance lessons. She wore a long, tunic-style white blouse, blue jeans and blue platform heels, and, at the moment, she was wishing she'd worn sneakers. Then she could have sprinted for some distance.

The minute that thought entered her mind, she dismissed it, though. Running through a crowd like a lunatic would only draw the notice she was trying to avoid.

"C'mon, babe, it's *lunch*. What could it hurt?"

"I don't eat," she told him, "I'm an oxygenarian."

He blinked at her. "What?"

"Nothing," she muttered, hurrying again. Stop talking to him, she told herself. Ignore him and he'll go away.

She headed for the landmark right ahead of her. The snow-topped mountain in the middle of Anaheim, California. This particular mountain was probably one of the best known peaks in the world. Alex smiled just looking at it. She lifted her gaze and watched as toboggans filled with screaming, laughing people jolted around curves and splashed through lagoons, sending waves of water into the air. The line for the mountain was a long one and as her gaze moved over the people there, she saw *him*. He was watching her. A big man with black hair, a stern jaw and a plump baby on his hip.

In one quick instant, she felt a jolt of something like "recognition." As if something inside her, *knew* him. Had been searching for him. Unfortunately, judging by the black-haired little girl he was holding, some other woman had found him first.

"Quit walking so fast, will ya?" the annoying guy behind her whined.

Alex fixed her gaze on the sharp-eyed man and felt his stare hit her as powerfully as a touch. Then his eyes shifted from her to the man behind her and back again. He seemed to understand the situation instantly.

"There you are, honey!" he called out, smiling directly at Alex. "What took you so long?"

Smiling broadly, she accepted the help he was offering and ran to him. He greeted her with a grin then dropped one arm around her shoulders, pulling her in close to his side. Only then did he shift his gaze to the disappointed man.

"There a problem here?" Her Knight in Shining Denim demanded.

"No," the guy muttered, shaking his head. "No problem. Later."

And he was gone.

Alex watched him go with a sigh of relief. Not that he had ever scared her or anything, but she hadn't wanted to waste her first day in Disneyland being irritated. The big man beside her still had his arm around her and Alex liked it. He was big and strong and it was hard not to appreciate a guy who had seen you needed help and offered it without a qualm.

"Boon!"

The little girl's voice shattered the moment and with that reminder that her hero was probably someone else's husband, Alex slipped out from under his arm. Glancing up at the little girl, she smiled. "You're a beauty, aren't you? Your daddy must be very proud."

"Oh, he is," the man beside her said, his voice so deep it seemed to sink right inside her. "And he's got two more just like her."

"Really." She wasn't sure why the news that he was the father of three was so disappointing, but there it was.

"Yeah. My cousin and his wife have the other two on the ride right now. I'm just watching this one for them."

"Oh." She smiled, pleasure rushing through her. "Then you're not her father?"

He smiled, too, as if he knew exactly what she was thinking. "Not a chance. I wouldn't do that to some poor, unsuspecting kid."

Alex looked into his eyes and enjoyed the sparkle she found there. He was relishing this little flirtation as much as she was. "Oh, I don't know. A hero might make a very good father."

"Hero? I'm hardly that."

"You were for me a minute ago," she said. "I couldn't seem to convince that man to leave me alone, so I really appreciate your help."

"You're welcome. But you could have gone to a security guard and had the guy thrown out. Probably should have."

No, going to a security guard would have involved making statements, filling out paperwork and then her identity would be revealed and the lovely day she'd planned would have been ruined.

She shook her head, pushed her long blond hair back from her face and turned to sweep her gaze across the manicured flower gardens, the happy kids and the brilliant blue sky overhead. "No, he wasn't dangerous. Just irritating."

He laughed and she liked the sound of it.

"Boon, Gar," the little girl said in a voice filled with the kind of determination only a single-minded toddler could manage.

"Right. Balloon." He lifted one hand to the balloon seller, and the guy stepped right up, gently tying the string of a bright pink balloon to the baby's wrist. While Garrett paid the man, the baby waved her arm, squealing with delight as the balloon danced and jumped to her whim.

"So, I think introductions are in order," he said. "This demanding female is Mara and I'm Garrett."

"Alexis, but call me Alex," she said, holding her right hand out to him.

He took her hand in his and the instant her skin brushed along his, Alex felt ripples of something really intriguing washing throughout her body. Then he let her go and the delightful heat dissipated.

"So, Alex, how's your day going?"

She laughed a little. "Until that one little moment, it was going great. I love it here. It's my first time, and I've heard so much about this place..."

"Ah," he said nodding, "that explains it."

She tensed. "Explains what?"

"If it's your first time here, you're having so much fun that all of these crowds don't bother you."

"Oh, no. I think it's wonderful. Everyone seems so nice, well, except for—"

"That one little moment?" he asked, repeating her words to her.

"Yes, exactly." Alex smiled again and reluctantly took a step back. As lovely as this was, talking to a handsome man who had no idea who she was, it would be better for her if she ended it now and went on her way. "Thank you again for the rescue, but I should really be going…"

He tipped his head to one side and looked at her. "Meeting someone?"

"No, but—"

"Then what's your hurry?"

Her heartbeat sped up at the invitation in his eyes. He didn't want her to leave. And how nice that was. He actually liked her.

The darling little girl was still playing with her balloon, paying no attention at all to the two adults with her.

Alex looked up into Garrett's pale blue eyes and did some fast thinking. She had to keep a low profile, true. But that didn't mean she had to be a hermit during her… vacation, did it? And what kind of holiday would it be if there were no "romance" included?

"What do you say," he added, "hang with us today. Rescue me from a day filled with too many kids?"

"*You* need rescuing?"

She saw the teasing glint in his eyes and responded to it with a smile.

"Trust me. My cousin's girls all have my number. If you're not there to protect me, who knows what might happen?"

Tempting, she thought. So very tempting. She'd only been in America for three days and already she was feeling a little isolated. Being on her own was liberating, but, as it turned out, *lonely*. And it wasn't as if she could call the few friends she had in the States—the moment she did, word would get back to her family and, just like that, her bid for freedom would end.

What could it hurt to spend the day with a man who made her toes curl and the family he clearly loved? She took a breath and made the leap. "All right, thank you. I would love to rescue you."

"Excellent. My cousin and his family should be back any minute now. So while we wait, why don't you tell me where you're from. I can't quite place your accent. It's British, but…not."

She jolted a little and fought to keep him from seeing it. "You've a good ear."

"So I've been told. But that's not really an answer, is it?"

No, it wasn't, and how astute of him to notice. She'd been trained in how to answer questions without really answering them from the time she was a child. Her father would have been proud. *Never answer a question directly, Alexis. Always be vague. Watch what you say, Alexis. You've a responsibility to your family. Your heritage. Your people…*

"Hey. Alex."

At the sound of his concerned voice, she shook her head, coming out of her thoughts with relief. That was the second time Garrett had rescued her today. She didn't want to think about her duties. Her role in history. She didn't want to be anything but Alex.

So instead of being evasive again, she said, "Why don't you try to figure out where I'm from and I'll let you know when you've got it right?"

One dark eyebrow lifted. "Oh, you're challenging the wrong guy. But you're on. Five bucks says I've got it by the end of the day."

Oh, she hoped not. If he did, that would ruin everything. But she braved it out and asked, "Five dollars? Not much of a wager."

He gave her a slow grin that sent new flashes of heat dancing through her system. "I'm open to negotiation."

She actually *felt* her blood sizzle and hum.

"No, no. That's all right." She backed up quickly. Maybe she wasn't as prepared for that zing of romance as she had thought. Or maybe Garrett the Gorgeous was just too much for her to handle. Either way, she was nervous enough to try to cool things down between them just a little. "Five dollars will do. It's a bargain."

"Agreed," he said, one corner of his mouth lifting tantalizingly. "But just so you know, you should never bet with me, Alex. I always win."

"Confident, aren't you?"

"You have no idea."

A thrill of something hot and delicious swept through her veins. Nerves or not, she really enjoyed what he was doing to her. What was it about him that affected her so?

"That was fun, Uncle Garrett!"

A tiny whirlwind rushed up to them and threw both arms around Garrett's knees. The girl gave him a wide smile then shifted suspicious eyes to Alex. "Who are you?"

"This is Alex," Garrett told her. "Alex, meet Mia."

She smiled at the child and couldn't help noticing that the little girl held on to Garrett's legs just a little more tightly.

"Mia, don't run from me in these crowds," a deep male voice shouted.

Alex turned to watch an impossibly attractive couple approach, the man holding on to a smaller version of the still-wary Mia.

"Alex," Garrett said briskly, "this is my cousin Jackson and his wife, Casey, and that pretty girl with them is Molly."

"It's lovely to meet you all."

Jackson gave her a quick up and down, then winked at his wife. "Wow, leave Garrett alone for a few minutes and he finds the most beautiful woman in the whole place—"

His wife nudged him with an elbow.

"—not counting you of course, sweetie. You're the most beautiful woman in the *world*."

"Nice recovery," Casey told him with a laugh and a smile for Alex.

"Always were a smooth one, Jackson," Garrett mused.

"It's why she loves me," his cousin answered, dropping a kiss on his wife's head.

Alex smiled at all of them. It was lovely to see the open affection in this family, though she felt a sharp pang of envy slice at her, as well. To get some time for herself she'd had to run from her own family. She missed them, even her dictatorial father, and being around these people only brought up their loss more sharply.

"It's nice to meet you, Alex," Casey said, extending her right hand in welcome.

"Thank you. I must admit I'm a little overwhelmed by everything. This is my first trip to Disneyland and—"

"Your *first* time?" Mia interrupted. "But you're *old*."

"Mia!" Casey was horrified.

Garrett and Jackson laughed and Alex joined them. Bending down slightly, she met Mia's gaze and said, "It's horrible I know. But I live very far away from here, so this is the first chance I've ever had to visit."

"Oh." Nodding her head, Mia thought about it for a minute then looked at her mother. "I think we should take Alex to the ghost ride."

"Mia, that's *your* favorite ride," her father said.

"But she would like it, wouldn't you, Alex?" She turned her eyes up and gave her a pleading look.

"You know," Alex said, "I was just wishing I knew how to find the ghost ride."

"I'll show you!" Mia took her hand and started walking, fully expecting her family to follow.

"Guess you'll be spending the day with us for sure, now," Garrett teased.

"Looks that way." She grinned, delighted with this turn of events. She was in a place she'd heard about her whole life and she wasn't alone. There were children to enjoy and people to talk to and it was very near to perfect.

Then she looked up at Garrett's blue eyes and told herself maybe it was closer to perfect than she knew.

"And after the ghost ride, we can ride the jungle boats and then the pirate one." Mia was talking a mile a minute.

"Molly, honey, don't pick up the bug," Jackson said patiently.

"Bug?" Casey repeated, horrified.

Still holding Mara, Garrett came up beside Alex and said softly, "I promise, after the ghost ride, I'll ride herd on my family and you can do what you want to do."

The funny thing was, he didn't know it, but she was already doing what she had always wanted to do.

She *wanted* to be accepted. To spend a day with nothing more to worry about than enjoying herself. And mostly, she wanted to meet people and have them like her because she was Alex Wells.

Not because she was Her Royal Highness Princess Alexis Morgan Wells of Cadria.

Two

She was driving Garrett just a little crazy.

And not only because she was beautiful and funny and smart. But because he'd never seen a woman let go and really enjoy herself so much. Most of the women who came and went from his life were more interested in how their hair looked. Or in being sophisticated enough that a ride on spinning teacups would never have entered their heads.

But Alex was different. She had the girls eating out of her hand, and, without even trying, she was reaching Garrett in ways that he never would have expected. He couldn't take his eyes off her.

That wide smile was inviting, sexy—and familiar, somehow.

He knew he'd seen her before somewhere, but damned if he could remember where. And that bothered him, too. Because a woman like Alex wasn't easily forgotten.

At lunch, she had bitten into a burger with a sigh of pleasure so rich that all he could think of was cool sheets and hot sex. She sat astride a carousel horse and he imagined her straddling him. She licked at an ice cream cone and he—

Garrett shook his head and mentally pulled back fast from that particular image. As it was, he was having a hard time walking. A few more thoughts like that one and he'd be paralyzed.

Alex loved everything about Disneyland. He saw it in her eyes because she didn't hide a thing. Another way she was different from the women he knew. They were all about artful lies, strategic moves and studied flirtation.

Alex was just…herself.

"You'll like this, Alex," said Mia, who had appointed herself Alex's personal tour guide. "The pirate ships shoot cannons and there's a fire and singing, too. And it's dark inside."

"Okay, kiddo," Jackson told his daughter, interrupting her flood of information, "how about we give Alex a little rest?" He grinned at her and Garrett as he steered his family into the front row of the boat.

Garrett took the hint gratefully and pulled Alexis into the last row. A bit of separation for the duration of the ride would give them a little time to themselves.

"She's wonderful," Alex murmured. "So bright. So talkative."

"Oh, she is that," Garrett said with a laugh. "Mia has an opinion on everything and doesn't hesitate to share it. Her kindergarten teacher calls her 'precocious.' I call her a busybody."

She laughed again and Garrett found himself smiling in response. There was no cautious titter. No careful chuckle. When Alex laughed, she threw her soul into it and every-

thing about her lit up. Oh, he was getting in way too deep.
This was ridiculous. Not only did he not even know her
last name, but he hadn't been able to pin down what country she was from, either.

Not for lack of trying, though.

The sense of familiarity he had for her was irritating
as hell. There was something there. Something just out of
reach, that would tell him how he knew her. Who she was.
And yet, he couldn't quite grab hold of it.

The ride jolted into motion and Alex leaned forward,
eager to see everything. He liked that about her, too. Her
curiosity. Her appreciation for whatever was happening. It wasn't something enough people did, living in the
moment. For most, it was all about "tomorrow." What they
would do when they had the time or the money or the
energy.

He'd seen it all too often. People who had everything
in the world and didn't seem to notice because they were
always looking forward to the next thing.

"Wonderful," she whispered. Their boat rocked lazily
on its tracks, water slapping at its hull. She looked behind
them at the people awaiting the next boat then shifted her
gaze to his.

Overhead, a night sky was filled with stars and ani-
matronic fireflies blinked on and off. A sultry, hot breeze
wafted past them. Even in the darkness, he saw delight
shining in her eyes and the curve of her mouth was something he just didn't want to resist any longer.

Leaning forward, he caught her by the back of the neck
and pulled her toward him. Then he slanted his mouth over
hers for a taste of the mouth that had been driving him
nuts for hours.

She was worth the wait.

After a second's surprise, she recovered and kissed him

back. Her mouth moved against his with a soft, languid touch that stirred fires back into life and made him wish they were all alone in the dark—rather than surrounded by singing pirates and chattering tourists.

She sighed and leaned into him and that fired him up so fast, it took his breath away. But who needed breathing anyway? She lifted one hand to his cheek and when she pulled back, breaking the kiss, her fingertips stroked his jaw. She drew a breath and let it go again with a smile. Leaning into him, she whispered, "That was lovely."

He took her hand in his and kissed the center of her palm. "It was way better than lovely."

A kid squealed, a pirate's gun erupted too close to the boat and Alex jolted in surprise. Then she laughed with delight and eased back against him, pillowing her head on his shoulder. He pulled her in more closely to him and, instead of watching the ride, indulged himself by watching her reactions to their surroundings instead.

Her eyes never stopped shifting. Her smile never faltered. She took it all in, as if she were soaking up experiences like a sponge. And in that moment, Garrett was pitifully glad Jackson had talked him into going to Disneyland.

"I'm having such a nice day," she whispered in a voice pitched low enough that Garrett almost missed it.

"*Nice?* That's it?"

She tipped her head back and smiled up at him. "*Very* nice."

"Oh, well then, that's better." He snorted and shook his head. Nothing a man liked better than hearing the woman he was fantasizing about telling him she was having a "nice" time.

"Oh, look! The dog has the jail cell keys!" She was off again, losing herself in the moment and Garrett was charmed. The pirates were singing, water lapped at the sides of their boat and up ahead of them he could hear Mia singing along. He smiled to himself and realized that astonishing as it was, he, too, was having a *very* nice day.

After the ride, they walked into twilight. Sunset stained the sky with the last shreds of color before night crept in. The girls were worn-out. Molly was dragging, Mara was asleep on Casey's shoulder and Mia was so far beyond tired, her smile was fixed more in a grimace. But before they could go home, they had to make their traditional last stop.

"You'll like the castle, Alex," Mia said through a yawn. "Me and Molly are gonna be princesses someday and we're gonna have a castle like this one and we'll have puppies, too…"

"Again with the dog," Jackson said with a sigh at what was apparently a very familiar topic.

Alex chuckled and slipped her hand into Garrett's. His fingers closed over hers as he cut a glance her way. In the soft light, her eyes shone with the same excitement he'd seen earlier. She wasn't tired out by all the kids and the crowds. She was thriving on this.

Her mouth curved slightly and another ping of recognition hit him. Frowning to himself, Garrett tried to pin down where he'd seen her before. He knew he'd never actually *met* her before today. He wouldn't have forgotten that. But she was so damned familiar…

The castle shone with a pink tinge and as they approached, lights carefully hidden behind rocks and in the shrubbery blinked on to make it seem even more of a fairy-tale palace.

Garrett shook his head and smiled as Mia cooed in delight. Swans were floating gracefully in the lake. A cool wind rustled the trees and lifted the scent of the neatly trimmed rosebushes into the air.

"Can I have a princess hat?" Mia asked.

"Sure you can, sweetie," Jackson said, scooping his oldest into his arms for a fast hug.

Garrett watched the byplay and, for the first time, felt a twinge of regret. Not that it would last long, but for the moment, he could admit that the thought of having kids like Mia and her sisters wasn't an entirely hideous idea. For other people, of course. Not for him.

"Alex, look!" Mia grabbed Alex's hand and half dragged her up to the stone balustrade overlooking the lake. The two of them stood together, watching the swans, the pink castle in the background and Garrett stopped dead. And stared.

In one blinding instant, he knew why she looked so familiar.

Several years ago, he'd done some work for her father.

Her father, the King of Cadria.

Which meant that Alex the delicious, Alex the sexiest woman he'd ever known, was actually the Crown Princess Alexis.

And he'd kissed her.

Damn.

He scrubbed one hand across the back of his neck, took a deep breath and held it. This changed things. Radically.

"Do you want to live in a castle, Alex?" Mia asked.

Garrett listened for her answer.

Alex ran one hand over Mia's long black hair and said, "I think a castle might get lonely. They're awfully big, you know. And drafty, as well."

Garrett watched her face as she described what he knew was her home. Funny, he'd never imagined that a princess might not like her life. After all, in the grand scheme,

being royalty had to be better than a lot of other alterna-
tives.

"But I could have lots of puppies," Mia said thought-
fully.

"Yes, but you'd never see them because princesses can't
play with puppies. They have more important things to
do. They have to say all the right things, do all the right
things. There's not a lot of time for playing."

Mia frowned at that.

So did Garrett. Was that how she really felt about her
life? Was that why she was here, trying to be incognito?
To escape her world? And what would she do if she knew
he had figured out her real identity? Would she bolt?

Alex smiled and said, "I think you might not like a real
castle as much as you do this one."

Nodding, the little girl murmured, "Maybe I'll just be
a pretend princess."

"Excellent idea," Alex told her with another smile. Then
she turned her head to look at Garrett and their gazes col-
lided.

He felt the slam of attraction hit him like a fist to the
chest. He was in deep trouble here. A princess, for God's
sake? He'd kissed a *princess*? He took a good long look at
her, from her platform heels to the blue jeans and the pair
of sunglasses perched on top of her head.

She had worked very hard to disguise herself, he
thought, and wondered why. As a princess, she could have
had a guided tour through the park, swept through all of
the lines and been treated like—well, royalty. Instead, she
had spent her day wandering through Disneyland just like
any other tourist.

Alone.

That word shouted through his mind and instantly,
his professional side sat up and took notice. Letting go,

for the moment, of the fact that she'd lied about who she was—where was her security detail? Where were her bodyguards? The entourage? Didn't she know how dangerous it was for someone like her to be unprotected? The world was a dangerous place and helping out the wackos by giving them a clear shot at you didn't seem like a good plan to him.

So just what was she up to?

As if reading his troubled thoughts from the emotions in his eyes, Alex's smile faded slightly. Garrett noticed and immediately put his game face on. She was keeping her identity a secret for a reason. Until he found out what that was, he'd play along.

And until he knew everything that was happening, he'd make damn sure she was safe.

In the huge parking lot, they all said goodbye and Jackson and Casey herded their girls off toward their car. The parking lot lights above them flickered weirdly as tourists streamed past like zombies in search of the best way home.

Garrett turned to look at Alex again. "Where's your car?"

"Oh, I don't have one," she said quickly. "I never learned to drive, so I took a cab here from the hotel."

A cab, he thought grimly. On her own. She was asking for disaster. It was a freaking miracle she'd made it here without somebody recognizing her and tipping off the press. "Where are you staying?"

"In Huntington Beach."

Not too far, he thought, but far enough that he didn't want her repeating the "grab a cab" thing. His gaze scanning the crowded lot and the people passing by them, he said, "I'll give you a ride back to your hotel."

"Oh, you don't have to do that," she argued automatically.

He wondered if it was sheer politeness or a reaction to his change in attitude. The closeness, the heat that had been between them earlier and definitely cooled. But how could it not? She was a runaway princess, and he was the guy who knew better than to give in to his urges, now that he knew the truth.

She was a *princess* for God's sake. Didn't matter that his bank account was probably close to hers. There was wealth and then there was *royalty.* The two didn't necessarily mix.

"Yeah," he told her, "I really do."

"I can take care of myself," she said.

"I'm sure you can. But why wait for a cab when I'm here and ready?"

No way was he going to let her out of his sight until he knew she was safe. She was too high-profile. Princess Alexis's pretty face had adorned more magazine covers than he could count. Reporters and photographers usually followed after her like rats after the Pied Piper. Her luck was bound to run out soon and once it did, she'd have people crowding all around her. And not all of them would be trustworthy.

Nope. He'd be with her until he got her back to her hotel, at least. Then he'd figure out what to do next.

"Well, all right then," she said with a smile. "Thank you."

The traffic gods were smiling on them and it didn't take more than twenty minutes before he was steering his BMW up to the waterfront hotel. He left his keys with the valet, took Alex's arm and escorted her into the hotel. His gaze never quit moving, checking out the area, the people, the situation. The hotel lobby was elegant and mostly empty. Live trees stood in huge, terra cotta pots on the inside of the double doors. A marble floor gleamed under pearly lights and tasteful paintings hung on cream-colored walls.

A couple of desk clerks were busily inputting things into computers. A guest stood at the concierge, asking questions, and an elevator hushed open to allow an elderly couple to exit. It all looked fine to his studied eyes, but as he knew all too well, things could change in an instant. An ordinary moment could become the stuff of nightmares in a heartbeat.

Alex was blissfully unaware of his tension, though, and kept up a steady stream of comments as they walked toward the bank of elevators. "It's this one," she said and used her key card to activate it.

While they waited, he took another quick look around and noted that no one had paid the slightest attention to them. Good. Seemed that her identity was still a secret. Somehow that made him feel a bit better about his own failure to recognize her.

But in his own defense, you didn't normally see a princess in blue jeans taking a cab to Disneyland.

She was staying in the penthouse suite, of course, and he was glad to see that there was a special elevator for that floor that required a key card. At least she had semiprotection. Not from the hotel staff of course, and he knew how easily bribed a staff member could be. For the right price, some people would sell off their souls.

When the elevator opened, they stepped into a marble-floored entryway with a locked door opposite them. He waited for her to open the door then before she could say anything, he stepped inside, to assure himself that all was as it should be. His practiced gaze swept over the interior of the plushly decorated suite. Midnight-blue couches and chairs made up conversation areas. An unlit fireplace took up most of one wall and the sliding glass doors along a wall of windows afforded an amazing view of the ocean. Starlight filled the dark sky and the moon shone down on the water with a sparkling silver light.

He stalked across the suite to the bedroom, gave it and the master bath a quick, thorough look then moved back into the living room. He checked the balcony then swept his gaze around the room. No sign of anything and just the stillness in the room told him that there hadn't been any intruders.

"What're you doing?" she asked, tossing the key card onto the nearest table.

"Just making sure you're okay." He brushed it off as if it were nothing more than any other guy would have done. But she was no dummy and her blue eyes narrowed slightly in suspicion.

Her nose was sunburned, her hair was a wild tangle and she looked, he thought, absolutely edible. His body stirred in reaction and he told himself to get a grip. There wouldn't be any more kisses. No more fantasies. Not now that he knew who she was.

Alex was strictly off-limits. Oh, he wanted her. Bad. But damned if he was going to start an international incident or something. He'd met her father. He knew the king was not the kind of man to take it lightly if some commoner was sniffing around the royal princess. And Garrett didn't need the extra hassle anyway. Yeah, she was gorgeous. And hot. And funny and smart. But that crown of hers was just getting in the way. And beside all that was the fact that she was here. Alone. Unprotected. Garrett was hardwired to think more of her safety than of his own wants. And mixing the two never worked well.

"Well, I appreciate it," she said softly, "but I'm really

fine. The hotel is a good one and they have excellent security."

Uh-huh. He wasn't so sure of that, but he'd be doing some checking into the situation, that was for damn sure. True, it was a five-star hotel and that usually meant guests were safe. But as he had found out the hard way, mistakes happened.

"Thank you again."

Alex walked toward him and everything in him wanted to reach out, grab her and pull her in close. He could still taste her, damn it, and he knew he wouldn't be forgetting anytime soon just how good she felt, pressed up against him. His body was hard and aching like a bad tooth, which didn't do much for his attitude.

"I had a wonderful day." Her smile widened and she threw her arms out. "Actually, it was perfect. Just as I'd always imagined my first day at Disneyland would be."

That statement caught him off guard and he laughed. "You imagined a five-year-old talking your ears off?"

"I imagined a day spent with friends and finding someone who—" She broke off there, letting the rest of what she might have said die unuttered.

Just as well, Garrett told himself. He might be a professional security expert, but he was also a guy. And knowing that she felt the same pulse of desire he did was almost more than he could take.

Hell, if he didn't get out of there soon, he might forget all about his principles and better judgment.

"Guess I'd better go," he said, stepping past her for the open doorway while he could still manage it.

"Oh. Are you sure?" She waved one hand at the wet bar across the room. "Maybe one drink first? Or I could call room service…"

She wasn't making this easy, he told himself. Need

grabbed him at the base of the throat and squeezed. It would be so easy to stay here. To kiss her again and take his time about it. To feel her body respond to his and to forget all about who she was. Who he was. And why this was a really bad idea.

"I don't think so," he said, "but thanks. Another time."

"Of course." Disappointment clouded her features briefly. And after a day of watching her smile and enjoy herself, damned if he could stand her feeling badly.

"How about breakfast?" He heard himself say it and couldn't call the words back.

That smile of hers appeared again and his heart thudded painfully in his chest. Garrett King, master of bad mistakes.

"I'd like that."

"I'll see you then," he said and stepped out of the penthouse, closing the door quietly behind him.

In the elevator, he stood perfectly still and let the annoying Muzak fill his mind and, temporarily at least, drive out his churning thoughts. But it couldn't last. He had to think about this. Figure out how to handle this situation.

Yes, he wanted Alex.

But his own code of behavior demanded that he protect—not bed—the princess.

He watched the numbers over the elevator doors flash and as they hit the first floor and those doors sighed open, he told himself that maybe he could do both.

The question was, should he?

Three

"Did you and Mickey have a good time?"

"Funny." Garrett dropped into his favorite, blood-red leather chair and propped his feet up on the matching hassock. Clutching his cell phone in one hand and a cold bottle of beer in the other, he listened to his twin's laughter.

"Sorry, man," Griff finally said, "but made me laugh all day thinking about you hauling your ass around the happiest place on Earth. All day. Still can't believe you let Jackson con you into going."

"Wasn't Jackson," Garrett told him. "It was Casey."

"Ah. Well then, that's different." Griffin sighed. "What is it about women? How do they get us to do things we would never ordinarily do?"

"Beats the hell outta me," Garrett said. In his mind, he was seeing Alex again as he said goodbye. Her eyes shining, her delectable mouth curved…

"So was it hideous?"

"What?"

"I swear, when I went to Knott's Berry Farm with them last summer, Mia about wore me into the ground. That kid is like the Tiny Terminator."

"Good description," Garrett agreed with a laugh. "And she was pumped today. Only time she sat down was when we were on a ride."

Sympathy in his tone, Griffin said, "Man, that sounds miserable."

"Would have been."

"Yeah...?"

Garrett took a breath, considered what he was about to do, then went with his gut. He was willing to keep Alex's secret, for the time being anyway, but not from Griffin. Not only were they twins, but they were partners in the security firm they had built together.

"So, talk. Explain what saved you from misery."

"Right to the point, as always," Garrett murmured. His gaze swept the room. His condo wasn't big, but it suited him. He'd tried living in hotels for a while like his cousin Rafe had done for years until meeting his wife, Katie. But hotels got damned impersonal and on the rare occasions when Garrett *wasn't* traveling all over the damn globe, he had wanted a place that was *his*. Something familiar to come home to.

He wasn't around enough to justify a house, and he didn't like the idea of leaving it empty for weeks at a stretch, either. But this condo had been just right. A home that he could walk away from knowing the home owner's association was looking after the property.

It was decorated for comfort, and the minute he walked in, he always felt whatever problems he was thinking about slide away. Maybe it was the view of the ocean.

Maybe it was the knowledge that this was his space, one that no one could take from him. Either way, over the past couple of years, it really had become *home*.

The study where he sat now was a man's room, from the dark paneling to the leather furniture to the stone hearth on the far wall. There were miles of bookshelves stuffed with novels, the classics and several gifts presented to him by grateful clients.

And beyond the glass doors, there was a small balcony where he could stand and watch the water. Just like the view from Alex's hotel room. Amazing how quickly his mind could turn and focus back on her.

"Hello? Garrett? You still there?"

"Yes, I'm here."

"Then talk. No more stalling. What's going on?"

"I met a woman today."

"Well, shout hallelujah and alert the media!" Griffin hooted a laugh that had Garrett wrenching the phone away from his ear. "'Bout time you got lucky. I've been telling you for months you needed to loosen up some. What's she like?"

"Believe me when I say she defies description."

"Right. You met a goddess at Disneyland."

"Not exactly."

"What's that mean?"

"She's a princess."

"Oh, no," Griffin groaned dramatically. "You didn't hook up with some snotty society type, did you? Because that's just wrong."

Frowning, Garrett said, "No, she's a *princess*."

"Now I'm confused. Are we talking a real princess? Crown? Throne?"

"Yep."

"What the—"

"Remember that job we did for the King of Cadria a few years ago?"

Silence, while his brother thought about it, then, "Yeah. I remember. They were doing some big show of the crown jewels and we set up the security for the event. Good job."

"Yeah. Remember the daughter?"

"Hah. Of course I remember her. Never met her face-to-face, but I saw her around the palace from a distance once or twice. Man she was—" Another long pause. "Are you kidding me?"

Garrett had gotten a few of those long-distance glances, too. He remembered not paying much attention to her, either. When he was on a job, his concentration was laser-like. Nothing but security concerns had registered for him and once that had been accomplished, he and his brother had left Cadria.

Since the small island nation was just off the coast of England, he and Griffin had flown to Ireland to visit their cousin Jefferson and his family. And never once had Garrett given the crown princess another thought.

Until today.

"Nope. Not kidding. Princess Alexis was at Disneyland today."

"I didn't see anything about it on the news."

"You won't, either." Garrett took a swig of his beer and hoped the icy brew would cool him off. His body was still thrumming, his groin hot and hard, and he had a feeling it was only going to get worse for him, the longer he spent in her company. "She's hiding out or some damn thing. Told us her name was Alex, that's all."

"What about her security?"

"Doesn't have any that I could see."

Griffin inhaled sharply. "That's not good, bro."

"No kidding?" Garrett shook his head as Griffin's concern flashed his own worries into higher gear. Alex was all alone in a hotel room and *Garrett* was the only one who knew where she was. He couldn't imagine her family allowing her to be unprotected, so that told him she had slipped away from her guards. Which left her vulnerable. Hell, anything could happen to her.

"What're you gonna do about it?"

He checked the time on the grandfather clock on the far wall. "I'm going to wait another hour or so, then I'm calling her father."

Griffin laughed. "Yeah, cuz it's that easy to just pick up a phone and call the palace. Hello, King? This is King."

Garrett rolled his eyes at his brother's lame joke. They'd heard plenty just like that one while they were doing the job for Alex's father. Kings working for kings and all that.

"Why am I talking to you again?"

"Because I'm your twin. The one that got all the brains."

"Must explain why I got all the looks," Garrett muttered with a smile.

"In your dreams."

It was an old game. Since they were identical, neither of them had anything to lose by the insults. Griffin was the one person in his life Garrett could always count on. There were four other King brothers in their branch of the family, and they were all close. But being twins had set Garrett and Griffin apart from the rest of their brothers. Growing up, they'd been a team, standing against their older brothers' teasing. They'd played ball together, learned how to drive together and dated cheerleaders together. They were still looking out for each other.

To Kings, nothing was more important than family. Family came first. Always.

Griffin finally stopped laughing and asked, "Seriously, what are you going to do?"

"Just what I said. I'm going to call her father. He gave us a private number, remember?"

"Oh, right."

Nodding, Garrett said, "First, I want to find out if the king knows where she is."

"You think she ran away?"

"I think she's going to a lot of trouble to avoid having people recognize her, so yeah." He remembered the blue jeans, the simple white shirt, the platform heels and her wild tangle of hair. Nope. Not how anyone would expect a princess to look. "Wouldn't be surprised to find out no one but us knows where she is. Anyway, I'll let the king know she's okay and find out how he wants me to handle this."

"And how do *you* want to handle it?" Griffin asked.

Garrett didn't say a word, which pretty much answered Griffin's question more eloquently than words could have. What could he possibly have said anyway? That he didn't want to handle the situation—he wanted to handle *Alex?* Yeah, that'd be good.

"She must be something else."

"Y'know? She really is," he said tightly. "And she's going to stay safe."

Memories flew around him like a cloud of mosquitoes. Nagging. Irritating. He couldn't stop them. Never had been able to make them fade. And that was as it should be, he told himself. He'd made a mistake and someone had died. He should never be allowed to forget.

"Garrett," Griffin said quietly, "you've got to let the past go."

He winced and took another drink of his beer. As twins, they had always been finely attuned to each other. Not exactly reading each other's minds or anything—thank God for small favors. But there was usually an undercurrent that each of them could pick up on. Clearly, Griffin's twin radar was on alert.

"Who's talking about the past?" Bristling, Garrett pushed haunting memories aside and told himself that Alex's situation had nothing to do with what had happened so long ago. And he would do whatever he could to see that it stayed that way.

"Fine. Be stubborn. Keep torturing yourself for something that you did. Not. Do."

"I'm done talking about it," Garrett told his brother.

"Whatever. Always were a hard head."

"Hello, pot? This is kettle. You're black."

"Hey," Griffin complained, "I'm the funny one, remember?"

"What was I thinking?" Garrett smiled to himself and sipped at his beer.

"Look, just keep me posted on this. Let me know what her father has to say and if you need backup, *call*."

"I will," he promised, even though he knew he wouldn't be calling. He didn't want backup with Alex. He wanted to watch over her himself. He trusted his brother with his life. But he would trust *no one* with Alex's. The only way to make sure she stayed safe was to take care of her himself.

Alex couldn't sleep.

Every time she closed her eyes, her mind dredged up images snatched from her memories of the day. Mostly, of course, images of Garrett—laughing, teasing his nieces, carrying a sleeping baby…and images of him as he leaned in to kiss her.

Oh, that kiss had been…well, way too short, but aside

from that, wonderful. She could still hear the water slosh-
ing against the boat, the singing from the pirates and feel
the hot wind buffeting their faces. Still feel his mouth
moving over hers.

It had been, she told herself with a small smile, *magic*.

She picked up her hot tea off the room service cart and
stepped onto the balcony of her suite. A summer wind
welcomed her with the cool kiss of the sea. She stared up
at the night sky then shifted her gaze to the ocean where
the moon's light danced across the surface of the water,
leaving a silvery trail, as if marking a path to be followed.
In the middle of the night, everything was quiet, as if the
whole world was dreaming.

And if she could sleep, Alex knew her dreams would
be filled with Garrett.

She took a sip of the tea and sighed in satisfaction.

Alexis knew she should feel guilty for having left
Cadria the way she had, but she just couldn't manage it.
Maybe it was because of the years she had spent doing all
the "right" things. She had been a dutiful daughter, a help-
ful sister, a perfect princess. She was always in the right
place at the right time saying the right things.

She loved her father, but the man was practically me-
dieval. If it weren't for her mother's restraining influence,
King Gregory of Cadria would probably have had his only
daughter fitted for a chastity belt and tucked away in a
tower. Until he picked out the right husband for her, of
course.

Alex had had to fight for every scrap of independence
she had found over the past few years. She hadn't wanted
to be seen only at state occasions. Or to christen a new
ship or open a new park. She wanted more. She wanted
her life to mean something.

And if that meant a twenty-eight-year-old woman had to run away from home—then so be it.

She only hoped her father would eventually forgive her. Maybe he would understand one day just how important her independence was to her.

Nothing had ever been *hers*. The palace deemed what she should do and when she should do it.

Even her work with single mothers in need, in the capital city of Cadria, had been co-opted by the palace press. They made her out to be a saint. To be the gently bred woman reaching out to the less fortunate. Which just infuriated her and embarrassed the women she was trying to help.

Her entire life had been built around a sense of duty and privilege, and it was choking her.

Shaking her head, she tried to push that thought aside because she knew very well how pitiful that sounded. Poor little rich girl, such a trying life. But being a princess was every bit as suffocating as she had tried to tell little Mia earlier.

Mia.

Alexis smiled to herself in spite of her rushing thoughts. That little girl and her family had given Alex one of the best days of her life. Back at the palace, she had felt as though her life was slipping away from her, disappearing into the day-to-day repetitiveness of the familiar. The safe.

There were no surprises in her world. No days of pure enjoyment. No rush of attraction or sizzle of sexual heat. Though she had longed for all of those for most of her life.

She had grown up on tales of magic. Romance. Her mom had always insisted that there was something special about Disneyland. That the joy that infused the place somehow made it more enchanted than anywhere else.

Alex's mother had been nineteen and working in one

of the gift shops on Main Street when she met the future
King of Cadria. Of course, Mom hadn't known then that
the handsome young man flirting with her was a prince.
She had simply fallen for his kind eyes and quiet smile. He
kept his title a secret until Alex's mother was in love—and
that, Alexis had always believed, was the secret. Find a
man who didn't know who she was. Someone who would
want her for herself, not for who her father was.

Today, she thought, she might have found him. And in
the same spot where her own mother had found the magic
that changed her life.

"I can't feel guilty because it was worth it," she murmured a moment later, not caring that she was talking to
herself. One of the downsides of being by yourself was that
you had no one to talk things over with. But the upside
was, if she talked to herself instead, there was no one to
notice or care.

Her mind drifted back to thoughts of her family and
she winced a little as she realized that they were probably
worried about her. No doubt her father was half crazed,
her mother was working to calm him down and her older
brothers were torn between exasperation and pride at what
she'd managed to do.

She would call them in a day or two and let them know
she was safe. But until then, she was simply going to *be*.
For the first time in her life, she was just like any other
woman. There was no one to dress her, advise her, hand
her the day's agenda. Her time was her own and she had
no one to answer to.

Freedom was a heady sensation.

Still, she couldn't believe she had actually gotten away
with it. Ditching her personal guards—who she really
hoped didn't get into too much trouble with her father—
disguising herself, buying an airplane ticket and slipping

out of Cadria unnoticed. Her father was no doubt furious, but truth to tell, all of this was really his fault. If he hadn't started making noises about Alex "settling down," finding an "appropriate" husband and taking up her royal duties, then maybe she wouldn't have run.

Not that her father was an ogre, she assured herself. He was really a nice man, but, in spite of the fact that he had married an American woman who had a mind of her own and a spine of steel, he couldn't see that his daughter needed to find her own way.

Which meant that today, she was going to make the most of what she might have found with Garrett—she frowned. God, she didn't even know his last name.

She laughed and shook her head. Names didn't matter. All that mattered was that the stories her mother had told her were true.

"Mom, you were *right*," she said, cradling her cup between her palms, allowing the heat to seep into her. "Disneyland is a special place filled with magic. And I think I found some for myself."

He had already been cleared for the penthouse elevator, so when Garrett arrived early in the morning, he went right up. The hum of the machinery was a white noise that almost drowned out the quiet strains of the Muzak pumping down on him from overhead speakers.

His eyes felt gritty from lack of sleep, but his body was wired. He was alert. Tense. And, he silently admitted, eager to see Alex again.

Stupid, he knew, but there it was. He had no business allowing desire to blind him. She was a princess, for God's sake and he was now, officially, her bodyguard.

Garrett caught his own reflection in the mirrored wall opposite him and scowled. He should have seen it coming, what had happened when he finally got through to the King of Cadria. The fact that he had been surprised only underlined exactly how off course his brain was.

In the seconds it took for the elevator to make its climb, he relived that conversation.

"She's in California?"

The king's thundering shout probably could have been heard even without the telephone.

Well, Garrett told himself, that answered his first question. He had been right. The king had had no idea where Alex was.

"Is she safe?"

"Yes," Garrett said quickly as his measure of the king went up a notch or two. Sure he was pissed, but he was also more concerned about his daughter's safety than anything else. "She's safe, but she's on her own. I'm not comfortable with that."

"Nor am I, Mr. King."

"Garrett, please."

"Garrett, then." He muttered to someone in the room with him, "Yes, yes, I will ask, give me a moment, Teresa," he paused, then said, "Pardon me. My wife is very concerned for Alexis, as are we all."

"I understand." In fact Garrett was willing to bet that "very concerned" was a major understatement.

"So, Garrett. My wife wished to know how you found Alexis."

"Interestingly enough, I was with my family at Disneyland," he said, still amused by it all. Imagine stumbling across a runaway princess in the heart of an amusement park. "We met outside one of the rides."

No point telling the king that Garrett had come to Alex's rescue, not knowing who she was. No point in mention-

*ing the kiss he had stolen in the darkness of a pirate ride,
either.*

"I knew it!" *The king shouted then spoke to his wife in
the room with him.* "Teresa, this is your fault, filling our
daughter's head with romantic nonsense until she—"

*Listening in on a royal argument just underscored
what Garrett had learned long ago. People were people.
Didn't matter if they wore a king's crown or a baseball
cap. They laughed, they fought, they cried—all of them.
And it sounded to Garrett that the King of Cadria, like any
other man, didn't have a clue how to deal with women.*

*The king's voice broke off and a moment later a soft,
feminine voice spoke up. The queen, Garrett guessed, and
smiled as he realized that she clearly didn't let her husband's blustering bother her.*

"Hello, Garrett?"

"Yes, ma'am."

"Is Alexis well?"

"Yes, ma'am, as I told your husband, she was fine when
I took her back to her hotel last night."

"Oh, that's such good news, thank you. You say you
met her at Disneyland?"

"Yes, ma'am."

More to herself than to him, the queen murmured, "She
always dreamed of visiting the park. I should have guessed
she would go there, but—"

*A princess dreaming about Disneyland. Well, other
young girls dreamed of being a princess, so he supposed
it made sense. Garrett heard the worry in the queen's
voice and he wondered if Alex was even the slightest bit
concerned about what her family was going through.*

"Thank you again for looking out for my daughter," *the
queen said,* "and now, my husband wants to speak to you
again."

Garrett smiled to himself imagining the phone shuffle going on in a palace a few thousand miles away. When the king came back on the line, his tone was quieter.

"Yes, my dear, you're right. Of course. Garrett?"

"I'm here, sir."

"I would like to hire you to protect our daughter."

Instantly, Garrett did a quick mental step backward. This wasn't what he'd had in mind. He didn't want to guard her body. He just wanted her. Not the best basis for a protection detail.

"I don't think that's a good idea—"

"We will pay whatever you ask, but frankly my wife feels that Alexis needs this time to herself so I can't very well drag her back home, much as I would prefer it. At the same time, I'm unwilling to risk her safety."

Good point, Garrett couldn't help but admit. Whether she thought so or not, there was potential danger all around Alexis. Which is why he had placed this call in the first place. He thought she should be protected—just not by him. "I agree that the princess needs a bodyguard, but..."

"Excellent." The king interrupted him neatly. "You will keep us informed of what she's doing, where she's going?"

Instantly, Garrett bristled. That wasn't protection; that was being an informant. Not once in all the years he and his twin had run their agency had they resorted to snapping pictures of cheating spouses and damned if he was going to start down that road now.

"I'm not interested in being a spy, your majesty."

A dismissive chuckle sounded. "A spy. This isn't the situation at all. I'm asking that you protect my daughter—for a handsome fee—and along the way that you merely observe and report. What, Teresa?" Garrett heard furious whispers during the long pause and finally the king came

*back on the line. "Fine, it is spying. Very well. Observe
and not report?"*

He still didn't like it. Then the king spoke again.

*"Garrett, my daughter wants her holiday, but she's
managed to lose every guard I've ever assigned her. We
would appreciate it very much if you would watch over
Alexis."*

Which was why he had finally agreed to this.

Garrett came back out of his memories with a thoughtful frown at his image. He had the distinct feeling that this
was not going to end well.

But what the hell else was he supposed to do? Tell a
man, a king, that he *wouldn't* protect his daughter? And
still, he would have refused outright if the king had insisted on the spying.

But damned if he could think of a way to get out of
guarding her. The king didn't want Alex's presence announced to the world, for obvious reasons, and since
Garrett had already met her, and was a trained security
specialist besides, how could he *not* take the assignment?

If he had said no and something happened to Alexis,
he'd never be able to live with himself. His frown deepened as he silently admitted that the truth was, he already
had one dead girl haunting him—he wouldn't survive another.

Four

At the knock on her door, Alex opened it and smiled up at Garrett.

The slam of what she had felt around him the day before came back harder and faster than ever. He was so tall. Broad shoulders, narrow hips. He wore black jeans, a dark green pullover shirt—open at the collar, with short sleeves that displayed tanned, muscular forearms. His boots were scuffed and well worn, just adding to the whole "danger" mystique. His features were stark, but somehow beautiful. His eyes shone like a summer sky and the mouth she had thought about way too often was quirked in a half smile.

"I'm impressed."

"You are?" she asked. "With what?"

"You're ready to go," he said, sweeping his gaze up and down her before meeting her gaze again. "Not going to have me sit in the living room while you finish your hair or put on makeup or decide what to wear?"

Her eyebrows lifted. He had no way of knowing of course, but she had been raised to be punctual. The King of Cadria never kept people waiting and he expected the same of his family.

"Well," she said, "that was completely sexist. Good morning to you, too."

He grinned, obviously unapologetic. "Wasn't meant to be sexist, merely grateful," he said, stepping past her into the living room of her suite. "I hate waiting around while a woman drags her feet just so she can make an entrance." He gave her a long, slow look, then said, "Although, you would have been worth the wait."

She flushed with pleasure. A simple compliment simply given, and it meant so much more than the flowery stuff she was used to hearing. As for "entrances," she got way too many of those when she was at home. People standing when she entered a room, crowds thronging for a chance at a handshake or a photo. A band striking up when she was escorted into a formal affair.

And none of those experiences gave her the same sort of pleasure she found in seeing Garrett's reaction to her. Alex threw her hair back over her shoulder and tugged at the hem of her short-sleeved, off-the-shoulder, dark red shirt. She had paired the top with white slacks and red, sky-high heels that gave her an extra three inches in height. Yet still she wasn't at eye level with Garrett.

And the gleam in his eyes sent pinpricks of expectation dancing along her skin. Funny, she'd been awake half the night, but Alex had never felt more alert. More...alive. She should have done this years ago, she thought. Striking out on her own. Going incognito, meeting people who had no idea who she was. But then, even as those thoughts raced through her mind, she had to admit, if only to herself, that the real reason she was feeling so wired wasn't her little holiday. It was Garrett.

She'd never known a man like him. Gorgeous, yes. But there was more to him than the kind of face that should be on the pages of a magazine. There was his laughter, his kindness to his little cousins—and the fact that he'd ridden to her rescue.

And the fact that the black jeans he wore looked amazing on him didn't hurt anything, either.

Alex watched him now as he scanned the perimeter of the room as if looking for people hiding behind the couches and chairs. Frowning slightly, she realized that she'd seen a similar concentrated, laserlike focus before. From the palace guards and her own personal protection detail. He had the air of a man on a mission. As if it were his *job* to keep her safe. Doubt wormed its way through her mind.

Was it possible this had all been a setup? Had her father somehow discovered her whereabouts and sent Garrett to watch over her?

Then she silently laughed and shook her head at the thought. Garrett had been at Disneyland with his family. Their meeting was accidental. Serendipity. She was reading too much into this, letting her imagination spiral out of control. Alex was projecting her concerns onto Garrett's presence with absolutely no reason at all to do so. The man was simply looking around the penthouse suite.

She was so used to staying in hotels like this one she tended to forget that not everyone in the world was blasé about a penthouse. Inwardly smiling at the wild turns paranoia could take, she ordered herself to calm down and patiently waited for Garrett's curiosity to be satiated.

Finally, he turned to look at her, his features unreadable. "So. Breakfast?"

"Yes, thanks. I'm starving."

He gave her that grin that seemed designed to melt her knees and leave her sprawling on the rug. Really, the man had a presence that was nearly overpowering.

"Another thing I like about you, Alex. You admit when you're hungry."

She shook off the sexual hunger clawing at her and smiled back at him. "Let me guess, most women you know don't eat?"

He shrugged as if the women in his life meant nothing and she really hoped that was the case.

"Let's just say the ones I've known consider splitting an M&M a hearty dessert."

She laughed at the image. "I know some women like that, too," she said, snatching up her red leather bag off the closest chair. "I've never understood it. Me, I love to eat."

"Good to know," he said, one corner of his mouth lifting.

And there went the swirl of something hot and delicious in the pit of her stomach. How was she supposed to keep a lid on her imagination if every look and smile he gave her set off incendiary devices inside her?

This holiday was becoming more interesting every minute. When he took her hand and drew her from the penthouse, Alex savored the heat of his skin against hers and told herself to stop overthinking everything and just enjoy every moment she was with him.

They had breakfast down the coast in Laguna Beach, at a small café on Pacific Coast Highway. On one side of the patio dining area, the busy street was clogged with cars and the sidewalks bustled with pedestrian traffic. On the other side, the Pacific Ocean stretched out to the horizon. Seagulls wheeled and dipped in the air currents, surfers rode waves in to shore and pleasure boats bobbed lazily on the water. And Alex was only vaguely aware of any of it. How could she be distracted by her surroundings when she could hardly take her eyes off Garrett? His thick, black hair lifted in a capricious breeze and she nearly sighed when he reached up to push his hair off his forehead. The man was completely edible, she thought, and wondered vaguely what he might look like in a suit. Probably just as gorgeous, she decided silently, but she preferred him like this. There were too many suits in her world.

This man was nothing like the other men in her life. Which was only one of the reasons he so intrigued her.

But Garrett seemed…different this morning. Less relaxed, somehow, although that was probably perfectly natural. People were bound to be more casual and laid-back at an amusement park than they were in everyday situations. The interesting part was she liked him even more now.

There was something about his air of casual danger that appealed to her. Not that she was afraid of him in any way, but the sense of tightly reined authority bristling off him said clearly that he was in charge and no one with him had to worry about a thing.

She laughed to herself. Funny, but the very thing she found so intriguing about him was what drove her the craziest about her father.

"Want to share the joke?" he asked, that deep voice of his rumbling along every single one of her nerve endings.

"No," she said abruptly. "Not really."

"Okay, but when a woman is chuckling to herself, a man always assumes she's laughing at *him*."

"Oh, I doubt that." Alex reached for her coffee cup and took a sip. When she set it down again, she added, "I can't imagine too many women laugh at you."

Amusement sparkled in his eyes. "Never more than once."

Now she did laugh and he gave her a reluctant smile.

"Not intimidated by me at all, are you?" he asked.

"Should I be?"

"Most people are."

"I'm not most people."

"Yeah," he said wryly, "I'm getting that." He leaned back in his chair and asked, "So what next, Alex? Anything else on your 'must see' list besides Disneyland?"

She grinned. It was wonderful. Being here. Alone. With him. No palace guards in attendance. No assistants or ministers or parents or brothers hovering nearby. She felt freer than she ever had and she didn't want to waste a moment of it. Already, her excitement had a bittersweet tinge to it because Alex knew this time away from home couldn't last.

All too soon, she would have to go back to Cadria. Duty was far too ingrained in her to allow for a permanent vacation. Another week was probably all she could manage before she would have to return and be Princess Alexis again. At the thought, she almost heard the palace doors close behind her. Almost sensed the weight of her crown pressing against her forehead. *Poor little rich girl,* she thought wryly and briefly remembered Garrett's tiny cousin wistfully dreaming of being a princess.

If only the little girl could realize that what she already had was worth so much more. A ripple of regret washed through Alex as she turned her gaze on the busy street.

She wondered how many of the people laughing, talking, planning a lazy day at the beach were like her—on holiday and already dreading the return to their real world.

"Alex?"

She turned her head to look at him and found his gaze locked on her. "Sorry. Must have been daydreaming."

"Didn't look like much of a daydream. What's got you frowning?"

He was far too perceptive, she thought and warned herself to guard her emotions more closely. "Just thinking that I don't want my holiday to end."

"Everything ends," he said quietly. "The trick is not to worry about the ending so much that you don't enjoy what you've got while you've got it."

Nodding, she said, "You're absolutely right."

"I usually am," he teased. "Ask anybody."

"You're insufferable, aren't you?"

"Among many other things," he told her, and she felt a tug of something inside her when his mouth curved just the slightest bit.

Then he turned his back on the busy street and looked out at the water. She followed his gaze, and nearly sighed at the perfection of the view. Tiny, quick-footed birds dashed in and out of the incoming tide. Lovers walked along the shore and children built castles in the sand.

Castles.

She sighed a little at the reminder of her daydream, of the world waiting for her return.

"So no big plans for today then?" he asked.

"No," she said with a suddenly determined sigh, "just to see as much as I can. To enjoy the day."

"Sounds like a good idea to me. How about we explore the town a little then take a drive along the coast?"

Relief sparkled inside her. She had been sure he'd have to leave. Go to work. Do whatever he normally did when not spending time with a runaway princess. "Really? That sounds wonderful. If you're sure you don't have to be somewhere…"

"I'm all yours," he said, spreading his arms as if offering himself to her.

And ooh, the lovely sizzle that thought caused. "You don't have to be at work?"

"Nope. I'm taking a few days off."

"Well, then, lucky me."

The waitress approached with the check, Garrett pulled a few bills from his wallet and handed them to her.

"Hmm, that reminds me," Alex said when the woman was gone again. "You owe me five dollars."

His eyebrows lifted. "For what?"

She folded her arms on the table. "We had a wager yesterday and you never did guess where I'm from."

He nodded, gaze locked on hers, and warmth dazzled her system. Honestly, if he were to reach out and touch her while staring at her as he was, Alex was sure she'd simply go up in flames.

"So we did," he said and reached into his wallet again.

"You don't have to actually pay me," she said, reaching out to stop him. Her hand touched his and just as she'd suspected, heat surged through her like an out of control wildfire. She pulled her hand back quickly, but still the heat lingered. "I just wanted you to admit you lost. You did buy breakfast after all."

"I always pay my debts," he said and pulled out a five. Before he could hand it over, though, Alex dug into her purse for a pen and gave it to him. "What's this for?"

"Sign it," she said with a shrug and a smile. "That way I'll always remember winning my first wager."

He snorted an unexpected laugh. "That was your first bet?"

No one but her brothers—and they didn't count—ever made bets with a princess. It would be considered tacky. A tiny sigh escaped her before she could stop it. How much

she had missed just because of how things might "look."
"You're my first—outside my family of course. And I did
pretty well, I think, don't you? I did earn five dollars."

"So you did," he said, clearly amused. "Okay then…"
He took her pen, scrawled a message, signed it and handed
both the pen and the money to her.

Alex looked down and read, "Payment in full to Alex
from Garrett." She lifted her gaze, cocked her head and
said, "I still don't know your last name."

He nodded. "Don't know yours, either."

"Seems odd, don't you think?" Her gaze dropped to his
signature. It was bold, strong and she had no doubt that a
handwriting analyst would say that Garrett was confident,
powerful and even a little arrogant.

"I'll tell you my name if you tell me yours," he taunted.

Her gaze snapped to his. Tell him her last name? She
considered it for a second or two. Wells was common
enough; maybe he wouldn't think anything of it. But then
again, if he put her first name with her last, it might ring
a familiar bell that she'd rather remain silent.

She was having too much fun as "just Alex" to want to
give it up this early in her holiday. So why risk it? Why
insist on last names when it didn't really matter anyway?
After all, when her holiday was over, they'd never see each
other again. Wasn't it better for both of them to keep things
light? Superficial?

He was still watching her. Waiting. She couldn't read
his expression and she really wished she could. Alex
would have loved to know what he was thinking about
this…whatever it was between them. If he was as intrigued, as filled with a heightened sense of anticipation
as she was.

"So?" he asked, a half smile curving his mouth as he
waited for her decision.

"First names only," she said with an emphatic nod. "It's more fun that way, don't you agree?"

"I think," Garrett said as he stood up and held one hand out to her, "the fun hasn't even started yet."

"Is that a promise?" she asked, slipping her hand into his and relishing the rush of heat and lust that immediately swamped her.

"It is," he said, "and I always keep my promises."

Garrett looked down at their joined hands then lifted his gaze to hers as the buzz between them sizzled and snapped like sparks lifting off a bonfire. "Fun. Coming right up."

They spent a couple of hours in Laguna, wandering down the sidewalks, drifting in and out of the eclectic mix of shops lining Pacific Coast Highway. There were art galleries, handmade ice cream parlors, jewelry stores and psychics. There were street performers, entertaining for the change dropped into open guitar cases and there were tree-shaded benches where elderly couples sat and watched the summer world roll by.

Alex was amazing. She never got tired, never got bored and absolutely everything caught her attention. She talked to everyone, too. It was as if she was trying to suck up as much life as possible. And he knew why. Soon she'd be going back behind palace walls and the freedom she was feeling at the moment would disappear.

Hard to blame her for wanting to escape. Who the hell didn't occasionally think about simply dropping off the radar and getting lost for a while? He'd done it himself after—Garrett shut that thought down fast. He didn't want to relive the past. Had no interest in wallowing in the pain and guilt that had ridden him so hard for so long. There was nothing to be gained by remembering. He'd learned his lesson, he assured himself, and that was why he was sticking to Alex like glue.

It had nothing to do with how she looked in those mile-high heels. Or the brilliance of her smile or the damn sparkle in her eyes.

He could tell himself whatever he wanted to, he thought, but even *he* didn't believe the lies.

"You're frowning," she said, snapping him out of his thoughts. He was pitifully grateful for the distraction.

"What?"

"Frowning," she repeated. "You. Do I look that hideous?"

He shook his head at the ridiculousness of the question, but dutifully looked at the drawing the caricature artist was doing of Alex. The guy had an easel set up under one of the trees along the highway and boxes of colored pastels sat at his elbow. Garrett watched him drawing and approved of the quick, sure strokes he made.

Alex was coming alive on the page, her smile wider, her eyes bigger and brighter and her long blond hair swirling in an unseen wind.

"So?" she asked.

"It looks great," he muttered, not really caring for how the artist had defined Alex's breasts and provided ample cleavage in the drawing.

"Thanks, man," the guy said, layering in a deeper blue to Alex's eyes. "I love faces. They fascinate me. Like you," he said to Alex, "your face is familiar, somehow. Like I've seen you before. But with that accent no way you're from around here."

Garrett's gaze snapped to her in time to see her face pale a bit and her eyes take on a wary sheen.

"I'm sure I've just got one of 'those' faces," she said, trying to make light of the guy's statement. "You know they say we all have a double out there, wandering the world."

"Yeah," the artist murmured, not really listening. "But you're different. You're…"

"You done?" Garrett asked abruptly.

"Huh?" The guy glanced up at him and whatever he saw in Garrett's eyes convinced him that he was indeed finished. "Sure. Let me just sign it."

A fast scrawl with a black chalk and he was tearing the page off the easel and handing it to Alex. She looked at it and grinned, obviously pleased with the results. In fact, she was so entranced by the drawing, she didn't notice the artist's eyes suddenly widen and his mouth drop open in shock.

Apparently, Garrett thought grimly, he'd finally remembered where he had seen Alex before. Moving fast, Garrett caught the other man's eye and gave him a warning glare that carried threats of retribution if he so much as said a single word.

His meaning got across with no problem. The tall, thin man with the straggly beard closed his mouth, wiped one hand across the back of his neck and nodded in silent agreement.

Garrett pulled out his wallet and handed over a wad of cash. Way more than the price of the drawing, this was also shut-the-hell-up-and-forget-you-ever-saw-her money. When the guy whistled low and long, Garrett knew the bribe was successful.

"Thank you!" Alex said and finally looked at the artist. "It's wonderful. I know just where I'll hang it when I get home."

"Yeah?" The artist grinned, obviously loving the idea that one of his drawings would soon be hanging in a castle.

"Well, cool. Glad you like it, Pr—" He stopped, shot a look at Garrett and finished up lamely, *"Miss."*

Alex missed the man's slipup. She reached into her purse. "How much do I owe you?"

"It's taken care of," Garrett said, stepping up beside her and dropping one arm around her shoulders. He shot another warning look at the artist. "Isn't it?"

"You bet," the guy said, nodding so hard Garrett half expected the man's head to fly off his neck. "All square. We're good. Thanks again."

Garrett steered her away from the artist, and got her walking toward where he'd parked his car. Best to get out of here before the guy forgot just how threatening Garrett could be and started bragging about how he had drawn the portrait of a princess.

"You didn't have to buy this for me, Garrett," she said, with a quick glance up at him. "I appreciate it, but it wasn't necessary."

"I know that. I wanted to."

"Well, I love it." She turned her head to study the portrait. "Whenever I look at it, I'll think of today and what a lovely time I had. I'll remember the ocean, the ice cream, the tide pools, the shops…"

She came to a stop and the people on the sidewalk moved past them like water rushing around a rock in a fast moving stream. She looked at him, reached up and cupped his cheek in her palm. He felt her touch all the way to his bones.

Her blue eyes shone with the glitter of promises when she said, "And I'll remember *you* most of all."

He knew with a soul-deep certainty that he'd never forget her, either.

Five

Decker King looked more like a beach bum than a successful businessman. And that was just how he liked it.

Garrett only shook his head while Decker flirted like crazy with Alex. Decker wore board shorts, flip flops and a T-shirt that read, Do it With a King.

And in smaller letters, King's Kustom Krafts.

The man might be annoying, but his company built the best luxury pleasure crafts in the world. His specialty was the classic, 1940s style wooden powerboats. Decker had customers all over the world sitting on waiting lists for one of his launches.

"You sure you want Garrett to take you out?" Decker was saying, giving Alex a smile meant to seduce.

"Yeah," Garrett interrupted. "She's sure."

Decker glanced at him and smirked. "Okay, then. My personal boat is moored at the dock out back." He tossed the keys to Garrett. "Don't scratch it."

"Thank you, Decker," Alex said with a smile as Garrett grabbed her hand and headed for the dock.

"My pleasure, Alex," he called back as she was hustled away. "Anytime you get tired of my dull cousin, just call me!"

"I don't think you're dull," Alex said on a laugh, her hand tightening around his.

"Decker thinks anyone with a regular job is dull. He's talented but he's also a flake."

"But he runs this business…"

"Yeah, like I said, talented. He's like a savant."

Alex laughed again as they stepped out into the sunlight, leaving the airy boat-building warehouse behind. "Oh, come on. He's very sweet."

"All women like Decker." Garrett looked down at her and smiled. "None of the cousins have figured out why, yet."

"None of you? How many cousins do you have?"

"I can't count that high," he said with a half laugh. "We're all over California. Like a biblical plague."

She laughed and Garrett let the sound ripple over him like sunlight on the water.

"Must be nice, having that much family."

"It can be," he admitted. "It can also be a pain in the ass from time to time."

They stopped at the end of the dock, and Garrett helped her into the sleek boat waiting for them. He untied the rope, tossed it aside then jumped in beside her. The wood planks of the hull gleamed a dark red-brown from layers of varnish and careful polishing. The red leather bench seats were soft and the engine, when Garrett fired it up, sounded like the purr of a mighty beast.

Alex laughed in delight and Garrett couldn't help grinning in response. In a few minutes, he was out of the harbor and headed for open water.

"I love this boat," she shouted over the engine noise. "It's like the ones in that Indiana Jones movie!"

"I love that you know that!" He grinned and gunned the engine harder, bringing the bow up to slap at the water as they careened across the surface.

When they were far enough out that Garrett was convinced that Alex was perfectly safe, he eased back on the throttle. The roar of the engine became a vibrating purr as the sleek powerboat shifted from a wild run into a lazy prowl.

Garrett slanted a look at her. "So, action movie fan are you?"

"Oh, yes." She turned her face up to the sun, closed her eyes and smiled. "It's having three brothers, I think. They had no time for comedies or romance, so movie night at our house meant explosions and gunfire."

"Sounds like my house," he said, remembering the many nights he and his brothers had spent reveling in movie violence. Garrett and Griffin especially had enjoyed the cops and robbers movies. The good guys tracking down the bad guys and saving the day in the end. Maybe that was why he and his twin had both ended up in the security business.

"You have brothers?"

"Four—one of them is my twin."

"A twin! I always thought it would be wonderful to be a twin. Was it?"

"Wonderful?" He shook his head. "Never really thought about it, I guess. But yeah, I suppose so. Especially when we were kids. There was always someone there to listen. To play with and, later, to raise hell with."

Being a twin was such a part of who and what he was

that he'd never really considered what it must look like from the outside. Griffin and he had done so much together, always right there, covering each other's backs that Garrett couldn't imagine *not* being a twin.

"Did you? Raise a lot of hell?"

"Our share," he mused, lost briefly in memories of parties, football games and women. "When we were kids, being identical was just fun. Swapping classes, tricking teachers. As we got older, the fun got a little more…creative."

"Identical?" She took a long look at him. "You're exactly alike?"

He shook his head and gave her a half smile. "Nah. I'm the good-looking one."

She laughed as he'd hoped she would.

"Must have been nice," she said, "raising a little hell once in a while. Having someone to have fun with."

"No hell-raising in your house?" he asked, though he couldn't imagine her and her brothers throwing any wild parties when the king and queen were out of town.

"Not that you'd notice," she said simply, then changed the subject. "Decker seemed very nice." She ran her fingertips across the small brass plaque on the gleaming teak dashboard. *King's Kustom Krafts.*

"Decker King is his name?"

"Yeah." He hadn't even considered that she would learn Decker's last name. And what kind of thing was that for a man like him to admit? Hell, he made his living by always thinking three steps ahead. By knowing what he was going to do long before he actually did it. By being able to guess at what might happen so that his clients were always safe. But around Alex, his brain wasn't really functioning. Nope, it was a completely different part of his body that was in charge now.

And it was damned humbling to admit he couldn't seem to get his blood flowing in the direction of his mind.

"Yeah. Decker's okay."

"He builds lovely boats."

"He really does," Garrett said, relaxing again when she didn't comment on Decker's last name. "So, you've heard about my family, tell me about these brothers of yours."

She looked at him and he read the wary suspicion in her eyes. "Why?"

"Curiosity." He shrugged and shifted his gaze to the sea. No other boats around. But for the surfers closer to shore, they were completely alone. Just the way he preferred it. Giving her a quick glance he saw her gaze was still fixed on him as if she were trying to make up her mind how much to say.

Finally, though, she sighed and nodded. "I've already told you I've got three brothers. They're all older than me. And very bossy." She turned her face into the wind and her long blond hair streamed out behind her. "In fact, they're much like my father in that regard. Always trying to order me about."

"Maybe they're just looking out for you," he said, mentally pitying the brothers Alex no doubt drove nuts. After all, the king himself had told Garrett that Alex managed to lose whatever bodyguards were assigned to her. He could only imagine that she made the lives of her brothers even crazier.

"Maybe they should realize I can look after myself." She shook her head and folded her arms over her chest in such a classic posture of self-protection that Garrett almost smiled.

But damned if he didn't feel bad for her in a way, too. He hated the idea of someone else running his life. Why should she be any different? Still, every instinct he possessed had him siding with her brothers and her father. Wasn't he here, protecting her, because he hadn't been able to stand the idea of her being on her own and vulnerable?

"Guys don't think like that," he told her. "It's got nothing to do with how capable they think you are. Men look out for our families. At least the decent guys do."

"And making us crazy while you do it?"

"Bonus," he said, grinning.

Her tense posture eased as she gave him a reluctant smile. "You're impossible."

"Among many other things," he agreed. Then, since he had her talking, he asked more questions. Maybe he could get her to admit who she was. Bring the truth out herself. *And then what?* Was he going to confess that he already knew? That her father was now *paying* him to spend time with her? Yeah, that'd go over well. How the hell had he gotten himself into this hole anyway?

Disgusted, he blew out a breath and asked, "So, you've got bossy brothers. What about your parents? What're they like?"

She frowned briefly and shifted her gaze back to the choppy sea, focusing on the foam of the whitecaps as if searching for the words she needed. Finally, on a sigh, she said, "They're lovely people, really. And I love them terribly. But they're too entrenched in the past to see that their way isn't the only way."

"Sound like normal parents to me," he mused. "At least, sounds like my dad. He was always telling us how things had been in his day, giving us advice on what we should do, who we should be."

She tucked her hair behind her ears and, instantly, it blew free again. Garrett was glad. He was getting very fond of that wild, tangled mane of curls.

"My parents don't understand that I want to do something different than what they've planned for me."

He imagined exactly what the royal couple had in mind for their only daughter and he couldn't picture it having anything to do with boat trips, ice cream and Disneyland. He knew enough about the life Alex lived to know that she would be in a constant bubble of scrutiny. How she dressed, what she said and who she said it to would be put under a microscope. Reporters would follow her everywhere and her slightest slip would be front page news. Her parents no doubt wanted her safely tucked behind palace walls. And damned if he could blame them for it.

"Give me an example," he said, steering the boat along the coastline. More surfers were gathered at the breakers and, on shore, towels were scattered across the sand like brightly colored jewels dropped by a careless hand.

"All right," she said and straightened her shoulders as if preparing to defend her position. Her voice was stronger, colored with the determination she felt to run her own life. "At home, I volunteer with a program for single mothers."

Her expression shifted, brightening, a smile curving her mouth. Enthusiasm lit up her eyes until they shone like a sunlit lake. When she started talking, he could hear pride in her voice along with a passion that stirred something inside him.

"Many of the women in the program simply need a little help in finding work or day care for their children," she said. "There are widows or divorcées who are trying to get on their feet again." Her eyes softened as she added, "But there are others. Girls who left school to have their babies and now don't have the tools they'll need to support themselves. Young women who've been abused or abandoned and have nowhere to turn.

"At the center, we offer parenting classes, continuing

education courses and a safe day care for the kids. These young women arrive, worried about the future and when they leave, they're ready to take on the world. It's amazing, really."

She turned on the bench seat, tucked one leg beneath her and rested one arm along the back of the seat. Facing him, she looked him in the eye and said, "The program has grown so much in the past couple of years. We've accomplished so many things and dozens of women are now able to care for their children and themselves. A few of our graduates have even taken jobs in the program to give back what they've received."

"It sounds great."

She smiled to herself and he saw the well-earned pride she felt. "It is, and it feels *good* to do something to actually help, you know? To step outside myself and really make a difference."

"Sounds like you're doing a good thing," Garrett said quietly.

"Thank you." She shrugged, but her smile only brightened. "I really feel as though I'm doing something important. These women have taught me so much, Garrett. They're scared and alone. But so brave, too. And being involved with the program is something I've come to love. On my own."

She sighed then and beneath the pride in her voice was a wistfulness that tore at him. "But my parents, sadly, don't see it that way. They're happy for me to volunteer—organizing fundraisers and writing checks. But they don't approve of me donating my time. They want me in the family business and don't want me, as they call it, 'splitting my focus.'"

"They're wrong," he said and cut back enough on the throttle so that they were more drifting now than actually motoring across the water. "You are making a difference. My mom could have used a program like that."

"Your mother?"

Garrett gave her a small smile. "Oh, my mom was one of the most stubborn people on the face of the planet. When she got pregnant with my brother Nathan, she didn't tell our father."

"Why ever not?"

"Always told us later that she wanted to be sure he loved *her.*" He smiled to himself, remembering the woman who had been the heart of their family. "She was alone and pregnant. No job skills. She supported herself working at In and Out Burgers. Then, a week before Nathan was born, my father showed up."

"Was he angry?"

"You could say that." Garrett laughed. "Mom insisted later that when he walked into the burger joint and shouted her name, there was steam coming out of his ears."

Alex laughed at the image.

"Dad demanded that she leave with him and get married. Mom told him to either buy a burger or get out of line and go away."

"What did he do?"

"What any man in my family would do," Garrett mused, thinking about the story he and his brothers had heard countless times growing up. "He demanded to see the owner and when the guy showed up, Dad bought the place."

"He bought the *restaurant?*"

"Yep." Grinning now, Garrett finished by saying, "He wrote the guy a check on the spot and the first thing he did as new owner? He fired my mother. Then he picked her up, carried her, kicking and screaming the whole way, to the closest courthouse and married her."

He was still smiling to himself when Alex sighed, "Your father's quite the romantic."

"More like hardheaded and single-minded," Garrett told her with a rueful shake of his head. "The men in our family know what they want, go after it and don't let anything get in their way. Well, except for my uncle Ben. He didn't marry *any* of the mothers of his kids."

"Any?" she asked. "There were a lot of them?"

"Oh, yeah," Garrett said. "That branch of the family still isn't sure they've met all of the half brothers that might be out there."

"I don't even know what to say to that," she admitted.

"No one does."

"Still, passion is hard to ignore," she told him, then asked, "are your parents still that way together?"

"They were," he said softly. "They did everything together. Even dying. We lost them about five years ago in a car accident. Drunk driver took them out when they were driving through the south of France."

"Garrett, I'm so sorry." She laid one hand on his arm and the touch of her fingers sent heat surging through him as surely as if he'd been struck by lightning.

He covered her hand with his and something…indefinable passed between them. Something that had him backing off, fast. He let her go and eased out from under her touch. "Thanks, but after the shock passed, all of us agreed that it was good that they had died together. Neither of them would have been really happy without the other."

"At least you have some wonderful memories. And your family."

"Yeah, I do. But you're lucky to still have your parents in your life. Even if they do make you nuts."

"I know," she said with a determined nod. "I just wish I could make them understand that—" She broke off and laughed. "Never mind. I'm wasting a lovely day with complaints. So I'm finished now."

Whatever he might have said went unspoken when he heard the approach of another boat. Garrett turned to look and saw a speedboat seemingly headed right for them. As casually as he could manage, he steered their boat in the opposite direction and stepped on the gas, putting some distance between them.

"What's wrong?"

He glowered briefly because he hadn't thought she was paying close attention to what he was doing. "Nothing's wrong. Just keeping my distance from that boat."

She looked over her shoulder at the boat that was fading into the distance. "Why? What're you worried about?"

"Everything," he admitted, swinging the little boat around to head back toward shore.

"Well, don't," she said and reached out to lay one hand on his forearm again. The heat from before had hardly faded when a new blast of blistering warmth shot through him. Instantly, his groin tightened and he was forced to grind his teeth together and clench his hands around the wheel to keep from shutting the damn engine off and grabbing her.

Seriously, he hadn't been this tempted by a woman in years.

Maybe never.

Shaking his head at the thought, he said, "Don't what?"

"Don't *worry,* Garrett." She released him and even with the heat of the sun pouring down on them, his skin felt suddenly cool now at the loss of her touch. "I'm taking a holiday from worry and so should you."

That wasn't going to happen. Garrett made his living worrying about possibilities. About danger around every corner. Possible assassins everywhere. Not an easy thing to turn off, and he wasn't sure he would even if he could.

"And what do you usually worry about?" he asked.

"Everything," she said, throwing his own word back at him. "But as I said, I'm taking a holiday. And so are you."

Then she laughed and tipped her face up to the sky. Closing her eyes, she sighed and said, "This is wonderful. The sea, the sun, this lovely boat and—"

"And—?"

She looked over at him. "You."

He nearly groaned. Her blue eyes were wide, her lush mouth curved and that off-the-shoulder blouse of hers was displaying *way* too much off-the-shoulder for his sanity's sake. Now it had dipped low over her left shoulder, baring enough of her chest that he could only think about getting the damn fabric down another two or three inches.

For God's sake, she was killing him without even trying. Garrett was forced to remind himself that he was on a job here. He was working for her father. It was his job to *guard* her luscious body, not *revel* in it.

Besides, if she knew the truth, knew who he was and that her father was paying him to spend time with her... hell, she'd probably toss his ass off the boat and then drive it over him just for good measure.

Knowing that didn't change a damn thing, though. He still wanted her. Bad.

"Alex..."

"I've been thinking." She slid closer. Their thighs were brushing now and he felt the heat of her through the layers of fabric separating them.

He almost didn't ask, but he had to. "About what?"

"That kiss."

Briefly, he closed his eyes. Throttling back, he cut the engine and the sudden silence was overwhelming. All they heard was the slap of water against the hull, the sigh of the wind across the ocean and the screech of seagulls wheeling in air currents overhead.

That kiss.

Oh, he'd been thinking about it, too. About what he would have done if they'd been alone in the dark and not surrounded by laughing kids and harassed parents. In fact, he'd already invested far too much time indulging his fantasies concerning Alex. So much so that if she moved another inch closer…pressed her body even tighter to his…

"Garrett?"

He turned his head to look at her and knew instantly that had been a mistake. Desire glittered like hard diamonds in her eyes. He recognized it, because the same thing was happening to him. He felt it. His whole damn body was on fire, and he couldn't seem to fight it. More, he didn't want to.

He hadn't asked for this. Hadn't expected it. Didn't need it, God knew. But the plain truth was he wanted Alex so badly he could hardly breathe.

The worst part?

He couldn't have her.

He was working for her father. She was a princess. He was responsible for her safety. In the real world, a holiday romance was right up his alley. No strings. No questions. No complications. But *this* woman was nothing *but* complications. If he started something with Alex, regret would be waiting in the wings.

All good reasons for avoiding this situation. For brushing her off and steering this damn boat back to Decker's yard as fast as possible. For dropping her at her hotel and keeping an eye on her from a distance.

And not one of those reasons meant a damn thing in the face of the clawing need shredding his insides.

"Not a good idea, Alex," he managed to say.

"Why ever not?" She smiled and the brilliance of it was blinding. She leaned in closer and he could smell the soft, flowery scent of her shampoo.

Her question reverberated in his mind. *Why not?* He couldn't give her any of the reasons he had for keeping his hands to himself. So what the hell was he supposed to say?

That he was actually a monk? That he didn't find her the least bit attractive? She wouldn't buy either of those.

"It's a beautiful day," she said, pressing her body along his on the bench seat. "We're both on holiday—" She stopped suddenly and looked at him. "Unless you're involved with someone already and—"

"No." One word, forced through clenched teeth. He took a breath. "If I were, I wouldn't be here with you."

"Good. Then Garrett…kiss me again."

He ground his teeth in a last ditch effort to hang on to his rampaging desires, or at least his professionalism. Then her scent came to him again on a soft wind and he knew he was lost. Maybe he'd *been* lost since the moment he met her.

Alex the princess might be easy enough to ignore, but Alex the woman was an entirely different story.

He grabbed her, pulled her onto his lap as he moved out from under the steering wheel and looked down into her eyes. "This isn't a good idea."

"I think it's a brilliant idea," she countered with a smile, then lifted her face to his.

Her eyes were bright, her mouth so close he could almost taste it and her hair flew about them like a blond cloud, drawing him in. He didn't need any more encouragement. Right or wrong, this was inevitable.

He took what she offered, what he needed more than

he'd like to admit. He'd curse himself later for surrendering. For now, there was Alex, a soft sea breeze and the gentle lap of water against the hull of the boat. They were alone and damned if he'd waste another minute.

Six

His mouth came down on hers and the first taste of her sent Garrett over the edge. The kiss they'd shared at Disneyland had haunted him until he had damn near convinced himself that no kiss could be as good as he remembered it.

He was wrong.

It was better.

He knew the contours of her mouth now, how her body folded into him, the sigh of her breath on his cheek. She wrapped her arms around his neck and pressed herself more tightly to him. Her hands swept up into his hair, and each touch of her fingers was like lightning through his bloodstream.

He parted her lips with his tongue and she met him eagerly, stroking, tasting, exploring. Mouths fused, breaths mingling, hearts hammering in time, they came together with a desperate need that charged the air around them.

Garrett set his hands at her hips and lifted her up, shifting her around until she was straddling him, her pelvis pressed to his hard, aching groin. It wasn't enough, but it was a start. She groaned into his mouth as his hips arched up against her.

Alex moved with him, rocking her body against his, as demanding as he felt. She slanted her head, giving as well as taking, tangling her tongue with his, losing herself in the heat that seemed to be searing both of them.

His hands swept up, beneath the hem of that red shirt that had been making him crazy all morning. He skimmed his fingers across her skin until he could cup her lace-covered breasts in his palms. Then he swept his thumb back and forth across her erect nipples until she was twisting and writhing against him, grinding her hips against his.

Her kiss grew hungrier, more desperate.

He knew the feeling.

Her moans enflamed him. Her touch, the scrape of her short, neat fingernails over the back of his neck, felt like accelerant thrown onto a bonfire. He was being engulfed and he welcomed it.

It was as if everything in his life had come down to this moment with her. As if his hands had always ached for the touch of her. His body hard and ready, all he wanted was to peel her out of her white slacks and panties and bury himself inside her.

The ocean air slid around them like a cool caress, keeping the heat at bay and adding new sensations to the mix. Hair rippled, clothing was tugged as if even nature wanted them together in the most basic way.

"You're killin' me," he muttered, tearing his mouth from hers long enough to drag in a deep breath of the salt-stained air.

"No," she said with a sigh and a grin as she licked her lips. "Not interested in killing you at all, Garrett."

He returned that smile, and slowly lifted the hem of her shirt, baring her abdomen and more to his gaze. When her lace-covered breasts were revealed, he reached behind her, unhooked her bra with a flick of his fingers then lifted the lacy cups for his first good look at her breasts.

Round and full, with dark pink, pebbled nipples, they made his mouth water. He lifted his gaze to hers and saw passion glazing her eyes. She licked her bottom lip, drew a shallow breath and leaned into him.

"Taste me," she whispered.

And it would have taken a stronger man than Garrett to turn down that offer. He bent his head and took first one nipple, then the other into his mouth. Moving back and forth between them, he licked and nibbled at her sensitive skin until she was a jangle of need, practically vibrating against him.

Finally, he suckled at her left breast while tugging at the nipple of her right with his fingers. His tongue traced damp circles around her areola and his mouth worked at her, sucking and pulling, drawing as much of her as he could into him.

"Garrett, yes," she whispered, holding his head to her, as if afraid he might stop.

But he had no intention of stopping. Now that they had crossed the barrier keeping them apart, nothing would keep him from having her completely.

"That feels so good." She was breathless, her body moving of its own accord, looking for the release she needed.

And as she moved on him, his groin tightened to the point of real pain and he wouldn't change anything. He dropped one hand to the juncture of her thighs and through the material of her white slacks, he felt her heat. Felt the dampness gathering there at her core.

He rubbed her, pressing hard against the nub of sensation he knew would be aching as he ached. She groaned again, louder this time, and moved restlessly on him. Dropping her hands to the snap and zipper, she undid them, giving him a view of the pale, ivory lace panties she wore before going up on her knees on the bench seat.

Garrett released her nipple, looked up into her eyes and lost himself in their passion-filled depths. He lifted one hand and deliberately, slowly dipped his fingers beneath the elastic band of her panties. She took a breath, let her head fall back and tensed, waiting for his first touch.

She looked like a pagan goddess.

Breasts bared to the sun, face lifted to the sky, hair flying in the wind and her center, open and waiting. He was rocked right down to his soul. She was magnificent. And the need clamoring inside him whipped into a churning frenzy.

He cupped her heat with his palm and was rewarded by a soft sigh of pleasure that slid from her elegant throat. Garrett's hand moved lower, his fingers reaching. She moved with him, giving him easier access. Her hands dropped to his shoulders to steady herself and when his thumb stroked over that one bud of passion, she jolted and gasped in a breath.

"Garrett...Garrett..." It was both plea and temptation.

He watched her, gaze fixed on her expressive face as he dipped first one finger, then two, inside her damp heat. He worked her body, making her rock and twist as she climbed that ladder of need to the climax that was waiting for her. His thumb moved over that nub again and again until she was practically whimpering. Her fingers dug into his shoulders, her sighs came fast and furious.

He stroked her, inside and out, until her body was bowed with building tension, until she was so blindly wrapped up in her own need, he, too, felt the gathering storm. When the first shocking jolt of release hit her, Garrett steadied her with one hand while with the other he pushed her higher, and higher, demanding more, always more.

"I can't," she whispered brokenly. "No more…"

"There's always more," he promised and then delivered—another orgasm, crashing down on her right after the first.

She wobbled on unsteady knees and finally dropped to his lap. Only then did she open her eyes and look into his. Only then did she lean forward and kiss him with a long, slow passion that left him as breathless as she felt.

Never before had he taken so much pleasure from his partner's climax. Never before had he been willing to put his own needs on hold for the simple joy of watching a woman shatter in his arms.

Dragging his hand free of her body, he reached up and smoothed her tangled hair back from her face. Then he cupped her cheek and drew her in close. He kissed her then, relishing the slow slide of her tongue against his.

Alex's mind splintered under the assault of too many sensations at once. His hands, his mouth, his breath. He was everything. The center of the universe, and she was left spinning wildly in his orbit. This moment, this touch, this kiss, was everything.

And in the aftermath of two amazing orgasms, it was all she could do to breathe.

She had thought she knew what it was to kiss Garrett. Truthfully, though, she'd had no idea. This was so much *more* than she had experienced before, there was no way she could have been prepared for what she would feel when it was more than a kiss. When his touch lit up her insides like the firework-lit skies over the palace on Cadria's Coronation Day.

Alex stared into his blue eyes, suddenly as dark and mysteriously hypnotic as the deepest seas, and tried to gather up the frayed threads of her mind. A useless endeavor.

Her brain had simply shut down. Her body was in charge now and all she knew was that she needed him. Needed to feel his skin against hers. Though she was still trembling with the reaction of her last orgasm, she wanted more. She wanted his body locked inside hers.

She traced her fingertips across his cheek, smiled and whispered, "That was amazing. But we're not finished... are we?"

"Not by a long shot," he told her before he gave her a quick, hard kiss that promised so much more.

"Thank heaven," she answered and dropped her hands to the hem of his shirt. As she went to tug it up, though, a deep, throaty noise intruded. A noise that was getting closer. They both turned to see the speedboat, racing toward them again.

Instantly, Alex pulled her shirt down, fastened her bra and quickly did up her pants. The other boat was too far away still for anyone to get a glimpse of bare skin, but the intimacy of the moment had been shattered anyway, and she didn't want to risk a stranger getting a peek at her.

Garrett's gaze narrowed on the approaching craft and his mouth firmed into a grim line. In seconds, he went from ravaging lover to alert protector. He lifted her off his lap, slid behind the wheel of the boat and fired up the engine. The throaty roar pulsed out around them and still, the racing boat's motor screamed loud enough that Alex wanted to cover her ears.

They watched as the speedboat came closer, its hull bouncing and crashing over the surface of the water. A huge spray of water fantailed in its wake as the driver swung in their direction.

"What's he doing?" Alex shouted.

"I don't know," Garrett called out, focus locked on the fast-approaching watercraft.

The boat was close enough now that Alex could see a couple up near the front of the boat and a child standing alone in the back. She whipped her head around, but saw no one else nearby. Just the far away surfers and the jet boat coming ever closer.

"Guy's an idiot," Garrett told her as the boat swung into a sharp turn. "If he doesn't throttle back, someone's going to—"

Before he could finish the sentence, the child flew off the back of the boat, hit the water hard and promptly sank. The boat kept going, the two other people on board apparently unaware they had lost the child.

"Oh, my God!" Alex stood up, frantically waving both arms at the driver to get his attention, but she went unnoticed. "The boy! He hasn't surfaced!"

Garrett shut off the engine, yanked his shirt over his head and tossed it to the deck then shouted, "Stay on the boat!" before he dove into the water.

His body knifed below the surface so cleanly he hardly made a splash. Terrified, Alex watched as he swam with swift, sure strokes, tanned arms flashing in and out of the water as he headed for the spot where the boy had gone under.

Alex's stomach jumped with nerves. With outright fear. She threw a glance at the jet boat, still flying across the water then looked back to where Garrett was swimming purposefully toward the child in trouble. She felt helpless. Useless. She had to *do* something.

Sliding behind the wheel, she fired up the engine and carefully eased the throttle forward, inching the boat closer to Garrett. She'd never driven a boat before and the power at her hands terrified her. One wrong move and she could endanger both Garrett and the child. Too much gas, she could run over them—if she didn't hit them outright. And there was the damage the propellers below the surface could do.

Tension gripping her, Alex's hands fisted on the steering wheel as she fought her own fears and her sense of dread for both the boy and Garrett. She kept her gaze locked on Garrett's sleek figure slicing through the water. Where was the boy? Why hadn't he come up? How could Garrett find him?

Fear ratcheted up another notch or two inside her as she inched ever closer. She risked another glance around; she was still alone out here. The jet boat hadn't returned.

"Do you see him?" she shouted.

Garrett shook his head, water spraying from the ends of his hair just before he suddenly dived deep, disappearing beneath the water entirely.

Alex cut the engine and stood up, watching the ever-churning water, hoping, waiting. What felt like *hours* ticked past.

"Come on, Garrett," she chanted, studying the water, looking for any sign of him. "Come back up. Come on!"

How could he hold his breath that long? What should she do? If she jumped in as well, would she make it that much more dangerous? One more person flailing about? She wasn't a strong swimmer anyway.

She heard a roar of sound and turned her head to see the jet boat hurtling toward them. If they didn't slow down…

"Stop!" Waving her arms and jumping up and down like a crazy woman, Alex screamed and shouted to get their attention. Idiots. Complete idiots. Didn't they realize that they could run over both Garrett and the child they must have finally realized was missing?

The boat slowed and when the engine cut off, the silence was deafening.

"Tommy!" The woman yelled as the man on board dived off the stern of his boat. Hanging over the railing, the woman was oblivious to Alex's presence, her focus concentrated solely on the dark water and what might be happening below.

Alex felt the same.

She didn't know how long Garrett had been underwater. She'd lost track of time. Couldn't think. Could hardly breathe. Dimly, she was aware that prayers were whipping through her mind at a furious rate and she hoped that someone upstairs was listening.

Apparently, they were. *"There!"*

Alex pointed at the shadow of movement in the dark water as it headed toward the surface. The woman on the boat behind her was still screaming and wailing. Alex hardly heard her.

Garrett shot out of the water, shaking his hair back from his face. In his arms, a boy of no more than five or six lay limply, eyes closed. A moment later, the man from the jet boat popped up beside Garrett and tried to take the boy.

Garrett ignored him and swam toward the jet boat. Alex followed his progress, her gaze locked on him and on the pale, young face he towed toward safety.

"Oh, God. Oh, God." The woman was babbling now,

tears streaming down her face, voice breaking on every word. "Is he breathing? Is he breathing?"

Garrett laid the boy on the cut out steps at the back of the boat and tipped the child's head back. While Alex watched, Garrett blew into the boy's mouth once. Twice. The waiting was the worst part. The quiet, but for the water continually slapping the hull and the now quiet weeping from the woman who had to be the boy's mother.

Again, Garrett breathed air into the boy's lungs and this time, there was a reaction.

Coughing, sputtering, retching what seemed a gallon of sea water, the little boy arched up off the deck of the boat, opened his eyes and cried, "Mommy!"

Instantly, the woman was on her knees, gathering her son to her chest. Rocking him, holding him, murmuring words only he could hear between the sobs racking her.

Tears streaked down Alex's cheeks, too, as she watched the man in the water grab Garrett and give him a hard hug. "Thanks, man. Seriously, thank you. I don't know what— If you hadn't been here—"

Garrett's gaze drifted to Alex and she felt his fury and relief as surely as she felt her own. But mixed in with those churning emotions, pride in what Garrett had done swelled inside her. He'd saved that child. If not for him, the boy would never have been recovered. His parents might have spent hours looking, wondering exactly where the boy had fallen in, having no idea where to search for him.

"Glad I could help," Garrett said tightly. "Next time slow down. And give that kid a life vest when you're on a damn boat."

"Right. Right." The man swiped one hand across his face, looked up at his family and Alex saw him pale at the realization of what might have happened.

"Yeah," he said. "I will. I swear it."

"Thank you," the woman said, lifting her head long enough to look first at Garrett and then at Alex. "Thank you so much. I don't know what else to say—"

She broke off, her gaze narrowing as she stared at Alex, a question in her eyes. "Aren't you…"

A knot of panic exploded in Alex's stomach. Would this woman recognize her? Say something?

"You'd better get him to a doctor," Garrett blurted. "Have him checked out."

"Yes," the woman said, tearing her gaze away from Alex long enough to nod, then stare down at her son again. "Good idea. Mike?"

"Coming," the man said, pushing himself out of the water and onto the boat. "Thanks again. It's not enough but it's all I can say."

Relieved that not only the boy was safe, but her secret as well, Alex watched Garrett swim toward her. She paid no attention when the speedboat owners fired up their powerful engine and took off—at a slower pace than they had been going previously. She was just glad to see them gone. Of course she was happy the child had survived. Happy that Garrett had been able to save him. But she was also grateful that her identity was still a secret. What were the odds, she wondered, of being in the middle of an ocean with a child near drowning and that boy's mother recognizing her?

She shoved those thoughts away as Garrett braced his hands on the edge of the boat and hoisted himself inside. Then he just sat there, holding his head in his hands. Alex sat down beside him, uncaring about the water sluicing off his clothes, soaking into hers.

Alex wrapped her arms around him and leaned her head on his shoulder.

"You were wonderful," she said softly.

"I was lucky," he corrected, lifting his head to look at her. "Saw a flash of the kid's white T-shirt and made a blind grab for him."

"You saved him," Alex said, cupping his cheek in her palm. "You were wonderful, Garrett."

A slow smile curved his mouth. "If you say so."

She smiled too. "I do."

"I learned a long time ago—never argue with a beautiful woman." He caught her hand in his, squeezed it briefly then leaned in to give her a fast kiss. "But, I think our boating trip is over."

Her heart tumbled in her chest. She didn't want the day to end. It had been filled with emotional ups and downs and moments of sheer terror. A boy's life had been saved and her own life had taken a wild turn in a direction she hadn't expected.

Alex looked at Garrett and couldn't even imagine *not* being with him. She'd known him only two days and he had touched her more deeply than anyone she had ever known. He was strong and capable and funny. He kissed her and her body exploded with need. He caressed her and the world fell away. She had never felt more alive than she did when she was with Garrett.

So no, she didn't want this day to end because every day that passed put her one day closer to leaving—and never seeing him again.

"Hey," he asked, brow furrowing, "what is it? What's wrong?"

"Nothing," she said. "It's nothing. I just…didn't want today to be over, I suppose."

He brushed a kiss across her mouth and eased back. "Day's not over, Alex. Just the boat ride."

"Really?"

"Really. Dress codes in five-star restaurants are a

lot looser in California than anywhere else, but…" He slapped one hand against his jeans and looked ruefully at his sodden boots. "I think they'll draw the line at soaking wet. I need to change clothes before I take you to dinner."

What he was saying made sense, but the look in his eyes told a different story. It was as if in saving the child, he'd closed a part of himself off from her, and Alex wanted to know why. He was pulling back, even sitting here beside him. She could feel a wall going up between them and wasn't sure what to do about it.

So for now, she let it go and gave him the answer she knew he was expecting.

"In that case," she told him, "we'd better get going."

Seven

The King Security company building was quiet. Halls were dark, phones silent and Garrett appreciated the peace. The light on his desk shone like a beam of sunlight in the darkness as he added his signature to a stack of papers Griffin had already signed in his absence.

The puddle of light from his desk lamp was bright and golden and threw the rest of the room into deep shadow. But Garrett didn't need light to find his way around. This place had pretty much been his life for the past ten years. He and Griffin had adjoining offices with a shared bathroom complete with shower separating them. There were plenty of times they had to leave fast for a job and having a shower and a change of clothes around came in damn handy.

There were bookcases on two of the walls and floor-to-ceiling windows overlooking the ocean on another. Family photographs and paintings hung on the remaining wall, and plush leather furniture completed the room. There was a fireplace, wet bar and a long couch comfortable enough to have served as Garrett's bed more than once.

This was the company he and Griffin had built with a lot of hard work, tenacity and the strength of their reputation. He was proud of it and until recently, hadn't so much as taken a day off. Garrett King lived and breathed the job. At least he *had,* until Alex came into his life.

And just like that, she was at the forefront of his thoughts again.

Instantly, his mind turned back to the afternoon on Decker's boat. His body reached for the sense memory of Alex trembling against him, but his brain went somewhere else. To the child falling into the water and nearly drowning. To Garrett's split-second decision to leave Alex alone and unprotected while he saved the child.

He couldn't have done it differently and he knew that, but still the decision haunted him. She had been alone. What if it had all been a setup? Some cleverly disguised assassination or kidnapping attempt on a crown princess? Sure, chances were slim, but they were *there.* The boy could have been a champion swimmer, doing exactly what he had been paid to do.

Absurd? he asked himself. Maybe. Paranoid? Absolutely. But stranger things had happened, and he'd been around to see a lot of them. Gritting his teeth, Garrett silently fumed at his complete lack of professionalism. He'd saved the boy but risked Alex and that was not acceptable.

He could still feel the slide of her skin beneath his fingers. Hear her whispered cries and the catch in her breath as her climax took her. His body went hard and tight as stone and he told himself the pain was only what he deserved.

Never should have let any of it happen, he told himself.

Hell, he knew better. Years ago, he'd learned the hard way that putting your own wants before the job was a dangerous practice that could end up costing lives.

Garrett threw the pen and swiped one arm across his desk, sending the stack of papers flying like a swarm of paper airplanes. Releasing his temper hadn't helped, though, and he pushed back from his desk, swiping one hand across his face. His eyeballs felt like sand-crusted rocks. He couldn't sleep for dreams of Alex.

That was why he was here, in the middle of the night. He had hoped that focusing his mind on work would keep thoughts of Alex at bay. So far he'd been there for two hours and it wasn't working.

Instead his brain insisted on replaying that scene in the boat over and over again. Those few, stolen, amazing moments that even now, he couldn't really regret. How the hell could he?

He had tried to tell himself that Alex was no different than any other celebrity or royal needing protection. That being with her didn't really mean a damn thing. But then she would laugh and his calm reason flew out the window.

The woman had a hell of a laugh.

It was just part of what he'd noticed about Alex at Disneyland. What set her apart from every other female Garrett had ever known.

She threw herself into life—she held nothing back. Even there in his arms, she had been open and vulnerable, offering him everything. It was damn sexy to watch, and every minute with her was a kind of enjoyable misery. His body was so tight and hard, he could hardly walk. He felt like a damn teenager again. No woman had ever affected him like this. Which was a big problem. She wasn't his. Not even temporarily.

She was a damn princess, and he was lying to her every

minute he was around her. She thought she was free and on her own, and he was being paid by her father to look out for her.

How much deeper was this hole he was in going to get?

Shaking his head, Garrett bent to scoop up the fallen papers and shuffle them back into some kind of order. Griffin had been right when he had ragged on Garrett for being practically monklike for months. Garrett had long ago burned out on women who were more interested in what being seen with a King could do for them than they were in him. And frankly, the women he knew were all the damn same. They all talked about the same things, thought the same way and, in general, bored the hell out of him.

Not Alex.

Nothing about her was ordinary. Or boring.

He never should have called the king. Never should have agreed to this bodyguard gig. Hell, he never should have gone to Disneyland.

Yeah, he told himself wryly. It was all Jackson's fault. If he'd never gone with his cousin and his family, if he'd never met Alex at all…he didn't like the thought of that, either.

"Son of a bitch." He tossed the papers to his desktop and glared at them hard enough to start a fire.

"Problem?"

Garrett snapped a look at the open doorway where his twin stood, one shoulder braced against the doorjamb. The shadows were so thick, he couldn't see Griffin's face, but the voice was unmistakable.

"What're you doing here in the middle of the night?" Garrett leaned back in his black leather chair and folded his hands atop his flat abdomen.

"Funny," Griffin said, pushing away from the doorway

to wander into his brother's office, "I was going to ask you the same thing." He dropped into one of the visitor's chairs opposite Garrett. "Was headed home from Amber's place and imagine my surprise when I spotted a single light on in the office. I figured it was either you or a really stupid burglar."

Garrett looked at his twin. His tuxedo was wrinkled, the collar of his shirt opened halfway down his chest and the undone bow tie was hanging down on both sides of his neck. Apparently at least *one* of them had had a good night.

"How is Amber?"

Griffin snorted and shoved one hand through his hair. "Still talking about getting that modeling job in Paris. I heard all about her packing tips, what she'll be wearing in the runway show and what kind of exfoliant will leave her skin—and I quote here—'shimmery.'"

He had to laugh. Shaking his head, he studied his brother and asked, "Why do you insist on dating women who don't have two active brain cells?"

"There are…compensations," Griffin said with a grin. "Besides, you date women who can walk and talk at the same time and you don't look happy."

"Yeah, well." What the hell could he say? He wasn't happy. Things with Alex were more complicated than ever.

He was tangled up in knots of hunger and frustration. Torn by his sense of duty and responsibility. For two days, he'd fought his every urge and instinct. All he wanted to do was get Alex naked and have her to himself for a few hours. Or weeks.

Instead, he'd made damn sure that the scene in the boat or anything remotely like it, hadn't happened again. For those few moments with Alex, Garrett had allowed himself to forget who and what she was. To put aside the reality of the situation. He'd indulged himself—putting her in a potentially dangerous situation—and now he was paying for it.

Every cell in his body was aching for her. He closed his eyes to sleep and he saw her. He caught her scent in his car, on his clothes. He was being haunted, damn it, and there didn't seem to be a thing he could do about it.

Disgusted, he said, "I'm happy."

"Yeah, I'm convinced." Griffin scowled at him.

He was really not in the mood to listen to his twin. He didn't want to hear about how he should let go of the past. Stop blaming himself for what had happened so long ago. He didn't want to talk. Period.

"Go away," he said, snatching up his pen again and re-focusing on the papers in an attempt to get Griffin moving. Of course, it didn't work.

"Princess giving you problems?"

Garrett's gaze snapped to his twin's.

"Whoa. Quite the reaction." Griffin's eyebrows lifted. "So she's getting to you, huh?"

He dropped the pen, scraped both hands across his face and then shoved them through his hair. When that didn't ease his tension, he pushed out of his chair and stalked to the window overlooking the ocean. The moon was out, shining down on the water, making its surface look diamond studded. It was a scene that had soothed him many times over the years. Now, all it did was remind him of Alex. Of being on that boat in the sunshine. Of holding her while she—

"She's not getting to me. Everything's fine. Leave it alone, Griff."

"I don't think so." His twin stood up and walked to join him at the window. "What's going on, Garrett?"

"Nothing. Absolutely *nothing*. That's the problem."

Griffin studied him for a long minute or two and even in the shadowy light, Garrett saw amusement flicker in his twin's eyes. "You've got it bad, don't you?"

"You don't know what you're talking about."

"Right. Everything's great with you. That's why you're here. In the middle of the night, sitting alone in the dark."

"My desk light's on."

"Not the point."

"What *is* the point, Griffin?"

His twin gave him a half smile. "The point is, the mighty Garrett King is falling for a princess."

"You're out of your mind."

"Sure I am."

"She's a job. Her father hired us, remember?"

"Uh-huh."

"She's a princess. And God knows I'm no prince."

"Rich as one," Griffin pointed out helpfully.

"It's not enough and you know it." He shook his head. "Royalty hangs with royalty. Period."

"Not lately." When Garrett glared at him, Griffin shrugged. "I'm just sayin'…

He shifted his gaze away from his twin and stared unseeing at the ocean. Alex's face swam into his mind and as much as he tried to ignore it, she wouldn't go away. He was getting in too deep here and he knew it. But damned if he could see a way out.

"She's a job," he repeated, and which of them he was trying harder to convince, Garrett wasn't sure.

"Sure she is." Griffin slapped him on the shoulder. "Look, making yourself nuts over this just isn't worth it, Garrett. Why not just tell her the truth? Tell her who you are, that you're working for her father."

He'd thought about it. But confessing all wouldn't solve

anything. He'd still want her. And he still wouldn't be able to have her. And as a bonus, she'd be hurt.

"Can't do that."

"Fine, then let me take over," Griffin said.

Garrett just stared at him. "What?"

"Wouldn't be the first time we twin-switched somebody."

"You can't be serious," Garrett said with a snort of laughter.

"Why not? If she's just a job, I'll show up as you, spend some time with her…"

"Stay the hell away from her, Griffin."

His twin grinned. "So I'm right. She *does* mean something to you."

Blowing out a breath, Garrett frowned and turned his face back to the window. His own reflection stared back at him.

"Yeah, guess she does," he murmured, talking to his brother but somehow hoping to reassure the man in the glass as well. "Damned if I know what, though. But in another week or so she'll be gone. Problem solved."

"You think so?"

"I know it." All he had to do was find a way to keep his hands off her. Then she'd be back behind palace doors and his life would go back to normal. If the man in the glass didn't look reassured at all, Garrett ignored it.

Glancing at his twin, he deliberately changed the subject. "As long as you're here, bring me up to speed on what's going on with the business."

"Garrett…"

"Drop it, Griff," he said tightly. "Just, drop it."

"The most stubborn son of a—fine. Okay then, we've got a new client." Griffin moved back to the chair and sat down, stretching out his legs and crossing them at the ankle. "He's opening a luxury resort in Georgia and apparently he's having trouble with some local protestors."

"What're they protesting?"

Griffin snorted. "He's building a golf course and apparently threatening the home ground of the three-legged-gnat-catcher-water-beast-frog or some damn thing. Anyway, to protect the insects, they're threatening our client, and he wants to hire us to protect his family."

"It's a weird world, brother," Garrett muttered. "Protect the gnats by killing people."

"You got that right. Still, upside is, the weirdness is good for business. Anyway..."

Garrett nodded and listened while his brother outlined his plans for their latest client. This was better. Work. Something definable. Something he could count on. All he had to do was keep his focus centered. Remember who he was and why it was so important to keep a hard demarcation line between him and Alex.

He took a seat behind his desk, picked up the pen and began making notes. King Security was his reality.

Not a runaway princess looking for a white knight.

Three days.

It had been three days since they were together on that boat. Three days since Garrett had touched her in any but the most impersonal way. Three days that Alex had spent in a constant state of turmoil, waiting for it all to happen again and then being crushed when *nothing* happened.

Which was making her insane.

"Honestly," she demanded out loud of the empty room, "what is he waiting for?"

She knew he wanted her as much as she did him. When they were together, she felt the tension rippling off him in waves. So *why* was he working so hard at keeping her at arm's length? And why was she allowing it? For heaven's sake, this wasn't the nineteenth century. If she wanted him, she should go after him. No subtlety. No more waiting. He was determined to ignore what was between them, and she was just as determined that he be unable to.

Time was running out for her, Alex thought grimly. Soon enough, she would be on a plane headed back to Cadria and all of this would be nothing but a memory. And damn it, if memories were all that was going to be left of her, then she wanted as many of them as she could make.

With that thought firmly in mind, she checked her mirror and gave herself an objective once-over. Garrett had had some business to take care of that morning and so she'd had a couple of hours to herself and hadn't wasted them. A cab had taken her to the nearest mall where she had shopped until her feet gave out.

It had been good, walking through the Bella Terra mall, just another woman shopping. The freedom she felt was still thrilling, and she didn't know how she would get used to being under the palace microscope once her bit of freedom had ended. Being just one of a crowd was so liberating. She'd laughed with salesgirls, had a hamburger in the food court and then spent a lovely hour in a bookstore.

In fact, it would have been a perfect morning but for the fact that she'd had the oddest sensation that she was being watched. Ridiculous really and probably her own nerves rattling around inside her. No one here knew who she was so why would anyone be interested in what she was doing? She simply wasn't totally accustomed to being alone, that was all. Since leaving her guards behind her, she had been with Garrett almost every moment. Of course she would feel a touch uncomfortable. But it meant nothing.

Brushing off those thoughts, she returned to studying her reflection with a critical eye.

Hair good, makeup perfect and the slinky black dress she'd purchased just that morning clung to her like a second skin. The neckline was deep, displaying cleavage that should surely catch Garrett's eye. And the hemline was just barely legal. Paired with a pair of four-inch black heels, she looked, if she had to say so herself, hot.

Which was her intention, after all.

Her insides swirled with anticipation as she imagined the look on Garrett's face when he saw her. "Let him try to ignore me *now.*"

A smile curved her mouth as she let her mind wander to all sorts of interesting places. Damp heat settled at her core and a throbbing ache beat in time with her pulse. She needed him as she had never needed anyone before. And tonight, she was going to make sure he knew it.

An extremely vivid memory rose up in her mind. In a flash, she recalled just how it felt to have Garrett kissing her, touching her. Showering her body with the kinds of sensations she'd never known before. And she wanted it again, blast it.

"What's missing in this holiday romance," she told her reflection sternly, "is *romance.*"

Her time here was almost over. She couldn't very well put off her return indefinitely. First of all, she wouldn't do that to her family. But secondly, even if she *tried,* her father would never stand for it. If she didn't go home soon, the king would have an army of investigators out searching for her and they *would* find her. Her father was nothing if not thorough.

Now that she considered it actually, she was a little surprised her father hadn't already sent a herd of search dogs after her. It wasn't like him to let her minirebellion stand.

Frowning at the girl in the mirror, Alex shifted her gaze to the telephone on the bedside table. Guilt gnawed at her as she thought about calling home. At least letting her mother know that she was safe. The problem was, reaching her mother wouldn't be easy. The queen didn't have an email account. And she refused to get a cell phone, despite the palace and the king's insistence, so Alex would have to go through the palace phone system. Then she would have to talk to who knew how many ladies-in-waiting, assistants and secretaries before finally reaching her mother.

And during that interminable wait, everyone she talked to could spill the beans to her father the king, and Alex was in no mood to hear another lecture on the evils of selfishness.

"No," she said, staring at the phone, "I'm sorry, Mother, but I'll be home soon enough."

Just thinking about home had Alex imagining the castle walls closing in around her. She took a deep breath and reminded herself that she was still free. Still on her own. She still had time to enjoy life in the real world. To enjoy her time with Garrett.

Garrett.

She frowned again and turned to the laptop computer sitting on the desk near the terrace. She still didn't know Garrett's last name. They'd never discussed it again after that first time when they had decided to keep their identities a mystery. But…she did know his *cousin's* last name.

Garrett had kept her so busy the past couple of days, she'd hardly had a moment to think about the possibilities that knowledge provided. Every day had been so filled with activities and rushing about that when he brought her back to the hotel at night, she was so exhausted she usually just fell into bed.

But tonight…

She chewed at her bottom lip and wondered. What if there was a reason Garrett hadn't made any further moves?

Maybe he had lied when he said he wasn't involved with someone. Maybe he had a *wife*. That thought jolted and rocked through her on an equal tide of disappointment and righteous indignation.

For the first time, she considered the fact that she actually had a *reason* for keeping her last name a secret. Perhaps Garrett did, too.

"Right, then," she told herself. "Time to find out more about Garrett."

Decision made, she walked quickly to the computer, booted it up and took a chance. She entered the name Garrett King in the search engine and hit Enter.

In seconds, her world tilted and her stomach dropped. The first listing read *King Security, Garrett and Griffin King.*

King Security?

She couldn't believe it. Mouth dry, heart pounding, she clicked on the link and watched as their website opened up. She clicked on the About Us tab and there he was.

Her Garrett.

Garrett King.

Security expert.

"Bloody hell."

Garrett waited outside the penthouse door. He shot his cuffs, smoothed the lapels of his tailored, navy blue suit and wondered what the hell was taking Alex so long. Damn, hadn't taken him much time to get used to her being painfully punctual. Now that she was taking a few seconds to open the door, he was both bothered and worried.

Was she safe?

He knocked again and the door flew open. Alex was there and she looked…amazing.

The misery of the past couple of days gathered into a twist of knots in his gut. Just looking at her was pure, unadulterated torture. How the hell was he supposed to not touch her?

Garrett took a breath and reminded himself *again* of just what had happened the last time he'd allowed his dick to make his decisions for him. He had thrown professionalism aside in favor of his own wants and someone else had paid the price.

He'd be damned before he'd do the same damn thing again and have Alex paying for it.

When she just stared at him, he finally said, "You're so beautiful, you're dangerous."

She inclined her head in what he could only call a "regal" gesture. "Thank you." Grabbing her black bag from a nearby table, she hooked her arm through his and stepped out of the suite. "Shall we go?"

"Sure." Frowning to himself, Garrett felt the first stirrings of unease creep through him.

If he were out in the field, he'd be checking for snipers or some other bad guy sneaking up on him. It was just a feeling, but it had never let him down before.

Something was wrong.

Damian's was the hottest new restaurant on the coast. Designed to mimic the lush, noir atmosphere of the forties, the restaurant boasted a view of the ocean, a teakwood dance floor, linen-draped tables dusted with candlelight and the best seafood in California.

The place had struck a solid chord with the public—older people loved coming here to remember their youth and the younger crowd seemed to enjoy the romance and elegance of another era. It was easier to get a private audience with the pope than it was to land a reservation at

Damian's. Not a problem for Garrett, of course. It paid to be related to the owner.

A singer on stage, backed by a small orchestra working to evoke the feel of the big band era crooned about apple trees and lost loves. Dancers swayed to the music, bathed in spotlights that continually swept the floor.

Garrett wasn't surprised this place was a rousing success. Damian King was known for running restaurants that became legendary. At the moment, Damian was in Scotland, brokering a deal for a new "ghost" theme club to be opened in Edinburgh.

Jefferson King was happily living in Ireland. Garrett's brother Nash called London home and now Damian was in Scotland. He smiled to himself as he realized the Kings of California were slowly but surely starting to take over the world.

"It's lovely," Alex said and he turned to look at her.

Those were the first words she'd spoken to him since they'd left her hotel. She'd been polite, cool and completely shut off from him. The complete opposite of the Alex he had come to know over the last several days. There was no joy in her eyes, no easy smile and her spine was so straight, her shoulders so squared, it was as if she were tied to her chair.

"Yeah," he said warily. "Damian did a nice job of it. But then he always does."

"This isn't his only restaurant?"

"No, he's got a string of 'em up and down California."

"Interesting."

Okay, this was not right. She couldn't have made it plainer that something was chewing at her insides. He studied her and tried to figure out what the hell was going on. It was his *business,* after all, to be able to read people.

But for the first time since he'd known Alex, he didn't have a clue what was going on in her mind.

Her eyes were cool, dispassionate. Her luscious mouth was curved in a half smile that didn't reach her eyes. She was the epitome of the kind of sophisticated, aloof woman he usually avoided. Who was she and what had she done with Alex?

"Your cousin. That would be Damian *King?*"

"Yeah."

She nodded again, letting her gaze slide from his briefly. When she looked back at him again it was as if she was looking at a stranger.

That eerie-ass feeling he'd had earlier rose up inside him again. This whole night had been off from the jump. Something was up with Alex, and she wasn't even trying to hide it. He watched her. Waited. And had the distinct sensation that he wasn't going to like what was coming. She stroked her fingertips along the stem of the crystal water glass, and he was damn near hypnotized by the action.

A waitress approached and Garrett waved her away. Whatever was coming, he didn't want an audience for it. Keeping his gaze locked on the woman opposite him, he asked, "What's going on, Alex?"

"I was just wondering," she said, icicles dripping from her tone, "how many lies you've told me since the day we met."

A sinking sensation opened up in the pit of his stomach. A dark, yawning emptiness that spread throughout his system as the seconds ticked past.

"How long have you known?" she demanded quietly, her blue gaze frosty as it locked with his. "How long have you known who I am, Mr. *King?*"

The proverbial crap was about to hit the fan. He

shouldn't have been surprised. Alex was a smart woman. Sooner or later she was going to figure things out. Put two and two together and, any way you added it up, he was going to look like an ass.

No wonder everything had felt off to him tonight, Garrett thought grimly.

The woman sitting opposite him wasn't the Alex he knew.

This was Princess Alexis.

Eight

He didn't say anything.

Alex watched him, saw the flicker of an emotion dart across his eyes, but it came and went so quickly she couldn't identify it. Why wasn't he talking? Explaining? Because there was nothing he could say? Because if he tried to explain, it would only result in *more* lies?

The anger that had filled her since she had found his website spiked and roiled inside her. It had cost her every ounce of her self-control to keep what she was feeling locked within. She'd waited, half hoping that he would tell her the truth spontaneously. But then, why would he, when he was such a consummate liar?

King Security.

Alex felt like an idiot.

She'd believed everything.

Had *trusted* him, when all along, it had been nothing more than a game. He'd pretended to *like* her. Pretended to be attracted to her. When all along, he had known that she was a princess. God, she was a fool.

Garrett and his company had actually *been* to the palace. Had done work for her father. She hadn't recognized him because when he was in Cadria to provide security for the crown jewel celebration, Alex had avoided the whole situation. At the time, she and her father had been feuding over her involvement with the women's shelter. She'd been so furious with her father that she'd refused to have anything to do with the palace goings-on. Including, it seemed, meeting the security man brought in for the occasion.

If she had, she would have noticed Garrett. Looking at him even now, she could admit that he was most definitely a hard man to ignore. And if she'd met him then, she would have recognized him at Disneyland.

None of this would have happened. Her heart wouldn't be bruised, her feelings wouldn't be battered and she wouldn't now be wrapped in what felt like an icy blanket from head to toe.

She never would have found something with him that she could convince herself was real. She never would have believed that she, too, had discovered the same kind of magic her mother had found at the famous amusement park.

Instead she was left feeling the fool and staring into the eyes of a man she had thought she knew.

"How long?" she demanded, keeping her voice low enough that no one but him could hear her.

The strains of the music rose up and swelled around them, and the irony of the slow, romantic sound wasn't lost on her. She had hoped for so much from tonight. She'd wanted to seduce Garrett. Now all she could hope for was that she wouldn't get angry enough to cry.

She *hated* crying when she was furious.

Tilting her head to one side, she watched him. "Did you know at Disneyland?"

"Not right away," he admitted, and the iron bands around her chest tightened another inch or so until every breath was a minor victory.

That statement told her that at least part of what she had thought of as a magical day had been colored with lies.

Betrayal slapped at her. Was it before he'd kissed her in the dark during the pirate ride? While they laughed with his nieces on the carousel?

She looked into his blue eyes and searched for the man who had been with her on his cousin's boat a few days ago. The man who had touched her, shown her just how amazing two people could be together. But Alex didn't see him. Instead, she saw a cool-eyed professional, already pulling back from her. A part of her wondered how he could turn his emotions on and off so easily. Because right at that moment, she'd like nothing better than to be able to do the same.

"I didn't know you at first," he was saying. "Not until you and Molly were standing at the castle, talking about being a princess."

She nodded, swallowed hard and said, "So that's why you insisted on taking me home that night."

"Partly," he admitted.

She laughed shortly, the sound scraping against her throat. "Partly. It wasn't about me that night, Garrett. Not *me,* Alex. It was about protecting a princess. And you've been with me every day since for the same reason, haven't you?"

Scraping one hand across the back of his neck, he said, "I called your father that first night."

"Oh, God…" Just when she thought the icy cold enveloping her couldn't get worse…it did.

"I told him where you were. That you were alone and that I was…concerned."

"You had no right."

"I had a responsibility."

"To *whom?*" she demanded.

"To myself," he snapped. "I couldn't walk away leaving you unprotected once I knew who you really were."

"No one asked for your help."

"Your father did."

She shook her head, not wanting to hear any more. But she knew that was a futile hope.

"That's wonderful. Really. Your responsibility. Your decision. Your phone call." She narrowed her gaze on him. "But *my* life. This was never about you, Garrett. This was about me. What I wanted. And it never mattered, did it? Not to you. Not to anyone."

"Alex—"

She looked around the restaurant as if searching for an exit. But all she saw were couples sitting at tables, laughing, talking, easy with each other. They were enjoying the restaurant, the music, the romance of the place, and Alex suddenly envied them all so much it choked her.

"I never intended to hurt you."

"How nice for you then," she said, looking back at him. "Because you haven't hurt me. You've enraged me."

"Now who's lying?"

That snapped her mouth shut and all she could do was glare at him. Yes, she was lying because she *was* hurt. Devastated, in fact, but damned if she would show him how much his lies had cut at her.

"There's more," he said.

"Of course there is."

"Like I said before, your father hired me to protect you."

His words sunk into her consciousness like a rock tossed to the bottom of a lake. The sense of betrayal she had felt before was *nothing* compared to this. Her mouth opened and closed a few times as she struggled to speak past the hard knot of something bitter lodged in her throat. Finally, though, she managed to blurt, "Yes, he's *paying* you to spend time with me."

Garrett huffed out a breath and glanced to each side of him before he spoke again and a small part of Alex's brain chided her for dismissing just how careful he was. For thinking that he was simply a cautious man. She remembered thinking not long after they met that he was acting a lot like one of the palace guards. Foolish of her not to realize just what that actually might mean.

Then she pushed those thoughts aside and concentrated solely on what he was saying.

"Your father hired me as a personal bodyguard. We were both worried about what might happen if you were on your own."

"Yes," she said tightly, amazed that she could form thoughts, let alone *words*. "Can't have Alex out and about behaving like an actual person. No, no. Can't have *that*."

"Damn it, Alex, you're deliberately misunderstanding."

"I don't think so," she snapped. "And you know? Maybe you and my father were right. Maybe poor Alex doesn't have a brain in her head. After all, she was foolish enough to think a handsome man wanted to know her better when, in reality, he was on her father's payroll." Her fingers clenched into useless fists. She wanted to throw something. To surrender to the temper frothing and boiling inside her. Unfortunately, her breeding and training had been too thorough. Duty and dignity ran through her veins along with the blood.

Circumspection was another watchword of the royal family and she was too steeped in its tradition to give rein to what she was feeling now. Still, she couldn't continue sitting across from him as if this were a date. She couldn't look at him now without feeling like a complete idiot. She couldn't watch his eyes, cool and dark, without remembering the heat and passion that had flared there so briefly.

At that thought, she gaped at him, horrified. "What about the boat? What happened there? Are you getting a bonus?"

"What?"

She leaned in toward him, pushing the flickering candle to one side. "Was that on the agenda? Show the princess a good time? Or did you just want bragging rights? Want to be able to tell your friends how you got a princess naked? Is that it?"

He leaned in, too, and the flare of the candle flame threw dancing patterns across his features. His eyes were more shadowed, his cheekbones more pronounced. "You know damn well that's not true."

"Do I?" she countered. "Do I really? I know! I should trust you on this because you've been so honest with me from the first, I suppose."

"You kept secrets, too," he argued.

That stopped her for a second. But only a second. "I did, but I wasn't *spying* on you."

"I'm not a damn spy!" His voice pitched a little too loud just as the song ended and several people turned to look. He glared them away before staring back at her. "I told your father I wouldn't be an informer, and I haven't been."

"Again," she said coolly, "with your sterling reputation, I should just take your word?"

His mouth worked furiously as though he were fighting an inner battle to keep his temper in check and angry words from spilling free. Well, she knew just how he felt.

Finally, he managed to say, "You're angry, I get it."

"Oh, I'm well beyond angry, Mr. King," she snapped and stood up. "Fury is a good word and still it doesn't capture exactly what I'm feeling. But thankfully, neither of us has to suffer the other's presence any further."

"Where do you think you're going?" he asked, standing up to look down at her.

Her body lit up inside and Alex silently cursed her response to him. What was it about this man that he could get to her even when she was more furious than she had ever been in her *life?* That simply wasn't right. "Anywhere but here. This *is* a free country, isn't it?"

"Alex, don't do anything foolish just because you're mad."

"I'll do what I please, Garrett King, and I'll thank you to stay away from me." She turned to go, but he caught her arm and held on to her.

She glared down at his hand and then lifted her gaze to his. "You know, when we first met, I thought you were a hero. Now I know you're the villain in the piece."

The muscle in his jaw twitched, and she knew he was grinding his teeth into powder. Good to know that she wasn't the only one feeling as if the top of her head was about to blow off.

"I'm not a hero. Never claimed to be. But I'm not a damn villain, either, Alex. I'm just a man."

"Doing his *job,*" she finished for him and jerked her arm free of his grasp. "Yes, I know."

Head up, chin lifted in a defiant tilt, she headed for the bar. He was just a step or two behind her. "What're you doing?"

"I think I need a drink."

"Don't be an idiot. Come back to the table. We'll talk about this."

"Now I'm an idiot, am I?"

"I didn't *say* that," he muttered.

"Well, you're right on one score. I have *been* an idiot. But not any longer." She hissed in a breath. "I don't want to talk to you, Garrett. Go away."

"Not a chance," he whispered, close to her ear.

His deep voice rumbled along her spine and lifted goose bumps across her flesh. She so wanted to be unaffected by him. But it looked as though *that* wasn't going to happen anytime soon.

The worst part of all of this? Beyond the humiliation of her father going behind her back and the man she was... involved with selling her out to the palace?

She still wanted Garrett.

Mingled in with the anger and the hurt were the underlying threads of desire that still had her wrapped up in knots. How could she still want him, knowing what she did now?

Alex stalked into the bar and gave a quick glance around. There were a dozen or so tall tables with singles and couples gathered at them. A long, gleaming bar snaked around the room in a semicircle. Three bartenders in World War II military uniforms hurried back and forth filling drink orders. Mirrors behind the bar reflected the candlelight and the stony face of the man standing behind her.

The face that had haunted her dreams from the day they met. Their gazes locked in the mirror and Alex felt a jolt of something hot and wicked sizzle through her system in spite of everything.

Deliberately, she tore her gaze from his and walked to

the bar, sliding onto one of the black leather stools. She crossed her legs, laid her bag on the bar top and ordered a gin and tonic.

In the bar mirror, she watched Garrett take a seat a few stools down from her. Not far enough, she thought, but better than nothing. She was only surprised that he was giving her this small amount of space.

"Hello, gorgeous." A deep voice spoke up from just behind her and Alex lifted her gaze to the mirror.

A tall, blond man wearing a black suit and a wide smile stood watching her. "You are way too beautiful to be alone," he said and sat down without waiting for an invitation.

"Thank you, that's very kind." She saw Garrett's reaction from the corner of her eye and seeing him fume made her smile a welcome at the man beside her.

"An accent, too?" He slapped one hand to his heart in a dramatic gesture that had Alex smiling. "You're going to fuel my dreams for weeks."

"That's a lovely thing to say," she told him, though truthfully she thought he was a little on the ridiculous side. With his glib lines, and over-the-top reactions, he was nothing like Garrett with his quiet, deadly, sexy air. Ordinarily, in fact, she wouldn't have been the slightest bit interested in the blond. Still, she caught a glimpse of Garrett's face in the mirror and noted the abject fury on his features. So she leaned toward her new admirer and asked, "What's your name, love?"

"I'm Derek. Who're you?"

"Alexis," she said, "but you can call me Alex."

"You're no 'Alex,' babe," he said with a wink. "So Alexis it is."

In the other room, the music started up again and Derek stood, holding out one hand. "Dance?"

From the corner of her eye, Alex saw Garrett stand up as if he was going to try to stop her. So she quickly took Derek's hand and let him lead her to the floor.

Damn woman.

She was doing this on purpose. Letting that slick guy give her a lame line and then sweep her off to the dance floor. Well, fine, if that's what she wanted, she could have the plastic blond guy. But she wouldn't be alone with him. Garrett was still working for her father and damned if he was going to leave a woman like Alex to the likes of *that* guy.

He followed them into the other room and stood to one side as the blond pulled Alex into his arms and started moving to the music. Alex looked like a vision. That wild mane of blond hair, those heels that made her legs look ten miles long and where the hell had she gotten that dress, anyway? Didn't she know he could practically see her *ass?*

Alex laughed at something Blondie had to say and Garrett's teeth crushed together. He'd known from the start that his lies would eventually catch up with him. Maybe, he told himself, he should have listened to Griffin and confessed the truth to Alex himself. Then at least he would have had the chance to smooth things over with the telling.

But how much smoothing could he have done, realistically? She would still have been hurt. Still have been pissed. And he'd *still* end up standing here watching as some other guy made moves on her.

Moves, he told himself, that she wasn't deflecting.

Irritated beyond belief, Garrett stood like a statue, arms crossed over his chest, feet braced wide apart in a fighting stance. His gaze never left the couple as he watched Blondie ooze his way across the dance floor. Surely, Alex wasn't buying this guy's lines? Any minute now in fact, she'd probably step out of the dance and walk away.

Any minute.

Walking.

Damn it, Alex.

The music slid around the room and the singer's voice wrapped them all in a sensual web. His arms ached to hold her. His hands warmed at the thought of touching her again and his mouth craved the taste of her.

His eyes narrowed as Blondie steered Alex off the dance floor and out onto the dark balcony overlooking the ocean. While the music played and couples danced, Garrett moved through the crowd with a quiet intensity. Focused on his target, he was aware of his surroundings in a heightened way, but all he could think about was reaching Alex.

He stepped onto the polished wood balcony and heard the rush of the sea pushing into shore. Moonlight washed the whole scene in a silvery glow and the wind sweeping across the ocean was nearly icy. Voices came to him and he turned his head in response. That's when he spotted them, at the end of the deck, in a puddle of darkness that lay between the more-decorative-than-useful balcony lights.

Alex was facing the water, and Blondie was plastered up behind her, as close as he could get. Garrett's mind splintered a little and he actually *saw* red around the edges of his vision.

Then his eyes nearly popped from his head in an onslaught of pure fury. Blondie had one hand on Alex's ass and was giving it a rub—and Alex wasn't even trying to stop him.

What the hell?

It only took a few, long strides to carry him to Alex's

side, where he dropped one hand on Blondie's shoulder and squeezed. Blondie looked up, annoyed at the interruption, but annoyance faded fast when he got a good look at Garrett's expression.

"Dude, we're having some private time here."

"Dude," Garrett corrected through gritted teeth. "You're done. Take off."

Alex whipped her windblown hair out of her face and glared at him. "Go away, Garrett."

Astonished, the handsome guy stared at her. "You know this guy?"

"Yes, but pay no attention to him," Alex said.

Garrett's hand on Blondie's shoulder tightened as he silently convinced the other man it would be a much better idea to disappear. Fast.

Message received.

"Yeah, right. Okay. Outta here." He hunched away from Garrett's grip, gave Alex a wistful look and shrugged. "Sorry, babe. I don't do violence. I think *he* does."

"Damn straight," Garrett assured him.

"Oh, for—" Alex set her hands at her hips and glared at Garrett as Blondie hurried back to the restaurant, in search of easier prey. "What do you think you're doing?"

"Hah!" Garrett backed her up against the railing, looming over her as he planted his hands at either side of her. His grip on the cold, damp, iron railing tightened as he looked down into her eyes. "What am I doing? I'm keeping you from getting mauled in public."

"We were hardly in public and what if I *liked* being mauled?" she snapped, her eyes flashing with the kind of heat that any sane man would accept as a warning.

Garrett, though, had passed "sane" a couple of exits back. He was too close to her, bodies aligned, that damn dress of hers displaying way too much beautiful, smooth skin. Heat seared his insides and his dick went to stone. Just the scent of her was enough to drive him insane. He fought for clarity. Fought for control.

"Damn it, Alex. I get that you're pissed at me. And fine. I can deal with it."

"Oh, how very gracious of you."

"But," he continued, leaning close enough that her breasts were pillowed against his chest. That she could feel his erection pressing into her abdomen. Her eyes widened and her lips parted on a sigh. "I'm not going to stand around and watch you make a mistake."

"Another one, you mean?"

In the background, the music was soft, tempting; the singer's voice a lure, drawing them into a world where it was just the two of them, locked together. He felt every inch of her luscious body aligned along his. And in a heartbeat, control and focus went out the window, and Garrett found he couldn't even give a good damn.

"You didn't want that guy's hands on you, Alex."

She let her head fall back. Her eyes met his and a long sigh slid from her throat. "Is that right? And how do you know that?"

"Because you want *my* hands on you," he muttered, his gaze raking over her features before settling on her eyes. "You want *me* touching you and no one else."

She opened her mouth to say something, but Garrett didn't let her speak. Instead, he cupped her face in his hands, leaned down and took her mouth with his.

Pissed or not, Alex wanted him, too. He felt it in her instant surrender. She wrapped her arms around his neck, held his head to her and gave him everything she had. Their tongues entwined, caressing, stroking. The cool air swept past them, and danced across their heated skin.

She shivered, and he wrapped his arms around her,

holding her closer, tighter, until he felt her frenzied heartbeat racing in time with his own. Every inch of his skin hummed with anticipation.

He knew they had been headed for this moment since the day they had met. It didn't matter that he had fought it. This was inevitable. Pulling his head back, he looked down into her glassy eyes and whispered, "Your hotel's only a few minutes from here."

Dragging in a breath, she shivered again and leaned into him. "Then why are we still standing here?"

A fierce grin split his face briefly. Then he took her hand and headed around the edge of the balcony toward the front of the place. Now he was glad he hadn't bothered with valet parking. He didn't have the patience to hang around while some kid ran to bring him his car.

No more waiting.

That first taste of her pushed him over the edge. Touching her wouldn't be enough this time.

This time, he had to have it all.

Nine

It was minutes that felt like hours.

Desire pumping in the air around them, making each heartbeat sound like a gong in their heads, the drive to Alex's hotel was bristling with sexual heat. Somehow, Garrett got the car parked, and Alex through the lobby into the private elevator. Somehow, they managed to walk through the door of the penthouse and slam it closed behind them.

And then all bets were off.

Hunger was king here and neither of them had the strength or the will to fight it any longer.

Garrett tore off his jacket and tossed it aside. Alex's hands fumbled at the buttons on his shirt while he ripped his tie off and discarded it, as well. The moment his shirt was undone, her hands moved over his chest and every one of her fingers felt as if it were imprinting itself on his skin. Heat sizzled back and forth between them, leaving each of them struggling for air. Sighs and groans were the only sounds as they kissed again, hungrily, frantically.

He stabbed his fingers through her wild mane of hair and let the silkiness slide across his skin like cool water. She opened her mouth under his, offering him everything and he took it. Garrett was through pretending that their relationship was strictly business.

At least for this one night, he wanted everything that he had been dreaming of, thinking of, for the past several days. He couldn't touch her enough. Couldn't kiss her enough. He wanted more. Wanted all. Had to have her.

"Now, Alex," he muttered, tearing his mouth from hers to drag his lips and tongue and teeth along the elegant sweep of her neck.

She sighed and tipped her head to one side, as she held his head to her throat. "Yes, Garrett. Yes, please, *now.*"

He unzipped the back of her dress and pushed the slender straps down her arms, letting it fall to the floor at her feet. She stepped out of the puddle of fabric and kicked it to one side.

"You're amazing," he whispered, gaze moving over her as she stood there, naked but for those high heels she loved and a tiny scrap of black lace panties. She looked like every man's fantasy and she was his. All his.

Garrett caught her, pulled her in close, then bent his head to take first one then the other erect, pink nipple into his mouth. Her fingers threaded through his hair and pressed his head to her breasts as if afraid he would stop.

He had no intention of stopping.

The taste of her filled him. Her scent surrounded him. A haze settled over his mind, shutting out everything but the present. All there was in the world was this woman.

His hands moved over her skin, up and down her back, around and across her abdomen to the tiny scrap of black lace she wore. His fingers gave a sharp tug and she was naked, open for his touch.

Still suckling at her, he dropped one hand to the juncture of her thighs and sighed against her when she parted
her legs for him. He stroked that single bud of pleasure
until she was whimpering and rocking against his hand.
Her hips twisted and moved in time with his touch, and
he smiled against her breast as he felt her climax build.

Lifting his head, he stared at her as his fingers worked
her body into a frenzy. She licked her lips, tossed her hair
back and took breath after greedy breath.

Her gaze locked with his and her voice was soft as she
said, "I want you inside me this time, Garrett. I need to
feel you inside me."

He wouldn't have thought he could get any harder. But
he did. Reluctantly, he let her go just long enough to strip
out of his clothes. He paused only long enough to take a
condom from his wallet and sheathe himself. When she
made to kick off her high heels, though, he shook his head.
"Leave 'em on."

She gave him a slow, wide smile, then dropped her
gaze to take in all of him. Her eyes widened and when she
looked up at him again, she was even more eager for him.
"Now, Garrett. Be with me. Be *in* me."

They were still in the damn living room of the suite and
Garrett knew that they'd never make it to the bedroom.
Neither of them was willing to wait that long.

He swept her close to him and when his erection pushed
at her, she moaned and moved into him, feeding the fires
that were already swallowing him. "That's it. Right here,
right now. We'll do it slow next time."

"Next time," she agreed.

He carried her a few short steps to the couch, set her
on the high back and stepped in between her thighs. She
opened herself wider for him and when he entered her,
Alex groaned aloud.

Garrett gritted his teeth to keep from shouting as his body invaded hers in one hard thrust. Her damp heat enveloped him, a tight glove, squeezing. When he was seated to the hilt, Alex held him even closer. She moved on the precarious edge of the couch as much as she could. Now she did kick off those heels so she could lock her legs around his hips and hold on as he set a fast, dizzying pace that pushed them both as high as they could go.

They raced to the edge together. Gazes locked, bodies joined, two halves of the same whole. Again and again, his hips pistoned against her and she took everything he had, urging him on.

As the first crash of her orgasm slammed into her, she called out his name and Garrett felt her body spasm around his. He watched her shatter, felt the strength of her climax shaking her. And Garrett realized he'd never known this before. Never been this connected to any woman before. He watched her pleasure and felt it as his own.

He heard her sighs and wanted to capture them forever. Heard his name on her lips and felt both humbled and victorious. Possession raged through him and his only thought as his own release finally claimed him was: *mine*.

Seconds ticked past, became minutes, and those could have been hours for all Alex knew. Or cared.

With Garrett's body still locked with hers, she had everything she had been craving for days. The incredible feel of him deep inside her. The dazzling orgasm that was so much better than anything she had ever felt before. The sweet sensation of his arms wrapped around her. It was all…perfect.

As if she really had found the magic she had been looking for when she first began this holiday.

But even as that thought flitted through her mind, she

knew it wasn't true. Despite what she was feeling, she knew now that Garrett didn't share it.

Want wasn't romance.

Desire wasn't love.

Love? Now where had that thought come from? She stiffened in his arms as the word circled round and round in her mind. She didn't want to believe it, but how could she not? What she felt for Garrett was so far beyond what she had ever known with anyone else.

What else could it be, but love?

Which put her in a very uncomfortable position.

She was in love with a man who was only with her because he had been hired by her father.

"Alex…" Garrett's voice thundered down around her, sounding like a summer storm, and she knew that their moment was over.

She looked up at him, watching his face as he spoke again.

"I'm sorry."

She blinked. "You're *sorry?*"

He pulled away from her and she instantly missed the feeling of his body pressed into hers. And she wanted to kick herself for it. How could she possibly love such a Neanderthal?

"It shouldn't have happened," he muttered, raking one hand through his hair and stepping back so she could slide off the back of the couch. "I let myself be distracted and allowed you to do the same."

"Allowed?" she echoed. "You *allowed* me?"

He didn't pick up on the temper in her voice, or if he did, he wasn't paying attention. His mistake.

"I take full responsibility for this, and I want you to know, it won't happen again."

"You…you…" She opened and closed her mouth several times, but nothing came out. Well, who knew that "stunned speechless" could actually happen? Her bare toes curled into the rug beneath her feet as if she needed all the help she could get just to keep her balance.

"I know what you're going to say," he told her, with a small, brief smile. "And you don't have to. I know you regret this as much as I do."

Oh, she wanted to do something to wipe that "understanding" expression off his face. But once again, her breeding rang true and she settled for quietly seething instead. When she could speak again, she did so quietly. "So you're writing my dialogue for me as well, are you?"

"What?"

Fury flashed inside her like an electrical storm. She actually *felt* bolts of white-hot anger stabbing through her system, and it was all she could do to keep from screaming. Looking up at him, Alex shook her head and said, "You pompous, arrogant, dim-witted, ego-maniacal... *twit!*"

He scowled at her. "What the hell?"

"Oh," she said, eyes widely innocent. "Weren't expecting that, were you?"

"What are you so pissed about *now?*"

"The very fact that you could even ask me that proves your twit-dom!"

"That's not even a word."

"It is now," she told him, stalking a few paces away because she was simply so furious she couldn't stand still. She should have been embarrassed, or, at the very least, uncomfortable, walking about her suite stark naked. But truthfully, she was too angry to care.

"I'm trying to do the right thing," he said, each word grinding out of his throat.

"For the both of us, it seems," she snapped. Her gaze

fixed on him, she said, "Did it even occur to you that what I might regret most is your ridiculous attitude?"

"Ridiculous? I'm taking responsibility for this mess. How is that ridiculous?"

"How is this a *mess?*" she countered.

"You know damn well how," he muttered. "Because I'm here to protect you."

"But not from pompous asses, apparently," she said.

"Okay, that's enough."

"Have you decided that, as well?" she asked, a sugary sweet tone to her voice.

"What the hell, Alex? We both know this shouldn't have happened."

"So sayeth the almighty arbiter of everything sexual."

"You're starting to piss me off."

"Well, join the bloody club!" Walking back to him, she stopped within a foot of his gorgeous body, tipped her head back and glared into those eyes that only moments ago had been glazed with passion. Now there were ice chips in those depths and damned if she didn't find them just as attractive. "I'm not a naive young virgin out for her first romp in the hay, you know. You're not the first man in my bed. You're simply the first to regret it the moment it was over. Well, thank you very much for that, Garrett King.

"Now, why don't you take your sense of responsibility and leave?"

"I'm not going anywhere until we settle this."

"Then I hope you packed a lunch," she quipped, "because I don't see that happening anytime soon."

"Maybe if you'd be reasonable…"

She sucked in a gulp of air and gave him a shove. He didn't budge an inch. Like shoving a bloody wall. "Reasonable? You think I'm *not* being reasonable? It's only my exceptional breeding and the training of my mother, not to mention countless governesses, that's keeping me from punching you in the nose!"

He laughed at the very idea, which infuriated her enough to curl her hand into a fist and take a wild swing at him, just as her brothers had taught her to. Garrett, though, was too fast for her and caught her hand in his before she could make contact.

"Nice 'breeding,'" he said with a half smile.

"You're insufferable."

"You've said that before."

"Then clearly I'm an astute human being."

He sighed. "Alex, look me in the eye and tell me you think this was a good thing. I'm not looking for a relationship. This is going nowhere."

His words slapped her, but she wouldn't let him see it. She wouldn't be the needy one while he tried to make light of something that had shaken her to her very foundations. So she took a page from his book…she lied. "What makes you think I'm looking for a future with you? Are you really that egotistical? Do you think one night in bed with you is enough to make a woman immediately start craving white picket fences? Start scribbling her name next to yours surrounded by lacy hearts?

"I'm a *princess,* Garrett. I may have run off for a holiday but I know what my duties are. I know what my life will be. God knows, it was planned for me practically from the moment I drew my first breath! And nowhere in that plan does it say *fall in love with a Neanderthal, move to California and remain barefoot and pregnant.*"

Her breath was coming fast, in and out of her lungs. Her heartbeat was racing and her blood was pumping. Being this close to him was feeding more than her anger. In spite of everything, she wanted him.

He was stupid and clueless and impossibly arrogant—
and, he was the most intriguing man she had ever known.
Even the fact that he had lied to her from the beginning
wasn't enough to cool off the fires licking at her insides.
And Alex had the distinct feeling that thirty years from
now, when he was nothing more than a hazy memory, she
would *still* want him.

"Neanderthal?"

Her fury abated for the moment, she only asked, "How
would you describe yourself at this moment?"

"Confused, angry—" he paused, tucked his fingers beneath her chin and lifted her face, her eyes, up to his "—and
more turned on than I was before."

He felt it, too. That soul-deep stirring. He didn't want
it, either, but it seemed as though neither of them had a
choice when it came to what lay sizzling between them.
Arguments didn't matter. Differences didn't matter.

All that mattered was the next touch. The next kiss.

"Oh," she admitted on a sigh, "me, too."

He kissed her and the rest of the world fell away. Alex
let go of her anger and gave herself up to the wonder of
what he could make her feel.

His arms came around her as his mouth took hers. He
carried her into the bedroom and laid her down atop the
silk duvet. The slide of the cool fabric against her skin was
just another sensation to pile onto the rest.

Sliding his hands up and down her body, Alex arched
into him, allowing her mind to drift free so that she could
concentrate solely on the moment. Every stroke was a
benediction. Every caress a promise of more to come.

Her body felt alive in a way it never had before. His
touch was magic…kindling sparks of flame at every spot
he touched. He leaned over her, kissing her, then sliding

along her body, nibbling his way down. Then he stopped, pulled back and slid off the bed.

"Where are you going?"

"Right back," he swore, his eyes fixed on hers.

True to his word, he was gone only moments and she saw that he had another condom with him, sheathing himself as he came closer.

A smile tugged at the corner of her mouth. "You always carry those in your wallet?"

"I have since I met you," he admitted, kneeling back on the bed, dropping his head for a quick kiss. "Just in case."

"Always prepared?" she asked.

"Babe, those are the Boy Scouts. And trust me when I say I'm no Boy Scout."

"No," she whispered as he moved down the length of her body again, letting his mouth and tongue blaze the trail, "you're really not."

Alex sighed deeply and stared up at the ceiling. Moonlight poured through the windows, along with a chill ocean breeze that ruffled the white sheers and sent them into a sensual dance that mimicked her own movements beneath Garrett's talented hands.

"You're torturing me," she whispered and arched into him as his lips crossed over her abdomen.

"That's the plan," Garrett assured her.

"You're an evil man," she said on a sigh. "Don't stop."

"Not a chance," he promised.

Then he moved, shifting down to kneel between her thighs and Alex looked at him. Slowly he scooped his hands beneath her bottom and lifted her from the bed. Everything in her tensed in expectation. Her gaze locked with his as he lowered his mouth to her center and—

She groaned at the first sweep of his tongue across a bud of flesh so sensitive it felt as if it had a life of its own.

Electric-like jolts of sensation shot through her, coiling the tension within her even tighter. Alex moved into him, loving the feel of his mouth on her.

Reaching down, she pushed her fingers through his hair as he pushed her higher and faster than she had gone before. This intimacy was so overwhelming; her system was flooded with emotions tangling together. She felt so much, wanted so much, *needed* so much.

It was close. She felt it. The orgasm hovering just out of reach was almost on her and she wanted him inside her when it hit. "Garrett, please."

Instantly, he pulled away from her, sat back on his thighs and lifted her onto his lap. Alex went up onto her knees and slowly, deliberately, lowered herself onto him. It was delicious. The tantalizingly slow slide of his hard thickness pushing into her depths. She gloried in every inch of him. She let her head fall back as she wrapped her arms around his neck and swiveled her hips against him, taking him even higher and deeper than she had before.

Until she was sure he was touching the tip of her heart.

"You feel so good," he whispered, kissing the base of her throat, locking his lips against her pulse point. His breath hot against her skin, he whispered words she couldn't hear—could only *feel*.

And then she moved on him and his hands settled at her hips, guiding her motions, helping her set a rhythm they both kept time with. Again and again, she rocked her body onto his, and, over and over, they tore apart and came together. They moved as one. Breathed as one.

And at last, they shattered as one.

Ten

In the dark, when it was quiet, reality crashed down on top of them again, and Alex was the first to feel its sharp tugs at the edges of her heart.

Grabbing up her short, blue silk robe, she slipped it on, then crossed her bedroom, opened the French doors leading to the balcony that wrapped around the entire penthouse suite and stepped outside. The stone floor was cool and damp beneath her feet and the wind off the ocean lifted her hair and teased her heated skin.

Staring out at the moonlit sea, Alex tried to get a handle on the rampaging emotions crashing through her. Her mind was alive with careening thoughts that rushed up to be noticed then were swallowed and replaced by the next one. In fact, the only thing she was truly sure of was that she did love Garrett King. Infuriating as he was, she loved him.

They'd known each other such a short time, it was hard

to believe. But the simple fact was, as her mother had always told her, love didn't come with a timetable. It was either there or it wasn't and no amount of waiting would change that.

Her heart ached and her mind whirled. There was misery along this road and she knew it. Garrett had made no secret of the fact that he wasn't interested in a relationship. And even if he were, their lives were so different. They didn't even live on the same *continent!* What possible chance was there for anything more than what they had already shared?

Taking hold of the iron railing in front of her, she squeezed tightly in response to the tension within.

A moment later, Garrett joined her, and her heart sped into a gallop. She glanced at him. He was wearing the slacks he'd abandoned what felt like hours ago, but he was barefoot and shirtless and his broad, sculpted chest seemed to be begging for her touch. She gripped the handrails to keep from giving in to that urge.

"Alex, we really need to talk."

"That never bodes well," she replied, deliberately turning her gaze on the ever-shifting surface of the water below.

He stood beside her. Close, but not touching and still, she felt the heat from his body sliding into hers.

"It's too late to do a damn thing about it, but none of that should have happened, Alex."

She stiffened. He still regretted being with her. How would he react, she wondered, if he knew she loved him? She glanced over the railing to the sand ten stories below. He'd probably jump.

"No doubt you're right."

"Huh." She felt more than saw him turn his gaze on her. "You surprise me. I expected a different reaction."

Alex steeled herself then turned to look up into his eyes. "What were you thinking? Keening? Gnashing of teeth?" She gave him a smile that felt stiff and wooden. "Sorry to disappoint."

"Not disappointed. Just surprised."

"Well, you shouldn't be," she said, silently congratulating herself on how calm and cool she sounded. Honestly, if she weren't a princess, she should think of going on the stage. "You'd already made yourself quite clear on the subject, and, as I've mentioned, I'm not an idiot, Garrett. I know that we don't suit. I know we mean nothing to each other and that this isn't going anywhere...."

Those words ripped a new hole in the fabric of her heart, but better *she* say them than him.

"I didn't say you mean nothing to me, Alex," he said, laying his hands on her shoulders and turning her so that she faced him.

God, she didn't want to look into his eyes. Didn't want to feel the heat of him spearing through her body. Didn't want to think about the pain she would feel when she was gone and back in the palace.

The only way to get through any of it was to pretend none of it mattered.

So she gave him that forced smile again and hoped he wouldn't notice. "Ah, yes, I forgot," she quipped. "I do mean something to you after all. Quite a hefty paycheck, I'm guessing."

"I didn't say that, either," he ground out.

"You haven't said much, Garrett," she told him. "What else am I to think?"

"That you're an amazing, smart, funny, incredibly sexy *princess*."

"It always comes back to that, doesn't it?" she mused, stepping out of his grip and turning to face the sea again.

"If I'd known how you would focus on that, I would have worn my crown while we were in bed together."

"I don't give a damn for your crown, Alex," he snapped, voice near growling now. "In fact this would all be a hell of a lot easier if you *weren't* a princess. You think your father would be thrilled to know that I'm here with you?"

"What's my father got to do with any of this?"

Clearly exasperated, he snapped, "I've done security work for royalty all over the globe. You know what's the *one* thing they all have in common? They don't get involved with non-royals. Hell, I've got more money than a lot of them, but I'm still a 'commoner.' You think your father feels any different?"

"Probably not."

"Exactly." Garrett shook his head. "It all comes down to that, Princess."

"Story of my life," she murmured, sliding a glance at him.

"What's that supposed to mean?"

"Please," she scoffed. "Do you think you're the only man who has run screaming into the night trying to escape the glare of the palace? You're not." Shaking her head she added, "And for all of those that run away, dozens more run *toward* the crown. None of them see me, Alex. They see the princess. Some hate the very idea of royalty and others covet it. People on the outside look at the royal family and think, *Isn't it wonderful? All the pomp and pageantry. How nice to shop wherever you like and not worry about the price.*

"Well," she continued, "there's *always* a price, Garrett. It's just one that most people never see. It's a lack of privacy. A lack of freedom and imagination. It's being locked into centuries of tradition whether you like it or not, and it's duty."

Her gaze narrowed, her breath coming fast and furious, she hurried on before he could say a word. She looked up into his eyes and watched them flash with emotion, but she didn't let that stop her.

"You think I don't understand your 'duty' to protect me? Trust me when I say that's the one thing I am all too aware of. Duty is the first thing I was taught. Duty to my country, to the citizens of Cadria and to my king. My family has ruled for centuries. Yes, Cadria is a small country, but she's proud and it's *our* duty to protect her. Keep her safe. So, yes. I understand your self-imposed duties, but it doesn't mean I like them any more than I like the golden chains linking me to my own set of duties."

He studied her for a long minute before speaking. When he did, he said only, "Quite a rant."

She huffed out a short laugh. "Apparently, I have what you Americans refer to as 'issues.'"

"I never use that word," he assured her, and reached out for her again.

Smiling, she let herself be held. Probably another monumental mistake, but she needed the comfort of his arms. The strength of him, wrapped around her. If she had one more thing to regret in the morning, then so be it.

"Why'd your father have to be a *king?*"

She laughed a little and linked her arms at the small of his back. "Your father was a King, too."

He gave her a squeeze. "Funny."

Tipping her head back, she looked up at him and whispered, "You may be willing to pretend that everything that happened tonight was a mistake, but I for one, enjoyed myself immensely."

"So did I, Alex. That's the problem."

"Doesn't have to be."

He shook his head. "I'm here to do a job and that doesn't include bedding *you*."

That barb hit home with a staggering force she didn't even want to admit to herself. So much for tender makeup scenes in the moonlight. "Yes," she said softly. "I wonder if you'll get a raise in pay for this? Maybe if I tell my father how very good you were?"

"Cut it out, Alex."

She felt like a fool. She'd spilled her heart out to him, laid it at his feet and he chose that moment to remind her that he was being paid by her father. How could she possibly *love* a man who only saw her as a job? How could she have forgotten, even for a minute, that he had lied to her from their first day together? That her father was paying him to watch over her?

Well, fine. If he wanted to turn his back on what they had together, then she wouldn't stop him. She might be fool enough to love him, but she wasn't so big a fool that she didn't know when to pull back from the edge of a very steep cliff. Releasing him, she steeled herself for the soul-deep cold that slipped inside her the instant she left the circle of his arms.

"You're the one who brought this up again," she reminded him.

"I just want you to understand is all. I didn't want to say yes to your dad, but he's a hard man to refuse."

"That much I know from personal experience."

He took a breath. "When I realized who you were, I was worried. I called your father and told him I was uncomfortable with you out on your own with no protection. And so was he. I talked to your mother, too."

She closed her eyes briefly and he felt the tension in her body tighten. "So they double-teamed you."

"Yeah," he said with a sharp nod. "Guess you could say that."

"They're very good at it," she mused, a half smile blooming and disappearing from her mouth in a fraction of a second. "It's how they deal with my brothers and me, as well."

"Then you can see why—"

"I can see why you said yes to my father," she cut him off neatly and speared him with a glance that had gone icy. "What I don't see is why you *lied* to me."

"I lied because I had to. Your father told me you're adept at escaping your guards."

"And because you lied, I never even tried to escape you," she whispered.

"I couldn't risk you escaping me, Alex. I had to keep you safe. As for fighting what was happening between us…" He paused and shook his head again as if he couldn't believe they were in this situation. "In my job, when I get distracted, people tend to *die.* I won't let that happen to you, Alex."

"Garrett, if you don't *live,* you might as well be dead already. Don't you see that?"

"What I see is that I let you get to me," he said, gaze moving over her face. "Didn't mean to. Didn't want you to. But you did anyway."

A part of her thrilled to hear it. But the more rational voice in her mind warned against it. The look in his eyes was far from warm and fuzzy. The set of his jaw and the tension in every line of his body screamed that he was a man who'd made his decision. Alex had come in second to his sense of honor. What he said next only defined it.

"As much as I want you, I can't let this happen again, Alex. Not while I'm responsible for your safety."

There it was. Duty first. She should respect that sentiment, seeing as she had been raised to believe the same. But somehow, that didn't make her feel any better.

A chill swept over her that had nothing at all to do with the cold wind still flying toward them. Garrett couldn't have made himself clearer.

"No worries, Garrett," she told him, keeping her voice light in spite of the knot of pain clogging her throat. "You're absolutely safe from me now as I'm just not interested anymore."

"Liar."

She laughed shortly. "Amazing that you even feel comfortable using that word against someone else."

"Amazing that you can be so pissed at me for doing something you're pretty good at yourself."

She ignored that and turned for the bedroom, suddenly more than ready for this conversation to be over. "Before you go, want to check the bathroom for hidden assassins?"

"Funny."

Stepping into the bedroom, she walked to the dressing table, picked up her hairbrush and started drawing the bristles through her tangled hair. Staring into the mirror, she caught his reflected gaze. "You're making far too much of this situation. You're assuming I want this 'relationship' to continue. But I don't."

"Lying again."

She tossed the brush down. "Stop telling me when I'm lying. It's rude."

"Then stop lying."

"Same to you."

"I'm not lying now," he said. "I still want you."

"Me, too."

"Damn it, Alex."

"Shut up and kiss me, Garrett."

He did and Alex's brain went on hiatus again. Soon,

she would be able to sit back and regret this at her leisure. But at the moment, all she could think was how right it felt. How good it was to be in his arms again. To have his mouth fused to hers.

He lifted her and carried her to the bed and when he set her down onto the mattress, she looked up into icy-blue eyes that sparked and shone with the kind of need that shook her to the bone.

For now, that was enough.

Three days later, Garrett was on the edge with no way out.

Now that she knew who he was, Alex seemed to delight in making him nuts. She insisted on walking down crowded sidewalks, going shopping through packed malls and even driving to San Diego to visit SeaWorld. It was as if she had determined to make him earn every dime of his paycheck from her father.

It was a security expert's nightmare.

Garrett knew damn well it was only a matter of time before her identity was revealed. Someone, somewhere, was going to recognize her and then he'd be hip-deep in paparazzi, reporters and general nutcases, all trying to get close to the visiting princess.

But short of locking her into her penthouse, he didn't have a clue how to keep her from being noticed. A woman like Alex got people's attention. She was tall, gorgeous and had a perpetual smile on her face that seemed to welcome conversations with strangers. He hovered as closely as he could and still it wasn't enough.

His mind filled with ugly possibilities. He'd seen enough damage done over the years to be prepared for the absolute worst—his brain dredging up any number of horrific scenarios. And it killed him to think of anything happening to Alex.

Which was only natural, he assured himself. After all, she was in his care. Of course he'd be worried about her—that was his *job*. And that was all it was.

Garrett's trained gaze swept the room as he deliberately tried to become invisible, as any good bodyguard would. But, being the only man in a homeless shelter that catered to women and kids made Garrett's job harder. He stood out like Death at the Party. He caught the glances tossed his way and was sorry to know he was making some of the women here really uncomfortable. But damned if he was going to let Alex out of his sight.

The woman continued to press her luck and push him closer and closer to the ragged edge of control. Today, she had insisted on visiting a women's shelter to compare their setup with the program she knew at home.

Jane, the woman in charge, hadn't had a problem with his presence—but she had asked him to stay out of the way and that he was willing to do. Better all the way around for a protection detail to blend into the background as much as possible. It gave him eyes and ears to the place without attracting attention himself.

Watching Alex move around the room with the director, Garrett felt his admiration for her grow. She wasn't here as a princess. She had introduced herself as a fellow volunteer, visiting from Europe. And in a few short minutes, she and Jane had been chatting like old friends.

While Alex looked at the facility and met a few of the residents, Garrett watched *her*. She fit in any damn where, he thought and wondered at how easily Alex dismissed *what* she was in favor of *who* she was. She was so much more than some dilettante royal. She was eager and involved and she *cared* for people and what she might do to help. It had nothing to do with her crown. This was her soul he was watching, and damned if he could look away.

"You a cop?"

Garrett jolted out of his daydreams, gave himself a mental kick for being caught unaware and then looked down at the little boy staring up at him with wide brown eyes. "No, I'm not a cop."

"Look like one," the boy said, giving Garrett a gap-toothed smile. "You're all straight and stiff like one."

Great. He was doing such a good job being invisible that a five-year-old had made him. Alex really was throwing him off his game.

One corner of his mouth lifted in a smile. "You stand up straight, you get taller."

Those brown eyes went as big as saucers. "Tall as you?"

"Taller," Garrett assured him and instantly, the kid squared his shoulders, straightened his spine and lifted his chin. All forty pounds of him.

"Is she your girlfriend?"

That question came unexpectedly, though why it had, he didn't know. He'd spent enough time around his cousin's kids to know that they said pretty much whatever popped into their heads. "No," he said, shifting his gaze back to Alex. "She's a friend."

"She's nice," the boy said. "Pretty, too, and she smells good."

"Yeah," Garrett said, still watching Alex. "You're right."

"You should make her your girlfriend."

Intrigued, he shot the kid a look and asked, "Yeah? Why's that?"

"Because she smiles when she looks at you and that's nice. Besides, she's *pretty*."

"Timmy!" A woman shouted from across the room and the little boy trotted off, leaving Garrett staring after him.

Out of the mouths of babes, he mused. He looked up, caught Alex's eye and she flashed him one of those smiles that seemed designed to knock him off balance. In a flash, he remembered her under him, over him. The feel of her skin, the taste of her mouth, the scent of her, surrounding him.

As if she knew exactly what he was thinking, her smile slipped into something more private. More…intimate. And Garrett was once again hit with the knowledge that he'd fallen into a hole that just kept getting deeper.

Alex very much enjoyed watching Garrett go quietly insane at the beach. It was a lovely day to sit on the sand and enjoy the last of summer. There were only a handful of people there, including a few children busily building sand walls in an attempt to hold back the inexorable rush of the tide. Sandpipers and seagulls strutted along the shoreline and surfers sat atop their boards waiting for the perfect ride.

Everyone was having a good time, she thought. Everyone, that is, but Garrett King.

Honestly, it was simply too easy to push the man's buttons. And Alex had discovered just how much fun it could be. The man was determined to keep her at a distance. He hadn't touched her since that one night they'd spent together. Her heart hurt and her body ached for his and so, she had decided to make him as uncomfortable as possible with his decision to leave her alone.

If she was going to be miserable, then she would do everything she could to make sure he was, too. She challenged him, worried him and in general made his time with her as difficult as possible. She flirted with him outrageously and watched him fight his own desires to keep his professionalism at the fore.

With his serious "bodyguard" expression, he kept most people at bay. But those who weren't the least bit intimidated slipped past him, much to Alex's delight. Because then she flirted with other men, just to watch Garrett's instant, infuriated response.

Take for example the surfer who was right now giving her a wink and a smile before heading for the water. If she weren't in love with a perfectly infuriating man, she would very well be tempted to take the other man up on his not-so-subtle offer.

"He's short," Garrett muttered from behind her.

She smiled to herself, nodded at the surfer and said, "He's at least six feet tall."

"Shorter than me, then," Garrett said tightly.

"Most people are," she returned. "Hardly a crime."

"He's at least thirty and he's at the beach in the middle of the week."

"So are you," she pointed out, glancing over her shoulder at the man in black who was glowering at the rest of humanity. Honestly, he looked like the Grim Reaper. No wonder most people tended to give her a wide berth.

"Yes, but I'm *working*," he told her.

"And you never let me forget that, do you?" Alex gritted her teeth and turned her head back to watch the handsome surfer carry his board out to the water. His black wet suit clung to a fairly amazing body and his long, light brown hair was sun-streaked, telling her he spent most of his days in the sun. Perhaps Garrett was right and he was a layabout. She frowned at the thought.

"Alex, don't start that again."

"I didn't start it, Garrett," she told him, now ignoring the surfer to concentrate on the conversation she was having with the man who refused to get close to her. "I never do. You're the one who consistently reminds me that I'm your *responsibility*. And I simply can't tell you how flattering that is."

He sighed. She heard it even from three feet away.

"But, even though it's your *job* to watch over me," she added, not for the first time, "it doesn't give you the right to chase away any man who dares to look at me."

"It is if I think they're dangerous."

She laughed outright at that comment and turned to stare at him. "Like the college student yesterday at the art gallery? That sweet young man who was so nervous he dropped his bottle of water?"

Garrett frowned. "He kept touching you."

"It was *crowded* in that shop."

"That's what he wanted you to think. He wasn't nervous, Alex. He was on the prowl. He kept bumping into you. *Touching* you." Scowling, he picked up a handful of sand and let it drift through his fingers. "It wasn't that crowded."

"Well, certainly not after you threw the poor soul up against a wall and frisked him!"

He smiled at the memory. "Did discourage him quick enough, didn't it?"

"And half the gallery," she pointed out. "People scattered, thinking you were a crazy person."

"Yeah…" He was still smiling.

"You're impossible. You know that, don't you?"

"If I hadn't known it before I met you, I do now. You tell me often enough."

"And yet you don't listen." Pushing up from the sand, Alex dusted off the seat of her white shorts and snatched up the sandals she had kicked off when they first arrived. Walking to him, she looked down into Garrett's eyes and said, "You might want to ask yourself why you take it so personally when another man looks at me. Or talks to me."

"You know why," he muttered, keeping his gaze fixed on hers.

"Yes, the job." She went down to one knee in front of him. "But I think it's more than that, Garrett. I think it's much more, but you're too much of a coward to admit it."

His features went like granite, and Alex knew she'd struck a nerve. Well, good. Happy to know it.

So quickly she hardly saw him move, he reached out, grabbed her and pulled her close. Then he gave her a brief, hard kiss before letting her go again. Shaking his head, he stood up, then took her hand and drew her to her feet as well.

"You keep pushing me, Alex, and you never know what might happen."

"And that, Garrett," she said, licking her lips and giving him a small victory smile, "is the fun part."

Eleven

"I quit."

"I beg your pardon?"

Garrett winced at the snooty tone the King of Cadria could produce. He had known going in that this phone call wouldn't go well, but there was nothing to be done about it. Garrett was through working for the king, and Alex's father was just going to have to deal with it.

"You heard me correctly, your majesty," he said, leaning back in his desk chair. The study in his home was dark, filled with shadows in every corner. A single lamp on his desk wasn't enough to chase them away—seemed like a pretty good metaphor for his life at the moment, he thought, surprised at the poetic train his mind was taking. But there were shadows in Garrett's past, too. Always there. Always ready to pounce. And the light that was Alex—though damn brighter than anything he'd ever known—still couldn't get rid of all those dark places.

So there was really only one thing to do. "I quit as your daughter's bodyguard."

The king blustered and shouted and Garrett let him go. He figured he owed it to the man to let him get it all out of his system. And while a royal father thousands of miles away ranted and raged, Garrett's mind turned to that afternoon on the beach. The look in Alex's eyes. The taste of her.

These past few days had been torturous. He couldn't be with her without wanting her and he couldn't have her as long as he was responsible for her safety. But the whole truth was, he couldn't have her, *period*.

Even if he gave in to what he wanted, what would it gain either of them? Soon she'd be going home to a damn palace. He would be here, in California running his business. He wasn't looking to be in love or to be married. But even if he were, she was a princess and there was just no way Garrett could compete with that. Oh, he was rich enough to give her the kind of house and servants she was used to. But he didn't have the pedigree her family would expect of a man wanting to be with Alex.

He was a King, and he was damn proud of it. The problem was, she was the daughter of a *king*.

No. There was nothing ahead for them but more misery and, thanks very much, but he'd rather skip that part of the festivities.

Sitting forward, he braced his elbow on the desktop and only half listened to the king on the other end of the line. Whatever the man said wouldn't change Garrett's mind. He already knew he was doing the only thing possible. For both of them.

"Mr. King," Alex's father was sputtering, "you cannot simply walk away from my daughter's safety without so much as a warning. I will need time to—"

Enough was enough.

"Sir, I won't take money from you to watch over Alex," Garrett finally interrupted the king and the other man's abrupt silence told him the king wasn't used to that kind of treatment. Just one more nugget of proof that Garrett King and royalty were never going to be a good mix. "But, that said," he continued into the quiet, "I won't leave her out there alone, either. On my own, I'll watch out for her until she's on a plane headed home."

"May I ask *why* you've decided to leave my employ?"

Touchy question, Garrett told himself. He could hardly confess to the king that he didn't want to be taking money from the father of the woman he wanted in his bed. That might be enough for a beheading in Cadria, for all Garrett knew.

"Let's just say, Alex and I have become friends. And I feel badly taking money from her father."

There was a long silence, and then the king gave a tired sigh. Garrett sympathized. Couldn't be easy being thousands of miles away from someone you worried about. "Fine then. I appreciate your help in this, Mr. King, and it won't be forgotten."

Long after the king hung up, Garrett sat in his darkened study and stared at nothing. No, he thought. None of this would be forgotten.

Ever.

The late-night knock on Alex's door startled her.

She tossed the book she had been reading to the sofa cushion beside her. Jumping up from the couch, she tugged at the belt of her blue silk robe and crossed the room with hesitant steps. She wasn't expecting anyone and the desk always called before they disturbed her. And just who would have been able to get onto the penthouse elevator besides… She looked through the peephole and saw Garrett staring back at her.

Her heart did a slow roll in her chest as her nerves drained away and an entirely different emotion charged to the surface. She leaned her forehead on the cool, painted surface of the door and took a breath. Would the man always have this effect on her? Would one look at him always be enough to turn her knees to water?

Shaking her head, she steadied herself, then fumbled with the locks and opened the door to him. "Garrett. I didn't expect to see you until tomorrow."

"Yeah," he muttered, stepping past her to enter the suite. "Something's come up."

She frowned as he walked into the room, careful not to get close enough to brush against her. Alex noticed that his features were grim, his cheeks shadowed by beard stubble and his hair looked as if he'd been running his fingers through it for hours.

"Garrett? Is something wrong?"

He laughed shortly and turned to look at her. His eyes were dark and filled with charged emotions too deep to name. Shoving his hands into the back pockets of his worn jeans, he just looked at her for a long minute before saying, "Just came to tell you something. You win."

"What?"

Shaking his head, he blew out a breath and said, "I talked to your father a while ago. Told him I quit."

"You did?" All right, she should be pleased, and yet, the look on his face told her that more was coming and that she wasn't going to like it.

"Told him I couldn't take money from him for keeping you safe."

She took a single step toward him. "Why, Garrett? Why would you do that?"

"You know why." His gaze swept her up and down before settling on her eyes again. "But that doesn't mean I'm backing off, Alex. I'm still going to be there. Every day. Making sure nothing happens to you."

"Garrett." She reached up and cupped his cheek in her palm. "Nothing's going to happen to me."

He caught her hand in his and held on. His shadow-filled eyes locked with hers and flashed with steely determination. "Damn straight, it's not."

Her hand trapped in his tight grip, she could only stare up at him. "Garrett, you're even more crazed about protecting me than the palace guards. Why?"

"Because I won't fail again."

"Fail? Fail how?"

He released her, turned and walked to the couch and looked down at the book, spine up on the cushions. He snorted. "Romance novel?"

"There's nothing wrong with a happy ending," she said.

"Happy endings are fictional, Alex."

"They don't have to be."

He turned back to face her. "You don't get it." A choked off laugh shot from his throat. "No reason why you should."

Alex was standing not two feet from him and yet she felt distance stretching out between them. The pale light of her reading lamp was a golden circle in the darkness, reaching for Garrett and not quite making it. Absently she noted the soft roar of the ocean, like an extra heartbeat in the room.

"Then explain it to me, Garrett. Tell me what's driving you."

He reached up, scraped both palms across his face and then shoved them through his hair. When he'd finished, he looked at her and his eyes were bleak, sending a thread of worry sliding through Alex's body.

When he spoke, his voice was rough and low, as if he regretted saying the words even before they were out of his mouth. "About ten years ago, I was hired to be a body-guard for the daughter of a very wealthy man."

Alex held her breath and stayed perfectly still. Finally, she was going to get to the heart of the problem and she didn't want to risk interrupting him. Yet at the same time, she couldn't fight the notion that once he said what he had to, nothing would be the same. For either of them.

"Her name was Kara." A smile briefly twisted his mouth and was gone again in a blink. "She was beautiful and stubborn and smart. A lot like you, really."

A trickle of cold began to snake down her spine and still, she remained quiet.

"I got…distracted," he said and once again shoved a hand through his hair as if somehow he could wipe away the memories swarming in his mind. "I fell in love with her—"

Pain was swift and sharp. Jealousy dug its talons into her heart and twisted. And just as quickly, it all faded away. He had loved, but it was ten years ago and obviously it hadn't ended well. She forced herself to ask, "What happened?"

"I quit my job," he said, and swept the room with his troubled gaze before looking back at her. "Knew I couldn't protect Kara with my focus splintered. Told her father I wouldn't be responsible for her life anymore and I left. Two days later, Kara ditched her new guard and ran away. The letter she left behind said she was running to me. She never got there. She was kidnapped and killed."

"God, Garrett…"

"I won't let that happen to you."

Sympathy briefly warred with frustration inside her. Frustration won. "What makes you think it would? One tragedy doesn't always signal another."

"I know. But even getting past that, it's not just Kara. It's you and me. We're too different, Alex. Our worlds are light years apart." He shook his head and she felt the finality of that one single action. His features were tight, implacable. His voice a promise as he added, "I'm not looking to fall in love, Alex. What would be the point?"

Her heart gave a sudden lurch in her chest, and it felt as if a ball of lead had dropped into the pit of her stomach. He was walking away from her. Without even trying. Without a backward glance. Tears filled her eyes but she furiously blinked them back. She wasn't about to let him see her *cry*. What would be the point anyway?

Whatever she had convinced herself they shared, in reality, it was no more than a holiday fling. A summer romance doomed to die at the end of the season. She loved a man determined to not love her back, and there didn't seem to be a thing she could do to change it.

And would she if she could?

She had her pride after all. And that emotion was leading the charge when she snapped, "I never said anything about love, Garrett."

"Please." He gave her a patient, tired smile that made her want to kick something. "I can see it in your face, feel it in your touch. Alex, you're looking for something I can't give you."

She felt the sting of those words, and actually swayed in place when they hit her. But she kept her chin lifted and her eyes defiant as she corrected, "Not can't. *Won't*."

"Same thing," he said, folding his arms across his chest and glaring down at her.

"For a man who prides himself on seeing every possible angle of every possible situation, you're surprisingly blind."

"Is that right?"

"It is," she answered and took a step closer to him. Her gaze fixed with his. "This isn't even about *me*, Garrett. It's about you and how you look at your life. I'm sorry about Kara. But that wasn't your fault. Bad things happen. You can't stop them. You can only live your life in spite of them."

"She left her guards because of me," he told her flatly. "If I hadn't gotten involved with her, she'd be alive today."

"You don't know that," she told him and saw denial in his eyes. "You're not God, Garrett. You don't have the power of life and death, and you can't personally protect everyone you care about."

"But I can limit those I care about," he said softly.

"So rather than love and risk the pain of losing it, you would make your own world smaller so maybe danger won't notice you? Maybe your circle of loved ones will be tiny enough that nothing bad will touch you?"

He didn't say anything to that, but then, he didn't have to. Alex knew now for certain that what they had was over. He could stay and watch over her as he'd said he would, but there would be no more lovemaking. No more flirtatious fun. No more laughter. There would be only Garrett, in his role of knight errant ready to do battle in defense of his charge.

And that wasn't enough for Alex. Not nearly enough.

Sadly, she shook her head and said, "The difference between you and me is, I won't deny myself something wonderful for fear of losing it."

"That's because you've never lost."

"Wrong again," she said, a half smile curving her mouth. "I just did."

"Alex—"

"I think you should go," she said, though the words tore at her.

This was over. He couldn't have made himself plainer. He didn't want her—he saw her only as his responsibility—and she wanted the magic.

The gulf lying between them was wider than ever.

"Fine. I'll go. But I'll be back in the morning," he said. "Don't leave the hotel without me."

She didn't answer because an order didn't require one. She simply stood, alone in the dim light and listened to the door close behind him.

First thing in the morning, though, the plan changed.

Griffin needed some backup with a client and Garrett had already dumped so much of the company work on his twin lately, he couldn't turn him down. Besides, he figured it might do both he and Alex some good to have some space.

He'd been up half the night, reliving that scene in her penthouse suite. He could still feel the chill in the room when he told her he wouldn't love her. Could still see her eyes when she told him to leave. A low, deep ache settled in his chest, but Garrett accepted it as the price he had to pay for screwing this up so badly.

And he knew that the pain was going to be with him a long, damn time. He was halfway to San Diego when he thought it was late enough that he could call Alex without waking her up. Punching in the phone number, Garrett steered his car down the 405 freeway and waited for what seemed forever for Alex to answer the damn phone. The moment she did, the sound of her voice sent another ping of regret shooting through him.

Mentally, he explained it away. Of course he regretted

that she'd be leaving. Why the hell wouldn't he? He'd spent practically every day with her for more than a week. Why wouldn't he be accustomed to her smile, her laughter? It was only natural that he'd listen for the sound of her accent and get a buzz when he knew he was going to see her.

Didn't mean he cared. Didn't *mean* anything. When she was gone, things would settle down. Get back to normal, he assured himself. Which was all he wanted. The regular world that didn't include runaway princesses.

"Alex, it's me," he said shortly, changing lanes to pass an RV moving at a snail-like speed in the sun-washed morning.

"What is it, Garrett?"

Her voice was clipped now, as if anger was churning just below the surface. He hated to hear it, but it was probably best, he told himself. If she was mad, then she wasn't hurting. He'd never meant to hurt her, God knew. But it had happened anyway and now the best thing he could do was keep up the wall he'd erected between them the night before.

"I won't be able to come over this morning," he said tightly. "Griffin needs some help on a case, and I—"

"No need to explain. I'm sure you're very busy."

The words might be right, but her tone said differently. He scowled at the phone. "Yeah. Well, anyway. You won't be alone. I sent one of our best agents over there. Terri Cooper. She's in the lobby now, waiting for a call from you to the front desk. She's the best in the business, so I know she'll keep you safe."

"Garrett, I don't need a babysitter."

"She's a bodyguard, Alex, and until I get back, she's sticking to you like glue."

"And I've no say in it."

He frowned to himself and downshifted as the flow of

traffic picked up a bit. "If you don't want to see Terri, don't leave the hotel. I'd prefer that anyway. I should be able to be back before dinner."

"I see," she said, her accent a little sharper, "and I'm to await you at your convenience, is that it?"

He punched the accelerator and swung around another car, which had no business driving in the fast lane. "Alex, don't start with me. We've been over this. You know it's not safe."

"No, Garrett," she argued, "*you* know it's not safe. But I've a mind of my own and am in no way burdened with your overwhelmingly cautious nature."

"Damn it, Alex." He thought about hitting the first off-ramp and heading back. Then he realized his twin was in La Jolla waiting for him, and Garrett was stuck between the proverbial rock and a hard place.

And he did *not* have a cautious nature.

Made him sound like some old lady afraid to leave her house. Nothing could be further from the truth. He faced down danger every damn day of his life. It was *Alex* facing danger he couldn't bear the thought of.

"I'm in charge of your safety."

"No, you're not. You said yourself last night that you're no longer working for my father. That makes you nothing more than a bossy ex-bed partner. And I don't take orders from my exes."

"You're making me crazy, Alex. Terri will be with you if you leave the hotel."

Someone cut him off and Garrett honked at them. Didn't do any good, but made him feel a little better.

"I won't promise anything. And if that makes you crazy, then I'll admit to enjoying your misery as a side benefit."

She was enjoying it, too. He heard it in her voice. God knew what she would do today just to prove to him that she could take care of herself. He didn't even want to think about it.

The stream of traffic was slowing down. Brake lights flashed ahead and cars were stacked up behind him, too. Just another day on Southern California's freeways. Once he was stopped dead, he muttered, "I'll be back as soon as I can. Just—be careful, okay?"

There was a long pause and, for a moment, he half wondered if she'd hung up on him and he hadn't noticed. Then finally, she said only, "Goodbye, Garrett."

Car horns blared, the radio in the car beside him was set to a volume probably audible in space and the only sound Garrett really noticed was the hum of the dial tone, telling him she was gone.

"She's making me nuts."

"In her defense," Griffin said helpfully, "she didn't have far to go."

"Thanks for that." Garrett gave his twin a dark look. "You're supposed to be on my side, remember? Blood thicker than water and all that?"

"Yeah, we're family, blah, blah," Griffin said, kicking back in the leather booth seat and pausing long enough to take a long pull on his bottle of beer. "But if the princess is getting to you this badly, then I'm all for it."

Garrett stared down at his own beer and then lifted his gaze to look around the half-empty pub. It was supposed to look Irish, but Garrett had seen the real thing not long ago when he did a job for his cousin Jefferson. Still, it wasn't bad, just touristy. Lots of dark wood, flags of Ireland all over the place and even a bronze leprechaun crouched on the bar.

He and Griffin had finished with their client early and had stopped in here for some lunch before facing the long drive home again. He was still worried about Alex, but she'd been on her own for hours already, doing God knew what—because the damn woman wouldn't answer her damn phone. All Terri sent him was a brief text saying everything was fine. So him taking a half hour for lunch wasn't going to make that much difference at this point.

"And did I mention," Griffin said with a knowing leer, "you look like *hell?*"

He had known that talking to Griffin about all of this wouldn't get him any sympathy. And maybe he didn't need any. What he needed was somebody to talk to.

He should have picked someone smarter.

"Doesn't matter if she's 'getting' to me or not—which she isn't," he added, after a pause for a sip of beer. "The point is she's a princess, Griff. Would never work."

"Man, I really did get all the brains," Griffin mused with a slow shake of his head. "The way you talk about her, she seems damn near perfect. And you don't want her because she's a princess? What is that?"

"It's not a question of want."

"Then what is it?"

"Even if I did admit to wanting Alex, the fact that she's a princess pretty much cools that whole idea."

"Because…"

Irritated, Garrett glared at his twin. "You think her family would want her with a security expert?"

"Who better?"

"Nice try. But royals prefer royals, and everyone knows that. Her father's probably got her future husband all picked out for her." The thought of that made him want to break something.

"Uh-huh. And what else?" Griffin shook his head. "There's more here, Garrett."

"Kara." He'd loved once and lost her. He wasn't sure he was willing to go through that again.

"Here we go," Griffin muttered. "You know, I've been hearing that excuse for years, and I'm just not buying it anymore."

"What the hell's that mean?"

"It means, that you've been hiding behind Kara. Yeah, it was terrible what happened to her. But you know damn well it wasn't your fault."

Garrett shifted in his seat, took a swig of beer and set the bottle down again.

"You loved her, and she died."

"Thanks for the news flash. But I don't need you to tell me that. I lived it."

Griffin ignored him. Leaning on the tabletop, he said, "Somewhere along the way, though, you died, too. Or at least you stopped living, which amounts to the same thing."

Garrett glared at his twin again, but it didn't do any good. Nothing could shut Griffin up if he had something to say and clearly he did. Seemed he'd been building up to this little speech for years.

"Now along comes the princess, shakes you up, makes you notice, *hey, not a bad world out here,* and *boom.*" He clapped both hands together for emphasis. "You shut down. Start pulling Kara out of the past and using her as a shield or some damn thing. The problem isn't Kara, Garrett. Never was. The problem is *you.*"

The waitress arrived with their lunch and while Griffin flirted and got an extra order of fries for his trouble, Garrett did some fast thinking. His twin might actually have a point. He had been enjoying his time with Alex. Had been relaxing the guard around his heart and the minute she got close, he'd pulled back. So was he using Kara as a shield? If that was true, then Alex had been right the night before when she'd accused him of making sure his world was small enough that tragedy would have a harder time striking.

When it was just the two of them again, Griffin noted, "Hmm. Looks like a lightbulb might have gone off in your head."

"Maybe," Garrett admitted, then added, "but even if you're right—"

"Can't hear that often enough," Griffin said with a grin just before popping a French fry into his mouth.

"—it doesn't change the fact that Alex is a princess and lives in a palace for God's sake. I live in a condo at the beach—"

"No, you don't," Griffin interrupted.

"Excuse me?" Seriously, he knew where he *lived*.

Taking another pull of his beer, Griffin said, "You don't live there. You live out of suitcases. Hell, you spend more time on King Jets than you do in that condo."

"What's that supposed to mean?"

"Means you don't live anywhere, Garrett. So what's keeping you here?"

He just stared at his twin. Was he the only one who could see the problems in this? Alex was oblivious and now Griffin, too? "Our *business?*"

"More excuses." Griff waved one hand at his brother, effectively dismissing him, then picked up his burger and took a bite. After chewing, he said, "We can run our place from anywhere. If you wanted to, you could set up a European branch and you damn well know it."

His chest felt tight. The noise in the pub fell away. All he could hear was himself, telling Alex that he wouldn't love her. That he couldn't. The problem was, he *did* love her.

A hell of a thing for a man to just be figuring out. But

there it was. He'd had to quit working for her father because he couldn't take money for protecting the woman he loved. He had kept his distance from her because he couldn't sleep with her knowing that he'd have to let her go.

But did he have to?

What if he was wrong? What if there was a chance a commoner might have a shot with a princess? Was he really ready to let Alex go without even *trying* to make it work? His brain raced with possibilities. Maybe he had been short-sighted. Stupid. But he didn't have to stay that way.

His phone rang, and he glanced at the readout. Instantly, he answered it and fought the sudden hot ball of worry in his guts. "Terri? What is it?"

"Boss, I'm sorry, but you *did* tell me to stick to her and—"

"What happened?" In his mind, he was seeing car wrecks, holdups, assassins...

"She had me drive her to L.A. and—"

"Uh, Garrett..."

"Shut up," he muttered, then to Terri he said, "L.A.? Why L.A.?"

"Garrett!"

His gaze snapped to Griffin.

Pointing to the bar, his twin said, "You need to see this."

He turned to look. Terri was still talking in his ear, but he hardly heard her. There was a flat screen TV above the bar, the sound muted. But he didn't need the sound. What he saw opened a hole in his chest. He snapped the phone shut and stared.

Alex was on the TV. But an Alex he hardly knew. Her long, thick hair was twisted into a complicated knot at the top of her head. Diamonds winked at her ears and blazed at the base of her throat. She wore a pale green dress that was tailored to fit her beautifully and she looked as remote as a…well, a *princess*.

Garrett pushed out of his seat, crossed the room and ordered the bartender to, "Turn it up, will you?"

The man did and Garrett listened over the roaring in his own ears. Someone shoved a microphone at Alex and shouted, "Princess, how long have you been here and why the big secret?"

She smiled into the camera, and Garrett could have sworn she was looking directly at him. His hands curled around the edge of the polished wood bar and squeezed until he was half afraid he was going to snap the thick wood in two.

"I've been in America almost two weeks," she said, her voice low, moderate, regal. "As for the secrecy of my visit, I wanted the opportunity to see the *real* America. To meet people and get to know them without the barriers of my name and background getting in the way."

People in the bar were listening. Griffin had moved up alongside him, but Garrett hardly noticed. His gaze was fixed on Alex. She looked so different. And already so far away.

"Did it work?" someone else shouted.

"It did," she said, her gaze still steady on the camera, staring directly into Garrett's soul. "I've enjoyed myself immensely. This is a wonderful country, and I've been met with nothing but kindness and warmth."

"You're headed home now, Princess," a reporter called out. "What're you going to miss the most?"

There was a long, thoughtful pause before Alex smiled into the camera and said, "It's a difficult question. I loved Disneyland, of course. And the beach. But I think what

I loved most were the people I met. *They* are what I'll miss when I go home. *They* are what will stay with me. Always."

She was leaving.

And maybe, he told himself darkly, it was better this way. But even he didn't believe that.

The camera pulled away and an excited news anchor came on to say, "Princess Alexis of Cadria, speaking to you from the Cadrian Consulate in Los Angeles. I can tell you we were all surprised to get the notice of her brief press conference. Speculation will be rife now, as to just where the princess has been for the last week or more.

"But this afternoon, a private jet will be taking her back to her home country. A shame we didn't get to see more of the lovely Princess Alexis while she was here."

Garrett had already turned away when the woman shifted gears and launched into another story. Walking back to their booth, Garrett sat down, picked up his burger and methodically took a bite. There was no reason to hurry through lunch now.

"Garrett—"

He glared his twin into silence and concentrated on the burger that suddenly tasted like sawdust.

Twelve

Everything was just as she'd left it.

Why that should have surprised Alex, she couldn't have said. But it did. Somehow, she felt so…changed, that she had expected to find the palace different as well.

Standing on the stone terrace outside the morning room, she turned to look up at the pink stone walls of the palace she called home. The leaded glass windows winked in the early morning sunlight and the flag of Cadria, flying high atop the far turret, snapped in the breeze.

She was both comforted and irritated that life in Cadria had marched inexorably on while she had been gone. But then, her emotions were swinging so wildly lately, that didn't surprise her, either. Since coming home a week ago, she had slipped seamlessly back into the life she had so briefly left behind. She had already visited two schools and presided over the planting of new trees in the city's park.

The papers were still talking about her spontaneous visit to the U.S. and photographers still haunted her every step.

Now, when she wanted to go shopping, she couldn't just walk to the closest mall or wander down to the neighborhood shops. A shopping excursion became more of a battle strategy. There were guards, which she told herself, Garrett would thoroughly approve of, there were state cars and flags flying from the bumpers. There were stores closed to all other shoppers and bowing deference from shopkeepers.

God, how she missed being a nobody.

Of course, her family didn't see it that way. They were all delighted to have her back. Her oldest brother was about to become engaged, and the other two were doing what they did best. Immersing themselves in royal duties with the occasional break for polo or auto racing. Her parents were the same, though her father hadn't yet interrogated her about her holiday and Alex suspected she had her mother to thank for that.

And she appreciated the reprieve. She just wasn't ready to talk about Garrett yet. Not to anybody. She was still hoping to somehow wipe him out of her mind. What was the point in torturing herself forever over a man who saw her as nothing more than an anvil around his neck?

"Bloody idiot," she muttered and kicked the stone barrier hard enough to send a jolt of pain through her foot and up her leg. But at least it was *physical* pain, which was a lot easier to deal with.

"Well," a familiar voice said from behind her, "that's more like it."

Alex looked over her shoulder at her mother. Queen Teresa of Cadria was still beautiful. Tall and elegant, Alex's mother kept her graying blond hair in a short cut that swung along her jawline. She wore green slacks, a white silk blouse and taupe flats. Her only jewelry was her wedding ring. Her blue eyes were sharp and fixed on her daughter.

"Mom. I didn't know you were there."

"Clearly," Teresa said as she strolled casually across the terrace, "care to tell me who the 'bloody idiot' is? Or will you make me guess?"

The queen calmly hitched herself up to sit on the stone parapet and demurely crossed her feet at the ankles. Alex couldn't help but smile. In public, Teresa of Cadria was dignified, elegant and all things proper. But when the family was alone, she became simply Teresa Hawkins Wells. A California girl who had married a king.

She had bowed to some traditions and had livened up other staid areas of the palace with her more casual flair. For instance, when she became queen, Teresa had made it clear that the "old" way of raising royal children wouldn't be happening anymore. She had been a hands-on mother and had remained that way. Naturally, there had also been governesses and tutors, but Alex and her brothers had grown up knowing their parents' love—and there were many royals who couldn't claim that.

None of Teresa's children had ever been able to keep a secret from her for long. And not one of them had ever successfully lied to their mother. So Alex didn't even bother trying now.

"Garrett King," she said.

"As I suspected." Teresa smiled as encouragement.

Alex didn't need much. Strange, she hadn't thought she wanted to talk about him, yet now that the opportunity was here, she found the words couldn't come fast enough. "He's arrogant and pompous and bossy. Always ordering me about, as bad as Dad, really. But he made me laugh as often as he made me angry and—"

"You love him," her mother finished for her.

"Yes, but I'll get over it," Alex said with determination.

"Why would you want to?"

The first sting of tears hit her eyes and that only made Alex more furious. She swiped at them with impatient fingers and said, "Because he doesn't want me." She shook her head and looked away from her mom's sympathetic eyes to stare out over the palace's formal gardens.

She focused on the box hedge maze. The maze had been constructed more than three hundred years ago, and Alex smiled, remembering how she and her brothers used to run through its long, twisting patterns at night, trying to scare each other.

The maze was so famous it was one of the most popular parts of the castle tour that was offered every summer. But the most beautiful part of the garden was the roses. They were Alex's mother's pride and joy. Teresa had brought slips of California roses with her when she'd given up her life to be queen. And she still nurtured those plants herself, despite grumblings from the head gardener.

Their thick scent wafted to them now, and Alex took a deep breath, letting the familiar become a salve to her wounded pride.

"Alex," her mother said, reaching out to lay one hand on her daughter's arm, "of course he wants you. Why else would he refuse to take money for protecting you?"

"Stubbornness?" Alex asked, shifting her gaze to her mother.

Teresa smiled and shook her head. "Now who's being stubborn?"

"You don't understand, Mom." Alex turned her back on

the garden and pushed herself up to sit beside her mother. The damp cold from the stones leached into her black slacks and slid into her bones, but she hardly noticed. "It was different for you. You met Dad at Disneyland, and it was magic. He fell in love and swept you off your feet and—"

She stopped and stared when her mother's laughter rang out around her. "What's so funny?"

"Oh, sweetie," Teresa said as she caught her breath again. "I didn't mean to laugh, but...maybe your father was right. When you were a little girl, he used to tell me I was spinning too many romantic stories. Filling your head with impossible expectations."

Confused, Alex just looked at her mother. "But you did meet at Disneyland. And you fell in love and became a queen."

"All true," her mother said, "but, that's not *all* of the story."

Intrigued, Alex let her own troubles move to the background as she listened to her mother.

"I did meet Gregory at Disneyland," she said, a half smile on her face. "I was working at the Emporium and he came in and bought half the merchandise at my station just so he'd have an excuse to keep standing there talking to me."

Alex could enjoy the story even more now that she had been to the famous park and could imagine the scene more clearly.

"We spent a lot of time together in the two weeks he was in California and, long story short, we fell in love." She smiled again, then picked up Alex's hand and gave it a squeeze. "But it wasn't happily ever after right away, sweetie."

"What happened?"

"Your dad left. He came back here, to the palace." She swept her gaze up to take in the pink castle and its centuries of tradition. "He told me he was going to be a king and that he couldn't marry me. That we couldn't possibly be together. His parents wouldn't have allowed it, and his country wouldn't stand for it."

"What? That's ridiculous!" Alex immediately defended her. "Cadria *loves* you."

"Yes," her mother said with a laugh. "*Now*. Back then, though, it was a different story. I was heartbroken and furious that he would walk away from love so easily."

She and her mother had more in common than Alex knew, she thought glumly. But at least her mom had eventually gotten a happy ending. But how? "What happened?"

"Your father missed me," Teresa said with a grin. "He called, but I wouldn't speak to him. He sent me gifts that I returned. Letters that went back unopened." Nudging Alex's shoulder with her own, Teresa admitted, "I drove him crazy."

"Good for you. I can't believe Dad walked away from you!"

"Centuries of tradition are hard to fight," Teresa said. "And so was your grandfather who had no interest in a commoner daughter-in-law."

"But—"

"I know, sweetie. Your grandfather loved me. Once he met me, everything was fine." She sighed a little. "But, your dad actually had to threaten to abdicate before his father would listen to reason."

"Dad was willing to give up the throne for you?"

"He was," Teresa said with another sigh of satisfaction. "Thankfully, it didn't come to that, since he's a very good king. But once his father saw how serious Gregory was, he promised to make it work. He went to the Law Chambers himself to see that the country's charter was rewritten to allow for a commoner as queen."

"Wow." She didn't know what else to say. Alex had had no idea of the intrigue and passion and clashes that had been involved in her parents getting together.

"Yes, wow," Teresa said, laughing again. "When it was all settled, in a record amount of time, thanks to your father being an impatient soul, Gregory came back to California with his grandmother's ring in hand and the rest, as they say, is history."

Holding up her left hand as proof, Teresa wiggled her fingers, letting the ancient diamond wink and glitter in the sunlight.

"I had no idea."

"Of course you didn't, and I should have told you the whole truth sooner. But, Alex, I had a point in telling you this now," her mother said and reached out to give her a one-armed hug. "And that is, don't give up on your young man. Love is a powerful thing and, once felt, it's impossible to walk away from. If your Garrett is anything like my Gregory…" She smiled again. "There's always hope."

"Excuse me, your majesty."

Teresa looked to the open doorway into the morning room. A maid stood in the shadows. "Yes, Christa?"

"I've laid the tea out, ma'am, for you and her highness."

"Thank you, Christa," Teresa said, "we'll be right in."

A quick curtsy and the maid was gone again. A moment later, Teresa scooted off the parapet, dusted off the seat of her slacks and said, "I'll pour the tea. You come in when you're ready, okay?"

Nodding, Alex watched her mother go, as her mind

whirled with possibilities. Was her mom right? Was there hope? Yes, her parents' love story had turned out well in the end, but the King of Cadria had been in love.

Whereas Garrett King *refused* to be in love with her.

She turned her head to stare out over the gardens, to the ocean beyond and to the man on the other side of the world. Hope, she thought wistfully, could be a both a blessing and a curse.

"She sent it back."

"What?" Griffin looked up as Garrett stormed into his office.

Tossing a small package onto his brother's desk, Garrett complained, "The necklace I sent to Alex two days ago. She returned it!"

"And this is my problem because…"

"You're my brother, and it's your job to listen to me," Garrett told him as he stalked the perimeter of his brother's office.

"Actually, it's my job to look into the file we just got on our Georgia client and—"

"Why would she return it?" Garrett asked no one in particular, thinking of the platinum and onyx piece he'd had commissioned just for her. He hadn't asked himself why it was so important for him to give her a memento of their time together. It simply was. He couldn't have her, but damned if he could entirely let go, either.

These past two weeks without her had nearly killed him. Nothing felt right to him anymore. Without Alex in his life, everything else was just white noise. He kept as busy as possible and *still* her absence chewed at him, widening the black hole inside him every damn day.

His fingers closed around the box that had been returned to him just a few minutes ago. Shaking it for emphasis, he blurted, "It was a trinket. Sort of a souvenir. You know, help her remember her holiday."

Griffin gave up and sat back in his chair. "Maybe she doesn't *want* to remember."

Garrett stopped dead and glared at his twin. "Why the hell wouldn't she want to remember? She had a great time."

"Yeah, but it's over, and she's back home at the palace."

"So, close the door? That's it?" Could she really cut him out of her life, her memories, that easily?

"Aren't you the one who closed the door?" Griffin asked.

"Not the point." Hell, Garrett knew he wasn't making any sense. He didn't need his twin stating the obvious.

Two weeks without her. Didn't seem to matter that he knew he'd done the right thing. Didn't matter that he knew there was no way they could have worked out anything between them. He missed her like he would an arm. Or a leg.

She was as much a part of him as his damn heart and without her, it was like he didn't have one.

This had not been a part of the plan. He'd expected to miss her, sure. But he hadn't counted on not being able to sleep or keep his mind on his damn work. He hadn't counted on seeing her everywhere, hearing her voice, her laugh in his mind at odd moments during the day.

"You're just going to prowl around my office, is that it?" Griffin asked.

Garrett stopped and glared at him. "What the hell am I supposed to do?"

"You know what I think you should do. Question is, what are you *going* to do?"

"If I knew that," he muttered darkly, "I'd be doing it."

"Well then, maybe this will help you decide," Griffin said and pulled the morning paper out from under a stack of files. "Wasn't going to show you this—but maybe you should see it after all."

"What?" Garrett took the paper, glanced at the picture on the front page and felt his heart stop.

Front and center, there was a photo of Alex, dressed in a flowing gown and a crown, holding on to the arm of an impossibly handsome man in a tux, wearing a damn sash across his chest that was loaded down with medals. The tagline above the photo screamed, *Royal Engagement In The Wind?*

"Oh, *hell* no," Garrett muttered.

"Looks to me like you'd better go get your woman back before it's too late," Griffin said, clearly amused at Garrett's reaction.

Garrett's vision fogged at the edges until all he could see was Alex's face staring up at him from the paper. He was about to really lose her. Permanently. Unless he took a chance.

Clutching the newspaper tight in one fist, Garrett grabbed the returned package and said, "Call the airport for me. Have one of the King Jets fueled up and ready to go when I get there."

Griffin was laughing as he made the call, but Garrett was already gone.

"Where is he?" Garrett stormed past the footman at the door to the castle and stomped loudly across the marble flooring. His head turned as if on a swivel as he scanned every hallway for signs of the king.

"If you'll follow me," the butler said, "his majesty is in the library."

Garrett hadn't slept in nearly twenty-four hours. He felt ragged and pushed to the edge of his endurance, but damned if he was going to wait another minute to talk to Alex's father. He'd gotten past the palace guards on the strength of his having done work for the crown before. But getting an audience with the king this easily was a plus.

The air smelled of roses and beeswax, and Garrett took a deep breath to steady himself for the coming confrontation. The sound of his footsteps as he followed after his guide rang out hollowly in the air, thudding like a heartbeat. He had a plan, of course. Wasn't much of one, but he'd use whatever he could. Alex was here, somewhere, and no matter what happened between him and the king in the next few minutes, he wasn't leaving until he spoke to her.

He stepped into the library and the butler left him with the king. The room was imposing, as it was meant to be. Dark paneling, bloodred leather furniture and floor-to-ceiling windows with a view of the sea. The man standing before a crackling fire was just as imposing. King Gregory was tall, muscular and the gray in his hair only made him look more formidable.

"Garrett, this is a surprise."

About to be an even bigger one, he thought and cut right to the chase. "Your majesty, Alex can't marry Duke Henrik."

"Is that right?" One eyebrow lifted.

Hell, Garrett couldn't believe the man would allow Alex *near* the duke. A quick online search had been enough to show Garrett that the man was more known for his string of women than for any work done in the House of Lords.

Well, the king might be okay with that, but damned if Garrett would let Alex end up with someone who didn't deserve her.

"How is this any of your business, Garrett?"

"It's my business because there's a good chance Alex is pregnant with my child."

Risky move, he told himself, since there was no way Alex was pregnant. But it was the one sure way he knew to delay any kind of wedding but for the one Garrett now wanted more than anything.

The king's face went red. "You—"

"Pregnant?"

Garrett whirled around at the deep voice behind him and was just in time to watch Alex's older brother Prince Christopher's fist collide with his face. Pain exploded inside his head, but he ducked before the prince could land another one.

Then he threw a fast right himself and watched the prince stagger backward. The other man recovered quickly and came at Garrett again, still furious.

The king was shouting, "Pregnant? *Pregnant?*"

Two more men ran into the room. They took in the scene at a glance and immediately joined their older brother in the fray.

"Perfect," Garrett muttered, turning a slow circle so he could keep an eye on all three of them. Seemed he wasn't going to come out of this without a few bruises. But he'd give as good as he got, too.

He blocked another blow, threw a punch himself and smiled when the youngest of the princes was laid out flat on his back. The king pushed past one of his sons and threw a punch of his own that Garrett managed to avoid.

He wasn't about to hit a king, either, so he focused on protecting himself and doing a lot of dodging.

As Garrett avoided another blow, he yelled, "Just let me talk to Alex and we can straighten this out."

"You stay away from my sister." This from the prince pushing up from the floor.

"No one is talking to anyone until I have some answers," the king shouted again.

"Why is everyone yelling?" Alex called into the mix.

Garrett turned at the sound of her voice and Christopher landed another solid jab on his jaw. "Damn it!"

Hands clapped loudly, followed by a sharp, feminine command. "Stop this at once! Christopher, no more fighting. Help Henry off the floor, and Jonathon, get your father some water."

The king was sputtering in rage, but everyone else moved to follow the queen's orders. Everyone but Alex. She just stood there in the doorway, staring at him as if she'd never seen him before. Her hair was tidy, her elegant dress and tasteful jewelry made her seem unapproachable. But somewhere beneath that cool exterior was *his* Alex. And Garrett wasn't leaving until he'd had a chance to reach her.

The capper for Garrett, though, was seeing the damn duke standing right behind her. That settled everything. No way in hell was Garrett letting his woman go. And she *was* his. Had been from that first day at Disneyland.

"Who's pregnant?" Alex demanded.

"Apparently, *you* are," Christopher told her.

"I'm *what?*" She fired a furious look on Garrett and he just glared right back.

"I said you could be."

"Pregnant?" Henrik repeated from behind her. "You're *pregnant*? I'll be leaving."

"Henrik!" The king's shout went unanswered as the duke scuttled out the door to disappear. Probably forever.

"What is going on here? I could hear the shouts all the way to the garden." The queen looked from one face to the next, her silent, accusatory stare demanding answers.

"Garrett King claims Alexis is pregnant with his child," the king managed to say through gritted teeth.

"And I was just about to beat him to a pulp," Christopher said helpfully.

"In your dreams," Garrett muttered, never taking his eyes off Alex.

"Well, it's a lie," she snapped. "I'm not pregnant."

No one was listening. The princes were arguing among themselves, the queen and the king were locked into battle and Alex was looking at Garrett through furious eyes. When she turned to leave, he bolted across the room, grabbed her hand and tugged her into the hall, away from her arguing family.

"Don't," she said, pulling her hand free. Looking up at him, she said, "You don't belong here, Garrett. Go home."

"No."

"You had your choice, and you made it. Now it's time we both live with it."

He grabbed her again, holding on to her shoulders half worried that she'd run if he let her go. It could take him *weeks* to find her again in this place. "Why did you return the package I sent you?"

"Because what we had is over. Now please, just *go*."

"I'm not going anywhere," he murmured and pulled her in close. Wrapping his arms around her, to hold on tight when she started to squirm, Garrett kissed her. He poured everything he'd been feeling for the last two weeks into that kiss. The longing. The pain. The regret. The joy at being with her again. For the first time in too damn long, he felt whole. As if the puzzle pieces of his life had fallen into place.

Her tongue tangled with his, her breath slid into his lungs and her heartbeat clamored in time with his own. Everything was right. He just had to convince her that he was a changed man.

Finally, he broke the kiss, stared down into those amazing eyes of hers and said, "Alex, I don't give a damn about your crown. I don't care that you're a princess. Don't care that our worlds are so different. I'll convince your father to let us be together. We can make it work, Alex. We *will* make it work."

"Garrett…" She sighed, and said, "I want to believe you. But you made yourself perfectly clear before. You didn't want me in California. So why now? What's changed?"

"Me," he told her, lifting his hands to cup her face. His thumbs moved over her cheekbones and just the feel of her soft, smooth skin beneath his eased the pain that had been tearing at him for what seemed forever. "I've changed. And I did want you in California, Alex. I always wanted you. From the first time I saw you in Disneyland, I wanted you. I was just too busy looking for trouble to see what I'd already found."

She shook her head, and Garrett's heart stopped briefly. But a King never backed away from a challenge. Especially one that meant more to him than his life.

"Alex, I know now what's really important." God, he had to make her believe him. Those eyes of hers were so deep, so rich with emotion, with *love*. Seeing it gave him enough hope to continue. To tell her everything he wanted her to know.

And he still hadn't even said the most important thing. "I love you. I *love* you, Alex, Princess Alexis Morgan Wells. I really do."

Her breath caught and a single tear rolled from the corner of her eye. He caught it with his thumb as if it were precious. Sunlight speared in from an overhead window and lay on her beautiful hair, now tightly controlled in a twist on top of her head.

"I love your laugh." His gaze moved over her and then he reached up to tug a few pins loose, letting her hair fall down around her shoulders. "And I love your hair, all wild and tangled. I love the way you find something beautiful in everything. I love your clever brain and your smart-ass mouth. I love that you're willing to call me out when you think I'm being an idiot."

Her lips quirked.

"And I love that you want to help women in need and I'd like to be a part of that."

She took a sharp breath.

"I want to be with you, Alex. Always. I want to build a life with you. In California *and* Cadria."

"How—"

"I'm opening a branch of King Security right here in Cadria. We'll be the European division."

"Garrett—" She shook her head sadly. "You're not used to this kind of life. I'm followed by reporters and photographers. We wouldn't be able to just buy a house in town and move in. We would have to live here in a wing of the palace. You'd hate that, you know you would."

He laughed shortly. "First off, you forget. I'm one of the Kings of California. We've got paparazzi following us all the damn time looking for a story. I'm used to life in a fishbowl. It's not always pretty, but if you want to badly enough, you can carve out a private life."

"But—"

"And it doesn't matter where we live, Alex," he said, "as long as we're together." He gave a glance around the wide hallway, with its priceless art hanging on the walls and the gleam of marble shining up at them. "I could learn to love the palace."

She laughed, and God, it sounded like music to him.

"I'll miss good Thai food at one in the morning, but if the craving gets bad, I'll have Griffin send me some on a King Jet."

"Oh, Garrett," she said on a chuckle.

"It'll work, Princess," he said quickly, giving her a quick kiss as if to seal a promise. "We'll blend our lives and build one together that will suit both of us."

Alex's breath caught in her chest. Everything she had ever dreamed of was right here, in front of her. All she had to do was reach out and take it. Returning the package he had sent her hadn't been easy, but she'd hoped that he would come to her, repeating family history. Now, here he was and Alex was half afraid to believe in it.

"I love you, Alex," he said softly. "Marry me. Love me back."

She sighed and lifted both arms to wrap them around his neck. "I do love you, Garrett King."

"Thank God," he said on a laugh, dropping his forehead to hers. "When you returned the necklace…"

"It was a necklace?"

"I brought it with me." He dipped one hand into his pocket and pulled out a flat, dark green jeweler's box.

Alex took it, opened the lid and sighed with pleasure.

"It's a seagull," he told her unnecessarily. "I had it made to remind you of the ocean. Of all the time we spent at the beach."

Tears stung her eyes as she lifted the beautifully crafted piece free of the box. She turned and lifted her hair so that he could put it around her neck and when it was lying against the base of her throat, she touched it and whispered, "I love it, Garrett, though I don't need a reminder. I'll never forget a moment of my time with you."

She had everything she had ever dreamed of, right there in her arms. Garrett King was looking at her with more love than she could have imagined possible. She felt the truth of it in his touch. Saw it plainly in his beautiful eyes that were no longer shadowed with old pain. Her heart felt full and yet...

"I'm still a princess, Garrett," she warned. "That won't change, ever. There will still be the chance of danger surrounding me and my family. It will still drive you crazy."

"Yeah," he said solemnly. "I know. But I'll be here to make sure you're safe. All of you." A small smile crooked one corner of his mouth. "King Security can be the palace's personal protection detail.

"Marry me, Alex. Together, you and I can do anything."

"I know we can," she said and went up on her toes to kiss him. "So yes, Garrett, I'll marry you."

He grinned and blew out a relieved breath. "Took you long enough."

Shaking her head, she said, "I can't believe you told my father I was pregnant."

"It was the only thing I could come up with on short notice."

She smiled up at him. "You used to be a much better liar, Mr. King."

"It's all in the past, Princess. No more lies. Not between us."

"Agreed," she said, a grin she felt might never go away curving her mouth.

"So," he asked as he leaned in to kiss her, "how do you feel about Disneyland for a honeymoon?"

"I think that sounds perfect."

Then he kissed her, and the world righted itself again. Alex reveled in the sensation of everything being just as it should be. She gave herself up to the wonder and the joy and wasn't even aware when her brothers and father burst into the hall to see why things had gotten so suddenly quiet.

And she didn't see when her mother ushered her men back into the study to allow her daughter time to enjoy the magic of a lifetime.

* * * * *

"You want me to come back as Molly's nanny?"

"Not as her nanny," Blake replied. "As my wife."

He could certainly understand Grace's slack-jawed astonishment. She'd wormed her way into his life and Molly's heart. She'd lied to him. Yet the hole she'd left behind had grown deeper with each hour she was gone.

Molly's unexpected arrival had already turned his calm, comfortable routine upside down. This doe-eyed blonde had kicked it all to hell. So he felt a savage satisfaction to see his chaotic feelings mirrored on her face.

"You're crazy! I can't marry you!"

"Why not?"

"Because…because… What about love, Blake? And…sex?"

With a smooth move, he pushed himself off the sofa. Grace wasn't prepared when he stopped mere inches away. With him standing so close, her chest rose and fell with every breath.

"That's not a problem, Grace. The sex is definitely doable."

Dear Reader,

When my husband and I spent a week in the small town of Saint-Rémy-de-Provence in the south of France, we absolutely fell in love with the place. And since I'm always on the lookout for exciting locales for books, I knew Saint-Rémy would eventually show up in one.

I didn't, however, expect the road that led my characters there would be so bumpy and pitted with tension, sexual and otherwise. I had great fun overcoming the roadblocks with Grace and Blake—hope you do, too!

All my best, and happy reading,

Merline Lovelace

THE PATERNITY PROMISE

BY
MERLINE LOVELACE

Published in Great Britain 2012
by Mills & Boon, an imprint of Harlequin (UK) Limited,
Eton House, 18-24 Paradise Road, Richmond, Surrey TW9 1SR

© Merline Lovelace 2012

ISBN: 978 0 263 89343 4
ebook ISBN: 978 1 408 97207 6

51-1112

Harlequin (UK) policy is to use papers that are natural, renewable and
recyclable products and made from wood grown in sustainable forests. The
logging and manufacturing processes conform to the legal environmental
regulations of the country of origin.

Printed and bound in Spain
by Blackprint CPI, Barcelona

A career Air Force officer, **Merline Lovelace** served at bases all over the world. When she hung up her uniform for the last time she decided to combine her love of adventure with a flair for storytelling, basing many of her tales on her own experiences in uniform. Since then she's produced more than ninety action-packed sizzlers, many of which have made the *USA TODAY* and Waldenbooks bestseller lists. Over eleven million copies of her books are available in some thirty countries.

When she's not tied to her keyboard, Merline enjoys reading, chasing little white balls around the fairways of Oklahoma and traveling to new and exotic locales with her handsome husband, Al. Check her website at www.merlinelovelace.com or friend her on Facebook for news and information about her latest releases.

To the Elite Eight, and the wonderful times we've
shared. Thanks for giving me such terrific fodder
for my books!

One

His fists balled inside the pockets of his tuxedo pants, Blake Dalton forced a smile as he stood amid the wedding guests jamming the black-and-white-tiled foyer of his mother's Oklahoma City mansion. The lavish reception was finally winding down. The newlyweds had just paused in their descent of the foyer's circular marble staircase so the bride could toss her bouquet. The couple were mere moments from departing for their honeymoon in Tuscany.

Blake was damned if he'd block their escape. His twin had waged a tumultuous battle to win the stubbornly independent pilot he'd finally finessed to the altar. Alex had earned these two weeks in Tuscany with his new bride, away from his heavy responsibilities as CEO of Dalton International.

Blake had no problem taking up the slack in his absence. An MBA, a law degree and almost a decade of

handling the corporation's complex legal affairs had
honed the leadership and managerial skills he'd devel-
oped as DI's CFO. He and Alex regularly took over sole
control of the multibillion-dollar conglomerate during
each other's frequent business trips.

No, the job wasn't the problem.

Nor was it their mother, who'd waged a fierce and
unrelenting campaign to get her sons married and settled down for over a year now.

Blake's glance cut to the matriarch of the Dalton clan.
Her hair was still jet-black, with only a hint of silver at
the temples. She wore a melon-colored Dior lace dress
and an expression of smug satisfaction as she surveyed
the newly married couple. Blake knew exactly what she
was thinking. One son down, one to go.

But it was the baby peering over his mother's shoulder that made his fist bunch even tighter and his heart
squeeze inside his chest. In the weeks since person or
persons unknown had left the six-month-old on his
mother's doorstep, Molly had become as essential to
Blake as breathing.

DNA testing had proved with 99.99 percent certainty
that the bright-eyed infant girl was a Dalton. Unfortunately, the tests hadn't returned the same accuracy as
to *which* of the Dalton brothers had fathered the baby.
Although even identical twins carried distinctive DNA,
there were enough similarities to fog the question of paternity. The report had indicated a seventy-seven percent probability that Alex was the father, but the issue
couldn't be completely resolved until the lab matched
the father's DNA with that of the mother.

As a result, the Dalton brothers had spent several uncomfortable weeks after Molly's arrival tracking down
the women they'd connected with early last year. Alex's

list had been considerably longer than Blake's, but none of the potential candidates—including the woman who'd just become Ms. Alex Dalton—had proved to be the baby's mother. Or so they'd thought.

A noisy round of farewells wrenched Blake's gaze from the baby. He looked up to find his brother searching the crowd. It was like looking in a mirror. Both he and Alex had their father's build. Like Big Jake Dalton, they carried six feet plus of solid muscle. They'd also inherited their father's electric blue eyes and tawny hair that the hot Oklahoma sun streaked to a dozen different shades of gold.

Blake caught Alex's eye and casually, so casually, shook his head. He had to forcibly blank both his face and his mind to block any more subtle signals. In the way of all twins, the Dalton brothers could pick up instantly on each other's vibes. Time enough for Alex and Julie to hear the news when they got back from Tuscany. By then Blake would have dealt with it. And with the shock and fury it had generated.

He rigidly suppressed both emotions until the newlyweds were on the way to the airport. Even then he did his duty and mingled until the last guests finally departed. His training as an attorney stood him in good stead. No one, not even his mother, suspected there was fury boiling in his gut.

"Whew!" Ebullient but drooping, Delilah Dalton kicked off her heels. "That was fun, but I'm glad it's over. Went off well, don't you think?"

"Very," Blake answered evenly.

"I'm going to check on Molly." She swooped up her shoes and padded on stockinged feet to the circular marble staircase. "Then I'm hitting the tub to soak for an hour. You staying here tonight?"

"No, I'll go back to my place." With a vicious exercise of will, he kept his voice calm. "Would you ask Grace to come down? I'd like to talk to her before I go."

His mother lifted a brow at his request to speak to the woman she'd hired to act as a temporary nanny. In the weeks since a baby had dropped into the lives of all three Daltons, Grace Templeton had proved indispensable. Become almost part of the family. So much so that she'd served as Julie's maid of honor while Blake stood up with Alex as best man.

She'd also started the wheels turning in Delilah's fertile mind. His mother had begun dropping unsubtle hints in recent days about how sweet Grace was. How well she interacted with Molly. And just tonight, how good Blake had looked standing beside her at the altar. The fact that he'd begun to think along those same lines only added to the fury simmering hot and heavy.

"Tell Grace I'll be in the library."

For once Delilah was too tired to pry. She merely waved her shoes and continued up the stairs. "Will do. Just don't keep her too long. She has to feel as whipped as I do."

She was about to feel a whole lot more whipped. Yanking on the ends of his black bow tie, Blake stalked down the hall to the oak-paneled library. The soft glow from the recessed lighting contrasted starkly with his black mood as he retrieved the report he'd stuffed into his pocket more than an hour ago. The facts were no less shattering now than they had been then. He was still trying to absorb their impact when Grace Templeton entered the library.

"Hey, Blake. Delilah said you wanted to talk to me."

His eyes narrowed on the slender blonde, seeing her in a wholly different light. She'd changed from the lilac, off-the-shoulder tea gown she'd worn for the wedding. She'd also released her pale, almost silvery hair from its sophisticated upsweep. The ends now brushed the shoulders of a sleeveless white blouse sporting several large splotches.

"'Scuze the wet spots," she said, brushing a hand down her front with a rueful laugh in her warm brown eyes. "Molly got a little lively during her bath."

Blake didn't respond. He merely stood with his shoulders rigid under his tux as she hitched a hip on the wide, rolled arm of the library's sofa.

"What did you want to talk about?"

Only then did she pick up on his silence. Or maybe it was his stance. Her head tilting, she gave him a puzzled half smile.

"Something wrong?"

He countered her question with one of his own. "Did you happen to notice the man who arrived at the reception just before Alex and Julie left?"

"The guy in the brown suit?" She nodded slowly, still trying to gauge his odd mood. "I saw him, and couldn't help wondering who he was. He looked so out of place among the other guests."

"His name's Del Jamison."

Her brow creased. Blake guessed she was mentally sorting through the host of people she'd met during her stint as Molly's temporary nanny. When she drew a blank, he supplied the details.

"Jamison's a private investigator. The one Alex and I hired to help search for Molly's mother."

She was good, he thought savagely. Very good. Her cinnamon eyes transmitted only a flicker of wariness, quickly suppressed, but she couldn't keep the color from leaching out of her cheeks. The sudden pallor gave him a vicious satisfaction.

"Oh, right." The shrug was an obvious attempt at nonchalance. "He was down in South America, wasn't he? Checking the places where Julie worked last year?"

"He was, but after Julie made it clear she wasn't Molly's mother, Jamison decided to check another lead. In California."

She couldn't hide her fear now. It was there in the quick hitch in her breath, the sudden stillness.

"California?"

"I'll summarize his report for you." Blake used his courtroom voice. The one he employed when he wanted to drive home a point. Cool, flat, utterly devoid of emotion. "Jamison discovered the woman I was told had died in a fiery bus crash was not, in fact, even on that bus. She didn't die until almost a year later."

The same woman he'd had a brief affair with. The woman who'd disappeared from his life with no goodbye, no note, no explanation of any kind. Aided and abetted, he now knew, by this brown-eyed, soft-spoken schemer who'd wormed her way into his mother's home.

And into Blake's consciousness, dammit. Every level of it. As disgusted by her duplicity as by the hunger she'd begun to stir in him, he stalked across the room. She sprang to her feet at his approach and tried to brazen it out.

"I don't see what that has to do with me."

Still he didn't lose control. But his muscles quivered with the effort of keeping his hands off her.

"According to Jamison, this woman gave birth to a baby girl just weeks before she died."

His baby! His Molly!

"She also had a friend who showed up at the hospital mere hours before her death." He planted his fists on the sofa arm, boxing her in, forcing her to lean back. "A *friend* with pale blond hair."

"Blake!" The gold-flecked brown eyes he'd begun to imagine turning liquid with desire widened in alarm. "Listen to me!"

"No, Grace—if that's really your name." His temper slipped through, adding a whiplash to his voice. "You listen, and listen good. I don't know how much you figured you could extort from our family, but the game ends now."

"It's not a game," she gasped, bent at an awkward angle.

"No?"

"No! I don't want your money!"

"What do you want?"

"Just… Just…!" She slapped her palms against his shirtfront. "Oh, for Pete's sake! Get off me."

He didn't budge. "Just what?"

"Dammit!" Goaded, she bunched a fist and pounded his chest. Her fear was gone. Fury now burned in her cheeks. "All I wanted, all I cared about, was making sure Molly had a good home!"

Slowly, Blake straightened. Just as slowly, he moved back a step and allowed her only enough space to push upright. Slapping a rigid lid on his anger, he folded his arms and locked his gaze on her face. Assessing. Considering. Evaluating.

"Let's start at the beginning. Who the hell are you?"

Grace balanced precariously on the sofa arm, her thoughts chaotic. After all she'd been through! So much fear and heartache. Now this? Just when she'd started to breathe easy for the first time in months. Just when she'd thought she and this man might...

"Who are you?"

He repeated the question in what she'd come to think of as his counselor's voice. She'd known Blake Dalton for almost two months now. In that time she'd learned to appreciate his even temperament. She admired even more his ability to smoothly, calmly arbitrate between his more outspoken twin and their equally strong-willed mother.

Oh, God! Delilah!

Grace cringed inside at the idea of divulging even part of the sordid truth to the woman who'd become as much of a friend as an employer. Sick at the thought, she lifted her chin and met Blake's cold, unwavering stare.

"I'm exactly who I claim to be. My name *is* Grace Templeton. I teach...I taught," she corrected, her throat tight, "junior high social studies in San Antonio until a few months ago."

She paused, trying not to think of the life she'd put on hold, forcing herself to blank out the image of the young teens she took such joy in teaching.

"Until a few months ago," Blake repeated in the heavy silence, "when you asked for an extended leave of absence to take care of a sick relative. That's the story you gave us, isn't it? And the principal of your school?"

She knew they'd checked her out. Neither Delilah nor her sons would allow a stranger near the baby unless they'd vetted her. But Grace had become so adept these past years at weaving just enough truth in with the lies that she'd passed their screening.

"It wasn't a story."

Dalton's breath hissed out. Those sexy blue eyes that

had begun to smile at her with something more than friendliness the past few weeks were now lethal.

"You and Anne Jordan were related?"

Anne Jordan. Emma Lang. Janet Blair. So many aliases. So many frantic phone calls and desperate escapes. Grace could hardly keep them straight anymore.

"Anne was my cousin."

That innocuous label didn't begin to describe Grace's relationship to the girl who'd grown up just a block away. They were far closer than cousins. They were best friends who'd played dolls and whispered secrets and shared every event in their young lives, big and small.

"Were you with her when she died?"

The question came at her as swiftly and mercilessly as a stiletto aimed for the heart. "Yes," she whispered, "I was with her."

"And the baby? Molly?"

"She's your daughter. Yours and…and Anne's."

Blake turned away, and Grace could only stare at the broad shoulders still encased in his tux. She ached to tell him she was sorry for all the lies and deception. Except the lies had been necessary, and the deception wasn't hers to tell.

"Anne called me," she said instead. "Told me she'd picked up a vicious infection. Begged me to come. I jumped a plane that same afternoon but when I got there, she was already slipping into a coma. She died that evening."

Blake angled back to face her. His eyes burned with an unspoken question. Grace answered this one as honestly as she could.

"Anne didn't name you as Molly's father. She was almost out of it from the drugs they'd pumped into her.

She was barely coherent... All I understood was the name Dalton. I knew she'd worked here, so...so..."

She broke off, her throat raw with the memory.

"So you brought Molly to Oklahoma City," Blake finished, spacing every word with frightening deliberation, "and left her on my mother's doorstep. Then you called Delilah and said you'd just happened to hear she needed a temporary nanny."

"Which she did!"

He gave that feeble response the disgust it deserved. "Did you enjoy watching my brother and me jump through hoops trying to determine which of us was Molly's father?"

"I told you! I didn't know which of you it was. Not until I'd spent some time with you."

Even then she hadn't been sure. The Dalton twins shared more than razor-sharp intelligence and devastating good looks. Grace could see how her cousin might have succumbed to Alex's charisma and self-confidence. She'd actually figured him for Molly's father until she'd come to appreciate the rock-solid strength in quiet, coolly competent Blake.

Unfortunately, Blake's self-contained personality had made her task so much more difficult. Although friendly and easygoing, he kept his thoughts to himself and his private life private. If he'd had a brief affair with a woman who'd worked for him, only he—and possibly his twin—had known about it.

Grace had hoped the DNA tests they'd run would settle the question of Molly's paternity. She'd been as frustrated as the Dalton brothers at the ambiguous results.

Then they'd launched a determined search for Molly's mother and thrown Grace in a state of near panic. She'd sworn to keep her cousin's secret. She had no choice but

to do just that. Molly's future depended on it. Now Blake
had unearthed at least a part of that secret. She couldn't
tell him the rest, but she could offer a tentative solution.

"As I understand it, Molly's parentage can't be absolutely established unless the father's DNA is matched
with the mother's. She…Anne…was cremated. I don't
have anything of hers to give you that would provide
a sample."

Not a hairbrush or a lipstick or even a postcard with
a stamp on it for Molly to cling to as a keepsake. The
baby's mother had lived in fear for so long. She'd died
the same way, mustering only enough strength at the end
to extract a promise from her cousin to keep Molly safe.

"You could test my DNA," Grace said, determined
to hold to that promise. "I've read that mitochondria are
inherited exclusively through the female line."

She'd done more than read. She'd hunched in front of
the computer for hours when not tending to Molly. Her
head had spun trying to decipher scientific articles laced
with terms like hypervariable control regions and HVR1
base pairs. It had taken some serious slogging, but she'd
finally come away with the knowledge that those four-
hundred-and-forty-four base pairs determined mater-
nal lineage. As such, they could theoretically be used
to trace a human's lineage all the way back to the mi-
tochondrial Eve. The Daltons didn't need to go that far
back to confirm Molly's heritage. They just needed to
hop over one branch on her family tree.

The same thought had obviously occurred to Blake.
His eyes were chips of blue ice as he delivered an ul-
timatum.

"Damn straight you'll give me a DNA sample. And
until the results come back, you'll stay away from
Molly."

"What?"

"You heard me. I want you out of this house. Now."

"You're kidding!"

She discovered an instant later that he wasn't. In two strides he'd closed the distance between them and wrapped his fist around her upper arm. One swift tug had her off the sofa arm and marching toward the library's door.

"Blake, for God's sake!" As surprised as she was angry, she fought his grip. "I've been taking care of Molly for weeks now. You can't seriously think I would do anything to hurt her."

"What I think," he returned in a voice as icy as his eyes, "is that there are a helluva lot of holes in your story. Until they're filled in, I want you where I can watch you day *and* night."

Two

"Get in."

Blake held open the passenger door of his two-seater Mercedes convertible. The heat of the muggy July evening wrapped around them, almost as smothering as the worry and fear that clogged Grace's throat.

"Where are we going?"

"Downtown."

"I need to tell Delilah that I'm leaving," she protested. "Get some of my things."

"I'll let my mother know what's happening. Right now all you need to do is plant your behind in that seat."

If Grace hadn't been so stunned by this unexpected turn of events, the brusque command might have made her blink. This was Blake. The kind, polite, always solicitous Dalton twin. In the weeks since she'd insinuated herself into Delilah's home, she'd never known him to be anything but patient with his sometimes overbearing mother, considerate with the servants and incredibly, achingly gentle with Molly.

"Get in."

She got. Even this late in the evening, the pale gray leather was warm and sticky from the July heat. The seat belt cracked like a rifle shot when she clicked it into place.

As the convertible rolled down the curved driveway, Grace fought to untangle her nerves. God knew she should be used to having her life turned upside down without warning. It had happened often enough in the past few years. One call. That's all it usually took. One frantic call from Hope.

No, she corrected fiercely. Not Hope. *Anne.* Although her cousin was dead, Grace had to remember to think and remember and refer to her as Anne.

She made that her mantra as the Mercedes sliced through the night. She was still repeating it when Blake pulled into the underground parking for Dalton International's headquarters building in downtown Oklahoma City. Although the clicker attached to the Mercedes's visor raised the arm, the booth attendant leaned out with cheerful greeting.

"Evenin', Mr. Dalton."

"Hi, Roy."

"Guess your brother 'n his bride are off on their honeymoon."

"Yes, they are."

"Sure wish 'em well." He leaned farther down and tipped a finger to his brow. "How're you doin', Ms. Templeton?"

She dredged up a smile. "Fine, thanks."

Grace wasn't surprised at the friendly greeting. She'd made many a trip to Dalton International's headquarters with Molly and her grandmother. Delilah had turned over control of the manufacturing empire she and Big Jake had scratched out of bare dirt to her sons. That didn't mean she'd surrendered her right to meddle as she saw fit in either DI's corporate affairs or in her sons' lives. So Delilah, with Molly and her nanny in tow, had regularly breezed into boardrooms and conferences. Just as often, she'd zoomed up to the top floor of the DI building, where her bachelor sons maintained their separate penthouse apartments.

The penthouse also boasted a luxurious guest suite for DI's visiting dignitaries. That, apparently, was where Blake had decided to plant her. Grace guessed as much when he stopped at the security desk in the lower lobby to retrieve a key card. Moments later the glass-enclosed elevator whisked them upward.

Once past the street level, Oklahoma City zoomed into view. On previous visits Grace had gasped at the skyline that rose story by eye-popping story. Tonight she barely noticed the panorama of lights and skyscrapers. Her entire focus was on the man crowding her against the elevator's glass wall.

She hadn't been able to tell which Dalton twin was which at first. With their dark gold hair, chiseled chins and broad shoulders, one was a feast for the eyes. Two of them standing side by side could make any woman drool.

It hadn't taken Grace long to separate the men. Alex was more outgoing, with a wicked grin that jump-started female hormones without him half trying. Blake was quieter. Less obvious. With a smile that was all the more seductive for being slow and warm and…

The ping of the elevator wrenched her back to the tor-tuous present. When the doors slid open, Blake grasped her arm again and marched her down a plushly carpeted hall toward a set of polished oak doors.

Okay, enough! Grace didn't get angry often. When she did, her temper flashed hot and fierce enough to burn through the fear still gripping her by the throat.

"That's it!" She yanked her arm free of his hold and stopped dead in the center of the hall. "You hustle me out of your mother's house like a thief caught stealing the silver. You order me into your bright, shiny convertible. You drag me up here in the middle of the night. I'm not taking another step until you stop acting like you're the Gestapo or KGB."

He arched a brow at her rant, then coolly, deliberately shot back the cuff of his pleated tux shirt to check his gold Rolex.

"It's nine-twenty-two. Hardly the middle of the night."

She wanted to hit him. Slap that stony expression right off his too-handsome face. Might have actually attempted it if she wasn't sure she would crack a couple of finger bones on his hard, unyielding jaw.

Besides which, he deserved some answers. The detective's report had obviously delivered a body blow. He'd loved her cousin once.

The fire drained from Grace's heart, leaving only sadness tinged now with an infinite weariness. "All right. I'll tell you what I can."

With a curt nod, he strode the last few feet to the guest suite. A swipe of the key card clicked the lock on the wide oak doors. Grace had visited the lavish guest suite a number of times. Each time she stepped inside, though, the sheer magnificence of the view stopped her breath in her throat.

Angled floor-to-ceiling glass walls gave a stunning, hundred-and-eighty-degree panorama of Oklahoma City's skyline. The view was spectacular during the day, offering an eagle's-eye glimpse of the domed capitol building, the Oklahoma River and the colorful barges that carried tourists past Bricktown Ballpark to the larger-than-life-size bronze sculptures commemorating the 1889 land run. That momentous event had opened some two million acres of unassigned land to settlers and, oh, by the way, created a tent city with a population of more than fifty thousand almost overnight.

The view on a clear summer night like this one was even more dazzling. Skyscrapers glowed like beacons. White lights twinkled in the trees lining the river spur that meandered through the downtown area. But it was the colossal bronze statue atop the floodlit capitol that drew Grace to the windows. She'd been born and bred in Texas, but as a social studies teacher she knew enough of the history of the Southwest to appreciate the deep symbolism in the twenty-two-foot-tall bronze statue. She'd also been given a detailed history of the statue by Delilah, who'd served on the committee that raised funds for it.

Erected in 2002, *The Guardian,* with his tall spear, muscular body and unbowed head, represented not only the thousands of Native Americans who'd been forced from their homes in the East and settled in what was then Indian Territory. The statue also embodied Oklahomans who'd wrestled pipe into red dirt as hard as brick to suck out the oil that fueled the just-born automobile industry. The sons and daughters who lived through the devastating Dust Bowl of the '30s. The proud Americans who'd worked rotating shifts at the Army Air Corps' Douglas Aircraft Plant in the '40s to overhaul, repair and build fighters and bombers. And, most recently, the grimly determined Oklahomans who'd dug through nine stories of rubble to recover the bodies of friends and coworkers killed in the Murrah Building bombing.

Grace and Hope... No! Grace and *Anne* had driven up from Texas during their junior year in high school to visit Oklahoma City's National Memorial & Museum. Neither of them had been able to comprehend how the homegrown terrorist Timothy McVeigh could be so evil, so twisted in both mind and morals. Then, less than a year later, her cousin met Jack Petrie.

Frost coated Grace's lungs. Feeling its sick chill, she wrapped both arms around her waist and turned away from *The Guardian* to face Blake Dalton.

"I can't tell you about Anne's past," she said bleakly. "I promised I would bury it with her. What I *can* say is that you're the only man she got close to in more years than you want to know."

"You think I'm going to be satisfied with that?"

"You have no choice."

"Wrong."

He yanked on the dangling end of his bow tie and threw it aside before shrugging out of his tuxedo jacket. His black satin cummerbund circled a trim waist. The pleated white shirt was still crisp, as might be expected from a tailor who catered exclusively to millionaires and movie stars.

Yet under the sleek sophistication was an edge that didn't fool Grace for a moment. Delilah bragged constantly about the variety of sports Blake and his twin had excelled at during their school years. Both men still carried an athlete's build—lean in the hips and flanks, with the solid chest and muscled shoulders of a former collegiate wrestler.

That chest loomed far too large in Grace's view at the moment. It invaded her space, distracted her thoughts and made her distinctly nervous.

"How many cousins do you have?" he asked with silky menace. "And how long do you think it will take Jamison to check each of them out?"

"Not long," she fired back. "But he won't find anything beyond Anne's birth certificate, driver's license and a few high school yearbook photos. We made sure of that."

"A person can't just erase her entire life after high school."

"As a matter of fact, she can."

Grace moved to the buckskin leather sofa and dropped onto a cushion. Blake folded his tall frame onto a matching sofa separated by a half acre of glass-topped coffee table.

"It's not easy. Or cheap," she added, thinking of her empty savings account. "But you can pull it off with the help of a very smart friend of a friend of a friend. Especially if said friend can tap into just about any computer system."

Like the Texas Vital Statistics agency. It had taken some serious hacking but they'd managed to delete the digital entry recording Hope Patricia Templeton's marriage to Jack David Petrie. By doing so, they'd also deleted the record of the last time Grace had used her maiden name and SSN.

A familiar sadness settled like a lump in Grace's middle. Her naive, trusting cousin had believed Petrie's promise to love and cherish and provide for her every need. As the bastard had explained in the months that followed, his wife didn't require access to their bank account. Or a credit card. Or a job. Nor did she have to register to vote. There weren't any candidates worth going to that trouble for. And they sure as hell didn't need to talk to a marriage counselor, he'd added when she finally realized he'd made her a virtual prisoner.

Financially dependent and emotionally battered, she'd spent long, isolated years as a shadow person. Jack trotted her out when he wanted to display his pretty wife, then shuffled her back into her proper place in his bed. It hadn't taken him long to cut off her ties with her friends and family, either. All except Grace. She refused to be cut, even after Petrie became furious over her meddling. Grace wondered whether those horrific moments when her gas pedal locked on the interstate were, in fact, due to mechanical failure.

Grace and Hope had become more cautious after that. No more visits. No letters or emails that could be intercepted. No calls to the house. Only to a pay phone in the one grocery store where Jack allowed his wife to shop. Even then it had taken a solid year of pleading before Hope worked up the courage to escape.

Grace didn't want to remember the desperate years that followed. The mindless fear. The countless moves. The series of false identities and fake SSNs, each one more expensive to procure than the last. Until finally—*finally!*—a woman with the name of Anne Jordan had found anonymity and a tenuous, tentative security at Dalton International. She'd been just one of DI's thousands of employees worldwide. An entry-level clerk with only a high school GED. Certainly not a position that would bring her into contact with the multinational corporation's CFO.

Yet it had.

"Please, Blake. Please believe me when I tell you Anne wanted her past to be buried with her. All she cared about in her last, agonizing moments was making sure Molly would know her father, if not her mother."

Or more accurately, that her baby would have the name and protection of someone completely unknown to Jack Petrie.

Grace prayed she'd convinced Blake. She hadn't, of course. The lawyer in him wouldn't be satisfied until he'd dug up and turned over every bit of evidence. But maybe she could deflect his inquisition.

"Will you tell me something?"

"Quid pro quo?" His mouth twisted. "You haven't given me much of a trade."

"Please. I...I wasn't able to talk or visit with Anne much in her last year."

She hadn't dared. Jack Petrie was a Texas state trooper, with a cop's wide connections. Grace knew he'd had her under surveillance at various times, maybe even bugged her phone or planted a tracking device on her car, hoping she would lead him to his wife. Grace had imposed on every friend she had, borrowing their cars or using their phones, to maintain even minimal contact with her cousin.

Jack didn't know about Grace's last, frantic flight to California. She'd made sure of that. She'd emptied her savings account, had a friend drive her to the airport and paid cash for a ticket to Vegas. There she'd rented a car for a desperate drive across the desert to the San Diego hospital where her cousin had been admitted.

Five heart-wrenching days later, she'd retraced that route with Molly. Instead of flying back to San Antonio with the baby, though, she'd paid cash for a bus ticket to Oklahoma City.

She hadn't used her cell phone or any credit cards in the weeks since she'd wrangled a job as Molly's temporary nanny. Nor had she cashed the checks Delilah had written for her salary. She'd planned to go back to her teaching job once Molly was settled with her father. The longer she spent with the baby, though, the more painful the prospect of leaving her became.

The thought of leaving Blake Dalton was almost as wrenching. Lately her mind had drifted to him more than it should. Especially at night, after she'd put Molly to bed. The increasingly erotic direction of that drift spurred pinpricks of guilt, then and now.

"Tell me how you and Anne met," she pleaded, reminding herself yet again Blake was her cousin's love, the man she'd let into her life despite all she'd been through. "How... Well..."

"How Molly happened?" he supplied.

"Yes. Anne was so shy around men."

For shy, read insecure and cowed and generally scared *shitless*. Grace couldn't imagine how Blake had breached those formidable barriers.

"Please," she said softly. "Tell me. I'd like to know she found a little happiness before she died."

He stared at her for long moments, then his breath eased out on a sigh.

"I think she was happy for the few weeks we were together. I was never sure, though. Took me forever to pry more than a murmured hello from her. Even after I got her to agree to go out with me, she didn't want anyone at DI to know we were seeing each other. Said it would look bad, the big boss dating a lowly file clerk."

He hooked his wrists on his knees and contemplated his black dress shoes. He must not have liked what he saw. A note of unmistakable self-disgust colored his deep voice.

"She wouldn't let me take her to dinner or to the theater or anywhere we might be seen together. It was always her place. Or a hotel."

It had to be that, Grace knew. Her cousin couldn't take the chance some society reporter or gossip columnist would start fanning rumors about rich, handsome Blake Dalton's latest love interest. Or worse, the paparazzi might snap a photo of them together and post it on the internet.

Yet she risked going to a hotel with him. She'd come out of her defensive crouch enough for that. And when she discovered she was pregnant with his child, she'd had no choice but to run away. She wanted the baby desperately, but she couldn't tell Dalton about the pregnancy. He would have wanted to give the child his name, or at least establish his legal rights as the father. Hope's false IDs wouldn't have held up under legal scrutiny, and her real one would have led Petrie to her. So she'd run. Again.

"Did you love her?"

Damn! Grace hadn't meant to let that slip out. And she sure as heck hadn't intended to feel jealous of her cousin's relationship with this man.

Yet she knew he had to have been so tender with her. So sensitive to her needs. His mouth would have played a gentle song on her skin. His hands, those strong, tanned hands, must have stroked and soothed even as they aroused and...

"I don't know."

With a flush of guilt, Grace jerked her attention back to his face.

"I cared for her," he said quietly, as much to himself

as to her. "Enough to press her into going to bed with me. But when she left without a word, I was angry as well as hurt."

Regret and remorse chased each other across his face.

"Then, when I got the report of the bus accident…"

He stopped and directed a look of fierce accusation at Grace.

"I wasn't with her when it happened," she said in feeble self-defense. "She was by herself, in her car. The bus spun out right in front of her and hit a bridge abutment. She was terrified, but she got out to help."

"And left her purse at the scene."

"Yes."

"Deliberately?"

"Yes."

"Why?"

Grace shook her head. "I can't tell you why. I can't tell you any more than I have. I promised Anne her past would die with her."

"But it didn't," he countered swiftly. "Molly's living proof of that."

She slipped off the sofa and onto her knees, desperate for him to let it go. "She's your daughter, Blake. Please, just accept that and take joy in her."

He was silent for so long she didn't think he would respond. When he did, the ice was back in his voice.

"All I have right now is your word that Anne and I had a child together. I'll send in the DNA sample you offered to provide. Once we have the results, we'll discuss where we go from here."

"Where I need to go is back to your mother's house! She's exhausted from the wedding. She told me tonight she was feeling every one of her sixty-two years. She can't take care of Molly by herself for the next few days."

"I'll help her, and when I can't be there I'll make sure someone else is. In the meantime, you stay put."

He pushed out of the chair and strode to the wet bar built into the far wall. For a moment Grace thought he intended to pour them both a drink to wash down the hurt and bitterness of the past hour, but he lifted only one crystal tumbler from one of the mirrored shelves. He returned with it and issued a terse command.

"Spit."

Three

The melodic chimes of a doorbell pierced Grace's groggy haze. When the chimes gave way to the hammer of an impatient fist, she propped herself up on one elbow and blinked at the digital clock beside the bed.

Oh, God! Seven-twenty! She'd slept right through Molly's first feeding.

She threw the covers aside and was half out of bed before reality hit. One, this wasn't her room in Delilah's mansion. Two, she was wearing only the lavender lace bikini briefs she left on when she'd changed her maid of honor gown. And three, she was no longer Molly's temporary nanny.

Last night's agonizing events came crashing down on her as the fist hammered again. Scrambling, Grace snatched up her now hopelessly wrinkled khaki crops and white blouse. She got the pants zipped and buttoned the blouse on her way to the front door. She had a good idea whose fist was pounding away. She'd spent almost a month now with Blake Dalton's often autocratic, occasionally irascible, always kindhearted mother.

So she expected to see the raven-haired matriarch. She *didn't* expect to see the baby riding on Delilah's chest, nested contentedly in a giraffe sling. Grace gripped the brass door latch, swamped by an avalanche of love and worry and guilt as she dragged her gaze from the infant to her grandmother.

"Delilah, I..."

"Don't you Delilah me!" She stomped inside, the soles of her high-topped sneakers slapping the marble foyer. "Don't you dare Delilah me!"

Grace closed the door and followed her into the living room. She wished she'd taken a few seconds to brush her hair and slap some water on her face before this showdown. And coffee! She needed coffee. Desperately.

She'd tossed and turned most of the night. The few hours she'd drifted into a doze, she'd dreamed of Anne. And Blake. Grace had been there, too, stunned when his fury at her swirled without warning into a passion that jerked her awake, breathless and wanting. Remnants of that mindless hunger still drifted like a steamy haze through her mind as Delilah slung a diaper bag from her shoulder onto the sofa and released Molly from the sling.

Grace couldn't help but note that her employer had gone all jungle today. The diaper bag was zebra-striped. Grinning monkeys frolicked and swung from vines on the baby's seersucker dress. Delilah herself was in knee-length leopard tights topped by an oversize black T-shirt with a neon message urging folks to come out and be amazed by Oklahoma City's new gorilla habitat—a habitat she'd coaxed, cajoled and strong-armed her friends into funding.

"Don't just stand there," she snapped at Grace. "Get the blanket out of the diaper bag."

Even the blanket was a riot of green and yellow and jungle red. Grace spread it a safe distance away from the glass coffee table. Molly was just learning to crawl. She could push herself onto her hands and knees and hold her head up to survey the world with bright, inquisitive eyes.

Delilah deposited the baby on the blanket and made sure she was centered before pointing an imperious finger at Grace.

"You. Sit." The older woman plunked herself down in the opposite chair, keeping the baby between them. "Now talk."

"You sure you wouldn't like some coffee first?" Grace asked with a hopeful glance at the suite's fully equipped kitchen. "I could make a quick pot."

"Screw coffee. Talk."

Grace blew out a sigh and raked her fingers through her unbrushed hair. Obviously Delilah had no intention of making this easy.

"I don't know how much Blake told you..." She let that dangle for a moment. Got no response. "Okay, here's the condensed version. Molly's mother was my cousin. When Anne worked at Dalton International, she had a brief affair with your son. She died before she could tell me *which* son, so I brought Molly to you and finessed a job as her nanny while Alex and Blake sorted out the paternity issue."

Delilah pinned Grace with a look that could have etched steel. "If one of my sons got this cousin of yours pregnant, why didn't she have the guts or the decency to let him know about the baby?"

Grace stiffened. Shielding Hope—*Anne!*—had become as much a part of her as breathing. No one knew what her cousin had endured. And Grace was damned if she'd allow anyone, even the formidable Delilah Dalton, to put her down.

"I told Blake and I'll tell you. Anne had good reasons for what she did, but she wanted those reasons to die with her. She didn't, however, want her baby to grow up without knowing either of her parents."

Delilah fired back with both barrels. "Don't get uppity with me, girl!"

The fierce retort startled the baby. Molly swung her head toward her grandmother, wobbled and plopped down on one diapered hip. Both women instinctively bent toward her, but she was already pushing back onto her knees.

Delilah moderated her tone if not her message. "I'm the one who bought your out-of-work schoolteacher story, remember? I took you into my home. I trusted you, dammit."

Grace didn't see any use in pointing out that she hadn't lied about being a teacher or temporarily out of work. The trust part stung enough.

"I'm sorry I couldn't tell you about my connection to Molly."

"Ha!"

"I promised my cousin I would make sure her child was loved and cared for." Her glance went again to the baby, happily drooling and rocking on hands and knees. Slowly, she brought her gaze back to Delilah. "And she is," Grace said softly. "Well cared for and very much loved."

Delilah huffed out something close to a snort but

didn't comment for long moments. "I pride myself on being a good judge of character," she said at last. "Even that horny goat I married lived up to almost everything I'd expected of him."

Grace didn't touch that one. She'd heard Delilah say more than once she wished to hell Big Jake Dalton hadn't died before she'd found out about his little gal pal. His passing would've been a lot less peaceful.

"Is all this you've just told me true?" the Dalton matriarch demanded.

"Yes, ma'am."

"Molly's mother was really your cousin?"

"Yes."

"Well, I guess we'll have proof of that soon enough. Damned lab is making a fortune off all these rush DNA tests we've ordered lately."

She pooched her lips and moved them from side to side before coming to an abrupt decision.

"I've watched you with Molly. I don't believe you're some schemer looking to extort big bucks from us. You'll have to work to convince Blake of that, though."

"I can't tell him any more than I have."

"You don't know him like I do. He has his ways of getting what he wants. So do I," she added as she pushed out of the chair and adjusted the sling. "So do I. C'mon, Mol, let's go see your daddy."

Without thinking Grace moved to help. Swooping the baby up, she planted wet, sloppy kisses on her cheeks before slipping the infant's feet through the sling's leg openings. While Delilah tightened the straps, Grace folded the jungle blanket back into the diaper bag and handed it to the older woman.

"I'm sorry Blake doesn't want me to help with Molly."

"We'll manage until this mess gets sorted out."

* * *

If it got sorted out. Grace grew more antsy as one day stretched into two, then three.

Blake had her things packed and delivered along with her purse. She tried to take that as a good sign. Apparently he wasn't afraid she would pull a disappearing act like her cousin had.

He didn't contact her personally, though, and that worried Grace. It also caused an annoyingly persistent ache. Only now that she'd been banished from their lives did she realize how attached she'd become to the Daltons, mother and son. And to Molly! Grace missed cooing to the baby and watching her count her toes and shampooing her soft, downy blond hair.

She'd known the time would come when she would have to drop out of Molly's life. The longer she stayed here, the greater the risk Jack Petrie might trace her to Oklahoma City and wonder what she was doing here. Yet she felt a sharp pang of dismay when Blake finally condescended to call a little past 6:00 p.m. with a curt announcement.

"I need to talk to you."

"All right."

"I'm downstairs," he informed her. "I'll be up in a few minutes."

At least she was a little better prepared for this face-to-face than she'd been for their last. Her hair was caught up in a smooth knot and she'd swiped on some lip gloss earlier. She debated whether to change her jeans and faded San Antonio SeaWorld T-shirt but decided to use the time to take deep, calming breaths.

Not that they did much good. The Blake Dalton she opened the door to wasn't one she'd seen before. He'd always appeared at his mother's house in suits or neatly

pressed shirts and slacks sporting creases sharp enough
to shave fuzz from a peach. Then, of course, there was
the tux he'd donned for the wedding. Armani should
wish for male models with builds like either of the Dalton twins.

This Blake was considerably less refined. Faded
jeans rode low on his hips. A black T-shirt stretched
across his taut shoulders. Bristles the same shade of
amber as his hair shadowed his cheeks and chin. He
looked tough and uncompromising, but the expression
in his laser blues wasn't as cold as the one he'd worn at
their last meeting, thank God.

"We got the lab report back."

Wordlessly she led the way into the living room.
Electric screens shielded the wall of windows from the
sun that hadn't yet slipped down behind the skyscrapers. Without the endless view, the room seemed smaller,
more intimate. *Too* intimate, she decided when she
turned and found Blake had stopped mere inches away.

"Aren't you going to ask the results?"

"I don't need to," she said with a shrug. "Unless the
lab screwed up the samples, their report confirms Molly
and I descend from the same family tree."

"They didn't screw up the samples."

"Okay." She crossed her arms. "Now what?"

Surprise flickered across his face.

"What'd you expect?" Grace asked, her chin angling.
"That I would throw myself into your arms for finally
acknowledging the truth?"

The surprise was still there, but then his gaze
dropped to her mouth and it took on a different qual-
ity. Darker. More intense. As though the idea of Grace
throwing herself at him was less of a shock than something to be considered, evaluated, assessed.

Now that the idea was out there, it didn't particularly shock her, either. Just the opposite. In fact, the urge grew stronger with each second it floated around in the realm of possibility. All she had to do was step forward. Slide her palms over his shoulders. Lean into his strength.

As her cousin had.

Guilt sent Grace back a pace, not forward. He'd been Anne's lover, she reminded herself fiercely. The father of her baby. At best, Grace was a problem he was being forced to solve.

"Now you know," she said with a shrug that disguised her true feelings. "You're Molly's father. And *I* know you'll be good with her. So it's time for me to pack and head back to San Antonio. I'll stop by to say goodbye to her on my way out of town."

"That's it?" His frown deepened. "You're just going to drop out of her life?"

"I'll see her when I can."

After she was certain Jack Petrie hadn't learned about her stay in Oklahoma City.

"There are legalities that have to be attended to," Blake protested. "I'll need Molly's birth certificate. Her mother's death certificate."

Both contained the false name and SSN her cousin had used in California. Grace could only pray the documents would be sufficient for Blake's needs. They should. With his legal connections and his family's political clout here in Oklahoma, he ought to be able to push whatever he wanted through the courts.

"I'll send you copies," she promised.

"Right." He paused, his jaw working. "I hope you know that whatever trouble Anne was in, I would have helped her."

"Yes," she said softly. "I know."

His eyes searched hers. "Anne couldn't bring herself to trust me, but you can, Grace."

She wanted to. God, how she wanted to! Somehow she managed to swallow the hard lump in her throat.

"I trust you to cherish Molly."

Saying goodbye to the baby was every bit as hard as it had been to say goodbye to Blake. Molly broke into delighted coos when she saw her nanny and lifted both arms, demanding to be cuddled.

Grace refused to cry until her rental car was on I-35 and heading south. Tears blurred the rolling Oklahoma countryside for the next fifty miles. By the time she crossed the Red River into Texas, her throat was raw and her eyes so puffy that she had to stop at the welcome center to douse them with cold water. Six hours later she hit the outskirts of San Antonio, still mourning her severed ties to Molly and the woman who'd been both cousin and best friend to her since earliest childhood.

Her tiny condo in one of the city's older suburbs felt stale and stuffy when she let herself in. With a gulp, she glanced from the living room she'd painted a warm terra-cotta to the closet-size kitchen. She loved her place, but the entire two-bedroom unit could fit in the foyer of Delilah Dalton's palatial mansion.

As soon as she'd unpacked and powered up her computer, Grace scanned the certificates she'd promised to send Blake. That done, she skimmed through the hundreds of emails that had piled up in her absence and tried to pick up the pieces of her life.

The next two weeks dragged interminably. School didn't start until the end of month. Unfortunately, the open-ended leave of absence Grace had requested had forced her principal to shuffle teachers to cover the fall semester. The best he could promise was hopefully steady work as a substitute until after Christmas.

At loose ends until school started, Grace had to cut as many corners as possible to make up for her depleted bank account. Even worse, she missed Molly more than she would have believed possible. The baby had taken up permanent residence in her heart.

Only at odd moments would she admit she missed Molly's father almost as much as she did the baby. Like everyone else swept up in the Daltons' orbit, she'd been overwhelmed by Delilah's forceful personality and dazzled by Alex's wicked grin and audacious charm. Now that she viewed the Dalton clan from a distance, however, Grace recognized Blake as the brick and mortar keeping the family together. Always there when his mother needed him to pull together the financing on yet another of her charitable ventures. Holding the reins at Dalton International's corporate headquarters while Alex jetted halfway around the world to consult with suppliers or customers. Grace missed seeing his tall form across the table at his mother's house, missed hearing his delighted chuckle when he tickled Molly's tummy and got her giggling.

The only bright spot in those last, endless days of summer was that she heard nothing from Jack Petrie. She began to breathe easy again, convinced she'd covered her tracks. That false sense of security lasted right up until she answered the doorbell on a rainy afternoon.

When she peered though the peephole, the shock of seeing who stood on the other side dropped her jaw. A second later, fear exploded in her chest. Her fingers scrabbled for the dead bolt. She got it unlocked and threw the door almost back on its hinges.

"Blake!"

He had to step back to keep from getting slammed by the glass storm door. Grace barely registered the neat black slacks, the white button-down shirt with the open collar and sleeves rolled up, the hair burnished to dark, gleaming gold by rain.

"Is...?" Her heart hammered. Her voice shook. "Is Molly okay?"

"No."

"Oh, God!" A dozen horrific scenarios spun through her head. "What happened?"

"She misses you."

Grace gaped at him stupidly. "What?"

"She misses you. She's been fretting since you left. Mother says she's teething."

The disaster scenes faded. Molly wasn't injured. She hadn't been kidnapped. Almost reeling with relief, Grace sagged against the doorjamb.

"That's what you came down to San Antonio to tell me?" she asked incredulously. "Molly's teething?"

"That, and the fact that she said her first word."

And Grace had missed both events! The loss hit like a blow as Blake's glance went past her and swept the comfortable living room.

"May I come in?"

"Huh? Oh. Yes, of course."

She moved inside, all too conscious now of her bare feet and the T-shirt hacked off to her midriff. The shirt topped a pair of ragged cutoffs that skimmed her butt cheeks.

The cutoffs were comfortable in the cozy privacy of her home but nothing she would have ever considered wearing while she'd worked for Delilah—or around her son. She caught Blake's gaze tracking to her legs, moving upward. Disconcerted by the sudden heat that slow once-over generated, she gulped and snatched at his reason for being there.

"What did Molly say?"

"We thought it was just a ga-ga," he said with a small, almost reluctant smile. "Mother insisted she was trying to say ga-ma, but it came out on a hiss."

She sounded it out in her head, and felt her stomach go hard and tight.

"Gace? Molly said Gace?"

"Several times now."

"I…uh…"

He waited a beat, but she couldn't pull it together enough for coherence. She was too lost in the stinging regret of missing those first words.

"We want you to come back, Grace."

Startled, she looked up to find Blake regarding her intently.

"Who's *we?*" she stammered.

"All of us. Mother, me, Julie and Alex."

"They're back from their honeymoon?"

"They flew in last night."

"And you…" She had to stop and suck in a shaky breath. "And you want me to come back and pick up where I left off as Molly's nanny?"

"Not as her nanny. As my wife."

Four

Blake could certainly understand Grace's slack-jawed astonishment. He'd spent the entire flight to San Antonio telling himself it was insane to propose marriage to a woman who refused to trust him with the truth.

It was even more insane for him to miss her the way he had. She'd wormed her way into his mother's house and Molly's heart. She'd lied to him—to all of them—by omission if nothing else. Yet the hole she'd left behind had grown deeper with each hour she was gone.

Molly's unexpected arrival had already turned his calm, comfortable routine upside down. This doe-eyed blonde had kicked it all to hell. So he felt a savage satisfaction to see his own chaotic feelings mirrored in her face.

"You're crazy! I can't marry you!"

"Why not?"

She was sputtering, almost incoherent. "Because...
Because..."

He thought she might break down and tell him then.
Trust him with the truth. When she didn't, he swallowed
a bitter pill of disappointment.

"Why don't we sit down?" he suggested with a calm
he was far from feeling. "Talk this through."

"Talk it through?" She gave a bubble of hysterical
laughter and swept a hand toward the living room. "My
first marriage proposal, and he wants to *talk* it though.
By all means, counselor, have a seat."

She regrouped during the few moments it took him
to move to a sofa upholstered in a nubby plaid that com-
plemented the earth-toned walls and framed prints of
Roman antiquities. As she dropped into a chair facing
him, Blake could see her astonishment giving way to
anger. The first hints of it fired her eyes and stiffened
her shoulders under her cottony T-shirt. He had to work
to keep his gaze from drifting to the expanse of creamy
skin exposed by the shirt's hem. And those legs. Christ!

He'd better remember what he'd come for. He had to
approach this challenge the same way he did all others.
Coolly and logically.

"I've had time to think since you left, Grace. You're
good with Molly. So good both she and my mother have
had difficulty adjusting to your absence."

So had he, dammit. It irritated Blake to no end that
he hadn't been able to shut this woman out of his head.
She'd lied to him and stubbornly refused to trust him.
Yet he'd found himself making excuses for the lies and
growing more determined by the hour to convince her
to open up.

"You're also Molly's closest blood relative on her
mother's side," he continued.

As far as he could determine at this point, anyway. He fully intended to keep digging. Whatever it took, however he got it, he wanted the truth.

"That's right," she confirmed with obvious reluctance. "Anne's parents are dead, and she was their only child."

He waited, willing her to share another scrap of information about her cousin. It hit Blake then that he could barely remember what Anne had looked like. They'd been together such a short time—if those few, furtive meetings outside their work environment could be termed togetherness.

Jaw locked, he tried to summon her image. She'd been an inch or two shorter than Grace. That much he remembered. And her eyes were several shades darker than her cousin's warm, caramel-brown. Beyond that, she was a faint memory when compared with the vibrant female now facing him.

Torn between guilt and regret, Blake presented his next argument. "I know you're facing monetary problems right now."

She bolted upright in her chair. "What'd you do? Have Jamison check my financials?"

"Yes." He offered no apology. "I'm guessing you drained your resources to help Anne and Molly. I owe you for that, Grace."

"Enough to marry me?" she bit out.

"That's part of the equation." He hesitated, aware he was about to enter treacherous territory. "There's another consideration, of course. Something frightened Anne enough to send her into hiding. It has to frighten you, too, or you wouldn't have gone to such lengths to protect her."

He'd struck a nerve. He could tell by the way she

wouldn't meet his eyes. Regret that he hadn't been able
to shield Anne from whoever or whatever had threatened her knifed into him. With it came an implacable
determination to protect Grace. Battling the fierce urge
to shake the truth out of her, he offered her not just his
name but every powerful resource at his disposal.

"I'll take care of you," he promised, his steady gaze
holding hers. "You *and* Molly."

She wanted to yield. He could see it in her eyes. He
congratulated himself, reveling in the potent mix of satisfaction at winning her confidence and a primal need
to protect his chosen mate.

His fierce exultation didn't last long. Only until she
shook her head.

"I appreciate the offer, Blake. You don't know how
much. But I can take care of myself."

He hadn't realized until that moment how determined
he was to put his ring on her finger. His expression hard-
ening, he played his trump card.

"There's another aspect to consider. Right now, you
can't—or won't—claim any degree of kinship to Molly.
That could impact your access to her."

Her back went rigid. "What are you saying? That you
wouldn't let me see her if I don't marry you?"

"No. I'm simply pointing out that you have no legal
rights where she's concerned. Mother's not getting any
younger," he reminded her coolly. "And if something
should happen to me or Alex…"

He was too good an attorney to overstate his case.
Shrugging, he let her mull over the possibilities.

Grace did, with ever increasing indignation. She
couldn't believe it! He'd trapped her in her own web of
lies and half-truths. If she wanted to see Molly—which

she did, desperately!—she would have to play the game by his rules.

But marriage? Could she tie her future to his for the sake of the baby? The prospect dismayed her enough to produce a sharp round of questions.

"What about love, Blake? And sex? And everything else that goes into a marriage? Don't you want that?"

With a smooth move, he pushed off the sofa. Grace rose hastily as well and was almost prepared when he stopped mere inches away.

"Do you?" he asked.

"Of course I do!"

For the first time she saw a glint of humor in his eyes. "Then I don't see a problem. The sex is certainly doable. We can work on the love."

Dammit! She couldn't form a coherent thought with him standing so close. Between that and the blood pounding in her ears, she was forced to fight for every breath. It had to be oxygen deprivation that made her agree to his outrageous proposal.

"All right, counselor. You've made your case. I want to be part of Molly's life. I'll marry you."

She thought that would elicit a positive response. At least a nod. Wasn't that what he wanted? What he'd flown down here for? So why the hell did his brows snap together and he looked as though he seriously regretted his offer?

Let them snap! They'd both gone too far to back down now. But there was one final gauntlet she had to throw down.

"I just have one condition."

"And that is?"

"We play this marriage very low-key. No formal announcement. No fancy ceremony. No big, expensive reception with pictures splashed across the society page."

She paced the room, thinking furiously. She'd covered her tracks in Oklahoma City. She was sure of it. Still, it was best to stick as close to the truth as possible.

"If anyone asks, we met several months ago. Fell in love, but needed time to be sure. Decided it was for real when you flew down here to see me this weekend, so we found a justice of the peace and did the deed. Period. End of story."

She turned, hands on hips, and waited for his response. It was slow coming. *Extremely* slow.

"Well?" she demanded, refusing to let his stony silence unnerve her. "Do we have a deal or don't we?"

He held out a hand. To shake on their bargain, she realized as the full ramifications of what she'd just agreed to sank in. If her cousin's horrific experience hadn't killed most of Grace's girlish fantasies about marriage, this coolly negotiated business arrangement would have done the trick.

Except Blake didn't take the hand she extended. To her surprise, he elbowed her arm aside, hooked her waist and brought her up against his chest.

"If we're going to project a pretense of being in love, we'd better practice for the cameras."

"No! No cameras, remember? No splashy… Mmmmph!"

She ended on a strangled note as his mouth came down on hers. The kiss was harder than it needed to be. It was also everything that she'd imagined it might be! Her blood leaping, she gloried in the press of his body against hers for a moment or two or ten.

Then reality hit. This was payback for the secrets she still refused to reveal. A taste of the sex he'd so generously offered to provide. She bristled, fully intending to jerk out of his hold, but he moved first.

Dropping his arm, he put a few inches between them. He'd lost that granite look, but she wasn't sure she liked the self-disgust much better.

"I'm sorry."

"You should be," she threw back. "Manhandling me isn't part of our deal."

"You're right. That was uncalled for."

It certainly was. Yet for some perverse reason, the apology irritated her more than the kiss.

"Do we need to negotiate an addendum?" she asked acidly. "Something to the effect that physical contact must be mutually agreed to?"

Red singed his cheeks. "Amendment accepted. If you still want to go through with the contract, that is."

"Do you?"

"Yes."

"Then I do, too."

"Fine." His glance swept over her, lingering again momentarily on her legs. "You'd better get changed."

"Excuse me?"

"You scripted the scenario. I flew down to see you. We decided it was for real. We hunted down a justice of the peace. Period. End of story."

She threw an incredulous glance at the window. Rain still banged against the panes. Thunder rumbled in the distance.

"You want to get married *today?*"

"Why not?"

She could think of a hundred reasons, not least of which was the fact that she had yet to completely recover from that kiss.

"What about blood tests?" she protested. "The seventy-two-hour mandatory waiting period?"

"Texas doesn't require blood tests. I've checked."

Of course he had.

"And the seventy-two-hour waiting period can be waived if you know the right people."

Which he did. Grace should have known he would cover every contingency with his usual attention to detail.

"We'll get the marriage license at the Bexar County Courthouse. One of my father's old cronies is a circuit judge. I'll call and see if he's available to perform the ceremony." He pulled out his cell phone. "Pack what you need to take back to Oklahoma with you. We'll arrange for a moving company to take care of the rest."

The speed of it, the meticulous preplanning and swift execution, left her breathless.

"You were that sure of me?" she asked, feeling dazed and off balance.

He paused in the act of scrolling through the phone's address book. "I was that sure of how much you love Molly."

They left for the county courthouse a little more than three hours later. Blake was driving the Lincoln town car his efficient staff had arranged for him. As Grace stared through the Lincoln's rain-streaked window, she grappled with a growing sense of unreality.

Like all young girls, she and her cousin had spent hours with an old lace tablecloth wrapped around their shoulders, playing bride. During giggly sleepovers, they'd imagined numerous iterations of her wedding day. Grace's favorite consisted of a church fragrant with flowers and perfumed candles, a radiant bride in filmy white and friends packed into the pews.

After that came the smaller, more intimate version. Just her, her cousin as her attendant, a handsome groom and the pastor in a shingle-roofed gazebo while her family beamed from white plastic folding chairs. She'd even toyed occasionally with the idea of Elvis walking her down the aisle in one of Vegas's wedding chapels. This hurried, unromantic version had never figured in her imagination, however.

The reality of it hit home when they walked across a rain-washed plaza to the Bexar County Courthouse. The building was listed on the National Register of Historic Places. Unfortunately the recent storm and still ominous thunderclouds hanging low in an angry sky tinted its sandstone turrets to prison-gray. The edifice looked both drab and foreboding as Blake escorted Grace up its granite steps.

The frosted window on the door of the county clerk's office welcomed walk-ins, but the bored counter attendant showed little interest in their application. He cracked a jaw-popping yawn when the prospective bride and groom filled out the application. Five minutes and thirty-five dollars later, they entered the chambers of Judge Victor Honeywell. *His* clerk, at least, seemed to feel some sense of the occasion.

The beaming, well-endowed matron hurried around her desk to shake their hands. "I can't remember the last time we got to perform a spur-of-the-moment wedding. Brides today seem to take a year just to decide on their gown."

Unlike Grace, who had slithered out of her cutoffs and into the white linen sundress she'd picked up on sale a few weeks ago.

Blake, on the other hand, had come prepared for every eventuality, a wedding included. While she'd packed, he'd retrieved a suit bag from the Lincoln. Dark worsted wool now molded his wide shoulders. An Italian silk tie that probably cost more than Grace had earned in a week was tied in a neat Windsor. The clerk's admiring gaze lingered on both shoulders and tie for noticeable moments before she turned to the bride.

"These just came for you."

She ducked behind a side counter and popped up again with a cellophane-wrapped cascade of white roses. Silver lace and sprays of white baby's breath framed the bouquet. A two-inch-wide strip of blue was looped into a floppy bow around the stems.

"The ribbon—such as it is—is the belt from my rain-coat," she said, her eyes twinkling. "You know, some-thing borrowed, something blue."

A lump blocked Grace's throat. She had to push air past it as she folded back the cellophane and traced a finger over the petals. "Thank you."

"You're welcome. And this is for you." Still beaming, the clerk pinned a white rose to Blake's lapel. "There! Now I'll take you to Judge Honeywell."

She ushered them into a set of chambers groaning with oak panels and red damask drapes. The flags of the United States and the state of Texas flanked a desk the size of a soccer field. A set of steer horns stretched across an eight-foot swath of wall behind the desk.

"It's Ms. Templeton and Mr. Dalton, Your Honor."

The man ensconced on what Grace could only term a leather throne jumped up. His black robe flapped as he rounded his desk, displaying a pair of hand-tooled cowboy boots. He was at least six-three or four and as whiskery as he was tall. When he thrust out a thorny palm, Blake had to tilt back to keep from getting stabbed by the exaggerated point of his stiff-as-a-spear handlebar mustache.

"Well, damn! So you're Big Jake Dalton's boy."

"One of them," Blake replied with a smile.

"He ever tell you 'bout the time the two of us busted up a saloon down to Nogales?"

"No, he didn't."

"Good. Some tales are best left untold." Honeywell shifted his squinty gaze to Grace. "I'd warn you against marrying up with any son of Big Jake if they didn't have the prettiest, smartest female in all fifty states for their mama." His nose twitched above the bushy mustache. "Speaking of Delilah, is she comin' to witness the ceremony?"

"No, but my brother is."

That was the first Grace had heard of it! She glanced at him in surprise while he confirmed the startling news.

"Alex should be here any moment. He was on final approach when we left the condo. In fact..."

He cocked his head. Grace followed suit and picked up the sound of footsteps in the tiled hallway. A moment later the judge's clerk reappeared with another couple in tow. The tall, tawny-haired male who entered the chambers was a mirror image of Blake. The copper-haired female with him elicited a joyous cry from Grace.

"Julie!"

She took an instinctive step toward the woman she'd grown so close to during her sojourn in Oklahoma. Guilt brought her to a dead stop. Grace hadn't lied to Julie or the Daltons, but she hadn't told the truth, either. Alex and his new wife had to be feeling the same anger Blake had when he'd first discovered her deception.

It wasn't anger she saw in her friend's distinctive green-brown eyes, however, but regret and exasperation.

"Grace, you idiot!" Brushing past Blake, Julie folded Grace into a fierce hug, roses and all. "You didn't need to go through what you did alone. You could have told me. I would've kept your secret."

Limp with relief, Grace gulped back a near sob. "The secret isn't mine to tell."

Her gaze slid to Blake's brother. Alex didn't appear quite as forgiving as his bride. She didn't blame him. She'd watched him interact with Molly these past months, knew he loved the baby every bit as much as Blake did. It had to hurt to transition so abruptly from possible father to uncle. Grace could offer only a soft apology.

"I'm sorry, Alex. I didn't know which of you was Molly's father. Honestly. Not until I'd been in Oklahoma City for a while, and by then you and Julie were, ah, working a separate set of issues."

The hard set to his jaw relaxed a fraction. "That's one way to describe the hell this stubborn woman put me through."

He stood for a moment, studying Grace's face. She braced herself, but his next words didn't carry either the condemnation or the sting she expected.

"Everyone, me included, will tell you that my brother is the better man. But once he sets his mind to something, he can be as ruthless as I am and as hardheaded as our mother. Blake's convinced us this marriage is what he wants. Is it what you want?"

Her fingers tightened on the stem of the roses. Their white velvet scent drifted upward as she turned to her groom. Blake stood tall and seemingly at ease, but his blue eyes were locked on hers.

"Yes," she said after only a minuscule hesitation. "I'm sure."

Was that satisfaction or relief or a brief flash of panic that rippled across his face? Grace was still trying to decide when the judge boomed out instructions.

"All right, folks. Y'all gather round so we can get these two hitched."

Blake held out a hand. Grace laid her palm in his, hoping he couldn't hear the violent thump of her heart against her ribs. As they faced the judge, she reminded herself she was doing this for Molly.

Mostly.

Five

It was actually happening. It was for real. Grace had to fight the urge to pinch herself as Blake slid a band of channel-cut diamonds onto her ring finger. Dazed, she heard the judge's prompt.

"With this ring…"

Her groom followed the cues in a deep, sure voice. "With this ring…"

"I thee wed."

"I thee wed."

The diamonds caught the light from the overhead lighting. Brilliant, multicolored sparks danced and dazzled. Grace couldn't begin to guess how many carats banded her finger. Four? Five? And she couldn't reciprocate with so much as a plain gold band.

"By the authority vested in me by the state of Texas," Judge Honeywell intoned, "I now pronounce you husband and wife."

He waited a beat before issuing another prompt. "Go ahead, Dalton. Kiss your bride."

For the second time that afternoon, Blake slipped an arm around her waist. Grace's pulse skittered. A shiver raced down her spine. Apprehension? Anticipation?

She knew which even before he bent toward her. Her whole body quivered in expectation. He was gentle this time, though. *Too* gentle! She ached to lean into him, but the deal they'd struck kept her rigid. Their marriage was first and foremost a business arrangement, a legal partnership with Molly as the focus. Grace might eventually accept Blake's oh-so-casual offer of sex, but she'd damned well better keep a close watch on her heart.

With that resolve firm in her mind, she accepted the hearty congratulations of Judge Honeywell, another fierce hug from Julie and a kiss on the cheek from her new brother-in-law. At that point Alex produced an envelope from his inside suit coat pocket.

"Mother wanted to be here, but Molly's cutting a tooth and was too fussy to fly. She sent this instead."

Grace took the envelope with some trepidation. Inside was a folded sheet of notepaper embossed with Delilah's raised monogram. Before unfolding the note, she looked a question at Blake. His small shrug told her this was as much a surprise to him as it was to her. Nervously, Grace skimmed the almost indecipherable scrawl.

I can't say I'm happy with the way you decided to do this. We'll discuss it when you get back from France. DI's corporate jet will fly you to Marseille. Contact Madame LeBlanc when you arrive. Blake has her number. Julie, Alex and I will take care of Molly.

For a wild moment Grace thought she was being hustled out of the country so Delilah could hammer some sense into Blake. Then the last line sank in. Julie, Alex and Delilah would care for Molly. She and her groom, apparently, were jetting off to France.

Wordlessly, she handed the note to Blake. After a quick read, he speared a glance at this twin. "Were you in on this?"

"I figured something was up when Mother had me ferry the Gulfstream V down to San Antonio. Where's she proposing it take you?"

"The south of France."

That produced a quick grin. "You get no sympathy from me, Bubba. She sent Julie and me to Tuscany on our wedding night. Good thing we're both pilots and know how to beat jet lag." He winked at his wife before addressing Grace. "Hope you have a passport."

"I do, but..."

But what? She'd decided in a scant few moments to turn her whole world upside down by accepting Blake's proposition. What possible objection could she have to capping an unreal marriage with a fake honeymoon?

"But Blake probably didn't bring his," she finished helplessly.

"He didn't," Julie interjected, fishing in her purse. "I did, however. Delilah had me race over and pick it up from your executive assistant," she explained as she slapped the passport into her brother-in-law's palm. "I forgot I had it until this moment."

He fingered the gold lettering for several moments, then shrugged. "Good thing you're packed," he said to Grace. "I can pick up whatever extras I need when we get to France."

* * *

They said their goodbyes at the airport. Then Alex and Julie boarded the smaller Dalton International jet that had flown Blake to San Antonio and the newlyweds crossed the tarmac to the larger, twin-engine Gulf-stream V.

The captain met them at planeside and tendered his sincere best wishes. "Congratulations, Mrs. Dalton."

"I…uh… Thank you."

Blake stepped in to cover his wife's surprise at hearing herself addressed by her new title. "I understand you just got back from Tuscany, Joe. Sorry you had to make such a quick turnaround."

"Not a problem. Alex and Julie were at the controls for most of the flight back, so the crew is rested and ready to go. We'll top off our gas in New York and have you basking in the sun a mere seven hours after that."

Blake made the swift mental calculation. Three hours to New York. Seven hours to cross the Atlantic. Another hour or more to contact Madame LeBlanc and travel to the villa DI maintained in Provence. Eight hours' time difference.

He was used to transatlantic flights, but he suspected Grace would be dead by the time they arrived at their final destination. Just as well. She could use the next few days to rest and get used to the idea of marriage.

So could he, for that matter. He'd lined up all his arguments, pro and con, before he'd flown down to San Antonio. Then Grace had opened the door in those cut-offs and he'd damned near forgotten every one. Only now could he admit that the hunger she stirred had him twisted in as many knots as her refusal to trust him with the truth. Helluva foundation to build a marriage on, he conceded grimly as he put a hand to the small of her back to guide her up the stairs.

A Filipino steward in a white jacket met them at the hatch, his seamed face creased into a smile. "Welcome aboard, Mr. Blake. I sure wouldn't have bet we'd be flying both you and Mr. Alex on honeymoons in almost the same month."

"I wouldn't have bet on it, either, Eualdo. This is my wife, Grace."

He bowed over her hand with a dignity that matched his years. "It's an honor to meet you, Ms. Grace."

"Thank you."

"If you'll follow me, I'll show you to your seats."

Blake had spent so many in-flight hours aboard the Gulfstream he'd long since come to regard it more as a necessity than a luxury. Grace's gasp when she entered the cabin reminded him not everyone would view it that way.

The interior was normally configured with high-backed, lumbar-support seats and generous workstations in addition to the galley, head and sleeping quarters. For personal or pleasure trips like this, however, the workstations were moved together to form an elegant dining area and the seats repositioned into a comfortable sitting area.

"Good grief." She gazed wide-eyed at the gleaming teak paneling and dove-gray leather. "I hope Dalton International isn't paying for all this."

"You're married to DI's chief financial officer," Blake replied dryly. "You can trust me to maintain our personal expenses separate and distinct from corporate accounts."

She flushed a little, either at the reminder that they'd

just merged or at the unspoken reminder that she *wouldn't* trust him with other, more important matters.

The pink in her cheeks deepened when they passed the open door to the sleeping quarters. A quick glance inside showed the twin beds had been repositioned into a queen-size sleeper complete with down pillows, satiny sheets and a duvet with DI's logo embroidered in gold thread. Blake didn't have the least doubt that Julie and Alex had put those sheets to good use every moment they weren't in the cockpit.

Different couple, completely different circumstances. Blake and *his* bride wouldn't share that wide bed. The reality of the situation didn't block his thought of it, though. Swearing under his breath, Blake was hit with a sudden and all-too-vivid mental image of Grace stretched out with her arms raised languidly above her head, her breasts bare, her nipples turgid from his tongue and his teeth.

"I've got a bottle of Cristal on ice, Mr. Blake."

He blinked away the searing image and focused on Eualdo's weathered face.

"Shall I pour you and Ms. Grace a glass now or wait until after takeoff?"

A glance at his bride provided the answer. She had the slightly wild-eyed look of someone who was wondering just what kind of quicksand she'd stumbled into. She needed a drink or two to loosen her up. So did he. This looked to be a *long* flight.

It wound up lasting even longer than either Blake or the captain had anticipated. When they put down at a small commercial airstrip outside New York City to refuel, a thick, soupy fog rolled in off the Atlantic and delayed their departure for another two hours. The same front that produced the fog necessitated a more northerly route than originally planned.

By the time they gained enough altitude for Eualdo to serve dinner, Grace's shoulders were drooping. The steward's honey-crusted squab on a bed of wild rice and a bottle of perfectly chilled Riesling revived her enough for dessert. When darkness dropped like a stone outside the cabin windows, however, she dropped with it.

The first time her chin hit her chest, she jerked her head up and protested she was wide-awake. The second time, she gave up all attempt at pretense.

"I'm sorry." She dragged the back of her hand across her eyes. "I shouldn't have piled wine on top of champagne. I'm feeling the kick."

"Altitude probably has something to do with that."

Blake's calm reply gave no hint of his thoughts. He'd never seduced a tipsy female, but the idea was pretty damned tempting at the moment.

"It's been a long day. Why don't you go to bed?"

Her glance zinged to the rear of the cabin, shot back. "Aren't you tired?"

"Some." He put the last of his willpower into another smile. "But Eualdo's used to me working my way across the Atlantic."

"On your wedding night?"

He had no trouble interpreting the question behind the question. "He's been with Dalton International for more than a decade," he said calmly. "You don't need to worry about what he'll think. Or anyone else, for that matter."

Her glance dropped to her hands. She played with the band of diamonds, and he added getting the ring resized to his mental list of tasks to be accomplished when they returned to Oklahoma City.

"Go to bed, Grace."

Nodding, she unhooked her seat belt. Blake's hooded gaze followed her progress. When she disappeared inside the stateroom, he downed the dregs of his Riesling and reclined his seat back.

Well, Grace thought as she crawled between the sheets fifteen minutes later, she could imagine worse wedding nights. The social studies teacher in her had read enough ancient history to shudder at some of the barbaric marriage rites and rituals practiced in previous times.

In contrast, this night epitomized the ultimate in comfort and luxury. She was being whisked across an ocean in a private jet. She'd found every amenity she'd needed in the surprisingly spacious bathroom. The cotton sheets were so smooth and soft they felt like whipped cream against her skin. Two million stars winked outside the curved windows built into the bulwark. The only thing she needed to perfect the scene was a groom.

With a vengeance, all those play-wedding scenes she and her cousin had enacted as girls came back to haunt her. Hope's marriage had brought her nothing but heartache and fear. Grace's...

Oh, hell! Disgusted by her twinge of poor-me self-pity, she rolled over and thumped the pillow. She'd made her bed. She'd damned well lie in it.

Now if only she could stop with the nasty urge to march back into the main cabin and reopen negotiations. As Blake had so bluntly suggested, the sex was certainly doable. *More* than doable. The mere thought of his hard, muscled body stretched out beside her, his hands on her breasts, his mouth hot against hers, made the muscles low in Grace's belly tighten.

She clenched her legs, felt the swift pull between her thighs. Need, fierce and raw, curled through her. Her breath got shorter, faster.

This was stupid! Blake was sitting just a few yards away! Two steps to the stateroom door, one signal, silent or otherwise, and he'd join her.

Sex could be enough for now, she told herself savagely. She didn't need the shared laughter, the private smiles, the silly jokes married couples added to their storehouse of memories.

And it wasn't as though she'd arrived at this point unprepared. Teaching high school kids repeatedly reinforced basic truths, including the fact that each individual had to take responsibility for his or her protection during sex. Grace had seen too many bright, talented students' lives derailed by their biological urges. She wasn't into one-night stands and hadn't had a serious relationship in longer than she cared to admit, but she'd remained prepared, just in case.

So why not ease out of bed and take those two steps to the door? Why not give the signal? She and Blake were married, for God's sake!

She kicked off the sheet. Rolled onto a hip. Stopped. The problem was she *wanted* the shared smiles and silly jokes. *Needed* more than casual sex.

"Dammit!"

Disgusted, she flopped down and hammered the pillow again. She was a throwback. An anachronism. And thoroughly, completely frustrated.

She didn't remember drifting off, but the wine and champagne must indeed have gotten to her. She went completely out and woke to a knock on the stateroom door and blinding sunlight pouring through the window she'd forgotten to shade. She squinted owlishly at her watch, saw it was the middle of the night Texas time, and had to stifle a groan when another knock sounded.

"It's Eualdo, Ms. Grace. Mr. Blake said to let you know we're ninety minutes out."

"Okay, thanks."

"I'll serve breakfast in the main cabin when you're ready."

She emerged from the stateroom a short time later, showered and dressed in a pair of white crops and a gauzy, off-one-shoulder top in a flowery print. A chunky white bracelet added a touch of panache. She figured she would need that touch to get through her first morning-after meeting with her groom.

Blake unbuckled his seat belt and rose when she approached. Except for the discarded tie and open shirt collar, he didn't look like a man who'd sat up all night. Only when she got closer did she spot the gold bristles on his cheeks and chin.

"'Morning."

"Good morning," he answered with a smile. "Did you get any sleep?"

"I did." God! Could this be any more awkward? "How about you?"

"All I need is a shower and shave and I'll be good to go. Eualdo just brewed a fresh pot of coffee. I'll join you for breakfast as soon as I get out of the shower."

He started past her, then stopped. A rueful gleam lighting his eyes, he brushed a knuckle across her cheek.

"We'll figure this out, Grace. We just need to give it time."

* * *

Time, she repeated silently as the Gulfstream swooped low over a dazzling turquoise sea in preparation for landing. Despite her inner agitation, the sweeping view of the Mediterranean enchanted her.

So did the balmy tropical climate that greeted them. Grace had watched several movies and travel specials featuring the south of France. She'd also read a good number of books with the same setting, most recently a Dan Brown–type thriller that had the protagonists searching for a long-lost fragment of the Jesus's cross at the popes' sprawling palace in Avignon. None of the books or movies or travelogues prepared her for Provence's cloudless skies and brilliant sunshine, however. She held up a hand to block the rays as she deplaned, breathing in the briny tang of the sea that surrounded the Marseille airport.

A driver was waiting at the small aircraft terminal with a sporty red convertible. After he'd stashed their bags in the trunk, he made a polite inquiry in French. Blake responded with a smile and a nod.

"Oui."

"C'est bien. Bon voyage."

Grace glanced at him curiously as he slid behind the wheel. "You speak French?"

"Not according to Cecile."

Right. Cecile. The chef who owned the restaurant where Alex and Julie had hosted their rehearsal dinner. The gorgeous, long-legged chef who'd draped herself all over Blake. That display of Gallic exuberance hadn't bothered Grace at the time. Much. It did now. With some effort, she squashed the memory and settled into the convertible.

Blake got behind the wheel. He'd changed into khakis and a fresh shirt and hooked a pair of aviator sunglasses on his shirt pocket.

"Just out of curiosity," she commented as he slipped on the glasses, "where are we going?"

"Saint-Rémy-de-Provence. It's a small town about an hour north of here." A smile played at the corners of his mouth. "A nationwide transportation strike stranded Mother there during one of her antique-hunting trips about five years ago. She used the downtime to buy a crumbling villa and turn it into a vacation resort for top-performing DI employees and their families."

Grace had to grin. That sounded just like her employer. Correction, her mother-in-law. Delilah Dalton possessed more energy and drive than any six people her age.

"The place was occupied most recently by DI's top three welding teams and their families," he added casually. "But Madame LeBlanc indicated we'll have it to ourselves for the next two weeks."

Not so casually, Grace's heart thumped hard against her ribs. The combustible mix of lust and longing she'd had to battle last night had been bad enough. How the heck was she going to get through the next two weeks? Alone. With Blake. Under the hot Provencal sun and starry, starry nights.

Slowly she sank into her seat.

Six

A little over an hour later Blake turned off the auto-route onto a two-lane road shaded by towering sycamores. Their branches met overhead to form a green tunnel that stretched for miles. The rocky pinnacles of the Alpilles thrust out of the earth to the left of the road. Sun-drenched vineyards and olive groves rolled out on the right, flashing through the sycamores' white, scaly trunks like a DVD run in fast-forward.

As delightful as the approach to Saint-Rémy was, the town itself enchanted Grace even more. Eighteenth-century mansions that Blake called *hôtels* lined the busy street encircling the town proper. Dolphins spouted in a fountain marking one quadrant of the circle, stone goddesses poured water from urns at another. In the pedestrians-only heart of the town, Grace caught glimpses of narrow lanes crammed with shops and open-air restaurants that invited patrons to sit and sip a cappuccino.

Blake noticed her craning her neck to peer down the intriguing alleyways. "We'll have lunch in town," he promised.

"I'd like that."

She studied her groom as he negotiated the busy street. He fit perfectly against this elegant eighteenth-century backdrop, Grace decided. The corporate executive had shed his suit and tie but not his sophistication. Sunlight glinted on the sleek watch banding his wrist and the light dusting of golden hair on his forearm. The aviator sunglasses and hand-tailored shirt left open at the neck to show the tanned column of his throat only added to the image.

"Madame LeBlanc will meet us at Hôtel des Elmes," he added as he skillfully wove through pedestrians, tourists and traffic.

She took a stab at a translation. "The Elms?"

"The Elms," he confirmed. "It used to be called the Hôtel Saint Jacques. Legend has it that the original owner claimed to have invented, or at least improved on, the scallop dish named in Saint James's honor."

Grace had to think for a moment. "Aha! Coquilles St. Jacques!"

"Right. You'll be pleased to know the current chef at the *hôtel* has followed in his predecessors' footsteps. Auguste's scallops au gratin will make you think you hear heavenly choirs."

The easy banter took them up to a pair of tall, wrought-iron gates left open in anticipation of their arrival. Once inside, Grace understood instantly the inspiration for the villa's new designation. Majestic elms that must have been planted more than a century ago formed a graceful arch above a crushed-stone drive. The curving drive wound through landscaped grounds dot-

ted with statuary and vine-shaded arbors, then ended in
a circle dominated by a twenty-foot fountain featuring
bronze steeds spouting arcs of silvery water.

And looming beyond the fountain was a masterpiece
in mellowed gray stone. The Hôtel des Elmes consisted
of a three-story central wing, with two-story wings on
each side. Wisteria vines softened its elaborate stone facade, drooping showy purple blossoms from wrought-
iron trellises. Grace breathed in the purple blossoms'
spicy vanilla scent as Blake braked to a stop.

The front door opened before he'd killed the engine.
The woman who emerged fit Grace's mental image of
the quintessential older French female—slender, charming, impossibly chic in silky black slacks and a cool
linen blouse.

"Bienvenue à Saint-Rémy, Monsieur Blake."

"It's good to be back," he replied in English.

After the obligatory cheek kissing, he introduced
Grace. She must have been getting used to being presented as his wife. She barely squirmed when Madame
LeBlanc grasped both her hands and offered a profuse
welcome.

"I am most happy to meet you." Madame's smile
took a roguish tilt. "Delilah has long despaired of getting her so-handsome sons to the altar. One can only
imagine how thrilled she must be that Alex and Blake
have taken brides within a month of each other. *Quelle
romantique!*"

"Yes, well…"

Blake's arm slid around Grace's waist. *"Trés romantique."*

His casual comment fed the fantasy of a honeymoon couple. Madame LeBlanc sighed her approval
and handed him a set of tagged keys.

"As you instructed, the staff will not report until to-morrow, but Auguste has prepared several dishes should you wish them. They need only to be reheated. And the upstairs maid has made up the bed in the Green Suite and left for the rest of the day. You will not be disturbed."

"Merci."

If the villa's grounds and exquisite eighteenth-century exterior evoked visions of aristocrats in silks and powered wigs, the interior had obviously been retro-fitted for twenty-first-century visitors. Grace spotted high-tech security cameras above the doors and an alarm panel just inside the entryway that looked as if it would take an MIT grad to program. The brass-accented elevator tucked discreetly behind a screen of potted palms was also a modern addition.

While Grace peeked around, Blake carried in their few bags and deposited them in the marbled foyer. "Would you like the ten-cent tour, or would you rather go upstairs and rest for a while first?"

"The tour, please! Unless…" Guilt tripped her. "I'm sorry. I zoned out on the plane, but you didn't. You're probably aching for bed."

Something shifted in his face. A mere ripple of skin across muscle and bone. Grace didn't have time to in-terpret the odd look before he masked it.

"I'm good." He made an exaggerated bow and swept an arm toward the central hall. "This way, madame."

Grace soon lost count of the downstairs rooms. There was the petite salon, the grand salon, the music room, the library, the card room, an exquisitely mirrored ball-room and several banquet and eating areas in addition to the kitchens and downstairs powder rooms. Each con-tained a mix of antiques and ultramodern conveniences cleverly integrated into an elegant yet inviting whole. Even the painted porcelain sinks in the powder rooms evoked an eighteenth-century feel, and the copper-and-spice-filled kitchen could accommodate cooks of all ages and eras.

The pool house with its marble columns and bougainvillea-draped pergola was a Greek fantasy come to life. The shimmering turquoise water in the pool made Grace itch to shed her clothes on the spot and dive in. But when they went back inside again and started for the stairs to the second floor, it was the painting of deep purple irises displayed in a lighted alcove that stopped her dead.

"Ooooh!" Grace was no art expert, but even she could recognize a Van Gogh when it smacked her between the eyes. "I have a poster of this same painting in my bedroom."

Blake paused behind her. "That's one of my mother's favorites, too. She donated the original to the Smithsonian's Museum of Modern Art but had this copy commissioned for the villa."

He was only an inch or two from her shoulder. So close she felt his breath wash warm and soft against her ear. The sensation zinged down her spine and stirred a reaction that almost made her miss Blake's next comment.

"This is one of the more than one hundred and fifty paintings Van Gogh painted during his year in Saint-Rémy. There's a walking tour that shows the various scenes he incorporated into his works. We can take it if you like."

"I would!"

The possibility of viewing sunflowers and olive groves through the eyes of one of the world's greatest artists tantalized Grace. Almost as much as the idea of viewing them with Blake.

Hard on that came the realization that she had no clue if her new husband was the least bit interested in impressionist art. Or what kind of music he preferred. Or how he spent his downtime when he wasn't doing his executive/corporate lawyer thing. She'd known him such a short time. And during those weeks he, his twin and his indomitable parent had focused exclusively on Molly and the hunt for the baby's mother.

Could be this enforced honeymoon wasn't such a bad idea after all. The main participants in every partnership, even a marriage of convenience, needed to establish a working relationship. Maybe Delilah had their best interests at heart when she'd arranged this getaway.

Maybe. It was hard to tell what really went on in the woman's Machiavellian mind. Withholding judgment, Grace accompanied Blake on a tour of the second story. He pointed out several fully contained guest suites, two additional salons, a reading room, even a video game room for the children of the Dalton employees and other guests who stayed at the *hôtel*. At the end of the hall, he opened a set of double doors fitted with gold-plated latches.

"This is the master suite." His mouth took a wry tilt. "Otherwise known as the Green Suite."

Grace could certainly see why! Awed, she let her gaze travel from floor-to-ceiling silk wall panels to elegantly looped drapes to the thick duvet and dozens of tasseled pillows mounded on the four-poster bed. They were all done in a shimmering, iridescent brocade that shaded from moss-green to dark jade depending on the angle of the light streaming through the French doors. The bed itself was inlaid mahogany chased with gold.

Lots of gold. So were the bombe chests and marble-topped tables scattered throughout the suite.

"Wow!" Mesmerized by the opulence, she spun in a slow circle. "This looks like Louis XV might have slept here."

"There's no record the king ever made it down," Blake returned with a grin, "but one of his mistresses reportedly entertained another of her lovers here on the sly."

Grace couldn't decide which hit with more of a wallop, that quick grin or the instant and totally erotic image his comment stirred. As vividly as any painting, she could picture a woman in white silk stockings, ribboned garters and an unlaced corset lolling against the four-poster's mounds of pillows. A bare-chested courtier with Blake Dalton's guinea-gold hair leaned over her. His blue eyes glinted with wicked promise as he slowly slid one of her garters from her thigh to her knee to her…

"…the adjoining suite."

Blinking, she zoomed out of the eighteenth century. "Sorry. I was, uh, thinking of powdered wigs and silk knee breeches. What did you say?"

"I said I'll be in the adjoining suite."

The last of the delicious image fizzled as Grace watched her husband open a connecting door. The bedroom beyond wasn't as large or as decadent as that of the Green Suite, but it did boast another four-poster and a marble fireplace big enough to roast an ox.

"It's almost noon Saint-Rémy time," Blake said after a quick glance at his watch. "If you're not too jet-lagged, we could reconvene in a half hour and walk into town for lunch."

"That works for me."

Calling herself an idiot for staring at the door long after it closed behind him, Grace extracted her toiletries from her tote bag and carried them into a bathroom fit for a queen. Or at least a royal mistress.

Maybe it was the glorious sun that sucked away her sense of awkwardness. Or the lazy, protracted lunch she and Blake shared at a dime-size table cornered next to a bubbling fountain. Or the two glasses of perfectly chilled rosé produced by a vineyard right outside Saint-Rémy.

Then again, it might have been Blake's obvious efforts to keep the conversation light and noncontroversial. He made no reference to the circumstances of their marriage or Grace's adamant refusal to betray her cousin's trust. As a consequence, she felt herself relaxing for the first time in longer than she could remember.

The still-raw ache of her cousin's death shifted to a corner of her heart. Jack Petrie, Oklahoma City, even Molly moved off center stage. Not completely, and certainly not for long. Yet these hours in the sun provided a hiatus from the worry she'd carted around for so many months. That was the only excuse she could come up with later for the stupidity that followed.

It happened during the walk back to their *hôtel*. Blake indulged her with a stroll through the town's pedestrian-only center, stopping repeatedly while she oooh'ed and aaaah'ed over shop windows displaying Provence's wares. One window was filled with colorful baskets containing every imaginable spice and herb. Another specialized in soaps and scented oils. *Hundreds* of soaps and oils. Delighted, Grace went inside and sniffed at products made from apple pear, lemon, peony, vanilla, honey almond and, of course, lavender. A dazzling display of stoppered vials offered bath oils and lotions in a rainbow of hues.

The clerk obviously knew her business. She sized up the diamonds circling Grace's finger in a single glance. With a knowing look, she produced a cut-crystal vial from a shelf behind the counter.

"Madame must try this. It is a special blend made only for our shop."

When she removed the stopper, an exquisitely delicate aroma drifted across the counter. Lavender and something else that Grace couldn't quite identify.

"The perfumers extract oil from the buds before they blossom. The fragrance is light, *oui?* So very light and yet, how do you say? So *sensuelle*."

She waved the stopper in the air to release more of its bouquet. Grace leaned forward, breathing deeply. She knew then that whatever else happened in this marriage, she would always associate the scent of lavender with sunshine and brilliant skies and the smile crinkling the skin at the corners of Blake's eyes as he watched her sniffing the air.

He didn't remain an observer for long. Sensing a sale, the shopkeeper dipped the stopper again. "Here, *monsieur,* you must dab some on your wife's wrist. The oil takes on a richer tone when applied to the skin."

With a good-natured nod, Blake took the stopper in one hand and reached for Grace's wrist with the other. His hold was loose, easy. As light as it was, though, the touch sent a ripple of pleasure along her nerves. The ripple swelled to a tidal wave when he raised her arm to a mere inch or so from his nose.

"She's right," he murmured. The blue in his eyes deepened as he caught Grace's gaze. "The warmth of your skin deepens the scent."

Warmth? Ha! She'd passed mere warmth the moment his fingers circled her wrist. And if he kept looking at her like that, she suspected she would spontaneously combust in the next five seconds.

Thankfully, the shop clerk claimed his attention. The distraction proved only temporary, however. Eager for a sale, the woman urged another test.

"Dab a little dab behind your wife's ear, *monsieur*. It is of all places the most seductive."

Grace's internal alarm went off like a klaxon. Every scrap of common sense she possessed urged her to decline the second sample. The sun and the wine and this man's touch were bringing her too close to the melting point. So she was damned if she knew why she just stood there and let Blake brush aside her hair.

The crystal stopper was cool and damp against the skin just below her earlobe. An instant later, her husband's breath seared that same patch of skin. Their only physical contact point was the hand caging back her hair. If the shock that went though her was any indication, however, they might have been locked together at chest and hip and thigh. Thoroughly shaken, Grace took a step back.

The abrupt move brought Blake's head up with a snap. He didn't need to see the confusion on his wife's face to know he'd crossed the line.

The line he'd been stupid enough to draw! He was the one who'd assured her they would work things out. He'd spouted that inane drivel about giving their arrangement time.

To hell with waiting. He ached to drag Grace out of the shop, hustle her back to The Elms and strip her down to the warm, perfumed flesh that was sending his senses into dangerous overload.

"Monsieur?"

The shop clerk's voice cut through his red haze. Before Blake could bring the woman into focus, he had to exercise the iron will that allowed him to appear calm before judges and juries.

She finally appeared, smiling and eager. "Do you wish to purchase a vial for your so-lovely wife?"

God, yes!

At his nod, she whipped out a sales slip. "Do you stay here in Saint-Rémy?"

He knew his address would up the asking price by at least half but was beyond caring. "We're at Hôtel des Elmes."

Her glance sharpened. "Ahhh. I recognize you now. You came to Saint-Rémy last year, *oui?* With… Er…" She broke off, then recovered after an infinitesimal pause. "With your so very charming mother."

Riiiight. Blake seriously doubted his twin had timed a visit to the villa to coincide with one of their mother's protracted stays. Alex and Delilah were both obviously well-known in town, however, so he didn't bother to correct the clerk's misconception.

"We'll take a bottle of that scent."

Beaming, she rattled off the price for a three-ounce bottle. He was reaching for his money clip when Grace gave a strangled gasp.

"Did you say two hundred euros?"

"Oui, madame."

"Two *hundred* euros?"

"Oui."

"That's like…"

Blake paused in the act of peeling off several euro notes while she did the mental math.

"Good grief! That's almost three hundred dollars

U.S." Horrified, she closed her hand over his. "That's too much."

A pained look crossed the salesclerk's face. "You will not find a more distinctive or more delicate scent in all Provence. And…"

Her glance cut to Blake. When she turned back to Grace, a conspiratorial smile tilted her lips.

"If I may say so, madame, your husband does not purchase this fragrance for you. He is the one who will detect its essence on your skin. If it pleases him…"

Her shoulders lifted in that most Gallic of all gestures, and Grace could only watch helplessly as Blake dropped the euro notes on the counter.

Seven

Even with Grace's seductive scent delivering a broadside every time Blake turned his head or leaned toward her, he didn't plan what happened when they returned to the villa. His conscience would always remain clear on that point. When he suggested a swim, his only intent was to continue the easy camaraderie established during lunch.

What he *hadn't* anticipated was the kick to his gut when Grace joined him poolside and slipped off her terry cloth cover-up. He'd already done a half dozen laps but wasn't the least winded until the sight of her slender, seductive curves sucked the air from his lungs.

"How's the water?"

Blake tried to untangle his tongue. Damned thing felt like it was wrapped in cotton wool. "Cool at first," he got out after an epic struggle. "Not so bad once you're in."

Oh, for God's sake! Her suit was a poppy-colored

one-piece that covered more than it revealed. Yet he was damned if he could stop his gaze from devouring the slopes of her breasts when she bent to deposit her towel on the lounger. That unexpected jolt was followed by another when she turned to dip a toe in the water and gave him an unimpeded view of the curve of her bottom cheeks.

"Yikes!" She jerked her foot back with a yelp and zinged him an indignant look. "You think this is *cool?* What's your definition of *cold?* Minus forty?"

He grinned and tread water as she dipped another cautious toe. Her face screwed into a grimace. She inched down a step, her shoulders hunched almost to her ears. Eased onto the next step. The water swirled around her calves, her thighs.

"Coward," he teased.

She took another tentative step, and his grin slipped. The water lapped the lower edge of her suit. The bright red material dampened at the apex of her thighs and provided a throat-closing outline of what lay beneath.

"Oh, hell."

He barely heard her mutter of self-disgust. Or felt the splash when she gathered her courage and flopped all the way in. She bobbed up a moment later, her hair a sleek waterfall of pale gold. Sparkling drops beaded her lashes. Laughter lit her eyes.

Something inside Blake shifted. He didn't see the woman who'd lied to him and his family by omission, or the conspirator who'd withheld crucial information about the mother of his child. There were no shadows haunting the eyes of this laughing, splashing water sprite. For the moment at least, no memories constrained her simple pleasure. It was a glimpse of the woman Grace must have been before she took on the burden of her cousin's secrets. An even more tantalizing hint of the woman who might reemerge if and when she shed that burden.

Without conscious thought, Blake realigned his priorities. Convincing his bride to trust him remained his primary goal. Getting her into bed ran a close second. But keeping that carefree laughter in her eyes was fast elbowing its way up close to the top of the list.

"All right," she gasped, dancing on her toes. "I'm in. When does it get to 'not so bad'?"

"Do a couple laps. You'll warm up quick enough."

She made a face but took his suggestion. He rolled into an easy breaststroke and kept pace with her. She had a smooth, clean stroke, he noted with approval, a nice kick. Two laps turned into three, then four. Or what would have been four.

She made the turn, pushed off the wall at an angle and submarined into him. They went under in a tangle of arms and legs. She came up sputtering. He came up with his bride plastered against his chest.

"Sorry!"

Blinking the water out of her eyes, she clung to him. They were at the deep end, in well over their heads. Literally, Blake thought, as her thighs scissored between his. Maybe figuratively.

Hell, there was no maybe about it. He wanted her with a raw need he didn't try to analyze. She must have seen it in his face, felt his muscles tighten under her slick, slippery hands. She looked up at him with a question in her eyes.

"According to our contract," he got out on a near rasp, "any and all physical contact must be by mutual consent. If you don't want this to go any further, you'd better say so now."

After a pause that just about ripped out Blake's guts, she clamped her lips shut and matched him look for look. With another growl, he claimed her mouth.

The kiss was swift and hot and hungry. If he'd interpreted her silence wrong, if she'd tried to push away, Blake would've released her. He was almost sure of that. She didn't, thank God, and he threw off every vestige of restraint.

They went under again, mouths and bodies fused. When they resurfaced, Blake kept her pinned, gave two swift kicks and took them to the wall. He flattened her against the tiles, using one hand to hold them both up while he attacked one strap of her suit with the other. The skin of her shoulder was soft and cool and slick. The mingled scents of lavender and chlorine acted like a spur, turning hunger into greed.

He switched hands, yanked down the other strap. She was as anxious now to shuck her bathing suit as he was to get her out of it. A wiggle, a shimmy, a kick, and it was gone. His followed two heartbeats later.

Her breast fit perfectly in his palm. The flesh was firm and smooth, the tip already stiff from the cold water. He rolled the nipple between his thumb and forefinger and damned near lost it when she arched her back to give him access to her other breast. He hiked her up a few inches, devouring her with teeth and tongue while he slicked his hand down her belly.

"Oh, God!"

Moaning, Grace threw her head back. She'd agreed to this. Had spent more than a few hours tossing around the idea of casual sex with this man. But this—this was nowhere near casual! Blake's mouth scorched her breasts, her shoulder, her throat. And her heart almost jumped out of her chest when he curved his fingers over her mound and parted her crease. She moaned again as he thrust into her and, to her utter mortification, exploded.

The orgasm ripped through her. She rode it blindly, mindlessly, until the spasms died and she flopped like a wet rag doll against his chest.

The thunder in her ears didn't subside. If anything, it grew louder. Only gradually did Grace realize that was Blake's heart tattooing against her ear. Gathering her shattered senses, she raised her head and curved her lips.

The skin at the corners of his blues eyes crinkled as he started to return her smile. Then she wrapped her legs around his hips and his expression froze. Slowly, sensually, she lifted her hips, positioning herself.

"Wait," he got out on a strangled grunt. "We need to take this inside."

"Why?"

"Protection. You need pro…" He broke off, hissing as she angled her hips. "Grace…"

He didn't say it, but she guessed he was thinking of Molly. She certainly was.

"It's okay," she said, breathless and urgent. "I'm covered."

He reacted to that bit of news with gratifying speed. Planting a foot against the tiles, he propelled them toward the shallow end. The sparkling water cascaded over his shoulders and chest as he took a wide stance and hefted her bottom with both palms.

A fresh wave of desire coiled deep in Grace's belly. Eager to give him some of the explosive pleasure he'd given her, she wrapped her legs around his waist. She didn't want slow. Didn't want gentle. When he thrust into her, she slapped her hips into his and clenched every muscle in her body.

He held out longer than she had. Much longer. Grace was close to losing control again when his fingers dug into her bottom cheeks. He went rigid and jammed her against him at an angle that put exquisite, unbearable pressure right where she wanted it the most. With a ragged groan, she arched into another shuddering, shattering climax. This time she took him with her.

Jet lag, a lack of sleep and the most intense sex he'd ever had combined to plow into Blake like an Abrams tank. He remembered helping Grace out of the water and savoring the view before she wrapped herself in one of the villa's blue-and-white-striped pool towels. He vaguely recalled diving back in to retrieve their bathing suits. He wasn't sure whether he'd suggested they stretch out in one of the loungers inside the vine-covered pergola, or she had. But the next time he opened his eyes, the sun had disappeared and hundreds of tiny white lights made a fairyland of the pool area.

He sat up, blinking, and scraped a hand across a sandpaper chin. The movement drew the attention of the woman on the lounger beside his.

"What time is it?" he asked, his voice still thick with sleep.

"I'm not sure. My internal clock is still set to Texas time." She glanced at the canopy of stars outside the pergola. "I'm guessing it's probably nine or nine-thirty."

Blake winced. Great! Absolutely great! Nothing demonstrated a man's virility like taking four or five hours to recharge after sex.

"Sorry I passed out on you."

"No problem." His obvious chagrin had a smile hovering at the corners of her mouth. "I napped, too."

Not for long, apparently. She'd used some of the time he was out cold to change into khaki shorts and a scoop-necked T-shirt. Her hair looked freshly washed, its shining length caught up in a plastic clip.

"Have you eaten?"

"I was waiting for you."

He was still in the swim trunks he'd brought up from the pool. They were dry now and rode low on his hips as he pushed off the lounger and reached out to help her up.

"Let's go raid the kitchen."

The hesitation before she took his hand was so brief he might have imagined it. He couldn't miss the constraint that kept her silent, though, once they'd settled in high-backed wrought-iron stools at the kitchen's monster, green-tiled island. As Madame LeBlanc had indicated, the chef had left a gourmand's dream of sumptuous choices in the fridge and on the counters. Grace opted for a bowl of cold, spicy gazpacho and a chunk of bread torn from one of the long, crusty baguettes poking out of a wire basket. Blake poured them both a glass of light, fruity chardonnay before heaping his plate with salad Niçoise and a man-size wedge of asparagus-and-goat-cheese quiche warmed in the microwave.

He forked down several bites of salad, savoring its red, ripe tomatoes and anchovies, eyeing Grace as she played with her bread, waiting for her to break the small silence. He had a good idea what was behind her sudden constraint. Morning-after nerves, or in this case, evening-after.

She validated his guess a few moments later. Drawing in a deep breath, she tackled the thorny subject head-on. "About what happened in the pool…"

He sensed what was coming and wasn't about to make it easy for her. "What about it?"

"I know we put the possibility of sex on the table when we negotiated this, uh, partnership."

"But?"

She looked down, crumbled her bread, met his gaze again. "But things just spun out of control. I'm as much to blame as you are," she added quickly. "Now that I've had time to think, though, it was too quick, Blake. Too fast."

"We'll take it slower next time."

The solemn promise almost won a smile.

"I *meant* it was too soon. I'm still trying to adjust to this whole marriage business."

"I know." Serious now, he laid down his fork. "But let's clarify one matter. Things didn't just spin out of control. I wanted you, Grace."

Color tinted her cheeks. "I'll concede that point, counselor. And it was obvious I wanted you."

"I understand this is an adjustment period for you, however. For both of us. We've a lot yet to learn about each other."

The deliberate reference to her hoard of secrets brought her chin up. "Exactly. Which is why we should avoid a repetition of what happened this afternoon until you're comfortable with who I am and vice versa."

What the hell would it take to get her to trust him? Irritation put a bite in Blake's voice. "So we just revert back to cool and polite? You think it'll be that easy?"

"No," she admitted, "but necessary if this arrangement of ours is going to work."

He swallowed the bitter aftertaste of anchovies and frustration. "All right. We'll take hot, wild sex off the agenda. For now."

* * *

Grace spent the second night of her honeymoon the same way she had her first, restless and conflicted and alone.

While moonlight streamed through windows left open to a soft night breeze, she punched the mounded pillow and replayed the scene in the kitchen. She'd been right to put the brakes on. The way she'd flamed in Blake's arms, lost every ounce of rational thought... She'd never gone so mindless with hunger before. Never craved a man's touch and the wild sensation of his hard, sculpted body crushing hers.

She'd had time to think while Blake dozed this afternoon, and the fact that she'd abandoned herself so completely had shaken her. Still shook her! She'd witnessed firsthand the misery her cousin endured, for God's sake. Had helped Anne run, hide, struggle painfully to regain her confidence and self-respect. Grace couldn't just throw off the brutal burden of those months and years. Nor could she dump it on Blake's broad, willing shoulders—much as she ached to.

No, she was right to pull back. Revert to cool and polite, to use his phrase. They both needed time to adjust to this awkward marriage before they took the next step. Whatever the heck that was.

It took a severe exercise of will, but she managed to block the mental image of Blake pinning her to the tiles and drop into sleep.

She remained firm in her resolve to back things up a step when she went down for breakfast the next morning.

The villa's staff had obviously reported for duty. The heavenly scent of fresh-baked bread wafted from the direction of the kitchen, and a maid in a pale blue uniform wielded a feather duster like a baton at the foot of the stairs. Her eyes lit with curiosity and a friendly welcome when she spotted Grace.

"*Bonjour,* Madame Dalton."

"*Bonjour.*"

That much Grace could manage. The quick spate that followed had her offering an apology.

"I'm sorry. I don't speak French."

"Ah, *excusez-moi.* I am Marie. The downstairs maid, yes? I am most happy to meet you."

"Thank you. It's nice to meet you, too."

She hesitated, not exactly embarrassed but not real eager to admit she didn't have a clue where her husband of two days might be. Luckily, Blake had primed the staff with the necessary information.

"Monsieur Dalton said to tell you that he takes coffee on the east terrace," Marie informed her cheerfully. "He waits for you to join him for breakfast."

"And the east terrace is…?"

"Just there, madame." She aimed the feather duster. "Through the petite salon."

"Thanks."

She crossed the salon's exquisitely thick carpet and made for a set of open French doors that gave onto a flagstone terrace enclosed by ivy-drenched stone walls. A white wrought-iron table held a silver coffee service and a basket of brioche. Blake held his Blackberry and was working the keyboard one-handed while he sipped from a gold-rimmed china cup with the other.

Grace stopped just inside the French doors to drag in several deep breaths. She needed them. The sight of her husband in the clear, shimmering light of a Provencal morning was something to behold. A stray sunbeam snuck through the elms shading the patio to gild his hair. His crisp blue shirt was open at the neck and rolled at the cuffs. He looked calm and collected and too gorgeous for words, dammit!

She sucked in another breath and stepped out onto the patio. "Good morning."

He set down both his coffee cup and the Blackberry and rose.

"Good morning." The greeting was as courteous and impersonal as his smile. "Did you sleep well?"

Right. Okay. This was how she wanted it. What she'd insisted on.

"Very well," she lied. "You?"

"As well as could be expected after yesterday afternoon."

When she flashed a warning look, he shed his polite mask and hooked a brow.

"I zoned out for a good four hours on that lounge chair," he reminded her. "As a consequence, I didn't need much sleep last night."

And if she bought that one, Blake thought sardonically, he had several more he could sell her.

He didn't have to sell them. The swift way she broke eye contact told him she suspected he was stretching the truth until it damned near screamed.

She had to know she'd kept him awake most of the night. She, and her absurd insistence they ignore the wildfire they'd sparked yesterday. As if they could. The heat of it still singed Blake's mind and burned in his gut.

In the small hours of the night he'd called himself every kind of an idiot for agreeing to this farcical facade. It made even less sense in the bright light of morning. They couldn't shove yesterday in a box, stick it on the closet shelf and pretend it never happened. Yet he *had* agreed, and now he was stuck with it.

It didn't improve his mood to discover she'd dabbed on some of the perfumed oil he'd bought her yesterday. The provocative scent tugged at his senses as he pulled out one of the heavy wrought-iron chairs for her.

"Why don't you pour yourself some coffee and I'll tell Auguste we're ready for... Ah, here he is."

At first glance few people would tag the individual who appeared in the open French doors as a graduate of Le Cordon Bleu and two-time winner of the *Coupe du Monde de la Patisserie*—the World Cup of pastry. He sported stooped shoulders, sparse gray hair and a hound-dog face with dewlaps that hung in mournful folds. If he'd cracked a smile anytime in the past two years, Blake sure hadn't seen it.

The great Auguste had been retired for a decade and, according to Delilah, going out of his gourd with boredom when she'd hunted him down. After subjecting the poor man to the full force of her personality, she'd convinced him to take over the kitchen of Hôtel des Elmes.

Blake had made his way to the kitchen earlier to say hello. He now introduced the chef to Grace. Auguste bowed over her hand and greeted her in tones of infinite sadness.

"I welcome you to Saint-Rémy."

Gulping, she threw Blake a what-in-the-world-did-I-do look? He stepped in smoothly.

"I've told Grace about your scallops au gratin, Auguste. Perhaps you'll prepare them for us one evening."

"But of course." He heaved a long-suffering sigh and turned his doleful gaze back to Grace. "Tonight, if you wish it, madame."

"That would be wonderful. Thank you."

"And now I shall prepare the eggs Benedict for you and *monsieur,* yes?"

"Er, yes. Please."

He bowed again and retreated, shoulders drooping. Grace followed his exit with awed eyes.

"Did someone close to him just die?" she whispered to Blake.

The question broke the ice that had crusted between them. Laughing, Blake went back to his own seat.

"Not that I know of. In fact, you're seeing him in one of his more cheerful moods."

"Riiight."

With a doubtful glance at the French doors, she spread her napkin across her lap. He waited until she'd filled a cup with rich, dark brew to offer the basket of fresh-baked brioche.

"We've got dinner taken care of," he said as she slathered on butter and thick strawberry jam. "What would you like to do until then?"

She sent him a quick look, saw he hadn't packed some hidden meaning into the suggestion, and relaxed into her first genuine smile of the morning.

"You mentioned a Van Gogh trail. I'd love to explore that, if you're up for it."

Resolutely, Blake suppressed the memory of his mother ruthlessly dragging Alex and him along every step of the route commemorating Saint-Rémy's most famous artist.

"I'm up for it."

Eight

Grace couldn't have asked for a more perfect day to explore. Sometime while they'd been over the Atlantic, August had rolled into September. The absolute best time to enjoy Provence's balmy breezes and dazzling sunshine, Blake assured her as the sporty red convertible crunched down the front drive. It was still warm enough for her to be glad she'd opted for linen slacks and a cap-sleeved black T-shirt with I ♥ Texas picked out in sparkly rhinestones. She'd caught her hair back in a similarly adorned ball cap to keep the ends from whipping her face.

Blake hadn't bothered with a hat, but his mirrored aviation sunglasses protected his eyes from the glare. With his blue shirt open at the neck and the cuffs rolled up on his forearms, he looked cool and comfortable and too damned sexy for his own or Grace's good.

"I wasn't sure how much you know about Vincent

van Gogh," he said with a sideways glance, "so I printed off a short bio while you were getting ready."

"Thanks." She gratefully accepted the folded page he pulled out of his shirt pocket. "I went to a traveling exhibit at the San Antonio Museum of Art that featured several of his sketches a few years ago. I don't know much about the man himself, though, except that he was Dutch and disturbed enough to cut off his left ear."

"He was certainly disturbed, but there's some dispute over whether he deliberately hacked off his ear or lost it in the scuffle when he went after his pal Gauguin with a straight razor."

While Blake navigated shaded streets toward the outskirts of Saint-Rémy, Grace absorbed the details in the life of the brilliant, tormented artist who killed himself at the age of thirty-seven.

"It says here Van Gogh only sold one painting during his lifetime and died thinking himself a failure. How sad."

"Very sad," Blake agreed.

"Especially since his self-portrait is listed here as one of the ten most expensive paintings ever sold," Grace read, her eyes widening. "It went for $71 million in 1998."

"Which would equate to about $90 million today, adjusted for inflation."

"Good grief!"

She couldn't imagine paying that kind of money for anything short of a supersonic jet transport. Then she remembered the painting of the irises at the villa, and Blake's casual comment that his mother had donated the original to the Smithsonian.

She'd known the Daltons operated in a rarified financial atmosphere, of course. She'd lived in Delilah's

rambling Oklahoma City mansion for several months
and assisted her with some of her pet charity projects.
She'd also picked up bits and pieces about the various
megadeals Alex and Blake had in the works at DI. And
she'd certainly gotten a firsthand taste of the luxury
she'd married into during the flight across the Atlantic
and at the Hôtel des Elmes. But for some reason the idea
of forking over eighty or ninety million for a painting
made it all seem surreal.

Her glance dropped to the diamonds banding her
finger. They were certainly real enough. A whole lot
more real than the union they supposedly symbolized.
Although yesterday, at the pool...

No! Better not go there! She'd just get all confused
and conflicted again. Best just to enjoy the sun and the
company of the intriguing man she'd married.

A flash of white diverted her attention to the right
side of the road. Eyes popping, she stared at a massive
arch and white marble tower spearing up toward the
sky. "What are those?"

"They're called *Les Antiques*. They're the most visible remnants of the Roman town of Glanum that once
occupied this site. The rest of the ruins are a little farther down the road. We'll save exploring them for another day."

He turned left instead of right and drove down a tree-
shaded lane bordered on one side by a vacant field and
on the other by tall cypresses and the twisted trunks of
an olive grove. Beyond the grove the rocky spine of the
Alpilles slashed across the horizon.

"Here we are."

"Here," Grace discovered, was the Saint-Paul de
Mausole Asylum, which Van Gogh had voluntarily entered in May 1889. Behind its ivy-covered gray stone

walls she glimpsed a church tower and a two- or three-story rectangular building.

"Saint-Paul's was originally an Augustine monastery," Blake explained as he maneuvered into a parking space next to two tour buses. "Built in the eleventh or twelfth century, I think. It was converted to an asylum in the 1800s and is still used as a psychiatric hospital. The hospital is off-limits, of course, but the church, the cloister and the rooms where Van Gogh lived and painted are open to the public."

A very interested public, it turned out. The tour buses had evidently just disgorged their passengers. Guides shepherded their charges through the gates and up to the ticket booth. After the chattering tourists clicked through the turnstile single file, Blake paid for two entries and picked up an informational brochure but caught Grace's elbow once they'd passed through the turnstile.

"Let them get a little way ahead. You'll want to experience some of the tranquility Van Gogh did when he was allowed outside to paint."

She had no problem dawdling. The path leading to the church and other buildings was long and shady and lined on both sides by glossy rhododendron and colorful flowers. Adding to her delight, plaques spaced along the walk highlighted a particular view and contrasted it with Van Gogh's interpretation of that same scene.

A depiction of one of his famous sunflower paintings was displayed above a row of almost identical bright yellow flowers nodding in the sun. A low point in the wall provided a sweeping view of silvery-leafed olive trees dominated by the razor-backed mountain peaks in the distance. Van Gogh's version of that scene was done with his signature intense colors and short, bold brushstrokes. Fascinated, Grace stood before the plaque and glanced repeatedly from the trees' gnarled, twisted trunks to the artist's interpretation.

"This is amazing!" she breathed. "It's like stepping into a painting and seeing everything that went into it through different eyes."

She lingered at that plaque for several moments before meandering down the shady path to the next. Blake followed, far more interested in her reaction to Van Gogh's masterpieces than the compositions themselves.

She was like one of the scenes the artist had painted, he mused. She'd come into his life shortly after Molly had, but he'd been so absorbed with the baby it had taken weeks for him to see her as something more than a quietly efficient nanny. The attraction had come slowly and built steadily, but the shock of learning that she'd deceived him—deceived them all—had altered the picture considerably. As had the annoying realization that he'd missed her as much as Molly had when she'd left Oklahoma City.

Yet every time he thought he had a handle on the woman, she added more layers, more bold brushstrokes to the composite. Her fierce loyalty to her cousin and refusal to betray Anne's trust irritated Blake to no end but he reluctantly, grudgingly respected her for it.

And Christ almighty! Yesterday's heat. That searing desire. He knew where his had sprung from. His hunger had been building since... Hell, he couldn't fix the exact point. He only knew that yesterday had stoked the need instead of satisfying it.

Now he'd found another layer to add to the mix—a woman in a black T-shirt and ball cap thoroughly enjoying the view of familiar images from a completely different perspective, just as Blake was viewing her. How many variations of her were there left to discover?

The question both intrigued and concerned him as he walked with her into the round-towered church that formed part of the original monastery. In keeping with the canons of poverty, chastity and obedience embraced by the Augustinian monks, the chapel was small and not overly ornate. The enclosed cloister beside it was also small, maybe thirty yards on each of its four sides. The cloister's outer walls were solid gray stone. Arched pillars framed the inner courtyard and formed a cool, shady colonnade. Sunlight angled through the intricately carved pillars to illuminate a stone sundial set amid a profusion of herbs and plants.

"Oooh," Grace murmured, her admiring gaze on the colonnade's intricately carved pillars. "I can almost see the monks walking two by two here, meditating or fingering their wooden rosaries. And Van Gogh aching to capture this juxtaposition of sunlight and shadow."

The artist couldn't have hurt any more than Blake did at the moment. The same intermingling of sun and shadow played across Grace's expressive face. The warm smile she tipped his way didn't help, either.

"I know you must have visited here several times during your stays in Saint-Rémy. Thanks for making another trek with me. I'm gaining a real appreciation for an artist I knew so little about before."

He masked his thoughts behind his customary calm. "You're welcome, but we're still at the beginning of the Van Gogh trail. You'll discover a good deal more about him as we go."

She made a sweeping gesture toward the far corner of the cloister. "Lead on, MacDuff."

They spent another half hour at Saint-Paul's. The windows in the two austere rooms where Van Gogh had lived and painted for more than a year gave narrow views of the gardens at the rear of the asylum and the rolling wheat fields beyond, both of which the artist had captured in numerous paintings. The garden's long rows of lavender had shed their purple blossoms, but the scent lingered in the air as Grace compared the scene with the plaques mounted along the garden's wall.

At the exit she lingered for a good five minutes in the spot reputedly depicted in *Starry Night,* arguably one of the artist's most celebrated canvases. The glowing golden balls flung across a dark cobalt sky utterly fascinated her and prompted Blake to purchase a framed print of the work at the gift shop. She started to protest that it was too expensive but bit back the words, knowing the stiff price wouldn't deter him any more than the price of the perfumed oil he'd purchased yesterday.

They stopped at the villa to drop off the purchase, then spent a leisurely two hours following the rest of the trail as it wound through the fields and narrow lanes Van Gogh painted when he was allowed to spend time away from the asylum. The trail ended in the center of town at the elegant eighteenth-century *hôtel* that had been converted to a museum and study center dedicated to the artist's life and unique style.

After another hour spent at the museum, Blake suggested lunch in town at a popular restaurant with more tables outside than in. Grace declared the location on one of Saint-Rémy's pedestrians-only streets perfect for people watching. Chin propped in both hands, she did just that while Blake scoped out the wine list. He went with a light, fruity local white and a melted ham-and-cheese sandwich, followed by a dessert of paper-thin crepes dribbling caramel sauce and powdered sugar. Grace opted for a crock of bouillabaisse brimming with carrots, peppers, tomatoes and celery in addition to five varieties of fresh fish, half-shelled oysters, shrimp and lobster. She passed on dessert after that feast, but couldn't resist sneaking a couple of bites of Blake's crepes.

They lingered at the restaurant, enjoying the wine and shade. Grace was sated and languid when they left, and distinctly sleepy-eyed when she settled into the sun-warmed leather of the convertible's passenger seat.

The crunch of tires on the villa's crushed-shell driveway woke her. She sat up, blinking, and laughed an apology.

"Sorry. I didn't mean to doze off on you."

"No problem." He braked to a halt just beyond the fountain of leaping, pawing horses. "At least you didn't go totally unconscious, like I did yesterday."

A hint of color rose in her cheeks. Blake sincerely hoped she was remembering the wild activity that had preceded yesterday's lengthy snooze. He certainly was. The color deepened when he asked with totally spurious nonchalance if she felt like a swim.

"I think I'll clean up a bit and see what's in the library. You go ahead if you want."

"I'll take a pass, too. I've got some emails I need to attend to."

"Okay. I'll, uh, see you later." She swung away, turned back. "Thanks again for sharing Van Gogh with me. I really enjoyed it."

"So did I."

This was what she'd wanted. What she'd insisted on. Grace muttered the mantra several times under her breath as she climbed the stairs to the second floor.

Tugging off her ball cap, she freed her wind-tangled hair and tried a futile finger comb. When she opened the door to the Green Suite, she took two steps inside and stopped dead.

"Omigosh!"

Starry Night held a place of honor above the marble fireplace, all but obscuring the faint outline of whatever painting had hung there before. The print's cool, dark colors seemed to add depth to the silk wall coverings. The swirling stars and crescent moon blazed luminescent trails across the night sky, while the slumbering village below created a sense of quiet and peace. The dark, irregular, almost brooding shape dominating the left side of the print might seem a little sinister to some, but to Grace it was one of the cypress trees Van Gogh had captured in so many of his other works.

She walked into the suite, took a few steps to the side and marveled at how the stars seemed to follow her movements. Then she just stood for long moments, drinking in the print's vibrant colors and thinking of the man who'd obviously instructed it be hung where she could enjoy it during her stay.

Okay, no sense denying the truth when it was there, right in front of her eyes. Blake Dalton was pretty much everything she'd ever dreamed of in a husband. Smart, considerate, fun to be with, too handsome for words. And soooooo good with his hands and mouth and that hard, honed body of his.

She could fall in love with him so easily. Already had, a little. All right, more than a little. She wouldn't let herself tumble all the way, though. Not with her cousin's memory hanging between them like a thin, dark curtain. As fragile as that curtain was, it formed an impenetrable barrier. Grace couldn't tell him the truth, and he couldn't trust her until she did.

Sighing, she turned away from the print and headed for the shower.

The curtain seemed even more impenetrable when she joined Blake for dinner that evening. As promised, Auguste had prepared his version of coquilles St. Jacques. It would be served, she'd been informed, in the small dining room. *Small* being a relative term, of course. Compared with the formal dining hall, which could seat thirty-six with elbow room to spare, this one was used for intimate dinners for ten or twelve. Silver candelabra anchored each end of the gleaming parquet-wood table. Between them sat a silver bowl containing a ginormous arrangement of white lilies and pink roses.

Blake had dressed for the occasion, Grace saw when she entered the room. She felt a funny pang when she recognized the suit he'd worn at their wedding. He'd opted for no tie and left his white shirt open at the neck, though. That quieted her sudden jitters and let her appreciate his casual elegance.

He in turn appeared to approve of the sapphire-colored jersey sundress that had thankfully emerged from her suitcase wrinkle-free. Its slightly gathered skirt fell from a strapless, elasticized bodice. Earrings and a necklace of bright, chunky beads picked up the dress's color and added touches of purple and green, as well.

"Nice dress," Blake commented. "You look good in that shade of blue."

Hell, she looked good in any dress, any shade. Even better out of one. Manfully, he redirected his thoughts from the soft elastic gathers and refused to contemplate on how one small tug could bring them down.

"Would you care for a drink before dinner?" He nodded to the silver ice bucket on its stand. "There's champagne chilling."

"Who can say no to champagne?"

The wine was bottled exclusively for The Elms by the small vintner just outside Epernay Delilah had stumbled across a few years ago. She got such a kick out of presenting her friends and acquaintances with a gift of the private label that her sons had given up trying to convince her not everyone appreciated their champagne ultra brut.

With that in mind, he filled two crystal flutes, angled them to let the bubbles fizz and handed one to Grace.

"What shall we drink to?"

"How about starry nights, as depicted so beautifully by the print you had hung in my bedroom? Thank you for that."

"You're welcome." He chinked his flute to hers. "Here's to many, many starry nights."

He savored the wine's sharp, clean purity but wasn't surprised when Grace wrinkled her nose and regarded her glass with something less than a connoisseur's eye.

"It's, uh…"

"Very dry?"

"Very something."

"They make it with absolutely no sugar," Blake explained, smiling. "It's the latest trend in champagne."

"If you say so."

"Try another sip. Mireille Guiliano highly recommends it in her book *French Women Don't Get Fat,*" he tacked on as additional inducement.

"Well, in that case…" She tipped her flute. The nose scrunch came a moment later. "Guess it takes some getting used to."

"Like our marriage," he agreed solemnly, then smiled as he relieved her of the drink. "We're learning to be nothing if not flexible, right? So I had another bottle put on ice just in case."

He made a serious dent in the ultra brut over dinner. Grace limited herself to one glass of the semi-sec but didn't debate or hesitate to accept a second serving of Auguste's decadent scallops au gratin. The chef himself presided over the serving tray and forked three shell-shaped ramekins onto her plate. Blake derived almost as much pleasure from her low, reverent groans of delight as he did from the succulent morsels and sinfully rich sauce.

The awkward moment came after dessert and coffee. Blake could think of a number of ways to fill the rest of the evening. Unfortunately, he'd agreed to take wild, hot sex off the agenda. He had *not* agreed to table slow and sweet, but he gritted his teeth and decided to keep that as his ace in the hole.

"I think there are some playing cards in the library. Want to try your hand at gin rummy?"

"We could. Or..." Her eyes telegraphed a challenge. "We could check out the video room upstairs. I saw it had a Wii console. I'm pretty good at Ubongo, if I do say so myself."

"What's Ubongo?"

"Ahhhh." She crooked a finger, batted her lashes and laid on a heavy French accent. "*Come avec moi, monsieur,* and I will show you, yes?"

A month, even a week ago, Blake would never have imagined he'd spend the second night of his honeymoon frantically jabbing red buttons with his thumbs while jungle critters duked it out on a flat-screen TV and his bride snorted with derision at each miss…or that each snort would only make him want her more.

He fell asleep long after midnight still trying to decide how getting his butt kicked at Ubongo could put such a fierce lock on his heart. But he didn't realize just how fierce until the next afternoon.

Nine

When Grace came downstairs, Blake was pacing the sunny breakfast room with his phone to his ear. He speared a glance at her gauzy peasant skirt topped by a white lacy camisole, waggled his brows and gave a thumbs-up of approval.

She preened a little and returned the compliment. He'd gone casual this morning, too. Instead of his usual hand-tailored oxford shirt with the cuffs rolled up, he'd chosen a black, short-sleeved crew neck tucked into his tan slacks. The clingy fabric faithfully outlined the corded muscles of his shoulders and chest. Grace was enjoying the view when he finished one call and made a quick apology before taking the next.

"Sorry. We've just been notified of a possible nationwide transportation strike that could affect delivery from one of our subs here in France. I've got the plant manager on hold."

She flapped a hand. "Go ahead."

That discussion led to a third, this one a conference call with Alex and DI's VP for manufacturing. Although it was still the middle of the night back in the States, both men were evidently working the problem hard. Grace caught snatches of their discussion while she scarfed down another of Auguste's incredible breakfasts.

Blake apologized again when he finished the call. "Looks like I'll have to hang close to the villa this morning while we refine our contingency plan. Alex said to tell you he's sorry for butting into your honeymoon."

Her honeymoon, she noted. Not his.

"No problem," she replied, shrugging off the little sting. "I want to do some shopping. I'll walk into town this morning."

When she left the villa an hour later, she saw vehicles jammed into every available parking space along the tree-shaded road leading into the heart of town. They were her first clue something was happening. The bright red umbrellas and canvas-topped booths that now sprouted like mushrooms in every nook and cranny of the town provided the second.

Delighted, Grace discovered it was market day in Saint-Rémy. Busy sellers offered everything from books and antiques to fresh vegetables, strings of sausages and giant wheels of cheese. A good many of the stalls displayed the products in the dreamy colors of Provence—pale yellows and pinks and lavenders of the soaps, earthy reds and golds in the pottery and linens.

She wandered the crowded streets and lanes, sniffing the heady scents, eagerly accepting free samples when offered. She bought boxed soaps for friends back in San Antonio, a hand-sewn sundress and floppy-brimmed hat exploding with sunflowers for Molly, a small but exquisitely worked antique cameo brooch as a peace offering for Delilah.

She'd thanked the dealer and was turning away when a wooden case at the back of the umbrella-shaded stall caught her eye. It held what looked like antique man stuff—intricately worked silver shoe buckles, pearl stickpins, a gold-rimmed monocle with a black ribbon loop.

And one ring.

Compared with the other ornate pieces in the case, the ring was relatively plain. The only design on the wide yellow gold band was a fleur-de-lis set in onyx. At least, Grace assumed those glittering black stones were onyx. She learned her mistake when the dealer lifted the ring from the case to give her a closer look.

"Madame has a good eye," he commented. "This piece is very old and very rare. From the seventeenth century. Those are black sapphires in the center."

"I didn't know there *were* black sapphires."

"But yes! Hold the ring to the light. You will see the fineness of their cut."

She did as instructed and couldn't tell squat about the cut, but the stones threw back a black fire that made Grace gasp and gave the dealer the scent of a deal in the making. He added subtle pressure by dropping some of the ring's history.

"It is rumored to have once belonged to the Count of Provence. But the last of the count's descendants lost his head in the Revolution and the rabble sacked and burned his *hôtel,* so we have no written records of this ring. No—how do you call it? Certificate of authenticity. Only this rumor, you understand."

Grace didn't care. She'd walked out of Judge Honeywell's office wearing a band of diamonds. Blake's ring finger was still bare. She didn't need a certificate to rectify the situation. Those shimmering black sparks were authentic enough for her.

"How much is it?"

He named a figure that made her gulp until she realized it was a starting point for further negotiations. She countered. He shook his head and came back with another price. She sighed and put the ring back in the case. He plucked it out again.

"But look at these stones, madame. This workmanship."

"I don't know if it will fit my husband," she argued.

"It can always be resized."

He dropped his glance to the sparkling gems circling her finger. His expression said she could certainly afford to have it fitted, but he cut the price by another fifty euros. Grace did the conversion to dollars in her head, gulped again and tried to remember the exact balance in her much-depleted bank account.

She could cover it. Barely. Squaring her shoulders, she took the plunge. "Do you take Visa?"

The velvet bag containing the ring remained tucked in her purse when she returned to the villa. A local official had delivered documents couriered in from some government source, and Blake had invited her to join them for lunch. The woman was lively company and was delighted to learn Blake intended to show his bride Saint-Rémy's ancient Roman ruins. She also warned they must go that very afternoon, as the archeological site could be affected if the transportation unions went on strike the following day as they'd threatened.

Grace couldn't see the connection but didn't argue

when Blake said he was satisfied with his review of the contingency plans and was free to roam for a few hours. Before they left the villa, though, he made sure his mobile phone was fully charged, then tucked it close at hand in the breast pocket of his shirt.

The monuments she'd spotted through the trees yesterday were even more impressive up close and personal. Blake parked in a dusty, unpaved lot filled with cars and what turned out to be school buses. Grace had to smile at the noisy, exuberant teens piling out of the buses.

"I've taken my classes on a few field trips like this one," she commented. "It's always tough to judge how much of what they'll see actually sinks in."

Not much, Blake guessed. At least for the young, would-be studs in the crowd. As both he and his brother could verify, the attention of boys that age centered a whole lot more on girls in tight jeans than ancient ruins.

Boys of any age, actually. Grace wasn't in jeans, but she snagged more than one admiring look from the male students and their teachers as she and Blake joined the line straggling along the dirt path to *Les Antiques*.

The two monuments gleamed white in the afternoon sun. Blake couldn't remember which triumph the massive arch was supposed to commemorate—the conquest of Marseille, he thought—but he knew the perfectly preserved marble tower beside the arch had served as a mausoleum for a prominent Roman family. Luckily, descriptive plaques alongside each monument provided the details in both French and English.

Blake wasn't surprised that the teacher in Grace had to read every word, much as she had on the Van Gogh trail yesterday. Peering over the heads of the kids, she glanced from the plaque to the intricate pattern decorating the underside of the arch.

"This is interesting. Those flowers and vines represent the fertility of 'the Roman Province,' aka *Provence.* I didn't know that's where the region's name came from."

Two of the teens obviously thought she'd addressed the comment to them. One turned and pulled an earbud from his ear. The other tucked what looked like a sketchbook under his arm and asked politely, *"Pardon, madame?"*

"The name, Provence." She gestured to the sign. "It's from the Latin."

"Ah, oui."

Blake hid a smile as the boys looked her over with the instinctive appreciation of the male of the species. They obviously liked what they saw. And who wouldn't? Her hair was a wind-tossed tangle of pale silk, and the skin displayed all too enticingly by the white lace camisole had been warmed to a golden tan by the hot Provencal sun. Not surprisingly, the boys lagged behind while the rest of their group posed and snapped pictures of each other under the watchful eyes of their teachers.

"You are from the U.S.?" the taller of the two asked.

"I am," she confirmed. "From Texas."

"Ahhh, Texas. Cowboys, yes? And cows with the horns like this."

When he extended his arms, Grace grinned and spread hers as far as they would go. "More like this."

"Oui?"

"Oui. And you? Where are you from?"

"Lyon, madame."

The shorter kid was as eager as his pal to show off his English. "We study the Romans," he informed Grace, his earbud dangling. "They were in Lyon, as in many

other parts of Provence. You have seen the coliseum in
Arles and the Pont du Gard?"

"Not yet."

"But you must!" The taller kid whipped his sketchbook from under his arm, flipped up the lid and riffled
through the pages. "Here is the Pont du Gard."

Grace was impressed. So was Blake. He'd visited the
famous aqueduct a number of times. The kid's drawings
captured both the incredible engineering and soaring
beauty of its three tiers of arches.

One of the teachers came over at that point to see
what his students were up to. When he discovered
Grace was a teacher, he joined the kids in describing
the Roman sites she should be sure to visit while in the
south of France. He also provided her a list of the archi-
tectural and historical items of interest he'd tasked his
students to search out at *Les Antiques* and the adjoining town of Glanum.

"What a good idea," Grace exclaimed as she skimmed
the Xeroxed four pages. "It's like a treasure hunt."

"The class searches in teams," the teacher explained.
"You should join us. You will gain a far better appreciation of this site."

"I'd love to but…" She threw Blake a questioning
glance. "Do we have time?"

"Sure."

"We can team up."

Blake gauged the boys' reaction to that with a single
glance. "You and these fellows do the hunting," he said
easily. "I'll follow along."

List in hand, she joined the search. Her unfeigned
interest and ready smile made willing slaves of her two
teammates. Preening like young gamecocks, they trans-
lated the background history of the first item on the list,

and crowed with delight when they collectively spotted the chained captives at the base of the arch representing Rome's might.

Blake found a shady spot and rested his hips against a fallen marble block, watching as Grace and her team searched out two additional items on the arch and three on the tall, pillared tower of the mausoleum. He wondered if the boys had any idea that she let them do the discovering. Or that her seemingly innocent questions about the translations forced them to delve much deeper into the history of the site than they otherwise would have. Those two, at least, were going home experts on *Les Antiques*.

The hunt took them across the street and down another hundred yards to the entrance to Glanum. Unlike the arch and mausoleum, access to the town itself was controlled and active excavations were under way at several spots along its broad main street. Despite the roped-off areas, there was still plenty to explore. The students poked into the thermal furnaces that heated the baths, clambered over the uneven stones of a Hellenistic temple and followed the narrow, twisty track through the ravine at the far end of town to the spring that had convinced Gauls to settle this site long before the Romans arrived.

Grace was right there with her team, carefully picking her way down a flight of broken marble steps to the pool fed by the sacred spring. The fact that she could translate the Latin inscription dedicating the pool to Valetudo, the Roman goddess of health, scored her considerable brownie points with the kids. The delight they took in her company scored even more with Blake.

He could guess the kind of dreams those boys would

have tonight. He'd had the same kind at their age. Still had 'em, he admitted wryly, his gaze locked on his wife.

The hunt finished, Grace exchanged email addresses with her teammates and their teacher before walking back to the car with Blake.

"You were really good with those kids," he commented.

"Thanks. I enjoy interacting with teens. Most of them have such lively minds, although the mood swings and raging hormones can be a pain at times."

Their footsteps stirred the dust on the unpaved path. A car whizzed by on the road to the mountain village high up in the Alpilles. The scents of summer lingered on the still air. Blake grasped her elbow to guide her around a rough patch, then slid his hand down to take hers.

He saw her glance down at the fingers interlacing hers. A small line creased her forehead, but she didn't ease her hand away until they reached the convertible. Blake chalked the frown up to the unsettled nature of their marriage and started to open the passenger door for her. She planted her hip against the door, stopping him.

"I bought you something while I was in town this morning." She fished a small velvet bag out of her purse. "It's not much. But I saw it and thought of you and our time here in France and… Well, I just wanted you to have it."

When he untied the strings, a heavy gold ring rolled into his palm. The fleur-de-lis embedded in its center flashed a rainbow of sparks.

"The dealer said it's an antique. He thinks it once belonged to the Count of Provence, but there's no documentation to support that claim." She looked from the ring to him with a mix of uncertainty and shyness. "Do you like it?"

"Very much. Thank you."

The heartfelt thanks dissolved both the shyness and uncertainty. "You're welcome."

The inquiries Blake had run into her finances told him she must have maxed out her credit card to buy the ring, but he knew better than to ruin the moment by asking if she needed a quick infusion of funds. He showed his appreciation instead by tilting the design up to the light.

"The stones are brilliantly cut."

"That's what the dealer said."

"He said right. You rarely find sapphires with so many facets."

"How'd you guess they're sapphires?"

Grinning, he lowered the ring. "Mother has me take care of insurance appraisals and certificates of authenticity for all her jewelry. She's got more rare stones in her collection than the Smithsonian."

"I don't doubt it. Here," she said when he started to slide it on. "Let me."

She eased the ring onto his finger, then hesitated with the band just above the knuckle.

"With this ring…"

The soft words hit with a jolt, ricocheting around in Blake's chest as she worked the ring over his knuckle. It was a tight fit, but the gold band finally slid on.

"…I thee wed."

Grace finished in a whisper and folded her hand over his. Blake didn't respond. He couldn't. His throat was as tight as a drum.

"I can recall every minute in Judge Honeywell's office," she confessed on a shaky laugh. "I can hear the words, replay the entire scene in vivid Technicolor. Yet..."

She glanced around the dusty parking lot, brought her gaze back to his.

"This is the first time I feel as though it's all for real."

"It is real. More than I imagined it could be back there in the judge's office."

His hand tightened, crushing hers against the heavy gold band. She glanced down, startled, then met his gaze again.

"Let me take you home and show you just how real it's become for me."

Blake had no doubts. None at all. He made the short drive to the villa on a surge of adrenaline and desire so thick and heavy it clamped his fists on the steering wheel.

Uncertainty didn't hit until he followed Grace up the stairs and into the cool confines of the Green Suite. When she turned to face him, he half expected her to retreat again, insist they go back to cool and polite.

He'd never wanted a woman the way he wanted this one. Never loved one the way he did his bright, engaging, sun-kissed bride. The fierce acknowledgment rattled him almost as much as the hunger gnawing at his insides. He could slam on the brakes if he had to, though. It would damned near kill him, but he could do it. All she had to do was...

"Lock the door."

It took a second or two for his brain to process the soft command. Another couple for him to click the old-fashioned latch into place. When he turned back, she reached for the top button on her camisole.

His uncharacteristic doubts went up in a blaze of

heat. With a low growl, he brushed her hands aside. "I've been fantasizing about popping these buttons since you came downstairs this morning."

He forced himself to undo them slowly. He wanted the pleasure of baring the slopes of her breasts inch by tantalizing inch. But his greedy pleasure splintered into something close to pain when he peeled back the cottony fabric and revealed the half bra underneath. With a concentration that popped sweat on his brow, he slid the camisole off her shoulders.

Damn! He was as jerky and eager as any of the adolescents they'd encountered this afternoon. Grace was the steady one. She displayed no hint of embarrassment or shyness when the camisole slithered down her arms and dropped to the carpet.

She reached back and unhooked her bra. The movement was so essentially female, so erotic and arousing. Blake ached for the feel of her smooth, firm flesh against his. But when he dragged his shirt free of his slacks, she copied his earlier move and brushed his hands aside.

"My turn."

Just as he had, she took her time. Her palms edged under the shirt, flattened on his stomach, glided upward. Blake bent so she could get it off over his head. His breath razored in, then out when her hands slid south again. A smile played in her eyes when she found his belt buckle.

"I've been fantasizing about *this* since I came downstairs this morning."

"Okay, that's it!"

He had her in his arms in one swoop and marched to the bed.

Ten

The session in the swimming pool had sprung the beast in Blake. This time, he was damned if he would let it slip its leash. He kept every move slow and deliberate as he dragged the brocade coverlet back and stretched Grace out on the soft, satiny sheets.

He took his time removing the rest of her clothes, and his. As he joined her on the cool, satiny sheets, his eyes feasted on her lithe curves. Tan lines made a noticeable demarcation at her shoulders and upper thighs. The skin between was soft and pale and his to explore.

"Too bad Van Gogh isn't around to paint you." He stroked the creamy slopes and valleys. "You would have inspired him to even greater genius."

"I seriously doubt that."

"Well, you certainly inspire me. Like here…"

He brushed a kiss across her mouth.

"And here…"

His lips traced her cheeks and feathered her lids. "And here…"

Mounding her breast, he teased the nipple with his teeth and tongue until it puckered stiff and tight. Blake gave the other breast equal attention and got a hint of the anguish Van Gogh must have suffered over his masterpieces. He was feeling more than a little tormented himself as he explored the landscape of his wife's body.

She didn't lay passive during the investigation. She flung one arm above her head, brought it down again to plane her hand over his shoulder and down his back. Fingers eager, she kneaded his hip and butt.

Blake felt the muscles low in his belly jerk in response but refused to rush the pace. His palm slid over her rib cage, down her belly. Her stomach hollowed under his touch, and a knee came up as he threaded the dark gold hair of her mound. He slid one finger inside the hot, slick lips, then two, and pressed the tight bud between with his thumb.

Her breath was a fast, shallow rasp now. His was almost as harsh. And when she rolled and nudged him onto his back, it shot damned near off the chart.

She went up on an elbow and conducted her own exploration. Just as slowly. Just as thoroughly. His chin and throat got soft kisses, his shoulder a nuzzle and a teasing nip. She followed by lightly scraping a fingertip down his chest and through hair that arrowed toward his groin.

"Now here," she said with a wicked grin as her fingers closed around him, "we have a real masterpiece."

"You won't hear me argue with that," he returned, his grin matching hers.

She gave a huff of laughter and stroked him, gently at first, then with increasing pressure. The friction coiled him as tight as a centrifuge, but he was confident in his ability to extend this period of mutual discovery awhile longer yet. Right up until she bent down, took him in her mouth and shot his confidence all to hell and back.

His breath left on a hiss. Everything below his waist went on red alert. He managed to hang on for a few moments longer but knew his control was about to blow.

"Grace…"

The low warning brought her head up. Her lips were wet and glistening, her eyes cloudy with desire. When he would have reversed positions, she preempted him by hooking a leg over his thighs. She guided him into her, gasping when he thrust upward, and dropped forward to plant her hands on his chest. The skin over her cheeks was stretched tight. Her hair formed a tangled curtain. Blake had never seen anything more beautiful or seductive in his life.

"Forget Van Gogh," he said gruffly. "Not even he could do you justice."

He shoved his hands through her hair and brought her down for a kiss that was as fierce as it was possessive.

Grace came awake with a twitch. Something rasped like fine sandpaper against her temple. Blake's chin, she decided after a hazy moment. Unshaven and bristly. Deciding to ignore the movement, she burrowed her nose deeper into the warm crevice between his neck and shoulder.

"Grace?"

"Mmmm."

"You awake?"

"Nuh-uh."

"No?"

He shifted, and the chin made another scrape. Grace

raised her head and squinted at the dim shadows wreathing the room.

"Whatimeizzit?"

"Close to six, I think."

"Jeez!"

Her head dropped. Her cheek thumped his chest. She tried to drift back into sleep but laughter rumbled annoyingly under her ear.

"Not a morning person, I take it."

"Not a 6:00 a.m. person," she mumbled, sounding sulky even to herself.

"I'll keep that in mind for future reference."

It took a few moments for that to penetrate her sleepy fog. When it did, she pushed up on an elbow and shoved her hair out of her eyes. She wasn't awake enough to address the subject of the future head-on. Or maybe she just didn't have the nerve. Still a little grumpy, she went at it sideways.

"Are you? A morning person, I mean?"

"Pretty much." An apologetic smile creased his whiskery cheeks. "I've been awake for an hour or so."

She groaned and would have made a dive for the pillows, but he shifted again. She ended up lying on her side, facing him, with her head propped on a hand and her thoughts hijacked by a worry about morning breath. She ran a quick tongue over her teeth. They didn't feel too fuzzy. And her lips weren't caked with drool, thank God! She refused to think about her uncombed hair and unwashed face. Or how much she needed to pee.

Blake, of course, looked totally gorgeous in the dim light. A lazy smile lit his wide-awake blue eyes, and he was tantalizingly naked above the rumpled sheets. He even smelled good. Sort of musky and masculine and warm.

When she finished inspecting the little swirl of dark gold hair around his navel and brought her gaze back to his face, she saw his smile had taken on a different slant. Less lazy. More serious.

"I did some thinking while I was lying here waiting for you to rejoin the living."

She guessed from his expression what he'd been cogitating over but asked anyway. "About?"

"Us."

The arm propping her up suddenly felt shaky. Did he want to alter their still-evolving relationship? Renegotiate the contract? After last night, she was certainly open to different terms and conditions. Still, she had to work to keep her voice steady.

"And what did you conclude, counselor?"

"I want to make this work, Grace. You, me, our marriage."

"I thought we were making it work."

"Bad word choice. I meant make it real."

He reached over to tuck a tangled strand behind her ear. She held her breath until he'd positioned it to his satisfaction.

"I want to spend the rest of my life with you. You and Molly and the children we might have together."

Oh, God! Were they really having this discussion with her teeth unbrushed and her face crumpled into sleep lines? She couldn't fall on his chest again, lock her mouth on his and show him how much she wanted the exact same things.

"Hold on."

Surprise blanked his face at the terse order. A swift frown followed almost instantly as she threw off the sheet.

"I'll be right back."

She spent all of three minutes in the bathroom. When she emerged, he was sitting with his back against the padded silk headboard. The scowl remained, but the fact that she was still naked seemed to reassure him. That, and the joy she didn't try to disguise when she scrambled onto the bed and knelt facing him.

"Okay, I can respond properly now. Repeat what you said, word for word."

He hooked a brow and repeated obediently, "I want to spend the rest of my life with you."

"Me and..." she prompted.

"You and Molly and the children we might have together."

A giddy happiness gathered in her throat, but she had to make sure. "And you can live with the fact that I won't...can't tell you Anne's secrets?"

"I don't like it," he admitted honestly, "but I can live with it."

"Then I say we go for it. Molly, more babies, the whole deal."

The laughter came back, and with it a tenderness that made her heart hurt.

"Whew! You had me worried there for a moment."

"Yes, well, for future reference, you probably want to wait until I've brushed my teeth to spring something like that on me."

"I'll add that to the list," he said as she framed his face with both hands.

She reveled in the scrape of his whiskery cheeks, amazed and humbled at the prospect of sharing the months and years ahead with this smart, handsome, incredible man. Every tumultuous hope for their future filled her heart as she leaned in and sealed their new contract.

* * *

Given the rocky start to her marriage, Grace would never have believed her honeymoon would turn into the stuff that dreams are made of.

Last-minute negotiations averted the threatened strike, so no further business issues intruded and Grace had her husband's undivided attention. As she'd already discovered, he woke early and disgustingly energized. She wasn't exactly a sloth, but she did prefer to open her eyes to sunshine versus a dark, shadowy dawn. They compromised by making love late into the night, every night, and in the morning only after she'd come fully alert. Afternoons and early evenings were up for grabs.

They also spent long hours learning about the person they'd married. Grace already knew Blake liked to read but until now had only seen him buried behind *The Wall Street Journal* or *The New York Times* or the latest nonfiction bestseller. She raided the library on one of Provence's rare rainy afternoons and wooed him away from the real world by curling up with a copy of one of her all-time favorites. He didn't exactly go into raptures over *Jane Eyre* but agreed the heroine did develop some backbone toward the end of the story.

Grace returned the favor by digging into the bestseller he'd picked up at a store in town that stocked books in English as well as French. Although she had a good grasp of American history, she never expected to lose herself in a biography of James Garfield. But historian Candace Millard packed high drama and nail-biting suspense into her riveting *Destiny of the Republic: A Tale of Madness, Medicine and the Murder of a President.*

Aside from that one rainy afternoon, they spent most of the daylight hours outside in the pool or in town or exploring Provence. The Roman ruins of Glanum had fired Grace's interest in the area's other sights. The coliseum at Arles and arch of ramparts in Orange more than lived up to her expectations. The undisputed highlight of their journey into the far-distant past, however, was the gastronomical masterpiece of a picnic Auguste had prepared for their jaunt to the three-tiered Pont du Gard aqueduct. They consumed truffle-stuffed breast of capon and julienne carrots with baby pearl onions in great style on the pebbly banks of the river meandering under the ancient aqueduct.

They jumped more than a dozen centuries when they toured the popes' palace at Avignon. Constructed when a feud between Rome and the French King Philip IV resulted in two competing papacies, the palace was a sprawling city of stone battlements and turrets that dominated a rocky outcropping overlooking the Rhône. From there the natural next step was a visit to Châteauneuf du Pape, another palace erected by the wine-loving French popes to promote the area's viticulture. It was set on a hilltop surrounded by vineyards and olive groves and offered a private, prearranged tasting of rich red blends made from grenache, counoise, Syrah and muscadine grapes.

Each day brought a new experience. And each day Grace fell a little more in love with her husband. The nights only added to the intensity of her feelings. The unabashed romantic in her wanted to spin out indefinitely this time when she had Blake all to herself. Her more practical self kept interrupting that idyllic daydream with questions. Like where they would live. And whether she would transfer her teaching certificate from Texas to Oklahoma. And how Delilah would react to the altered relationship between her son and Grace.

Her two sides came into direct conflict the bright, sunny morning they drove to the open-air market in a small town some twenty miles away. L'Isle sur la Sorgue's market was much larger than Saint-Rémy's and jam-packed with tourists in addition to serious shoppers laying in the day's provisions, but the exuberant atmosphere and lovely old town bisected by the Sorgue River made browsing the colorful stalls a delight.

For a late breakfast they shared a cup of cappuccino and a waffle cone of succulent strawberries capped with real whipped cream. They followed that with samples of countless varieties of cheese and sausage and fresh-baked pastries. So many that when Blake suggested lunch at one of the little bistros lining the town's main street, Grace shook her head and held up the paper bag containing the wrapped leek-and-goat-cheese tarts they'd just purchased.

"One of these is enough for me. All I need is something to wash it down with."

He pointed her to the benches set amid the weeping willows gracing the riverbank. The trees' leafy ribbons trailed in the gently flowing water and threw a welcome blanket of shade over the grassy bank.

"Sit tight," Blake instructed. "We passed a fresh-fruit stand a few stalls back. They mix up smoothies like you wouldn't believe. Any flavor favorites?"

"I'm good for anything except kiwi. I can't stand the hairy little things."

"No kiwi in yours. Got it. One more item to add to our future reference list."

The list was getting longer, Grace thought with a smile as she sat on the grass and stretched out her legs. Other people were scattered along the bank. Mothers and fathers and grandparents lounged at ease, with each generation keeping a vigilant eye on the young-sters tempting fate at the river's edge. A little farther away one young couple had gone horizontal, so caught up in the throes of youthful passion that they appeared in imminent danger of locking nose rings. Their moves started slow but soon gathered enough steam to earn a gentle rebuke from two nuns walking by on the side-walk above and a not-so-gentle admonition from a father entertaining two lively daughters while his wife nursed a third. His words were low and in French, but Grace caught the drift. So did the lovers. Shrugging, they rolled onto their stomachs and confined their erotic exchange to whispers and Eskimo nose rubs.

Grace's glance drifted from them to the mother nurs-ing her child. As serene as a Madonna in a painting by a grand master, she held the baby in the crook of her elbow and gently eased the nipple between the gummy lips. She didn't bother with a drape or cover over her shoulder, but performed the most natural task in the world oblivious to passersby. Men quickly averted their eyes. Some women smiled, some looked as though they were recounting memories of performing this same act, and one or two showed an expression of envy.

The scene stirred a welter of emotions in Grace she'd thought long buried. She'd prayed during Anne's trou-bled marriage that her cousin wouldn't get pregnant and produce a child to tie her even more to Jack Petrie. So what did Anne do after escaping the nightmare of her marriage and slowly, agonizingly regaining her self-respect? She fell for a high-powered attorney, turned up pregnant, panicked and ran again. Only this time she didn't run far or fast enough to escape her fear. Anne landed in a hospital in San Diego, and her baby landed in Grace's arms.

Grace had done her damndest not to let Molly wrap her soft, chubby arms wrap around her heart. It had been a losing battle right from the start. Almost the first moment she held Anne's daughter in her arms, she'd started working a contingency plan in her mind. She would keep Molly under wraps while she let it leak to friends that she was pregnant. Once she was sure word had gotten back to Anne's sadistic husband, she would take a leave of absence from her job and play out a fake pregnancy somewhere where no one knew her. Then she'd raise Molly as her own.

Instead, her dying cousin had begged Grace to deliver the baby to her father. Grace had conceded. Reluctantly. She understood the rationale, accepted that the child belonged with her father. The weeks Grace had spent with the Daltons as Molly's temporary nanny had only reinforced that inescapable fact. But the bond between her and Molly had become a chain around her heart. She'd dreaded with every ounce of her soul breaking that chain and walking away from both the child and the dynamic, charismatic Daltons. Now the chain remained intact.

Drawing up her legs, Grace rested her chin on her knees. She still needed to put a contingency plan into operation. She couldn't take the chance that Anne's sadistic husband might discover Grace had married a man with a young baby. Petrie would check Blake out, discover he wasn't a widower, wonder how he'd acquired an infant daughter just about the same time Grace came into his life.

She would contact a few of her friends in San Antonio, she decided grimly. Imply she'd met someone late last year, maybe during the Christmas break, and had spent the spring semester and summer vacation adjusting to the unexpected result. Then Blake Dalton had swooped in and convinced her to marry him.

Those deliberately vague seeds would sprout and spread to other coworkers. Eventually some version of the story might reach Jack Petrie. It should be enough to throw him off Molly's scent. It had to be!

Lost in her contingency planning, she didn't hear Blake's return until he came up beside her.

"One strawberry-peach-mango combo for you. One blueberry-banana for me."

She moved the sack with the tarts to make room for him on the patch of grass. Legs folded, he sank down with a loose-limbed athletic grace and passed her a plastic cup heaped with whipped cream and a dark red cherry. They ate in companionable silence, enjoying the scene.

The Sorgue River flowed smooth and green just yards away. The young lovers were still stretched out nose-to-nose. The father was hunkered down at the river's bank within arm's reach of his two laughing, wading daughters. His wife held the baby against her shoulder now and was patting up a burp.

Grace let a spoonful of her smoothie slide down a throat that suddenly felt raw and tight. This baby looked nothing like Molly. Her eyes were nowhere near as bright a blue, and instead of Mol's golden curls, she had feathery, flyaway black hair her mother had obviously tried to tame with a jaunty pink bow. Yet when she waved tiny, dimpled fists and gummed a smile, Grace laughed and returned it.

Blake caught the sound and followed her line of sight. Hooking an elbow on his knee, he watched the baby's antics until she let loose with a burp that carried clearly across the grass. After another, quieter encore, her mother slid her down into nursing position.

When Grace gave a small sigh, Blake studied her profile. He wasn't surprised by what he saw there, or by the plea in her eyes when she turned to him.

"I've had an incredible time in Provence," she said slowly. "Every day, every night with you has been a fantasy come true."

She threw another look at the baby, and he read her thoughts.

"I miss Molly, too," he admitted with a wry grin. "Let's go home."

Eleven

His mind made up, Blake moved with characteristic speed and decisiveness. While he and Grace threaded through the crowded market to their car, he used his cell phone to run a quick check of flight schedules for Dalton International's air fleet. The corporate jet was on the wrong side of the Atlantic, so he booked first-class seats on a commercial nonstop flight to Dallas leaving late that afternoon. With the time differential and the short hop to Oklahoma, they would get home at almost the same hour they departed France.

That left Grace barely an hour to throw her things together and say goodbye to Auguste and the rest of the staff. Blake's farewells included exorbitant gratuities for each member of the staff and a promise to bring madame back for a longer stay very soon.

The rush of leaving and her eagerness to get back to Molly carried Grace halfway across the Atlantic. Hav-

ing Blake beside her in the luxurious first-class cabin
staved off fatigue during the remainder of the trip. His
low-voiced, less than complimentary commentary on
the action flick they watched together had her giggling
helplessly and the other passengers craning to see what
was on their screens.

Fatigue didn't factor in until after the plane change
in Dallas. Fatigue, and a serious case of nerves about
coming face-to-face with Blake's mother again. Delilah
had let loose with both barrels at her last meeting with
Grace. The note from her that Alex delivered in San Antonio had much the same tone. She hadn't been happy
about the hurry-up wedding and warned that she'd have
something to say about it when the newlyweds returned
from France.

Grace couldn't imagine how the redoubtable Dalton
matriarch would react to the altered relationship between her son and his bride. Delilah must have known
Blake proposed for strictly utilitarian reasons. Mostly
utilitarian, anyway. Would she believe his feelings could
undergo a major shift in such a short time? Probably not.
Grace could hardly believe it herself.

By the time they turned onto the sweeping drive that
led to Delilah's Nichols Hills mansion, dread curled like
witches' fingers in her stomach. Then the front door
flew open and she saw at a glance she'd underestimated
Delilah. The older woman took one look at them and
gave a whoop that boomed like a cannon shot in the
brisk September air.

"I knew it!" she announced gleefully as they mounted
the front steps. "No one can resist the fatal combination
of Provence and Auguste. Especially two people who
were so danged hot for each other."

"Don't you ever get tired of being right?" Blake drawled as he bent to kiss her cheek.

"Never." Blue eyes only a shade lighter than her son's skewered Grace. "And that's something for you to remember, too, missy. Now get over here and so I can give my newest daughter-in-law a hug."

Enfolded in a bone-crunching embrace and a cloud of outrageously expensive perfume, Grace made the instant transition from employee and former nanny to member of the family. She was so grateful to this fierce and occasionally overbearing woman that she found herself battling tears.

"Thank you for trusting me with Molly and for…and for…everything."

"We should be thanking you." The hug got tighter, Delilah's voice gruffer. "You brought Molly to us in the first place."

Both women were sniffling when they separated. Embarrassed by her uncharacteristic descent into sentimentality, Delilah flapped a hand toward the stairs.

"I expect you want to see the baby. She's up in the nursery. I just heard her on the monitor, waking up from her nap."

The last time Grace had climbed this magnificent circular staircase was as an employee in Delilah's home. She couldn't quite get a grip on her feelings as she ascended them alongside Blake, anxious to embrace the baby now making come-get-me noises from the room on the left at the top of the stairs. Nerves played a major role. Excitement and eagerness bubbled in there, too. But mostly it was sheer incredulity that she now had the right to claim this man and this child as hers.

When they swept into the nursery Delilah had furnished so swiftly and so lavishly, Molly was standing up in the crib. Her downy blond hair formed a spiky halo and her blue eyes tracked their entrance with a touch of impatience, as if asking what took them so long.

Grace's heart melted into a puddle of mush at the sight of her. It disintegrated even more when Molly gave a gurgle of delight and raised her arms.

"Gace!"

Half laughing, half sobbing, Grace swept the baby out of the crib.

September rolled out and October came in with a nighttime temperature dip into the forties and fifties. As the weeks flew by, a nasty little corner of Grace's mind kept insisting this couldn't last. Sometime, somehow, she would pay for the joy she woke up with every morning. But her busy, busy days and nights spent in Blake's arms buried that niggling thought under an avalanche of others.

Their first order of business was finding a house. Rather than move Molly's nursery to Blake's bachelor pad during the hectic process of inspecting available properties, they accepted Delilah's invitation to occupy the guest wing of her mansion. So naturally both Molly and Delilah went with Grace to check out the possibilities when Blake got tied up at work. Julie, too, when she wasn't flying or distracted by the business of setting up the home she and Alex had recently moved into.

Grace worried at first that Delilah might try to push her toward something big and splashy, but her mother-in-law was motivated by only one goal. She wanted her granddaughter close enough to spoil at will. So she was thrilled when Grace settled on a recently renovated half-timbered home less than a mile from the Dalton mansion. The two-story house sat well back from the street

on a one-acre lot shaded by tall pines. Grace had fallen
in love with its oak floors and open, sunny kitchen at
first sight, but balked at the five bedrooms until Blake
convinced her they could convert one to an entertain-
ment center and one to an exercise room unless and
until they needed it for other purposes.

Once the house was theirs, Grace faced the daunting
prospect of filling its empty rooms. She thought about
tackling one room at a time, but Delilah graciously offered the services of her decorator to coordinate the
overall scheme.

"Take her up on it," Julie urged during a weekend
brunch at their mother-in-law's.

The two brides lolled on the sunlit terrace, keeping
a lazy eye on Molly in her net playpen while their husbands checked football scores in the den. Delilah had
taken her other guest to the library to show him some
faded photographs she'd unearthed from her early days
working the oil fields with her husband. Grace found
it extremely interesting that Julie's irascible partner,
Dusty Jones, had apparently become a regular visitor
to the Nichols Hills mansion.

"The decorator is good," her new sister-in-law asserted. "Really good."

Grace could hardly disagree. She'd lived in these op-
ulent surroundings for several months as Molly's nanny.
The Lalique chandeliers and magnificent antiques suited
Delilah's flair and flamboyance, but Grace had lived in
constant dread of Molly spitting up all over one of the
hand-woven Italian silk seat cushions.

"Trust me," Julie urged. "Victor will help you achieve
just the look you want. He understood right away that
I wanted to go clean and uncluttered in our place. I've
agreed with almost everything he's suggested so far."

"Surprising everyone concerned," Grace drawled, "yourself included."

"True," the redhead agreed, laughing. "I do tend to formulate strong opinions about things…as Alex frequently points out."

Marriage agreed with her, Grace thought. She looked so relaxed and happy with her auburn hair spilling over her shoulders and her fingers playing with the gold pendant Alex had given her as an engagement gift. The figure depicted on the intricately carved disk was the Inca god who supposedly rose from Lake Titicaca in the time of darkness to create the sun, the moon and the stars. Julie, who'd spent several years ferrying cargo in and out of remote airstrips in South America, had told Grace the god's name but she could never remember it.

"Might as well bow to the inevitable and give Victor a call," Julie advised, stretching languidly. "If you don't, Delilah will just invite him for cocktails one evening and make the poor guy go over your house plans room by room while she pours martinis down his throat."

"Okay, okay. I'll call him."

The two women sat in companionable silence. They'd known each other for only a few months but had become friends in that short time. Marrying twins had solidified the bond. It had also given them unique perspectives into each other's lives.

Grace had worried that her being the one to provide indisputable proof that Blake was Molly's father might drive a wedge between the brothers. Or between her and Alex. Until those final DNA results had come back, the preponderance of evidence had pointed to Alex as the most likely father. He'd taken the baby into his heart and had rearranged his life around her. The home he and Julie had just moved into had been bought with Molly in mind.

Alex appeared to have adjusted to being the baby's uncle instead of her father. He was just as attentive, and every bit as loving. Still, Grace struggled with a twinge of guilt as his wife got up to retrieve the stuffed turtle Molly had chucked out of her playpen.

"Tell me the truth," she said quietly when Julie dropped into her chair again. "Did Alex resent me for keeping my cousin's secret?"

"He did, for maybe a day or two after Blake showed him the final DNA results. He's a big boy, though. He worked through his disappointment." Her eyes took on a wicked glint. "I might have helped the process by redirecting his thoughts whenever I thought they needed it."

"Yes, I bet you... Oops, that's Blake's phone. He said something about expecting a call from Singapore. This may be it."

She scooped up the device he'd left on the table and checked caller ID. The number was a local one.

"Guess it's not Singapore."

Evidently the caller decided his message was too urgent to go to voice mail. Grace had no sooner set the phone down than it buzzed again, this time with a flashing icon indicating a text message.

"I'd better take this in to him. Keep an eye on Molly for me."

"Will do."

Phone in hand, she followed the sound of football fans in midroar to the den. Hoping it was the Dallas Cowboys who'd precipitated that roar, Grace shifted the phone to her other hand.

She honestly didn't mean to hit the text icon. Or read

the brief message that came up. But a single glance at the screen stopped her dead in her tracks.

Have an update on Petrie. Call me.

Ice crawled along Grace's veins. The hubbub in the den faded. The papered walls of the hall seemed to close in on her. She couldn't move, could barely breathe as Jack Petrie's image shoved everything else out of her mind. Smooth and handsome at first. Then smooth and sneering, as he was the last time he'd allowed Grace to visit his home. *His* home. Not her cousin's. Not one they'd made together. The house was his, the car was his, every friggin' dollar in the bank was his, to be doled out to *his* wife penny by penny.

The ice splintered. An almost forgotten fury now speared through Grace. Caught in its vicious maw, she let an animal cry rip from her throat and hurled the phone at the wall.

The Dalton men came running almost before the pieces hit the floor. Alex erupted from the den first.

"What the...?"

"Grace!" Blake shoved past his brother. "Are you okay?"

She didn't answer. *Couldn't* answer. Fury still clawed at her throat.

"Has something happened to Molly?" He gripped her upper arms. "Alex! Go check on Julie and the baby!"

He could have saved his breath. His brother was already pounding down the hall.

"Talk to me, Grace." Blake's fingers bit into her flesh. "Tell me what's happened."

"You got a call. That's what happened."

"What?"

She wrenched out of his hold. With a scathing look, she directed his attention to the shattered phone. He frowned at the pieces in obvious confusion.

"It was a text message." She fought to choke out the words. "My thumb hit the icon by mistake. I didn't intend to read the message. Wasn't intended to read it, obviously."

"What are you talking about? What message? Who was it from?"

"I'm guessing your friend, the P.I. What's his name? Jerrold? James?"

His jaw went tight. "Jamison."

"Right," she said venomously. "Jamison. He wants you to call him. For an update on Petrie."

"Oh, hell."

The soft expletive said it all. Spinning, Grace stalked down the hall and almost bowled over the two who emerged from the library. Any other time she might have noted with interest that a good portion of Delilah's crimson lipstick had transferred from her mouth to Dusty Jones's. At the moment all she could do was snap a curt response when Delilah demanded to know what was going on.

"Ask your son."

She brushed past them, wishing to hell she'd pocketed the keys to the snazzy new Jaguar Blake had insisted on buying her. She needed to get out. Think through this shock. But the keys were on the dresser. Upstairs. In the guest suite. Grace hit the stairs, grinding her teeth in mingled fury and frustration.

By the time she reached the luxuriously appointed suite, she'd added a searing sense of betrayal to the mix. She snatched the keys off the dresser, digging the jagged edges into her palm, staring unseeing at other objects scattered across the polished mahogany.

"Going somewhere?"

She jerked her head up and locked angry eyes on her husband. "I'm thinking about it."

"Mind if I ask where?" he asked calmly.

Too calmly, damn him! She'd always admired his steady thinking and cool composure. Not now. Not with this hurt knifing into her.

"I believed you," she threw at him. "When you said you could live with my refusal to betray Anne's trust, I actually believed you!"

"I am living with it."

"Like hell!"

His eyes narrowed but he kept his movements steady and unhurried as he turned, shut the door and faced her again.

"When you wouldn't trust me with Anne's secrets…"

"I couldn't! Some of us," she added viciously, "hold to our promises."

"When you *couldn't* trust me with Anne's secrets," he amended, his mouth thinning a little, "I had Jamison keep digging. I know now her real name was Hope Templeton."

The telltale signs that he was holding on to his temper with an effort took some of the edge off Grace's own anger. The hurt remained.

"I only had one cousin. Her birth is a matter of record. I'm surprised it took your hotshot P.I. so long to discover her real name."

"I also know she got married at the age of seventeen."

"How did you…? I mean, we…"

"Altered the record? I won't bother to remind you that's a crime."

He was in full lawyer mode now. Legs spread, arms crossed. Relentlessly presenting the evidence. The two of them would have to have this out, Grace realized. Once, and hopefully for all.

Reining in the last of her temper, she sank onto the bed. "Go on."

"What my hotshot P.I. did not find was any record of divorce. I can only assume Anne was still married when she and I met. I can also assume the marriage wasn't a happy one."

"And how did you reach this brilliant deduction?"

He shrugged aside the sarcasm. "The fact that Anne had left him, obviously. And that she used an assumed name, presumably to prevent him from finding her."

Grace could add so much more to the list. Like Anne's aversion to public places for fear Petrie or one of his friends would spot her. Her bone-deep distrust of all men until this one. Her abrupt disappearance from Blake's life, even though she must have loved him.

"I had Jamison check out her husband," he said, breaking into the dark, sad memories. "According to Texas Highway Patrol records, Jack Petrie is a highly decorated officer with two citations for risking his life in the line of duty. One for dragging a man and his son out of a burning vehicle. Another for taking down a drug smuggler who shot a fellow officer during a routine traffic stop."

"You didn't contact him, did you?" Grace asked with her heart in her throat.

"No. Neither did Jamison. But he made discreet inquiries."

She breathed in, out. "And?"

"Jamison came away with the impression Petrie was a devoted husband who liked to show off his pretty young wife. Rumor has it he was devastated when she walked out on him."

Blake waited for her to deny the rumor. When she didn't, he got to the real issue. "That leaves Molly."

"She's your child, Blake!" The exclamation burst out, quick and passionate. "Not Petrie's!"

"I know that. Even without the DNA evidence, Jamison's sources confirmed Anne left her husband almost a year before she and I met. Still, they were married when she gave birth to Molly, and under the law…"

"To hell with the law! You've run the tests. If it ever came to a legal battle, you've got more than enough evidence to support your paternity."

She came off the bed, pleading now.

"But it doesn't need come to a battle. Anne's dead. Petrie has no idea she had a child. Just leave it that way."

"What are you so afraid of, Grace? What was Anne afraid of? Did Petrie hurt her? Use his fists on her?"

"I…"

"Tell me, for God's sake!"

She almost broke down then. She would have given her soul at that point to share the whole, degrading truth, but her promise hung like an anchor around her neck. All she would respond to was one specific question.

"It wasn't physical. Not that I know of, anyway. But mental cruelty can be just as vicious."

"All the more reason for me to protect Molly from this jerk."

He had the training, the extensive network of connections to enact all sorts of legal sanctions. She knew that. She also knew the mere fact he'd had an affair with Anne would drive Jack Petrie to a jealous rage. The man was a sadist. He'd strangled his wife with a warped kind of love that others mistook for devotion. Anne was beyond his reach now, but her child wasn't. Or her lover.

"You've just proved my point," Grace countered with a touch of desperation. "You think Anne's husband won't want vengeance? He'll try to milk you for millions. Drag a paternity suit out in court for years. Have you thought of that?"

"Of course," he snapped. "I'm not afraid of a fight, legal or otherwise."

Okay. All right. She had to breathe deep. Slow down. Remember she wasn't dealing with someone as unbalanced as Jack Petrie.

"Put your own feelings aside for a moment, Blake. Think what a long, drawn-out court battle could do to Molly. When she's older she'll be curious about her mother. All she'd have to do is surf the Net. You can imagine the headlines she'll stumble across. Billionaire's Love Child Center of Vicious Paternity Dispute. Decorated Police Officer Calls Wife a Whore. Secretary Hooks Rich Boss with Sex And…"

"I've got the picture."

He got it, and he didn't like it. She didn't, either, but they couldn't ignore it.

"Don't dig any further, Blake. Please! In a year, two years, everyone outside our immediate circle will just assume Molly's our child. Petrie won't have any reason to question it."

He looked as if she'd punched him in the gut. Or square in his sense of right and wrong. His eyes went cold, his voice flat and hard.

"So you want to live a lie. Like your cousin."

For Molly's sake she gave the only answer she could. "Yes."

Twelve

"She just can't bring herself to trust me."

Blake gripped his beer and ignored the buzz from the crowd gathered in the watering spot a few blocks from Dalton International's corporate headquarters. He and his brother had wrapped a bitch of a meeting with senior executives from Nippon Steel earlier that evening, then taken their Japanese visitors to dinner at one of Oklahoma City's finest steak houses. The Nippon execs had taken a limo back to their hotel, leaving Blake and Alex to lick their wounds over a beer and a bucket of peanuts before heading home to their respective spouses. Despite the round of tough negotiations, it was Blake's spouse who occupied his mind more than the Japanese.

"I accept that Grace promised to keep Anne's secrets," he said, stretching his long legs out beneath a tabletop littered with peanut shells. "I respect her for holding to that vow, but Christ! We've been married almost a month now and she still doesn't think I can handle this character Petrie."

Shrugging, Alex attempted to take the middle road on the subject he and his twin had already beaten into the ground a number of times. "Grace knows Petrie. We don't."

"We know enough! The bastard terrorized his wife and forced her into a shadow life. Now he's doing the same thing to *my* wife."

Frustration ate like acid at Blake's gut. It was doing a serious number on his pride, too. He yanked at the knot of his tie and popped the top button of his shirt before downing a slug of beer.

"Mother says Grace stays in the background at the charity functions she's involved her in and ducks whenever a photographer shows up. She does the same when we attend a concert or some black-tie affair. The woman is fixated on maintaining a low profile until our marriage is old news."

"So? You don't exactly chase after the spotlight yourself."

"Dammit, bro, you're not helping here."

"You wanted a sounding board, I'm doing my best board act." Peanut shells crunched as his twin leaned his elbows on the table. "I've told you what I really think."

"Yeah, I know. You think I should take a quick trip to San Antonio and confront this guy. Let him know who he'd be dealing with if he got any smart ideas."

"Correction. I think *we* should take a quick trip to San Antonio."

"It's my problem! I'll handle it."

"You're doing a helluva job with it so far."

Blake's lips drew back in a snarl. He managed to choke it off. Barely. Alex knew damned well he was spoiling for a fight. Obviously, his twin was prepared to step in and draw the punches.

"Well, at least you've got Jamison's sources keeping an eye on Petrie," Alex commented.

"I'm getting regular updates."

"Does Grace know?"

"She knows."

That had caused another rough scene. Grace argued that Petrie was a cop. Sooner or later he would pick up on a surveillance, become suspicious, track it to the source. Blake countered with the assertion that Jamison and his associate in San Antonio were pros. They wouldn't tip their hands. In either case, Blake flatly refused to turn a blind eye to a potential threat.

Grace had conceded that point. Reluctantly, but she'd conceded. Still, the fact they were living with this guy Petrie's shadow hanging over them locked Blake's jaw every time he thought about it. He'd promised his wife he wouldn't confront the man without talking it over with her first. That discussion was fast approaching. In the meantime, he and Grace each pretended they understood and accepted the other's viewpoint.

"I get that Grace saw firsthand the hell Petrie put her cousin through," Alex said, attacking the matter from another angle. "What I don't get is why she doesn't want to take him on. I didn't know Anne all that well, but I do know Grace. My sense is she's much stronger than her cousin was."

"Stronger, and a whole bunch more stubborn," Blake agreed with a grimace.

"She's also got us to do the muscle work. All of us. Mother and Julie want in on this. Dusty, too."

Momentarily diverted, Blake raised a brow. "Yeah,

what's with that? The old coot's at Mom's house just about every time I stop by there these days."

"They're consulting," Alex replied, deadpan. "As Julie's business partner and coowner of one of Dalton International's subsidiaries, Dusty prefers to talk shop with someone who worked the same oil patches he did."

"Oh, Lord! I'm not going to tell you the image that just jumped into my head. But…" Blake raised his beer. "Here's to 'em."

Grinning, the brothers clinked bottles. Alex signaled the waitress to bring two fresh ones before returning to the issue digging at them both.

"Back to Grace. She's got to know she can count on you, on all of us, to protect her from this asshole Petrie."

"She knows," Blake said grimly. "The problem is she thinks she's protecting us. Or Molly and me, anyway."

His brother winced. "That's got to stick in your craw."

"Like you wouldn't believe."

He didn't go into further detail. As a kid Alex had been the one to wade fist-first into battle. Blake had always had his brother's back, though, and Alex his. The fact that his wife didn't trust him to have hers rubbed him raw. Feeling the grate yet again, he circled his beer bottle on the littered table and sent a shower of peanut shells to the already carpeted floor.

"So how long are you going to play this by her rules?" Alex wanted to know.

Blake's head snapped up. The uncompromising answer came fast. "The rules change the moment I sense so much as a hint of a real threat."

Grace was perched on one of the kitchen counter stools when she heard the muted rumble of the garage door going up. She'd put Molly down for the night at seven-thirty and indulged in the sybaritic luxury of an hour-long soak in scented bath oil that evoked instant memories of Provence's hot sun and endless lavender fields. Barefoot and supremely comfortable in a well-washed, black-and-silver San Antonio Spurs jersey that came almost to her knees, she'd curled up with a biography of Van Gogh before deciding to treat herself to a bowl of double chocolate fudge ripple. After so many years of busy days in the classroom and nights grading papers, she loved having the time and the freedom to read whatever struck her fancy. She loved even more reading to Molly, which she'd started doing before they'd moved into the house Grace was having such fun furnishing.

All in all, her days were perfect. The nights came pretty darn close.

Grace had gotten past her anger over Blake directing his P.I. to dig into the past her cousin had tried so desperately to escape. She'd also recovered—mostly—from the stinging sense of betrayal that he'd done it after she'd begged him to let that past stay buried. She understood his rationale. She didn't agree with it, but she understood it.

Unfortunately, a difference of opinion on something so crucial couldn't help but affect their continually evolving relationship. The strain it had caused was like a small but irritating itch they'd mutually decided to ignore.

Despite the itch, they still took pleasure in discovering new facets to each other's personalities. The quirks, the unconscious gestures, the ingrained habits. What's more, they still shared the sheer joy of Molly.

And Grace's pulse still bumped whenever her husband walked into a room.

Like now. She swiveled the stool, cradling her bowl of double chocolate fudge ripple, and felt the flutter as Blake entered the kitchen through the utility room connected to the garage. He moved with the athletic ease she so admired and looked as classy as ever, although the open shirt collar and the tie dangling from his suit coat pocket added a definite touch of sex to the sophisticated image.

They hadn't reached the stage of casual, hello-honey-I'm-home kisses yet. Grace wasn't sure they ever would, although she knew darn well they couldn't sustain indefinitely the searing heat they'd ignited during their honeymoon. She felt it sizzle now, though, as he nudged her knees apart so he could stand between them and cupped her nape.

"Did you and Alex get your Japanese execs all wined and dined?"

"We did."

His palm was warm against her skin, his eyes a smoky blue as his head bent toward hers. Tipping her chin, Grace welcomed him home with a kiss that left her breathless and Blake demanding a second one just like the first. She gave both willingly, as greedy as he was, but had to jerk back when the fudge ripple threatened to slide into her lap.

Blake eyed the bowl's contents with interest. "That looks good."

"Sit down, I'll get you some."

"I'll just share yours."

"Hmmmm." Her brow furrowed in a mock scowl. "In the 'just for future reference' category, I don't usually share my ice cream. Or my fries."

"Noted. But you'll make an exception in this instance, right?"

Since he was still wedged between her thighs and didn't look as though he planned to move anytime soon, she yielded the point.

"Okay. Here you go."

He downed the heaping spoonful in one try, prompting a quick warning.

"Whoa! You'll get a brain freeze gobbling it down like that."

A slow, predatory smile curved his mouth. "No part of me is liable to freeze like this."

He moved closer, spreading her wider. The Spurs jersey rode up, and Grace felt him harden against her.

"I see what you mean," she got out on a gasp when he exerted an exquisite pressure at the juncture of her thighs. "No danger of frost down there."

Or anywhere else!

The pressure increased. The muscles low in her belly clenched. He splayed his hands on her hips to keep her anchored, and the wild, throbbing sensation built with each rhythmic move of his lower body against hers.

"Blake!" She tried to wiggle away but the counter dug into her back. "We'd better slow down. I can't... You've got me too..."

"Hold on."

Like she could? Especially when he spanned her waist and lifted her in a smooth, easy move from the stool to the counter. She didn't even realize she still held the now-melted ice cream until he took the bowl and let it clatter into the sink. Then the jersey came up and over her head. Her bikini briefs got peeled off. Her mouth was level with his now, her hips in line with his belt. She should have felt completely, nakedly exposed. All she experienced was the urgent need to get him naked, too.

"Your jacket... Shirt..."

He shed the top half of his clothing with minimum movement and maximum speed. The bottom half stayed intact as he buried a fist in her hair, and took her mouth with his.

There was something different in this kiss, in the maddening pressure he exerted against her. He was a little rougher, a little harder, yet somehow more deliberate. As though he could demonstrate some sort of mastery over her if he wanted to but chose to restrain himself. Or not. Grace didn't register more than that hazy impression before he replaced his lower body with his hand and drove everything resembling rational thought out of her head.

She came mere moments later in a burst of bright colors and pure sensation. The explosive climax arched her spine and brought her head back. She slapped her palms on the counter to support her taut, shuddering body, but her arms folded like overstretched elastic.

Blake scooped her off the counter before she went horizontal and carried her limp and still quivering with pleasure to the bedroom. When he shed the rest of his clothes and joined her in bed for the grand finale, he was so gentle and tender Grace completely forgot that odd moment in the kitchen.

It came back with a vengeance less than a week later.

Yielding to her mother-in-law's indomitable will, she strapped Molly into her car seat to drive her over to the Nichols Hills mansion for some grandmother-granddaughter time. Grace herself had been instructed to shop for a cocktail dress for the big-dollar fundraiser

Delilah insisted her sons and their wives attend the following evening.

"Which I really do *not* want to go to," she said via the
rearview mirror to the infant happily banging a teething ring against the side window.

Her eyes on the baby, she had to jam on the brakes
to avoid an SUV cruising past the end of the drive. The
near miss rattled Grace and reminded her to keep her
attention on the road. The brief visit with Delilah didn't
exactly soothe her somewhat frayed nerves.

"You should get your nails done while you're out,"
her mother-in-law suggested after a prolonged exchange
of Eskimo kisses with a joyously squealing Molly. "Your
hair trimmed, too."

"I look that bad, huh?"

"You look gorgeous and you know it." She hitched
the baby on her hip and skewered her daughter-in-law
with one of her rapier stares. "Just not as glowing as you
did when you got back from Provence. Don't tell me you
and Blake have taken the sex down a notch already."

"I won't," Grace countered coolly.

"Don't get on your high horse with me, girl. If it's
not sex, it has to be that business with Jamison. Look,
I don't like to meddle in my sons' lives but…"

She paused and waited with a reluctant grin for Grace
to finish snorting.

"Okay, okay. Meddling is my favorite occupation.
But I thought you and Blake had come to an understanding on that matter."

"We have. More or less."

The older woman let Molly play with her sapphire-
and-diamond wrist bangle and skinned Grace with another serrated look. "I'm only going to say this once.
I'll never mention it again, I swear."

Grace believed that as much as she believed her former employer could keep her nose out of her sons' affairs. Once Delilah got the bit between her teeth, she kept it there.

"You did right standing by your promise to your cousin," she said, "but she's dead and you're married now. You need to decide where your loyalty lies."

Grace went rigid, her eyes flashing danger signals. They bounced off Delilah's thick hide.

"Go," she ordered brusquely. "Shop, have your nails done, and for God's sake think about what I just said."

Grace fumed all the way to the exclusive boutique she and Julie had discovered some months ago. She pulled into a parking slot two doors down and killed the Jag's engine, then sat with her fists gripping the leather-wrapped steering wheel.

She didn't need Delilah to lecture her about loyalty, dammit! She'd spent what felt like half her life and every penny of her income shielding Anne from her sadistic husband. If she closed her eyes, she could still see her cousin fighting desperately for her last breaths. Hear her rasping plea for Grace to take Molly to her father and please, *please* don't let Jack know about her.

Her knuckles whitened on the wheel. She stared at the shop window in front of the Jag. The window was bare except for a For Lease sign, but Grace barely noticed the empty expanse of glass and darkened interior.

Maybe…

Maybe the habit of protecting her cousin had become too ingrained. Maybe she'd been following instincts tainted by Anne's bone-deep fear when she should be trusting Blake's. He was calm and cool in a crisis. And more intelligent than any six people she knew. He could also wield resources every bit as if not more power-ful than Jack Petrie's. Most important, he was Molly's father. He'd strangle anyone who tried to harm her with his bare hands.

Groaning, Grace dropped her forehead to the wheel. Heart and soul, she ached to hold to the promise she made her cousin. She couldn't. Not any longer. Delilah was right. She had to let go of Anne's past. Her future revolved around Molly and Blake. With a silent plea to her cousin to understand, she raised her head and fum-bled in her purse for her cell phone.

She pressed one speed-dial key. Her husband's su-perefficient executive assistant answered before the sec-ond ring.

"Blake Dalton's office."

"Hi, Patrice, it's Grace. Is Blake free?"

"Hi, Grace. Sorry, but he's in the middle of a confer-ence call with the Association of Corporate Counsel's executive committee. They want him to chair the next symposium, you know."

"Yes, I do."

"Shall I pass him a note to let him know you're on the line?"

"No, just tell him… Tell him I was thinking about my cousin and…"

Hell! She couldn't put what she wanted to say on a yellow call slip.

"Just tell him I called."

"I will."

"Thanks."

She tapped End, feeling much like Julius Caesar must have when he brought his legionnaires across the Rubicon. She couldn't go back now. She didn't *want* to go back. She'd charge full steam ahead with Blake and Molly and a life without the specter of Jack Petrie hanging over it.

She was still riding the relief of that decision when she emerged from Helen Jasper's boutique some time later. As usual, the shop owner's eye had proved as unerring as her taste. She'd purchased the entire line of a young Oklahoma designer she was sure would make a splash in the fashion world. Grace ended up buying not only a tea-length cocktail dress in dreamy shades of green, but two beaded tops and a pair of slinky palazzo pants with accessories to match. She'd also had Helen bundle up the outfit she'd worn into the store and now felt very autumnal in heavyweight linen slacks in cinnamon-brown, a matching tank top and a pumpkin-colored silk overblouse left unbuttoned to show off a faux lizardskin belt as wide, if not as clanky, as Delilah's.

Smiling at the thought of Blake's reaction to the backless and darned near frontless cocktail dress, she bunched her shopping bags in one hand and fumbled in her purse for the car keys. She popped the door locks, dropped her purse on the front seat and was about to add the shopping bags when a black SUV wheeled into the slot next to hers. The idiot driver cut into the space so sharply she had to quickly yank on the open door to avoid having it dinged.

Mentally giving him the bird, she bent to retrieve the tissue-stuffed bags her quick move had sent tumbling to the floor mat. When she straightened, she caught a glimpse of the other driver from the corner of one eye. He'd exited his vehicle but hadn't moved away from it.

A prickly sense of unease raced along her spine. He

was standing close to her Jag. Too close. A half dozen tips from the various self-defense articles she'd read crowded into her mind. She went with the only one she could.

Jamming her car keys between her fingers, she closed her fist to form a spiked gauntlet and started to turn. She didn't get even halfway around before something hard rammed against her shoulder blade and her world turned red.

Thirteen

"She doesn't answer her phone."

Blake paced his brother's office on the twentieth floor of Dalton International's headquarters. Wall-to-wall windows offered a different perspective of downtown Oklahoma City than that in his own office at the opposite end of the long corridor bisecting the CEO's suites. But Blake had no interest in the sweeping panorama of the round-domed capitol building in the distance or the colorful barges meandering along the river in the foreground. He took another few paces, his fists jammed in the pocket of his slacks.

"I've left three voice mails. The first was around ten-thirty, the last one a half hour ago."

Although it was now just a little past two, Alex understood his brother's concern. He'd spent several tense hours himself when Julie took off in search of a missing Dusty Jones, her cell phone died and Alex didn't know where the hell she'd disappeared to. When he reminded Blake of that knuckle-cracking episode, his brother shook his head.

"I thought of that, but her phone was sitting in the charger next to mine when I left the house this morning. It's fully juiced."

"And Mother didn't know where Grace was heading?"

"Not specifically. Just that she was going shopping and maybe to get her hair or nails done."

"That sure narrows it down," Alex said drily as he reached for the phone on the broad plane of his desk. "I'll call Julie. I remember her mentioning some boutique or other that she and Grace really like."

Luckily, he caught his wife on the ground between crop-dusting runs. Julie had come to a reluctant decision to quit flying agro-air, worried that its high concentration of chemicals could affect the baby she and Alex had decided to try for. She was in the process of training a replacement now—and acclimating the poor guy to the challenges and dubious joys of working with Dusty.

Blake tried to suppress his nagging worry while his brother explained the situation to his wife and scribbled a couple of numbers on a notepad before promising to call back once they'd located Grace.

"She said to try a boutique owned by a woman named Helen Jasper." Alex punched in the first number. "Also a nail salon on… Hello? Ms. Jasper? This is Alex Dalton."

He listened a moment and smiled.

"Yes, I am. Very lucky. So is my brother. That's why I'm calling, actually. We need to get in touch with Grace, but her cell phone's not working. She was going shopping, and Julie said to try your place." His glance cut to Blake. "She did? All right, thanks."

Some of the tension riding Blake's shoulders left when Alex reported his wife had spent several hours and what sounded like a big chunk of change in the boutique.

"She left a little before noon. Maybe she stopped somewhere for a leisurely lunch."

"Maybe." The tension ratcheted up again. "But I can't see her lingering over a long lunch without calling to check on Molly."

"Let's try this nail place. She could have…"

Alex broke off, frowning when the door to his office opened. His executive assistant sent him an apologetic look as Delilah swept in pushing Molly's stroller, unannounced as usual. The matriarch of the Dalton clan—and nominal president of DI's board of directors—saw no reason why she had to wait for an underling to grant her access to either of her sons.

She halted the stroller in front of Blake. "Your assistant said you were here with Alex."

He barely had time to absorb her knee-high boots, black leggings and rust-colored tunic cinched with a monster leather belt decorated with an assortment of dangling, clinking zoo animals in silver and gold before Molly gave a joyous screech.

"Da-da!"

His heart turning over, Blake responded to his daughter's outstretched arms by unclipping the stroller's safety belt and gathering her in his. She brought with her that ever-fascinating, always changing combination of baby smells. Today it was powder and strained peaches and a faint, yeasty scent he couldn't identify.

"Have you heard from Grace?" Delilah demanded while Molly planted wet kisses on his cheek.

"No, but we know she left her favorite boutique a couple of hours ago."

"I was just saying she may be treating herself to a late lunch," Alex put in.

"She wouldn't do that," Delilah asserted flatly. "Not without giving me a call first to check on Molly."

The skin at the back of Blake's neck stretched taut. His mother had just confirmed his own thoughts.

"Patrice said Grace left a message for you earlier," she continued. "She didn't communicate her plans for the rest of the day?"

"Just that she wanted me to call her."

"That's it?"

"No." Blake's jaw tightened. "After she didn't reply to my second voice message, I grilled Patrice. She said Grace mentioned wanting to talk about her cousin, then changed her mind and just asked Patrice to tell me she called."

"Her cousin?"

Despite the distraction of Molly's palm slapping his cheek, he didn't miss the sudden flicker of guilt in his mother's eyes.

"What do you know that I don't?"

"Well…"

With a sudden premonition of disaster, Blake passed Molly across the desk to her uncle and locked on his mother. "Tell me what you did."

"I didn't *do* anything," she huffed. "I merely suggested to my daughter-in-law that she might want to think about whether she owes her loyalty to her dead cousin or her very much alive family."

"Dammit! I told you not to interfere in this."

"You're raising a daughter," she fired back. "You

should know by now that being a parent gives you the inalienable right to interfere when necessary."

Too furious to counter that broadside, Blake strode to the windows. He knew damned well that Grace *did* think about where her loyalty lay. Continuously. The matter twisted her in as many knots as it did him.

Had she gotten fed up with the pressure he and now Delilah had put on her? Was that why she hadn't responded to his return calls? Had she decided she needed some downtime, away from the Daltons, mother and son?

Christ! Would she just disappear? Walk out of his life as Anne had?

The thought put a hard, fast kink in his gut. Just as fast, Blake unkinked it. There was no way Grace would do that to him. She had too much integrity, too strong a sense of fair play. They'd argued over this whole mess, sure, but she knew he loved her too much to let her just disappear from his life.

Didn't she?

Brought up short, he tried to remember if he'd articulated the actual words. Maybe not, but he'd sure as hell showed her how he felt. The fact that he couldn't keep his hands off her spoke louder than words. As if it were an implied-in-fact contract, the attorney in him asserted, she could certainly infer his feelings from his actions.

Right, the less legalistic side of his mind sneered. Just as he could now infer why she hadn't returned his calls.

Well, there was one possible reason he could address right now. Cell phone in hand, he brought up the address book and hit Jamison's number.

"It's Blake Dalton," he said tersely. "I need an update on Petrie."

"Got a report a half hour ago," the P.I. informed him. "I was just going to email it to you."

"Give me the gist."

"Hang on, let me pull it up. Okay, here it is. Electronic surveillance of Petrie's residence showed him returning there yesterday afternoon at fourteen-thirty hours. My associate checked with his source in his highway patrol unit. Petrie and his partner testified in court in the morning. Reportedly, he felt queasy afterward, said he was coming down with something. He took the rest of the day off and called in for sick leave again this morning, saying he had a doctor's appointment. Surveillance showed him leaving his residence in civilian clothes at oh-six-fifteen."

Blake's eyes narrowed. "Pretty early for a doctor's appointment."

"That's what I thought, too. I've got my guy digging deeper."

"Call me as soon as… Wait. Back up a minute. You said Petrie testified in court yesterday morning?"

"Right. On a drug-stop case that crossed state lines and involved the feds. I've got the specifics here if you…"

"I don't need the specifics. Just tell me which court."

"Bexar County, 73rd Judicial District," Jamison reported after a moment. "Judge Honeywell presiding."

It might not mean anything. Honeywell heard dozens of cases every week. But the possibility, however remote, that Petrie might have picked up something about Grace from the judge or his assistant put the crimp back in Blake's gut.

"Call your associate in San Antonio. Tell him to put everything he's got on this. I want him to know Petrie's exact whereabouts, like fast."

"Will do."

He palmed the phone and was just turning to update the others when Alex's intercom buzzed. Shifting Molly to his right arm, his twin reached for the phone. Blake felt a surge of hope that Patrice had forwarded a call from Grace to his brother's office. That hope sank like a stone when Alex flashed him a quick frown.

"Yes, I'll take the call." He jiggled Molly, waited a moment and identified himself. "This is Alex Dalton."

Blake cut across the office. He pressed against the front edge of Alex's desk as the groove between his twin's brows dug deeper.

"Right. Thanks for calling."

"What?" Blake demanded before Alex had dropped the instrument back on the hook.

"That was Helen Jasper, the woman who owns the boutique where Grace shopped this morning. She just went out for a late lunch break and spotted Grace's car parked a couple doors down from her shop."

His voice was as grim as his face.

"She looked in the Jag's window. Said she could see the bags from her store spilling off the front passenger seat. Grace's purse is on the floor with them."

Delilah took Molly back to her house while her sons set out across town. Alex navigated, and Blake drove with a fierce concentration that was only minimally directed at the road. He tried to tell himself there were a number of reasons Grace might have left the Jag parked outside the boutique for so long. But none of reasons he dredged up explained her leaving her purse inside, in full view of anyone tempted to smash a window and empty it of wallet and credit cards.

"There's the boutique," Alex said when Blake pulled into the parking lot of an upscale strip mall. "And there's Grace's Jag."

Blake screeched into a slot beside the midnight-blue sedan and jammed his own vehicle into Park. He carried a spare key to the Jag on his key ring and was aiming it to beep the locks when Alex put out a restraining hand.

"There could be fingerprints or fibers or other evidence."

Like blood. He didn't say it. He didn't have to.

"Sure you want to contaminate the scene?"

"I've driven this car dozens of times. My prints, clothing fibers and DNA are all over it, but I'll be careful."

As it turned out, the doors weren't locked. Blake used the underside of the handle to open one. The baby seat sat empty in the back with some of Molly's toys scattered beside it. The front passenger seat held a jumble of shopping bags. Additional bags had obviously tumbled off the seat onto the floor. Grace's purse lay half-buried amid the silver tissue paper and pale blue bags. Her cell phone was clearly visible in the purse's side pocket.

Jaw clenched, Blake moved to the rear of the vehicle and used the key to pop the trunk. His breath escaped in a hiss of sheer relief when he found it empty. Alex gave him a silent, sympathetic thump on the shoulder. Blake knew he'd imagined the worst, too, although the empty trunk provided only temporary respite from those grim scenarios.

"I'll call Harkins," Alex said curtly.

Phil Harkins was a friend as well as a supremely competent chief of police. Alex had his phone out when Blake yanked on his arm.

"Wait!"

He ducked under the raised trunk lid and came back up with a half-folded sheet of paper he'd missed on the first, anxious sweep. The message inside was scrawled in bold black ink.

> You took my wife. I took yours. If you want to see the bitch alive again, you'd better keep this between you and me. A rich prick like you shouldn't have much trouble finding us. We'll be waiting for you.

Blake swore savagely and passed the note to Alex. His brother was still reading it when Blake's cell phone pinged. He checked caller ID, saw it was Jamison and cut right to the chase.

"What have you got?"

"Petrie flew out of San Antonio on a oh-seven-ten flight direct to Oklahoma City. He landed at eight-twenty, picked up one checked bag and rented a black Chevy Traverse from Hertz, Oklahoma tag six-three-two-delta-hotel-eight."

"Does the rental have a vehicle-tracking device?" Blake bit out.

"It does, but Hertz wouldn't give me access to their system."

"I'll take care of that."

He skimmed his contacts and pulled up Phil Harkins's number. The DA was in his office, thank God.

"Hey, pardner," he said with the affable geniality he showed to everyone except the worst of the bottom feeders his office prosecuted. "How's it hanging?"

"I need a favor, Phil. Fast, with no questions asked."

"Shoot."

* * *

Ten nerve-twisting minutes later, Harkins delivered.

"Hertz just transmitted the GPS tracking data. Your boy departed the airport, drove to your neighborhood and cruised your street. Didn't stop, but made a sharp U-turn at nine-fifty-four and drove to Nichols Hills."

Hell! He'd been following Grace. Blake was sure of it.

"He idled a block from your mother's place for eighteen minutes," Harkins recited, "then drove to your present location, where he sat for almost two hours."

Watching Helen Jasper's boutique. Waiting for Grace.

"Do your people have a lock on him now?" Blake asked, his insides ice-cold.

"Roger. He's heading south on I-35, three miles from the Texas border." Harkins hesitated. "I don't know what you have going on here, but I can ask the Texas Highway Patrol to make a stop."

Blake couldn't chance it. Petrie was a Texas state trooper. He could have his radio with him and be listening in on their net.

"No, don't alert the troopers. Just keep tracking him and let me know if he deviates from I-35." He shot his brother a fast look. "I'll be in the air."

Alex was punching the speed call number for his chief of air operations before Blake disconnected.

"What have we got ready to go?" He listened then issued a terse instruction. "Top off the fuel tank on the Skylane. We'll be there in fifteen minutes."

Blake didn't question the choice of a single-engine turboprop over one of Dalton International's bigger, faster corporate jets. Alex could put the Skylane down in a cow pasture if he had to.

* * *

They were in the air less than a half hour later. Alex laid on max airspeed and made a swift calculation.

"We should catch them between Austin and San Antonio…if that's where the bastard's headed."

Blake nodded, his eyes shielded by the sunglasses he'd put on to protect them from the unfiltered sunlight. He kept his narrowed, intent gaze trained on the wide ribbon of concrete cutting across the rolling hills and checkered fields below.

Petrie was down there, a thousand feet below and almost two hours ahead, driving a black Chevy Traverse. Blake could only pray he'd stuck to his end of the deal and had Grace sitting alive and unhurt beside him.

Fourteen

Grace shifted in the bucket seat, biting down hard on her lip when the SUV jounced over a rut. With her arms cuffed behind her, the ache between her shoulder blades had magnified to sheer torture in the interminable hour since she'd regained consciousness.

She turned her face to the window to hide a wince and searched for a landmark, any kind of a landmark. All she could see was a dense forest of stunted live oaks poking above an impenetrable wall of scrub. Refusing to give in to the desperation squeezing her chest like a vise, she faced front again and forced herself to speak coolly.

"Where are we going?"

Buzz-cut, tanned and clean-shaven, the outwardly all-American guy in the driver's seat wrenched his gaze from the single-lane dirt road ahead and shot her a look of smiling malevolence.

"I told you. You'll know when we get there. Now un-

less you want to talk to me about that rich bastard who
screwed my wife..."

Grace set her jaw.

"That's okay, cuz. You'll be squealing soon enough.
Now shut the hell up. I don't want to miss the turn."

This was how it had gone since Grace had come to,
dizzy and nauseous and aching all over. Petrie had refused to tell her how he'd found her. Refused to do more
than smile with amused contempt when Grace warned
he wouldn't get away with snatching her off the street.

She knew without being told that kidnapping wasn't
all he intended. He was a cop. He wouldn't leave a live
victim to bring him down. She also knew he intended
to use her as bait to get to Blake.

She'd been so careful! How had he made the connection between Blake and Anne? No, not Anne! Hope!
She had to think of her cousin as Hope again, use that
name when referring to her, or she'd feed into the rage
smoldering behind Petrie's careful facade.

Ten minutes later Grace caught a glimpse of blue
water through the screen of trees. Five minutes more,
and Petrie slowed to a near crawl, then turned onto an
overgrown dirt track. Grace had no idea how he spotted
the track. There was no mailbox, no scrap of cloth tied
to a bush, nothing but two sunken ruts cutting through
the heavy underbrush.

Thorny vines and ranches scraped the SUV's sides.
He was doing one helluva number on the paint job, she
thought with vicious satisfaction, then gritted her teeth
as the SUV bounced over the ruts and white-hot nee-
dles stabbed into her aching shoulders. She wanted to
sob with relief when the brush finally thinned and the
dirt track gave onto a clearing that sloped down to a
good-size lake.

A cedar-shingled cabin sat at the top of the slope, well above the waterline. Cinder blocks supported a screened-in porch. Additional cinder blocks formed columns to hold up the roof that shaded the porch. Grace whipped her gaze from the cabin to tree-studded opposite shore and spotted two or three similar structures. Most looked as if they were boarded up. None was within screaming distance.

Petrie pulled well off the track, killed the engine and got out. Leaving his door open, he extracted something from the floor behind his seat. A rifle case, Grace saw. Hand-tooled leather. Padded handle. Housing for the high-powered hunting rifle she'd seen him clean at his kitchen table more than once.

The case terrified her. Not for herself. For Blake. He would come after her. Find her somehow. Walk right into Petrie's gun sight.

The terror spiked again when Petrie got out and propped the rifle against the fender before extracting a soft-sided pistol case from his door's side bin. The case was half-zipped, providing easy access to the blue steel semiautomatic he slid out. It wasn't his service weapon. Grace had seen his state-issued black leather holster and Sig Sauer often enough to recognize the difference. This had to be a throwaway, one of those weapons reportedly confiscated during traffic stops that somehow never made it into evidence logs. Untraceable to the man who now coolly ejected the magazine and checked to verify a round was chambered before snapping the magazine back in place and thumbing the safety lock.

Just as coolly, he settled the pistol in the waistband of his jeans and picked up the rifle case. Grace's heart was racing when he rounded the hood, yanked open the passenger door and popped her seat belt.

"Let's go."

He hooked a hand around her upper arm and dragged her out, firing the pain in her shoulders to white-hot agony. It took every ounce of will she had not to moan as he hauled her up to the cabin. The screen door screeched when Petrie pulled it open, then groped above the main door for the key he obviously knew was there.

When he shoved Grace inside, the stink of old, dank blankets and used fishing tackle hit like a slap to the face. Grimacing, she inspected the dim interior. Bunk beds lined one wall. A rough-plank picnic table, a worn sofa with mismatched cushions and a lumpy armchair took up most of the remaining floorspace. The kitchen consisted of a counter with a sink, hot plate and half-size fridge. An unpainted door hung on its hinges at the far end of the room and gave a glimpse into a cubby-hole of a bathroom.

"Nice place you got here," Grace commented with a credible sneer.

"Belongs to a friend of mine. He's invited me up here a couple times to fish and drink. I know it offends your delicate sensibilities, but it'll do fine for what I have in mind, cuz."

"Stop calling me that, you dog turd. You and I are in no way related, thank God."

"You always were the feisty one."

She didn't like the slow, up-and-down look he gave her.

"I might just have to train you to heel, like I did Hope."

"You want to bet that's gonna happen?"

The face her cousin had once rhapsodized about being so strong and stamped with character now radiated nothing but amused contempt.

"We'll see how full of piss and vinegar you are when I'm done with you."

Dragging her across the room, he spun her so she was nose to nose with the rolled-up mattress on one of the top bunks. She felt him working the cuffs on her left wrist, felt it spring free and the screaming agony when her arm dropped to her side. She knew she had only three or four seconds to whirl and claw and fight for her freedom, but before she could do more than curl her numbed fingers Petrie had spun her around again. In a quick move he snapped the free end of the cuff to the metal pole supporting the upper bunk. Steel rattled against steel as the cuff shimmied down the pole.

"Make yourself comfortable, cuz. I figure we've got some time before the fun starts."

With unhurried calm, he placed the tooled leather case on the table, unzipped it and began to assemble his hunting rifle.

Grace watched him, her arms dangling uselessly at her sides. They felt as though they'd parted company with her aching shoulders. When the blood finally pulsed back into them, she angled around as far as the cuff would allow and yanked at the rolled-up mattress on the lower bunk.

"All right, Jack," she said after she sank onto the dank ticking. "You may as well tell me. I know you're itching to rub my face in it."

"How I found you, you mean? Or how I found out about my whore of a wife and the rich dick you married?"

"Both."

"Took some doing," he admitted as he snapped the rifle's bolt into place. "I've been searching ever since Hope walked out on me. Checking state and county court records, making calls to various police departments, screening NamUS—the National Missing Persons Data System," he clarified gratuitously.

Grace knew damned well what NamUS was. The data system was open to anyone with a computer. She'd screened it regularly herself for updates on her cousin.

"It wasn't until your marriage license popped in the Texas Vital Statistics database that I finally got a solid lead, though. I saw Judge Honeywell had married you and talked up his assistant. She gushed about what a handsome couple you'd made, how the judge and the Daltons went way back. I went right home from the courthouse and got on the computer."

He lifted his gaze, gave her a mocking smile.

"Found plenty of coverage about the Daltons of Oklahoma City but didn't see much mention of you. Made me think you were keeping a low profile for a reason, so I dug deeper and found a petition filed with the Oklahoma County clerk's office to establish paternity of the infant referred to as Margaret 'Molly' Dalton."

The smile took a hard twist.

"So I made some calls, cuz, and discovered a woman matching your description showed up at Dalton's mama's place almost the same day as the infant. I knew the kid wasn't yours. I'd been watching you too close. So there could only be one reason why you'd take a leave of absence from your job to work as a nanny."

The mask slipped, releasing the fury behind it.

"The brat is Hope's, isn't it? My whore of a wife had a kid by this guy Dalton, and noble, do-gooding Cousin Grace rushed to the rescue just like she always did."

"Jack…"

"Shut up! Don't even try to lie your way out of this. The kid's birth certificate was included in the paternity petition. Didn't take a genius to link her birth to the death certificate filed in the same California courthouse."

He shoved away from the table, the hate now a living thing. Grace tried not to flinch as he stalked across the room.

"She died out there," he raged. "Hope died, and you didn't even let me bury my wife."

"Jack, please. She…"

"Shut up!"

The backhand exploded against her cheek and slammed her head against the metal pole. Tasting blood, Grace fought to blink away the black spots blurring her vision.

"You're going to pay for what you did, bitch. You and Dalton."

With that implacable promise, Petrie went back to the table and picked up the rifle. Grace was still swallowing hot, coppery blood when the door banged shut and the screen door screeched behind him.

Her head swam. The whole side of her face hurt. She slumped against the metal post until she gritted her teeth and forced herself to think through the pain.

The cabin sat on a high slope that gave a commanding view of the only road in. Anyone approaching by boat would be similarly exposed. Grace couldn't wait for Petrie to pick Blake off. She wouldn't!

Breathing through her nose, she twisted to look up at the bunk above her. Its mattress was rolled up, too, revealing a crosshatch of springs hooked through the rectangular metal frame bolted to support poles.

No, wait! She blinked again, praying her still spinning head wasn't registering a blurred image. The frame wasn't bolted. With the first thrill of hope she'd felt since she'd regained consciousness, Grace saw the frame fit into Y-shaped supports.

If she could lift the frame out of the supports…

Slide the cuff up and off the pole…

She stretched out on the dank mattress and listened for any sound indicating Petrie's return, but all she could hear was the thunder of her own heart. Keeping a wary eye on the door, she rolled up on her hips and planted her feet against a corner of the frame above her.

It didn't budge. Jaw clenched, she pushed again. There was a squeak of rusted metal, an infinitesimal shift. Grunting with effort, Grace applied more leverage and got the frame half out of the support. The cry of the screen door made her drop it and her legs instantly.

"Had to set up a few electronic trip wires," Petrie informed her when he entered. With brutal nonchalance as he dropped some kind of a battery-operated device on the table. "We don't want your husband to burst in on us unannounced, do we? Now all we have to do is wait."

Neither Grace nor Petrie had any way of knowing his electronic sensors would work against, not for, him.

She lay in stark terror for what felt like hours, alternately praying the black box wouldn't beep and praying it would signal the arrival of an entire SWAT team. When the box finally gave two loud, distinctive pings, her heart stopped dead in her chest.

Then everything seemed to happen in fast-forward. She didn't have time to think, barely had time to choke back a sob before Petrie grabbed the rifle and charged for the door. He left it open, giving her a partial view of his body shielded by one of the concrete block columns and the rifle nested snug against his shoulder. Frantic, she rolled onto her hips and jabbed her feet at the upper bunk's metal frame.

"That you, Dalton?"

The answer came just as Grace got the corner of the frame off the supports.

"It's me. I'm coming in."

The frame dropped at a sharp angle, its rusted edges almost slicing into her face. She rolled out from under them just in time and somehow managed to keep the handcuffs from making more than a brief rattle. Petrie didn't hear it, thank God. His focus and his aim were both on the figure climbing the slope.

"Walk slow," he bellowed, "and keep your hands in the air."

Panting with fear and desperation, Grace eased off the bunk and then slid the cuff up, off the metal pole. The steel bracelet dangled from her other wrist as she searched frantically for a weapon, any kind of a weapon. The only thing within reach that wasn't nailed down were the fishing rods. If nothing else, she could slash and whip one of them. She scooped one up and was frantically trying to disengage it from the others when Petrie bellowed a warning.

"You can stop there."

Grace could see Blake now, unarmed, more than close enough for a high-powered hunting rifle to drill a hole through his heart.

"I got a score to settle with you, Dalton. I'm going to do it slow, though. I think maybe I'll put the first bullet in your kneecap."

"You can put a bullet wherever the hell you want, Petrie. Just let my wife go first."

"I don't think so, pal. She's got as much to answer for as..."

Two loud pings stopped him cold. Instinctively, he tilted his head an inch or two toward the intrusion detection device still sitting on the table. Grace knew that was all the break she'd get. She lunged through the open door, arm raised, fist wrapped around the rubber handle of the fishing pole, and lashed into Petrie's face with everything she had.

"Sunuvabitch!"

He flung out an arm, caught her broadside and sent her crashing. She slammed into the hard ground and caught only a brief glimpse of Blake hurtling past her in a flying tackle. She was rolling onto a hip, dazed and shaken, when a second figure burst out of the brush on the opposite side of the clearing and raced for the cabin.

Alex pounded past her onto the porch. Blake didn't need his brother's help, Grace saw as she staggered to her feet. He had Petrie on his back, straddling his hips while he smashed a fist into his face with lethal precision.

A dazed corner of her mind wondered how a corporate attorney could take down a trained cop. Then she remembered the tales Delilah had recounted about her sons' rough-and-tumble childhood in Oklahoma's oil fields and saw firsthand the rage her husband put into every blow.

Finally, Alex had to intervene. "That's enough. Jesus, you'll kill him."

He caught his brother's arm and hauled him off a now almost unrecognizable Petrie.

"He's... He's got another gun." Still winded from her fall, Grace steadied herself with a hand on the cinder blocks and gasped for breath. "In his waistband, at his back."

Blake rolled the man over and took possession of

the pistol. Thumbing the safety with practiced ease, he passed it to his brother.

"If the bastard tries to get up, blow his head off."

Then he was beside her, his blue eyes savage when he took in the bruise she knew had flowered after Petrie's backhanded blow.

"I'm okay," she said before he could spin around and add to the punishment he'd already inflicted. "Just winded...and scared."

"Me, too," he admitted hoarsely, cupping her unbruised cheek with a bloody palm. "God, I was terrified we wouldn't get here in time."

She didn't ask how he'd found her. The details didn't matter now. All she needed, all she wanted at that moment was to lean into his hard, welcoming body.

He held her off and looked down at her with grim intent. "I never told you I love you. That ripped at me the whole time we tracked you."

She managed a shaky smile. "Well, now that you're here..."

"I love you, Grace. I'm sorry it took almost losing you to make me realize how much. Maybe someday you'll forgive me for that."

"I will. I do. And you have to forgive me for almost letting my promise to Anne blind me to the promise I made you."

"I will. I do."

She went up on tiptoe and brushed her mouth over his—very carefully.

"I love you, too." She put her whole heart into the simple words. "So much I can't remember what it was like to *not* love you. Now take me home so we can clean our scrapes and bruises and start our marriage over."

Epilogue

Delilah insisted on celebrating her granddaughter's first birthday with her usual flamboyance and flair. As one of the Oklahoma City Zoo's most generous benefactors, she chose that as the venue for the momentous event and marshaled her entire staff to prepare for it.

Her social secretary drew up the guest list, which included fifty of Delilah's closest friends—all potential donors for a new exotic bird aviary—as well as every child enrolled in the Oklahoma City Special Olympics.

Louis, her majestic butler, came up with the design for the colorful invitations. They featured a talking parrot who squawked out the delights in store.

Her chef baked the six-layer jungle-themed main cake himself but graciously allowed a caterer to handle the rest of the menu items.

Naturally, Delilah also marshaled her daughters-in-law for party duty. She brushed aside the fact that Julie had turned over crop-dusting operations to her partners and the two additional pilots they'd brought on board. Julie's current responsibilities as director of flight operations for Dalton International kept her twice as busy, but Delilah blithely announced she could take the necessary time off to help with this once-in-a-lifetime event, as could Blake and Alex. Grace, who had delayed going back to teaching for a year or two, was totally immersed in the early preparations and event itself.

When the big day arrived, Delilah assigned her daughters-in-law the job of welcoming invitees and handing out goody bags crammed with beak-billed ball caps, macaw whistles, parrot sunglasses and canary-shaped marshmallow bars. Alex she put to work matching golf carts with drivers for kids who had difficulty walking. Blake had been tasked to assist a Special Olympics coordinator organize games suitable for children with varying disabilities. Bow-legged Dusty Jones and various volunteers from DI manned the lemonade, popcorn and cotton-candy stands set up throughout the zoo.

Even Molly participated. Spouting gibberish only she could understand, she played pat-a-cake with anyone who would reciprocate and toddled on wobbly legs after brightly colored beach balls in the infants' roller-derby. She also locked her arms around several other kids and refused to let go.

"She's at the hugging and kissing stage," Grace explained apologetically as she disentangled her daughter from a red-faced three year old. "C'mon, Mol-i-gans, it's time to blow out your candle and cut the cake."

Molly came into her arms with a smile so joyous that Grace's chest squeezed. She could see more of her cousin in the baby now. Not the frightened, cowed woman Hope had become, but the happy, laughing girl Grace had skated and played hop scotch and made mud pies with. Tears stung as she stood for a moment amid the bird calls and colorful chaos, nuzzling the squirming infant.

Oh, Hope! She's so bright and beautiful. Just like you.

Then she spotted her husband weaving his way through the crowd. A grinning boy in leg braces rode on his shoulders, waving energetically with one hand while he kept a death grip on Blake's hair with the other. When they reached his mother, Blake dipped so she could lift her son down and stopped to exchange a few words with her.

Grace's chest went tight again. Could her life be any fuller? Could her heart? This kind, thoughtful, incredibly sexy man filled every nook and cranny of her being. He and Molly and the child just beginning to take shape in her belly. She'd never dreamed she could feel such all-consuming happiness—and such a sharp stab of panic as when Molly gave a joyous cry and all but launched herself from her arms.

"Dada!"

Experience had taught Grace to keep a secure lock on the chubby little legs, thank goodness. Laughing in delight at her neat trick, Molly hung upside down until Blake righted her.

"Think you're pretty smart, don't you?"

"Smart," she echoed from the nest of his arms, adding to her growing vocabulary of one-syllable words. "Molly smart."

"Yes, you are. Very smart."

He angled her against his chest and slipped his free arm around Grace's waist. "Mother texted me with orders to convene for the cake cutting."

"Me, too. Guess we'd better comply."

They met Alex and Julie where the paths to the aviary converged.

"Un-ca!"

Molly reached out imperious arms and was duly passed to her uncle. While he and Blake led the way to the tables groaning with cake and other goodies, Julie fell into step with Grace.

"When are you going to tell Delilah you're pregnant?"

"We were thinking after the party might be a good time. She'll be too pooped to rush over to our house and start redecorating the nursery."

"Ha! Don't bet on it." The auburn-haired pilot hesitated for a moment, a rueful smile in her unusual eyes. "Listen, sweetie, I don't want to steal your thunder, but... Well..."

"Julie!" Grace swung around. "You, too?"

"Me, too, unless the stick I peed on this morning is defective."

"Omigod! This is wonderful! Delilah will have to divide her energy between the two of us!"

Julie burst out laughing. "I thought that advantage might occur to you. It certainly did to me."

They waited to spring the news on their mother-in-law until after the last of the guests had left. The family sat amid the party debris to catch their breath before pitching in to help the clean-up crews. Molly was sound asleep in the stroller parked between Grace and Blake. Alex sprawled long-limbed and loose at a picnic table with Julie beside him. Delilah drooped in a folding chair, sighing in ecstasy when Dusty pushed his battered straw Stetson back on his head and began to knead her shoulders. Weariness etched lines in her face but she essayed a smile as she surveyed the deflating balloons and animal-shaped confetti littering the scene.

"The party went well, don't you think?"

"I'd say so," Blake agreed lazily. "How much in pledges did you strong-arm out of your friends?"

His mother's smile turned smug. "Just over a hundred thousand. They could hardly balk when I promised my sons would match them dollar for dollar."

Neither son so much as blinked at this blithe reach into their pockets.

"Half goes to Special Olympics," Delilah continued, wincing a bit as Dusty's gnarled fingers found a knot. "The other half should cover the new exotic bird aviary. The Zoo Director was thrilled at the news."

Grace and Julie exchanged glances, then both women telegraphed unspoken signals to their husbands. Blake took the cue first.

"Grace and I have some exciting news, too."

Delilah shot upright and skewered Grace with keen blue eyes. "I knew it! You're pregnant!" Chortling, she twisted to give Dusty a triumphant grin. "Didn't I tell you that wasn't the flu that had her tossing up her breakfast last week?"

"Yep, you did."

The matriarch faced front again and trained her laser eyes on Julie. "What about you? I figure there was a reason you quit working with chemicals six months ago. You and Alex trying for a baby?"

"Not trying," Julie admitted. "Having."

"Whooeee!"

Dusty's gleeful shout made Molly jerk in her stroller. Startled, she puckered her lips and blinked once or twice, then settled back into sleep while the crop duster danced a quick jig.

"I'm gonna be a three-time grandpa. Not honorary, either," he added when he spun to a stop. Under his bushy white brows, his glance turned to Delilah. "Guess this would be a good time we tell 'em our news, Del."

"Guess so."

The sapphire bangle she always wore winked on her wrist as she reached for the thorny palm he held out to her. She didn't have to go into detail, though. Both sons and daughters-in-law were already on their feet.

"About time you made an honest man out of him," Alex said with a wide grin as he pulled her out of her chair and wrapped her in a fierce hug. He yielded his place to Blake, who echoed his brother's sentiments.

"We've been wondering when you two were going to come out of the closet. Literally."

To the amazement of all present, Delilah blushed a rosy red. Dusty merely beamed while Julie enveloped his bride-to-be in another hug.

"I'm so happy for you." Her laughing glance went to her former partner. "And if anyone can keep you out of the casinos, you old reprobate, it's Delilah."

Grace waited her turn, her heart so full it was almost a physical ache. She'd promised during Hope's last, anguished hours to deliver Molly to her father and make sure she was loved.

She is, Hope. So very loved.

So was Grace. She felt its embrace when she walked

into Delilah's arms and met her husband's eyes over his mother's shoulder.

Whatever happened, whatever came in the years ahead, this was one promise she and Blake would always keep.

* * * * *

& *A sneaky peek at next month...*

Desire

PASSIONATE AND DRAMATIC LOVE STORIES

My wish list for next month's titles...

In stores from 16th November 2012:

2 stories in each book - only £5.49!

☐ The Sheikh's Redemption – Olivia Gates

& Up Close and Personal – Maureen Child

☐ Texas Wild – Brenda Jackson

& Caroselli's Christmas Baby – Michelle Celmer

☐ Losing Control – Robyn Grady

& A Man of Distinction – Sarah M. Anderson

☐ Secrets, Lies & Lullabies – Heidi Betts

& Worth the Risk – Charlene Sands

Available at WHSmith, Tesco, Asda, Eason, Amazon and Apple

Just can't wait?

Special Offers

Every month we put together collections and longer reads written by your favourite authors.

Here are some of next month's highlights— and don't miss our fabulous discount online!

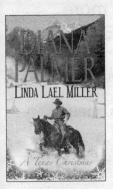

On sale 16th November   On sale 16th November   On sale 7th December

Save 20% on all Special Releases

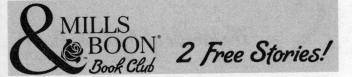

MILLS & BOON® Book Club

2 Free Stories!

Get your free stories now at

www.millsandboon.co.uk/freebookoffer

Or fill in the form below and post it back to us

THE MILLS & BOON® BOOK CLUB™—HERE'S HOW IT WORKS: Accepting your free stories places you under no obligation to buy anything. You may keep the stories and return the despatch note marked 'Cancel'. If we do not hear from you, about a month later we'll send you 2 Desire™ 2-in-1 books priced at £5.49* each. There is no extra charge for post and packaging. You may cancel at any time, otherwise we will send you 4 stories a month which you may purchase or return to us—the choice is yours. *Terms and prices subject to change without notice. Offer valid in UK only. Applicants must be 18 or over. Offer expires 31st January 2013. **For full terms and conditions, please go to www.millsandboon.co.uk/freebookoffer**

Mrs/Miss/Ms/Mr (please circle)
_____

First Name
_____

Surname
_____

Address
_____

_____
Postcode

E-mail
_____

Send this completed page to: Mills & Boon Book Club, Free Book Offer, FREEPOST NAT 10298, Richmond, Surrey, TW9 1BR

Find out more at
www.millsandboon.co.uk/freebookoffer

Visit us Online

0712/D2YEA

The World of Mills & Boon®

There's a Mills & Boon® series that's perfect for you. We publish ten series and, with new titles every month, you never have to wait long for your favourite to come along.

Blaze

Scorching hot, sexy reads
4 new stories every month

By Request

Relive the romance with the best of the best
9 new stories every month

Cherish

Romance to melt the heart every time
12 new stories every month

Desire

Passionate and dramatic love stories
8 new stories every month